HISTORICAL TALES
FROM
SHAKESPEARE

HISTORICAL TALES

FROM

SHAKESPEARE

by

Arthur Quiller-Couch

YESTERDAY'S CLASSICS

ITHACA, NEW YORK

This edition, first published in 2019 by Yesterday's Classics, an imprint of Yesterday's Classics, LLC, is an unabridged republication of the text originally published by Charles Scribner's Sons in 1900. For the complete listing of the books that are published by Yesterday's Classics, please visit www.yesterdaysclassics.com. Yesterday's Classics is the publishing arm of Gateway to the Classics which presents the complete text of hundreds of classic books for children at www.gatewaytotheclassics.com.

ISBN: 978-1-59915-492-3

Yesterday's Classics, LLC
PO Box 339
Ithaca, NY 14851

PREFACE

ALTHOUGH in the following pages I have chosen those plays, or most of them, which Charles and Mary Lamb omitted from their *Tales from Shakespeare*, and although I have taken a title very like theirs, my attempt has not been to round off or tag a conclusion to their inimitable work. They, as wise judges of what their book should be, found that a certain class of play lay outside their purpose. It is just these plays—the historical ones—which, with a different purpose, are here cast into narrative form.

It appeared to the friend who suggested this book, and to me, that nowhere, in spite of many inaccuracies, can historical pictures be found so vivid or in the main so just as in these historical plays of Shakespeare. We were thinking especially of the plays from English history. But our own experience seemed to show that many young readers fight shy of them, and so miss much which might quicken their interest in history and their early patriotism, being deterred perhaps by the dramatic form and partly by the sophisticated language. (For although even a very young reader may delight in Shakespeare, it takes a grown one and a wise one to understand his full meaning.) And we asked ourselves, 'Is it possible, by throwing the stories into plain narrative form and making the language more ordinary, to represent these vivid pictures so that young readers may be attracted to them—yet reverently, and in the hope that from our pale, if simple, copies they may be led on and attracted to his rich and wonderful work?'

This, at any rate, was my task: not to extract pleasant and profitable stories, as one might (and as the Lambs did) from the masterpieces of Shakespeare's invention, but to follow him into his dealings with history, where things cannot be forced to happen so neatly as in a made-up tale, and to persuade my young audience that history (in spite of their natural distrust) is by no means a dull business when handled by one who marvellously understood the human heart and was able so to put life into the figures of men and women long passed away that they become real to us as we follow their thoughts and motions and watch them making love, making war, plotting, succeeding, or accepting reverses, playing once more the big drama which they played on earth.

For although 'history' means properly 'enquiry' or 'research', and threatens nowadays to be a pursuit only enjoyable by a few grown-up persons, when taken in hand by such a poet—or 'maker'—it becomes again a story in the familiar sense, a moving tale which everyone can understand and enjoy, children no less than their elders. There had to be this difference, however, between the Lambs' stories and those which I set myself to repeat from Shakespeare — that whereas they had only to rehearse the plot of *The Merchant of Venice*, for instance, and the result was a pretty and, for their readers, a novel tale, if I contented myself with doing this to the historical plays I should be telling children little more than they already knew from their text-books. It seemed necessary, therefore, to lay more stress on the *characters* in these plays, and on the many springs of action, often small and subtle ones, by uncovering which Shakespeare made history visible; to keep to the story indeed, but to make it a story of men's motives and feelings, as well as of the actual events they gave rise to or were derived from.

For the sake of the story in this sense I have often followed Shakespeare where he is inaccurate, though I have sometimes corrected without comment where a slight correction could do no harm. It seemed to me equally uncalled-for on the one hand to talk of *Decius* Brutus and on the other to omit the tremendous reappearance of Queen Margaret in *Richard the Third*; equally idle to tie myself to the stage-chronology of *King John* and to set it elaborately right; alike unnecessary to repeat Shakespeare's confusion of the two Edmund Mortimers in one play and officious to cut out Mortimer's farewell in another on the ground that it is untrue to fact. The tale's the thing; else what becomes of Faulconbridge, Falstaff, Fluellen? In general, therefore, I have made it my rule to follow Shakespeare so long as he tells his story with fairness and justice.

It would be a great pleasure to believe that Shakespeare was always fair and just; to be convinced (with the illustrious poet who allows me to dedicate my book to him) that Shakespeare had no hand in the slanderous portrait of Joan of Arc sent down to us under his name. But convinced or not, no writer with a conscience could repeat that portrait for the children in whom are bound up our hopes of a better England than we shall see. Were he to do so, I believe that, thanks to such books as Green's *Short History of the English People*[1] and Mr. Andrew Lang's *A Monk of Fife*, our schoolboys would reject it with scornful disgust. It is enough to say that here they will not be given the chance; since to-day, if ever, it is necessary to insist that no patriotism can be true which gives to a boy no knightliness or to a girl no gentleness of heart.

Of true and fervent patriotism these plays are full. Indeed though they are, in Charles Lamb's words, 'strengtheners of virtue' in many ways, that remains their great lesson. It has been said that the real hero of Shakespeare's historical plays is England; and no one can read them and be deaf to the ringing, vibrating note of pride, of almost fierce joy to be an Englishman, to have inherited the liberties of so great a country and be a partaker in her glory. And this love of England is the sincerer for the courage with which he owns and grieves that she has been sometimes humiliated, sometimes untrue to herself. But as if this were not enough, he has left us—in Faulconbridge, in King Harry, in the two Talbots—lofty yet diverse examples of what patriotism can do; and again in Coriolanus and Marcus Brutus particular warnings of how even able men who love their country may, by a little unwisdom, injure her and wreck themselves. In short, and with the single exception named, these plays might almost serve as a

---

[1]To which, as to a classic, I have gone for what the play denies; even for some of its language, remembering the effect it had upon me as a boy.

handbook to patriotism, did that sacred passion need one. For nowhere surely in literature is it so confidently nourished and at the same time so wisely and anxiously directed.

And now, having excused my purpose, let me try to excuse my method also. I started, in my reverence for Charles and Mary Lamb, with some thought of tying myself by their rules of diction, and admitting no word which had not at least a warrant somewhere in Shakespeare. But I soon found (1) that the difference of design baulked my pen, and often in an irritating manner; and (2) that although I might hope to ape their example with success enough to deceive many, yet in my heart I was conscious how far short the attempt must fall of that natural easy grace which was theirs alike by genius and by years of loving familiarity with Shakespeare. Every man whose lot it is to write a great deal discovers his own manner, and does his best in that. So I resolved to use my own, and trust to telling the tales as simply and straightforwardly as I could. Now for my purpose it was necessary to be continually breaking up the rhythm of Shakespeare's majestic lines, and reducing them to ordinary prose; and there remains an apology to make to the critics who, with Shakespeare's lines in their memory, find this hard to tolerate. I ask them to remember that these stories are not intended for grown-up persons who know Shakespeare more or less by heart, but for children to whom their first reading of him is a pleasure to come.

A. T. QUILLER-COUCH.

CONTENTS

CORIOLANUS

FIVE HUNDRED years before the birth of Christ there lived in Rome a man of noble family named Caius Marcius. One of his ancestors, Ancus Marcius, had been King of Rome, and of the same house were afterwards descended the Marcius who was surnamed Censorinus, from having twice held the censorship, the most venerable office in the commonwealth, and Publius and Quintus Marcius, who together built the great aqueduct which supplied the city with pure water. So that altogether this house of Marcius was a very important one in Rome, and also a very proud one.

But of all its members none was ever so proud as this Caius Marcius, whose story we have to tell. His father died when he was quite a child, and thus his training fell into the hands of his widowed mother, the Lady Volumnia. In some respects it could not have fallen into better, for in those days the quality honoured above all others in Rome was manliness, and Volumnia, like a true Roman mother, set herself from the first to encourage her boy in all those manly pursuits to which she saw him inclined by nature. As a child he was taught to handle weapons, to exercise his body, and to endure hard living, so that he became swift in running,

1

dexterous in sword-play, and so strong in wrestling that no man could ever throw him. And when he was but sixteen she sent him off to the wars. "For," said she, "had I a dozen sons, and each one as dear to me as my Caius, I had rather have eleven die nobly for their country than one live at home in idle indulgence."

The war to which she sent Caius had been stirred up by Tarquin the Proud, the expelled King of Rome, in the hope of winning back his kingdom. The boy distinguished himself in his first battle, bestriding a Roman soldier who had been beaten to the ground beside him, and slaying the assailant with his own hands. For this feat, when the fight was over and the Roman side victorious, his general caused Caius Marcius to be crowned with a garland of oak-leaves, a coveted honour and only bestowed on one who saved the life of a fellow-Roman. Deep was Volumnia's joy when he returned to her with his brows thus bound; while, as for Caius, this first success so spurred his valour, that he soon became known as the bravest fighter in Rome, and though not yet one of her generals—by reason of his youth—yet the first of her warriors, and the swordsman on whom her armies doted and her generals depended.

To this his love and passionate pursuit of honour had led him. But what he and his mother forgot, or perhaps never saw clearly, was this—that the love and pursuit of honour may be so mixed up with pride as to become but a kind of selfishness; a very sublime kind of selfishness, no doubt, but none the less a disease. Caius Marcius was arrogantly proud, proud of his family, and, as time went on, insufferably proud on his own account; and this self-esteem, while it taught him to scorn all mean actions and petty personal gain, made him churlish and uncivil of speech to all whom he looked upon as his inferiors.

Now the Romans at this time, and for long years after, were divided into two classes, the Patricians and the Plebeians. To the Patricians belonged the old governing families of Rome, descendants of the first founders of the city, a nobility keeping the chief power in their own hands, trained in war and looking upon war as the one occupation which became their dignity. The Plebeians, on the other hand, were an undisciplined and oppressed crowd of traders, handicraftsmen, labourers, and idlers, having this on their side, that they grew in numbers with the growth of the city, until the Patricians, though they still despised, could no longer ignore them.

The chief ground of the Plebeians' complaint, among many, lay in the usury practised upon them by their rich masters. The poor man, unable to pay the heavy interest charged, was not only deprived of his goods but taken and sold into bondage, notwithstanding the wounds and scars he showed which he had received in fighting for Rome; and this, they urged, was a violation of the pledge given in the late wars, when they had been persuaded to fight, and had, indeed, fought faithfully, under a promise of gentler treatment. But when the war was done this promise had not been kept. The common people, indeed, were very nearly starving, and the angrier because the city held great stores of corn, which they firmly believed were being kept by the Patricians for their own use.

Their discontent began to break out in tumults and street riots, and word of this soon came to the ears of the neighbouring states, which were jealous of Rome (with very good reason) and watching for an opportunity to do her a mischief. They believed this opportunity to be come, and prepared to invade her; and to meet them the Roman Senate made proclamation by sound of trumpet that all men who were of age to carry weapons should come and enter their names on the muster-roll. The Plebeians refused to come; they had been tricked once with promises (they said), and would not give their masters another chance.

In this fix it began to occur to some of the Senators that they had been too hard upon the poor Plebeians, and many were now for softening the law. But others held out against this, and none so stubbornly as Caius Marcius. In his proud opinion these Plebeians were vile dogs and the scum of the earth, and he never scrupled to tell them so to their faces. That he and this dirty, cowardly rabble were men of like flesh and blood was a thing past belief, and since he never opened his mouth to them but to call them curs and worse, it may be fancied how they hated him even while they admired him for a brave soldier.

The Senate consulted for many days, but thanks to Marcius and his party no good came of their discussions. The Plebeians, seeing no redress, took a bold step; they gathered themselves together and marched out of the city in a body, using no violence, but crying as they went that Rome had no place for them, and that therefore they must go into wide Italy to find free air, water, and earth to bury them; and so passing out beyond the gates, they encamped on a hill beside the Tiber, called the Sacred Mount.

This stroke fairly disconcerted the Senators, who now sent out some of their number to treat with the malcontents, and among them one Menenius Agrippa, a friend of Caius Marcius. This Menenius was an old man, not over-wise, and certainly no great friend to the Plebeians; but having a blunt, hail-fellow way with him which the people liked. He could use his tongue roughly, but for all that he knew how to tackle a crowd in its own humour, and put in just the shrewd hits which folk of that class enjoy in a public speaker. He wasted no fine words on them, but went straight to the point with a homely proverb. "What is this? You say that while you sweat and starve, your rich masters eat and grow fat? Did you ever hear tell of the Belly and the Members? Once upon a time all the members of man's body rebelled against the belly, complaining that it alone remained in the midst of the body, eating all the food and doing nothing, while the rest of them toiled early and late for the body's maintenance—the eye seeing, the ear hearing, the legs walking, and so with the rest. But the belly smiled—by the way, you never heard of such a thing as a belly smiling, did you? Well, it did though; and it answered, 'That's true enough that I first receive and (so to speak) cupboard all the meats which nourish man's body; but afterwards, look you, I send out nourishment to all the other parts and limbs.' And just so, my friends, the Senate of Rome digests and sends out that which benefits you and all members of the state."

Menenius told this old tale so aptly, singling out one who interrupted, and addressing him as the Great Toe, that he very soon had his audience laughing; and in this good humour they consented with the Senate to come back, on condition that there should be chosen every year five magistrates, called Tribunes, whose special business should be to protect the poor people from violence and oppression.

Caius Marcius was furious when he heard of this concession. He had scoffed at the people's stale complaints—that they were hungry, that even dogs must eat, that meat was made for mouths, and the gods did not send corn for rich men only. "The rabble," he declared, "should have pulled the roof off the city before I would have given way and granted them these five fellows to defend their vulgar wisdom."

His rage was diverted for the moment by the news that the Volscians, the chief enemies of Rome, had taken up arms and were in full march upon the city. They had a leader, too, Tullus Aufidius, whom Marcius longed to encounter. The two had met before this, and found each other worthy foes; and between them, apart from their countries' quarrel, there had grown up a fierce but generous rivalry. "He is a lion I am proud to hunt," said Marcius; and with his own big arrogance, "Were I anything but what I am, I would wish to be Tullus Aufidius." In the campaign for which he was now eager the chief command did not fall to Marcius. By Roman rule this rested with the Consul for the year, Cominius, a gallant commander under whom he was proud to serve as Cominius was glad to have his services. But as Marcius, always courteous to his equals, begged Cominius to precede him and lead the way, he could not resist turning for a parting shot at the assembled rabble. "The Volscians have much corn. Shall we take these rats with us to gnaw their granaries?" But at the mention of fighting the crowd had begun to melt. "Worshipful mutineers, your valour comes forward bravely! *Pray follow!*"

So Marcius departed for the wars, followed by the sullen hatred of the poorer citizens and their newly-chosen Tribunes, and by the prayers of his own women-kind, sitting at home at their household work and waiting for news. But no two prayers could well have been more different in spirit than those offered up by Volumnia, his mother, and Virgilia, his gentle-hearted wife. The one rejoiced that her son had gone to win honour and prove his manhood once more, and her pictures of him as the two sat at their sewing terrified the softer Virgilia, who shuddered at the name of bloodshed, and besought Heaven to spare her husband from death. "The gods bless him from that fell Aufidius!" "Aufidius!" cried Volumnia; "he'll beat Aufidius' head lower than his knee, and then tread on his neck!" But Virgilia could not be quite comforted by this lively picture. She sat and quaked, and would not be tempted out of doors even when her gossiping acquaintances came with news of the campaign, which was now centred upon the Volscian town of Corioli.

Upon this important town the Consul Cominius had directed his march. But hearing that the rest of the Volscians were massing their forces to relieve it, he divided his army into two parts. To the one part, which included Marcius and was commanded by Titus Lartius, one of the bravest of the Roman generals, he entrusted the siege of Corioli; while with the other he himself marched out into the country to meet and grapple with the relieving forces.

The men of Corioli, disdaining the numbers of the division he left behind, were not slow in making a sortie, and at the first onset succeeded in beating back the Romans to their trenches. But Marcius, heaping curses on the runaways and calling on the stoutest fighters to rally and follow him, replied with a superb charge which drove the assailants back to their open gates, through which he hurled himself at their heels—almost alone, for the rain of arrows and javelins from the walls brought his followers to a halt. The Coriolans thereupon slammed to the city gates, shutting him inside, and Titus Lartius, arriving a little later, was fully persuaded he must have perished. But Marcius meanwhile had laid about him with incredible spirit, and actually hewed his way back to the gates; so that even while Titus lamented him, these flew open again and our hero appeared, covered with blood, but keeping his pursuers well at bay.

Now was the Romans' chance. They poured in to his rescue, and in a very short time the city was theirs. The baser soldiery then and there fell to sacking and plundering, though across the plain could be distinctly heard the noise of fighting where Cominius and his division had fallen in with the relieving force under Tullus Aufidius, and was being hotly beset. Marcius abhorred this vulgar pillaging, and most of all at such a time when, for aught they knew, their general urgently needed help. The thought of his rival, too, and the chance of encountering him, spurred him to fresh exertions, and he begged Titus Lartius to retain only a force sufficient to hold the city, and dispatch him with the rest to Cominius' relief. To this the old commander readily assented, and Marcius flew on his errand.

His aid was needed. Cominius had been forced to give ground before Tullus Aufidius' attack, and was drawing his men off, albeit in good order, and with none of the violent scolding to which Marcius would have given way in a like reverse. Still the position grave, and was not made more cheerful by the report of a messenger who had seen Titus Lartius and his men driven back on the trenches at the beginning of the fight, and knew nothing of their later success. But the well-known shout of Marcius as he dashed up to the rescue, and his brief tidings that Corioli had fallen, quickly dispelled this gloom and gave the men heart for a second attack. He demanded to be told of the Volscians' order of battle, and on which side they had placed their best fighting men; and learning that the flower of their warriors, the Antiates, were in the van and led by Aufidius, he besought leave to be set directly against these. This Cominius granted, and as the two armies advanced to their second encounter, Marcius outstripped his company, and so fiercely charged and cut a lane through the Antiates that the press of Romans following into the gap cut the Volscian array in half, and broke it up. Even so he would not desist from fighting, but calling out that it was not for conquerors to faint, pressed forward until the defeat became a rout and the Volscians were chased off the field with great slaughter. In their last rally Marcius for a moment had the joy of finding himself face to face with Aufidius, and the two were exchanging blows when a knot of Volscians came to the succour of their commander and against his will bore him off, to nurse a fiercer longing than ever for revenge. Up to this his hatred of Marcius had been a soldierly one, but now, in the bitterness of defeat, he felt, for the moment at any rate, that he could stick at nothing to be even with the man who had met him already these five times, and always come off with the advantage. "Were he sick, asleep, naked, in sanctuary, nay, my own brother's guest, none of these protections," swore Aufidius, "should hinder me from washing my fierce hand in his heart!"

The next morning the Consul Cominius, having entered Corioli, mounted a chair of state, and in the presence of the whole army gave thanks to the gods for the great victory. Especially he thanked them that Rome had such a soldier as Caius Marcius, and engaged that the citizens at home should echo him. But Marcius would have none of this praise. With a humility which really covered an insane pride—a pride which resented even the suggestion that valour in him could possibly be surprising—he protested that he had done no more than Lartius, for instance, had done: "and that's the best I can." His wounds (he said) smarted to hear themselves thus recognised. When Cominius offered him a tithe of all the horses and treasure captured, he begged to be forgiven for refusing this "bribe to pay his sword," as he put it. To his credit he had an entire contempt for private riches; but this refusal again smacked at least as much of pride as of disinterestedness. "You are too modest," Cominius insisted; "and if you will indeed be such an enemy to your own deserts, give us leave to treat you as they treat madmen who seek their own hurt—that is, put you in handcuffs first and then reason with you. Be it known, then," he raised his voice, "that for his valour I present Caius Marcius with the crown of this war, that I beg him to accept my own horse and harness, and in addition proclaim that henceforth, for his deeds before Corioli, he be known to all the world as we here applaud him—CAIUS MARCIUS CORIOLANUS!"

This compliment, paid before the whole army and acclaimed with shouts and the noise of drum and trumpet, our hero could not refuse. "Let me go wash the blood from my face," he answered, "and then you shall perceive whether I blush or no. But, sir, although I have received princely gifts, I have a boon yet to beg." "It is yours before you ask it," said Cominius. "There is among the Volscians an old friend and host of mine, a man who once used me kindly. I saw him taken prisoner yesterday, but I was pursuing Aufidius, and in my heat I neglected him. It would do me great pleasure if I could save him from being sold as a slave." "A noble request and readily granted. What is your friend's name?" "By Jupiter, I have forgotten!" It was his own fine action, not the prisoner, he was thinking of; and so at the moment when nothing seemed too small for his magnanimous remembrance his selfishness betrayed him.

Caius Marcius—or Coriolanus as we shall henceforth call him—had reached the height of his renown. At home even the discontented Plebeians were awed by the lustre of his exploits, and the path lay open before him to the Consulship, the highest honour Rome could bestow, and beyond that to a great and useful career. Volumnia and Virgilia went forth with the crowd that welcomed him into the city, the one praising the gods for his honourable wounds, the other stopping her tender ears at the mention of them. And such a crowd it was! Dignified priests jostled with nursemaids and kitchen wenches for a sight of the hero; fine ladies, regardless of their complexions, having found their stations, sat for hours in the sun's eye to await his coming and throw him their gloves and kerchiefs as he passed. Stalls, windows, parapets, ridge-roofs were thronged. It was faces, faces everywhere; faces of all complexions, but all agreeing in their earnestness to catch one glimpse of Coriolanus. His worst enemies, the Tribunes, marked all this and agreed among themselves that the great prize of the state, the Consulship—the one gift left for his mother to desire for him—lay within his grasp. And they foresaw well enough that should Coriolanus be Consul their own office might (as they put it) "go to sleep."

But among these Tribunes were two, Junius Brutus and Sicinius Velutus, astuter than the rest. They watched the exultant entry, and kept their tempers even while Menenius Agrippa (our old friend of the "Belly and the Members" story) jibed at them for envying the Patrician triumph. They bided their time.

For a Roman who sought the Consulship had to observe certain formalities which they foresaw must go sorely against the grain with Coriolanus. In particular, custom required him to appear on the day of canvassing in a humble dress, wearing only a white tunic like any mere workman, without the flowing cloak, or toga, which marked a Roman of birth; and to solicit each vote as a favour, giving reasons why he thought himself worthy to be Consul, and perhaps even displaying the wounds he had earned in his country's service. For the moment, no doubt, the Plebeians were disposed to forgive Coriolanus' past rancour and to let bygones be bygones. But a very little offensiveness might revive the old dislike and turn the scale against him, and these two clever Tribunes believed they might count on his turning restive and showing some of his old arrogance during the canvass.

As it turned out, they were right. At first Coriolanus' candidature went well enough. He had the Senate's support, and this his commander Cominius announced before a public assembly in a speech which lauded him to the skies. Coriolanus would not stay to listen to it; he had already undergone too much of this praise for his taste, and he had not the least desire to hear all his exploits recounted once more, and himself compared as a warrior to a ship in sail and treading men like weeds under its stem. But he returned to hear that the Senate approved his election, and it only remained for him to speak to the people. Upon this (as the Tribunes had expected) he asked leave to be excused the indignity of the canvass, a permission which they were too cunning to grant. Assured now that there were difficulties ahead, they went off to drill the people, so that the questions put to him, and the manner of putting them, might be providentially irritating to his temper.

The day of canvass arrived, and Coriolanus appeared in the market-place clad in his candidate's tunic, and feeling hot and very much ashamed of himself. The citizens, who had gathered in knots to await his coming, dispersed at once, and, as their cue was, advanced by ones, twos, and threes to put their questions. From the first Coriolanus was not happy in his manner towards them. "What am I to say?" he asked Menenius Agrippa by his side: "Surely you would not have me ask, 'What, do you want to see my wounds? Here they are then—I got them in my country's service when some of your brethren roared and ran away from the sound of our own drums.'" "Good heavens!" cried Menenius, "you must not speak of that! Talk to them reasonably, as for their good." "For their good? Shall I tell them to go home, then, and wash their faces?"

The very first knot of citizens began to catechise him in a style not likely to improve his temper. This was a great day for them, and they felt a high sense of their own importance. "Tell us, sir, what brings you to stand here?" They insisted upon all the formalities. "My own desert," snapped Coriolanus. "Your own desert?" "Ay, not my own desire." "How not your own desire?" "No, sir; it was never my desire yet to beg of the poor." "You must think, sir," put in one specially offensive catechiser, "that if we give you anything we hope to gain something from you." Coriolanus appeared to be vastly impressed by this, which, to be sure, was a somewhat shopkeeper-like view of the position. "Ah," he answered, "pray tell me then your price for the Consulship." "The price, sir," interposed another with better sense, "is to ask it kindly." "Kindly?" Coriolanus pitched his voice in a mocking key: "Sir, I pray you let me have it. I have wounds to show, and will show them to you—in private. Your good vote, sir; what say you? May I count on it?" "You shall have it, worthy sir," promised a citizen, whose wits happened to be too thick to catch the sarcasm. "That makes two worthy votes begged then. I have your alms. Good-day!" Coriolanus turned on his heel. "There's something odd about this," grumbled the voter who had talked about exchange; and even the thick-witted one muttered that "if his vote could be given again—but no matter!"

The truth is that even the meanest of us feels a certain importance when he has something to give, and likes to be asked for it politely. Coriolanus was at once too narrowly proud to see what every great leader of men must see, that all men have their feelings, and these must not be rough-ridden but understood, and too honestly proud to stoop to devices which other politicians used while despising them. He did, indeed, go through the form of observance, but with an insolent carelessness which made it worse than omission. Nor was his a noble carelessness, as one humble and mistaken observer had termed it. It was not that he did not care, but that in his heart he hated these Plebeians. He felt all the while how false his position was, and by and by, as this feeling became intolerable, he broke out bitterly, "Here come more votes! Your votes, pray! For your votes I have fought and kept watch; for your votes I carry two dozen odd wounds, and have seen thrice six battles—or heard of them. Pray, pray, give me your votes then, for indeed I want to be Consul!"

Puzzled and angered, yet remembering his past services, they gave him their votes. To this—as their Tribunes presently discovered with some dismay—they stood committed. Coriolanus had gone off to change his detestable garments, and, as he put it, "know himself again." Nothing remained but to confirm the election. Yet the temper of the people was sulky, and Brutus and Sicinius quickly perceived that all was not lost. "What? Could you not see he was mocking you? Could you not have insisted that as Consul he would be the state's servant, and have pressed your claims and tied him by a promise to serve you instead of speaking, as he always has spoken, against your liberties and charters? Had you not a man's heart amongst you, that you suffered all his contempt and gave him just what he asked?" "It is not too late yet," cried the citizen who had talked about exchange; "the election is not yet confirmed!" "Be quick then, and revoke this ignorant choice of yours! Stay— put the fault on us. Say that we, your Tribunes, over-persuaded you by laying stress on his great deeds and his ancestry, but that on second thoughts you find him your fixed enemy and regret our advice—our advice, mind! Harp on that." "We will!" shouted the crowd, who by this time repented the election almost to a man. They rushed off to the Capitol, and Brutus and Sicinius followed to watch this pretty storm of their raising.

Coriolanus, who fully deemed himself Consul elect, and was so deemed by the Senators, was talking among them with Titus Lartius, newly returned from Corioli. Tullus Aufidius, so Titus reported, had raised new troops, and in the face of them the Romans had been the quicker in offering terms of peace and coming away. In short, the Volscians, though checked for a while, were still dangerous. Their general, Aufidius, in wrath at their yielding Corioli so cheaply, had retired to his own house in the neighbouring town of Antium. "I wish I had cause to seek him there," muttered Coriolanus, little thinking that he would indeed be seeking Aufidius very soon, but not as Consul of Rome.

For while he came along the street discussing this news, he found his way unexpectedly barred by the Tribunes Brutus and Sicinius. "Pass no further," they commanded; "there will be mischief if this man goes to the market-place." "Why," cried the Senators, "is not Coriolanus elected by nobles and commons both?" "No; for the people are incensed against him. They cry out that they have been mocked, and call to mind his late opposition when corn was distributed to them free." "And so," Coriolanus broke out, "on that account they take back their votes, and I am not to be Consul! I'd better deserve the worst of them, then, and be made a vulgar Tribune like yourself!" "Let me tell you," answered Sicinius, "that if you wish to attain whither you're bound, you had better inquire your way, which you're out of, more gently, or you'll never be either Consul or Tribune." Menenius and Cominius here interposed, imploring calm; but Coriolanus broke out, "Talk to me of corn! What I said then I'll repeat." It was in vain that the Senators tried to check him. "No; I will say it. This shifty, foul-smelling rabble shall learn that I do not flatter. I say again that in truckling to them we are feeding a harvest of tares, of insolence, and sedition, which we ourselves have ploughed for and sown in our folly!" "No more, we beseech you!" his friends entreated. But Coriolanus' anger had passed completely out of control. He rated the Senators for their past lenity. "The rabble had well deserved corn! How? By shirking to fight for their country? By mutinies and revolts during the campaign? No; they demanded it, and the Senate, terrorised by their voting strength, gave way. 'Enough!' you say? Nay, take more—hear it all. When gentry, title, wisdom cannot conclude without the 'yes' or 'no' of general ignorance, then I say you must neglect the true necessity of the state for unstable vanity. I bid you—those of you who prefer a noble life to a long one—pluck out this multitude's tongue! Cease to let it lick poison because it finds poison sweet! Put an end to this dishonour which takes from your state the power to do good by submitting it to the control of that which only knows, or can do, evil!"

"Enough!" cried the Tribunes. "He has spoken like a traitor, and shall answer as a traitor! This man a Consul? Never!" They shouted for their officers, the ædiles, to summon the people. Sicinius laid hands on Coriolanus to arrest him. The Senators offered to be surety, but Coriolanus flung him off. "Hence, old goat! Hence, rotten thing! or I will shake your bones out of your garments." "Help! help!" shouted Sicinius, and the

ædiles and rabble came running together to his rescue.
For a while, as they hustled about Coriolanus and tried
to lay hands on him, their cries and the counter-cries
of the Patricians deafened the air. At length Menenius
appealed to the Tribunes to speak to the people, and
between them they managed to get a hearing. But
when they spoke it was not to soothe the feeling against
Coriolanus. "The city of Rome is the people, and we are
the people's magistrates. We must stand to that authority
or lose it, and in the name of the people we pronounce
Marcius worthy of death, and command that he be
carried hence and hurled from the Tarpeian rock,"—
for this was the form of death set apart for traitors by
Roman custom. "Ædiles, seize him!" Coriolanus drew
his sword. "No, no!"—Menenius would have prevented
him, calling on the Tribunes to withdraw for a while.
But it was too late, and a moment after he was shouting
to his fellow-nobles to help Coriolanus, as the rabble
made a rush crying, "Down with him! down with him!"

In the skirmish which followed the men of birth
had the upper hand, and beat Tribunes, ædiles, and
mob together out of the street. "On fair ground I could
whip forty such curs," panted Coriolanus; but Cominius
knew that their advantage was a short one, and he and
Menenius persuaded Coriolanus to escape to his house
before the crowd came pouring back—as it presently did,
demanding his instant death without trial for resisting
the law. It taxed all Menenius' powers of persuasion
to patch up a truce for the moment, engaging that if
the Tribunes would promise a regular form of trial he
would produce Coriolanus to submit to it. To this the

Tribunes, after some dispute, declared themselves ready; and dispersed their followers, commanding them, however, to reassemble in the market-place where the trial should be held.

It was no easy matter to persuade Coriolanus to attend. At home he raged up and down, swearing the rabble should pull his house about his ears and pile ten Tarpeian rocks one on another, or tear him in pieces by wild horses before he would submit. His friends could do nothing with him, and it was Volumnia who at length persuaded him to go. Coriolanus had always the deepest respect, as well as love, for his mother. From her he had learnt that passion for honour which he followed with so headstrong a will, and when she besought him to go and use fair speech, insisting that this could not disgrace him, he sullenly consented. "We'll prompt you," promised Cominius; "remember 'mildly' is the word." And "mildly" echoed Menenius. "Mildly be it then," grumbled Coriolanus, "mildly!"

In the market-place the people were awaiting him, well drilled by Brutus and Sicinius to echo whatever cry the Tribunes should raise. These two felt confident that they had only to put Coriolanus in a passion and he would be in their power. Coriolanus entered, his friends following close and standing about him to hold him in check, and Sicinius began to question him. "Do you submit to the people's voice and acknowledge their officers? and are content to suffer such legal censure as may be pronounced on you?" "I am content," was the answer. "There! you see he is content," put in the delighted Menenius: "he is a soldier, remember; you must not expect a soldier to be over-gentle in his language." "Well, well, no more of that," commented Cominius, who did not feel easy just yet. And in his very next words Coriolanus began to take the offensive, demanding why, after being elected Consul, he was dishonoured by having his election annulled. "It is your business here to answer, not to ask questions," said Sicinius. Still Coriolanus kept down his temper. "True, so it is." "We charge you that you have deprived Rome of her constitutional government and taken to yourself tyrannical power, for which you are a traitor to the people of Rome." This was too much. The charge, a new and unexpected one, had no justification. But it was the word "traitor" which stuck in Coriolanus' throat. " 'Traitor!' "—in a moment he was past holding. "May the fires of lowest hell wrap this people! Call me their traitor! If this lying Tribune had twenty thousand deaths for me, I would call him the liar that he is!" "To the rock! To the rock!" bawled the multitude. Still his friends implored, but Coriolanus was now utterly deaf. "Be it the rock, or be it exile, flaying, starvation, I would not buy their mercy with a single word."

Exile was the sentence the Tribunes had determined on, and in the name of the people Sicinius now pronounced it. Perhaps they hardly dared to exact the last penalty of the Tarpeian rock, but this they promised awaited Coriolanus if he ever again set foot within the gates of Rome.

"Curs!" answered Coriolanus, "it is I who banish *you!* Remain, and tremble at every rumour of war, shake whenever you see the plumes of your invaders nodding. Banish your defenders one by one, until your ignorance delivers you captive without a blow. For your sakes I despise Rome, and thus turn my back on her. There is a world elsewhere." And so he turned and departed, while they flung up their caps and shouted, "The people's enemy is gone!"

His wife, his mother, and a few friends escorted him to the gate. "Do not weep; a brief farewell is the best. Nay, mother, remember your ancient courage." Volumnia called curses upon the "many-headed beast" that treated her son so ungratefully. Virgilia could only weep. Old Cominius, that true friend, would have gone with him for a while, but Coriolanus forbade it and went his way alone.

Whither was Coriolanus bound? He was, as we have seen, a man with many great elements; and yet not an entirely great man, for selfishness infected them all. Even his high worship of honour had its roots in selfishness. He could say, and he believed, that he had fought and bled for his country, but at heart he thought first of self. He, the brave and noble Coriolanus, had been insulted, abused, treated with shameful ingratitude. The wound to his self-love poisoned all his thoughts. He forgot his boasted affection for his country, forgot everything but his one desire—to be revenged.

It was twilight in the Volscian town of Antium when a stranger, dressed in mean apparel and wearing a muffler about his face, entered the gate and wandered along the streets like a man uncertain of his way. Many people passed, but no man knew him. Of one of these he asked to be directed to the house of Tullus Aufidius.

Tullus Aufidius was dining and (as it chanced) entertaining the Senators of Antium, for the Volscians were even now on the eve of launching a fresh invasion into Roman territory under his guidance. The troops were mustered, Aufidius had made his preparations, and the Senators had gathered to-night to wish him good speed. From the banqueting-room where they feasted the sound of music poured through the doors into the outer hall, where the serving-men ran to and fro with dishes or shouted for more wine. Such was the scene upon which Coriolanus entered, still in his disguise, and stood for a moment looking about him. "A goodly house! And the feast smells well; but I have scarcely the look of a guest." "Hullo, friend!" called out one of the slaves, "what's your business, and where do you come from? Here's no place for you; go to the door, pray." "And whence are you, sir?" demanded another: "has the porter no eyes, that he admits such fellows? Pray, get you out." "Away!" Coriolanus thrust him aside. "Away? It's for you to go away. I'll have you talked with in a moment." "What fellow's this?" inquired a third. "A strange one as ever I saw. I cannot get him out of the house. Prithee, call my master to him." "Let me but stand here," said Coriolanus; "I will not hurt your hearth." But the fellow insisted that he must begone, and so insolently that Coriolanus lost his temper and caught him a sound buffet. In the midst of this hubbub Aufidius himself entered, having been summoned to deal with the intruder. "Where is this fellow?" he asked; and perceiving Coriolanus, "Your business, pray? and your name? Be quick, if you please—your name, sir!"

Coriolanus unwound the muffler from his face. "A name, Tullus, not musical in the Volscians' ears, and I believe harsh to thine."

Still Aufidius did not recognise him, being unprepared for this visitor, of all men. "Thou hast a face of command, and seemest a noble ship though thy tackle is torn. But I know thee not."

"I am Caius Marcius, once thy foe in particular, and foe of all the Volscians, as my surname Coriolanus may witness. That name is all my thankless country requites me with. The cruelty and envy of the rabble, by leave of the dastard nobles who forsook me, have swallowed all the rest and hounded me out of Rome. Therefore I am come to your hearth—not in hope to save my life—but in spite, to be revenged on my banishers. If thou, too, desirest revenge on Rome, make my misery serve thy turn; use me, and I will fight against my country with the spleen of all the devils below. If thou dare not, if it weary thee to try thy fortune afresh, then I am weary, weary to live, and offer my life here to thee and our old grudge."

While he spoke Aufidius had drawn back in amazement. But he was a man of generous impulse, and in a moment he fought down his present incredulity and his old malice together:—

"O Marcius, Marcius! Each word of thine plucks up a root of our ancient envy!" He embraced the foe whose body he had so often and vainly assailed with sword and lance. "Not when my wedded wife first crossed my threshold did my heart dance as it dances now to see thee here, thou noble thing! Why, thou Mars! I tell thee we have a power on foot now, at this moment; and once more I was purposing to hew thy shield from thine arm or lose my own arm in the endeavour. Time upon time thou hast beaten me, and night after night I have dreamed of new encounters—in my sleep we have been down together, tearing loose our helms, fisting each other's throat—and so waked half-dead with nothing. Worthy Marcius! Had we no other quarrel with Rome than her banishing thee, we would muster all from youngest to oldest to avenge thee. Come, come in; take our friendly Senators by the hand—they are here to wish me good speed. Take the half of my command, and direct thine own revenge. Thou shouldst know best when and how to strike Rome. Come in, I say. They shall say yes to all thy desires. Welcome a thousand times! more a friend than ever an enemy—and yet that was much, Marcius! Your hand, come!"

They passed together into the banqueting-room, and soon the disconcerted slaves had plenty to gossip about as they saw the strange visitor seated at the upper table and feasted, questioned, and consulted amid the deferential awe of the Senators. Aufidius was as good as his word, and readily gave up to Coriolanus the half of his commission. With this undreamt ally there was no division and no hesitation in the counsels of Antium. It was war now, and war without delay.

In Rome the Tribunes were congratulating them-selves. Their enemy was gone, and they had heard no more of him. It was pleasant to see the tradesmen singing in their shops, or going amicably about their business instead of running about the streets in tumult as in the days when they had Caius Marcius to provoke them. The Tribunes took great credit for this and for having rid Rome of one who aimed at kingship. They could repeat this false accusation safely; and Menenius and his fellow-Senators, while they shook their heads, took care to treat the Tribunes with consideration. As for Coriolanus, even his mother and wife heard nothing from him.

The first warning of something amiss came from a slave, who reported that the Volscians were astir again and had crossed the Roman frontiers with two separate armies. He carried this news to the ædiles, and was by those wiseacres promptly clapped into prison for a liar. "Have him whipped," commanded Brutus. Menenius suggested that it might be as well to make a few inquiries before whipping him.

And while Brutus and Sicinius protested that the tale could not be true—it was not possible—there arrived a messenger with word that the nobles had received news, and were crowding to the Senate House. The slave's report had been confirmed by a second. Marcius had joined with Aufidius, and was marching on Rome to revenge himself.

"A likely story!" sneered Sicinius. "Ay," added Brutus, "and raised no doubt to make the weaker spirits wish him home again." But this messenger was followed by another, and he again by Cominius in a towering rage. "You've made good work!" he broke out, addressing the Tribunes. "What news? What news?" asked Menenius eagerly; and being told it, he too rounded on the Tribunes. "You've made good work, you and your apron-men! Oh, you've made fine work!" "But is this true, sir?" Brutus stammered. "True? You'll look pale enough before you find it anything else. He will shake Rome about your ears. Who can blame him? And who can beg his mercy? Not you Tribunes—you who deserve such pity as a wolf deserves of the shepherd. Yes, indeed, you've made good work of it! You've brought Rome to a pretty pass!" "Say not we brought it." "Who, then?" snapped Menenius: "Was it we? We loved him; but, cowards that we were, we gave way and allowed your crew of danglers to hoot him out of the city. Here they come, your danglers!" as the crowd poured around them discussing the news. "Well, sirs, how do you like your handiwork?" The crowd was scared, but clamorous after its wont, each man noisily anxious to shift the blame off his own shoulders. "For my part, when I voted to banish him I said 'twas a pity." "I always said we were in the wrong." "So did we all." "You are goodly things, you voters," said Cominius, with bitter contempt.

The peril was urgent. Town after town yielded before Coriolanus without a blow, and Rome, divided within her gates, lay apparently at his mercy. In name he shared the command with Aufidius, but in fact Coriolanus was the sole hero of the campaign. The Volscian soldiery swore by their new leader, and his popularity began to teach Aufidius that the roots of ancient envy are not so easily plucked up after all. Aufidius was a generous man, up to a point; he had proved it by a highly generous action. But to obey a generous impulse is easier than to keep a magnanimous temper constant in face of a rival's success. Something of the old jealousy awoke in the Volscian leader; he saw, or thought he saw, that Coriolanus behaved more haughtily towards him than at first; his near friends and lieutenants encouraged the suspicion; he began to repent that he had given up half his command. Too big a man to deny his rival's merit, he was little enough to be galled by it, and to spy out faults which might some day serve for an accusation. "Coriolanus has merit; yet something brought him to grief once in spite of it. He has merit enough to silence criticism; yet he fell. Our virtues are as men choose to interpret them; a man may have power and be conscious of his own deserts, yet he will not find in an epitaph what he lacked in the praise of the living. Fire drives out fire, one nail another, and one man's reputation another's. When Rome has fallen, and Caius Marcius thinks himself strongest, my time shall come."

In Rome there was absolute dismay, and no attempt even to disguise it. Panic-stricken women ran wailing about the streets; the temples were filled with old folks weeping bitterly and entreating the gods; nor could a man be found wise or strong enough to provide for the city's defence. At the suit of the Tribunes (humble enough by this time) Cominius had been persuaded to visit the Volscian camp and supplicate Coriolanus in person. Coriolanus would not listen to his old commander; but as he knelt and pleaded their old acquaintance and blood shed together for Rome's sake, bade him rise, and with no more words, but a wave of the hand only, dismissed him back to the city. Where Cominius had failed would Menenius succeed? It was not likely; yet Menenius had strong claims on Coriolanus' love, and at length suffered himself to be persuaded. Cominius had perhaps chosen an unhappy moment. Menenius, a firm believer in the influence of the stomach over men's actions, would choose a propitious one, after dinner. The mission flattered his sense of importance; he might be able to show these huckstering Tribunes something, these fellows who were likely to cheapen coals by getting Rome burnt to the ground. After all he did not despair.

So he too set out for the Volscian camp. But his reception there was scarcely encouraging. The sentries at first would not let him pass, and seemed as little impressed by his name as by his recital of friendly services done for Coriolanus in the past. "You are mistaken," they assured him, "if you think to blow out the fire preparing for Rome with such weak breath as this." While they wrangled, Coriolanus himself came by in talk with Aufidius. "Now, you fellow," Menenius promised, "you shall see in what estimation I am held, and if a Jack-in-office can keep me from my son Coriolanus without hanging for it or worse"; and approaching Coriolanus, "The glorious gods sit in hourly synod about thy particular prosperity, and love thee no worse than thy old father Menenius does! O my son, my son! I was hardly moved to come to thee; but being assured that none but myself could move thee, I have been blown out of our gates with sighs, and conjure thee to pardon Rome and thy petitioning countrymen. The good gods assuage thy wrath, and turn the dregs of it upon this varlet here—this blockhead, who like a block hath denied my access to thee!" "Away!" answered Coriolanus. "Eh? How? Away?" stammered Menenius. "Away! I know not wife, mother, or child; I am servant to the Volscians now. My ears are closed against your petitions more firmly than your gates against me. Not another word!" He turned to Aufidius. "This man was my dear friend in Rome, yet thou see'st." "You keep a constant temper," said Aufidius. The two generals turned away and left Menenius standing red and discomfited before the jeers of the sentinels. "As for you, I take no account of such fellows. I say to you as I was said to, Away!" and away he stalked, followed by their laughter.

There was yet one plea left for Rome. While Coriolanus sat within his tent, grieved to have sent this old friend home (as he said) with a cracked heart, and resolute to listen to no more embassies, a stir arose without in the camp. No man had the cruelty to disturb or forbid this new procession. At the head of it in deepest mourning walked Virgilia, and behind her Volumnia leading Coriolanus' little son Marcius by the hand, and behind them again a train of Roman ladies, all in sorrowful black. They entered the tent and knelt before him, while Coriolanus rose, divided between his heart's instinct and his resolution to deny it.

"My lord and husband!" murmured Virgilia, and ceased.

"These eyes"—Coriolanus tried to recover his

firmness—"are not the same I wore in Rome."

"Sorrow—the sorrow that has changed us—makes you think so."

He could hold back his love no longer. "Best of my flesh, forgive me; but do not say, 'Forgive our Romans.' One kiss—a kiss as long as my exile, as sweet as my revenge!" He turned to his mother and knelt to salute her.

But Volumnia bade him rise, and, in spite of his protestation, sank herself upon her knees, and the child Marcius beside her. "Thou art my warrior; I helped to frame thee; this is thy son, and thyself in little." "The god of soldiers," said Coriolanus, "make him a noble soldier, proof against shame, and give him to stand in war like a great sea-mark, steadfast, the salvation of men who look upon him!" "And it is we who plead with you," said Volumnia.

"Nay, I beseech. Or, if you will plead, bid me not dismiss my soldiers or capitulate a second time with Rome's mechanics; plead not against my revenge, for to that I have sworn."

"You deny beforehand all we ask, yet we will and must ask." "Then all the Volscians shall hear it," said Coriolanus, and he called them to stand around.

"My son," said Volumnia, "should we hold our peace, yet the sight of us and our raiment would bewray what manner of life we have led since thy exile. Think how far more unfortunate than all living women are we, since the sight of thee, which should make our eyes flow with joy, our hearts dance with comfort, constrains them to weep and shake with sorrow and terror, making us, thy wife, thy mother, thy child, to see thee besieging the walls of his native country. Ah, it is worst for us; for others may pray to the gods, but we cannot. How can we pray for our country and for thy victory—both so dear to us—when one must destroy the other? when, whichever wins, a curse is bound up in the prayer? Either my son must be led, a foreign recreant, in manacles through our streets, or march in triumph through them, trampling on his country's ruin. But, for me, I will not see that day. If I cannot persuade thee, thou shalt march to assault thy country over thy mother's body that brought thee into the world."

"Ay," echoed Virgilia, "and over mine that brought thy son into the world to keep thy name alive."

Coriolanus groaned. "I do wrong to look on women's faces; they turn a man to womanish tenderness." He turned to leave them.

"Nay," commanded Volumnia, "go not thus from us. Did we implore thee to save the Romans by destroying the Volscians, thou mightst condemn us as aiming against thine honour. But we plead only to reconcile them, so that the Volscians may say, 'This mercy we have shown'; and the Romans, 'This mercy we have received,' and both unite in blessing thee as the maker of this peace. Son, the end of war is uncertain; but this is certain, that if thou conquer Rome it will be to reap a name which shall be dogged with curses, and its chronicle thus written, 'The man was noble, but with his last attempt he wiped out the remembrance of it and destroyed his country, and his name remains abhorred.'"

Yet Coriolanus sat silent. He could not trust himself to speak.

"Answer me, my son. Dost thou think it honourable for a noble man to remember the wrongs and injuries done him? Daughter, speak to him. He cares not for your weeping. Speak to him, boy; thy childishness may move him more than our reasoning. Son, no son in the world owes his mother more than thou owest; never in thy life hast thou shown thy mother any courtesy; not when she, poor soul, fond of no other child, doted on thee going to the wars, doted on thee returning laden with honour. Is my plea unjust? Spurn it, then. But if it be just, as thou fearest heaven, deny not thy mother her due."

A last time he would have turned away, but she and Virgilia and the child flung themselves on their knees together, uplifting their hands.

And seeing this, Coriolanus was mastered. He stepped to his mother, and lifting her, held her by the hand for a moment, silent. Then with a cry speech broke from him—"O mother, mother, what have you done to me!" Still he held her hand, fighting for words. "O mother, you have won a happy victory for your country, but—though you know it not—mortal and unhappy for your son!" He turned to Aufidius. "Sir, though I cannot make this war as I promised, I can and will make a peace to suit you. Say," he added, almost wistfully, since he had come to trust Aufidius, "could you in my place have listened to a mother less? or have granted less?" "I was moved myself," owned Aufidius, but this was all he would say. "I dare be sworn you were. But advise me, my friend, touching what peace you will make. I remain here, and I pray you stand by me in this matter." He would fain have gone to Rome with them whose dearness to him he had just so dearly proved; but his honour held him among the Volscians. "By and by," he promised; and dismissed them back on their happy errand. "You deserve to have a temple built to you; all the swords in Italy could not have made this peace."

Meanwhile in Rome the citizens swayed between hope and despair. Watchers lined the walls, their eyes bent on the Volscian camp. Within the city the mob had seized upon Brutus, and haled him up and down, promising him a lingering death if the petitioners brought back no comfort.

At length a cry went up from the walls, a shout. The Volscian camp was moving, retiring. Messengers came running, one after another, with the tidings; and soon, like the blown tide through an archway, the glad throng poured in through the gates. Trumpets sounded, drums, all instruments of music half-drowned in a tumult of cheering. And when at length Volumnia and her ladies appeared, escorted by the Senators, the crowd pressed about them rapturously, strewing flowers and shouting, "Welcome! Welcome!" Some lit triumphal fires; others ran and flung open the gates of all the temples, which soon were filled with men crowned with garlands and doing sacrifice as though news had come of a great victory.

Coriolanus was not to share this joy. He had spoken truth when he told his mother that she had won a victory most mortal for him. He turned his back upon the rejoicing city, and went, as his honour summoned him, friendless back to his fate. For as he led the Volscian troops homeward, Aufidius hurried before him, and before he reached Antium with drum and colours, Aufidius had made ready to receive him. "He has betrayed us. For a few women's tears he has bartered all the blood and labour of our great actions"; such was the charge forwarded by Aufidius in letters to the Senators. So when Coriolanus halted in the market-place, and delivered up the terms of peace, Aufidius stepped forward. "Read it not, noble lords! But tell this man he is a traitor!"

"Traitor!" Coriolanus turned on him fierce and amazed. "Ay, traitor," Aufidius repeated doggedly, "traitor and coward." "My lords," Coriolanus faced the Senators, "you shall judge me, and your judgment shall give this cur the lie, as he—he who shall carry the marks of my past whippings to his grave—already knows himself to be a liar." The Senators would have interposed, but the crowd had been instructed beforehand. Many had cause to hate Coriolanus for sons, fathers, kinsmen lost to them in fighting Rome. They pressed about him, crying, "Kill! Kill!"—and pierced with stroke upon stroke of their daggers, Coriolanus fell.

They had killed him believing him their enemy; but, their rage spent, they knew that they had slain a great man. Lifting the body, they bore it with military

35

honours through the streets of Antium, and buried it
as became its rank and its great deeds.

JULIUS CÆSAR

FOUR HUNDRED AND FIFTY years had passed and the Rome of Coriolanus had become the mistress of the world. But all these years had not healed the quarrel between the patricians and plebeians; for as the city increased in size and dignity and empire, so her citizens increased in numbers and grew less and less inclined to submit to the rule of a few noble and privileged families. And these civil quarrels became more bloody and dangerous as Rome lost that fear of the foreigner which had once bound her citizens together in self-defence.

To hold and garrison her vast possessions, too, she needed soldiers, and drew them from far and wide to fight under her eagles. And in times of peace these soldiers, being out of employment, were only too apt to meddle with civil affairs; until at length it became clear that whoever wanted the upper hand must get the support of the army. The man who perceived this most clearly was himself a soldier and one of the greatest generals the world has ever known—Julius Cæsar; and his hope was, by making himself master of the army, to rule alone and supreme and by strong and steady government to put an end to the miserable dissensions from which the state suffered.

To this he attained after a long struggle with his great rival Pompey. When it was over and the sons of Pompey, after their father's death, had been crushed in the battle of Munda, Cæsar treated the vanquished party with great leniency, no doubt because he wanted as few enemies as possible in the work of steady government to which, as master of the whole Roman world, he was now to turn his mind.

But he had made more enemies than he bargained for, and some quite unsuspected ones. To begin with, the beaten Pompeians were not men of the sort to understand his generosity or to be grateful for it. Then some of his own followers were angry because their rewards had fallen short of what they believed themselves entitled to; and also because Cæsar, though he had given them high appointments, went his own way, as strong men will, without consulting them. There were others again—noble spirits—who loved him and yet believed that so much power in the hands of one man was a danger to that Liberty on which the Romans had always prided themselves. As for the mob, they cheered for the man who was up, after the manner of mobs. A few months ago they had climbed the walls and house-tops and shouted themselves hoarse for Pompey. Now that Pompey was dead, and Cæsar returned in triumph from his victory over Pompey's sons, they shouted with equal enthusiasm for Cæsar.

And Cæsar, in the glow of his triumph, had parted with some of his old wisdom. Men of his great achievements become what we call "men of destiny"; and just as their enemies fail to see that success so mighty must contain something *fatal*, and cannot wholly depend on one man's cleverness or good luck, so they themselves are apt to forget that they are but the instruments of Heaven, and to take all the credit and become vain and puffed up. Thus the moment of Cæsar's triumph was the moment of his most dangerous weakness; for fancying himself almost a god, he began to talk and act in a way which persuaded his enemies that he was no more than a man with an ordinary man's frailties. Both were mistaken, and Destiny as usual turned the mistakes of both to her own sure purposes.

As usual, too, she gave warning; and at first in that small and seemingly casual voice which men disregard at the time and remember afterwards. There was an annual festival at Rome called the Lupercalia, held on the 15th of February, at the foot of the Aventine Hill, where Romulus and Remus, the founders of the city, had been discovered as infants with a she-wolf for their nurse. No doubt in the beginning it had been a rude shepherd's festival; but the Romans, proud to be reminded of their city's small beginnings, had appointed a company of priests who yearly on this date made a sacrifice of goats in honour of the old mother-wolf, and afterwards cut their skins into thongs. And the custom was for many noble youths to strip naked and run with these thongs, with which they playfully struck the bystanders. One of the runners this year was Mark Antony, a young man of pleasure, but of ambition too and excellent parts, when his love of pleasure allowed him to use them, and an especial friend of Cæsar's. Cæsar himself attended in state with his train of followers and flatterers, among whom one Casca was foremost calling "Silence!" to the crowd whenever the great man so much as opened his mouth.

The great man just now was talking familiarly with Antony, who stood ready stripped for the course, when a shrill voice from the throng cried "Cæsar!" "Ha! who calls?" asked Cæsar, turning about, and the officious Casca ordered silence again. "Beware the Ides of March!"—It was a soothsayer who gave this warning, and repeated it when Casca called him forward; but Cæsar lightly dismissed him as a "dreamer," and passed on to see the show.[1]

The crowd followed at his heels, and left two men standing—noble Romans both of them. Their names were Marcus Brutus and Caius Cassius, and a close friendship united them in spite of their very different natures. No citizen of Rome was more upright than Brutus, more single-minded, more unselfishly patriotic. A philosopher and a man of books rather than of action, he was in some ways as simple as a child; and being perfectly honest himself, doubted not that every one else must be honest. Privately he liked Cæsar and was respected by Cæsar; but he believed from the bottom of his heart that all this power in the hands of one man was a monstrous treason to the old Roman idea of liberty,

[1] The Romans marked off their months by three points: the Kalends or 1st day, and the Nones and Ides, which were the 7th and 15th of March, May, July, October, and the 5th and 13th of other months. They began by reckoning the number of days before the Nones, then the Ides, then the Kalends of next month. The Ides of March were the 15th.

and a danger to the commonwealth, and he watched it with a growing sadness and indignation.

Cassius, too, was indignant; but for reasons less lofty than those which moved Brutus. He felt the wrong done to the state; but being of a splenetic and angry temper, he disliked and was jealous of Cæsar. And Cæsar paid back this feeling with suspicion. "That Cassius," he said once to Antony, "has a lean and hungry look. He thinks too much, and such men are dangerous." "Fear him not, Cæsar," replied Antony, "he is a noble Roman and well disposed." "I would he were fatter," Cæsar persisted, who liked to have sleek and contented men about him: "If I, Cæsar, were liable to fear, I do not know whom I should avoid so soon as that spare Cassius. He reads much, is a great observer; he loves no plays as thou dost, Antony; hears no music; smiles seldom, and then as if he scorned himself for smiling. Men such as he are never easy of heart while they behold a greater than themselves; and therefore they are very dangerous." And Cæsar was right, though he fancied himself too great to fear this danger which he pointed out.

"Will you go see the runners?" asked Cassius, as he and Brutus were left alone.

"Not I," said Brutus, "I am not inclined for sport, and lack Antony's lively spirits. But do not let me hinder you, Cassius."

"Brutus, how comes it that your manner to me has changed of late? I miss the old gentleness and show of love, and observe that you bear yourself stiffly towards the friend who loves you."

"Pardon me, Cassius. I am troubled in mind, at war with myself; and it is this which makes me seem negligent in my behaviour to my good friends."

"Then," said Cassius, "I have mistaken you, and my mistake has made me keep buried in my breast some thoughts of mine well worth imparting. Tell me, Brutus," he asked abruptly, "can you see your face? . . . I wish you could; and I have heard men of the best respect in Rome—except *immortal* Cæsar," he put in with a sneer; "men groaning under this present yoke—declare how they wished Brutus would but use his eyes."

"Cassius, into what dangers would you lead me?"

"Well, my friend, let me be your glass; and look on me that you may discover more of yourself than you yet know." And he was beginning to protest what Brutus well knew, that he was no common flatterer or loose talker in company, when the noise of distant shouting interrupted him.

"What means this shouting?" said Brutus; "I fear the people are acclaiming Cæsar for their king."

"Ay, do you *fear* that? Then I must think you would not have it so."

"No, Cassius, though I love him well. But what is it you would impart to me? If it be aught toward the public good, you know that I prize what is honourable more than I fear death."

Thus encouraged, Cassius unfolded his tale of grievance. "Is it honour that we should all stand in awe of this one Cæsar, a man like ourselves? You and

I were born free as Cæsar. Is he in any way more of a man? He is a great swimmer; yet I have swum the roaring Tiber with him, and he has called to me to save him from drowning. I have seen him in Spain, sick of a fever—this god of ours—shaking and pallid, and calling for drink like a sick girl."

"Hark!" said Brutus, "they are shouting again. I do believe this applause must be for some new honours heaped on him."

"Why, man, he bestrides this narrow world like a Colossus, and we petty men walk under his huge legs and peep about to find ourselves dishonourable graves. Men at one time or another are masters of their own fate, and if we are underlings, we, and not our stars, not our destinies, are to blame. Brutus and Cæsar! Why Cæsar more than Brutus? Is Rome so degenerate that in this last age it holds but one man, and makes him king? There was a Brutus once who would have brooked the devil himself in Rome as easily as a king." He spoke of that Lucius Junius Brutus, his friend's ancestor, who had in old times expelled the Tarquins. Cassius was indeed no common flatterer, but knew exactly how to touch his friend's pride. Brutus was moved. He confessed that he guessed Cassius' meaning; he would think of what had been said; would talk of it further at some other time. Meanwhile let Cassius sustain himself with this— "Brutus had rather be a villager than repute himself a son of Rome under such conditions as he foresees will be laid upon Romans."

The re-entry of Cæsar and his train broke off their

talk. Something had clearly happened at the games to annoy the great man, for his face wore an angry spot, and his wife Calpurnia was pale, while the great orator Cicero had the look he put on when crossed in debate. As they went by Cassius plucked Casca by the sleeve and delayed him to know what the matter was. "Oh," said Casca, "there was a crown offered to Cæsar, or a kind of crown. It was mere foolery, and I did not mark it. Antony offered it, and Cæsar refused it thrice, and then he fell down in a fit." Casca had a bluff hearty manner with him, but he was really a sly unstable man who took his cue from his company. "A fit?" said Brutus; "that is likely enough, he suffers from the falling-sickness." [2] "Nay," interposed Cassius, with meaning, "it is not Cæsar, but you and I and honest Casca here that suffer from the *falling*-sickness." Casca scented the hint at once, and still keeping his jolly good-fellow-well-met way of speaking, let fall another in answer. "The tag-rag people," said he, "clapped and hissed Cæsar, just as if he were playing a part; and what's more, he gave them excuse enough, for just before he fell down he plucked open his doublet and offered me his throat to cut! If I had only been a practical fellow instead of the easy-going one you see, I swear I'd have taken him at his word." "And when all was over," said Brutus, "Cæsar came away sad, as we saw him?" "Ay." "Did Cicero say anything?" asked Cassius (for Cicero might or might not join the plot, and it was worth while to find out how he behaved). "Ay, he spoke Greek." "To what effect?" "Nay," said Casca, with a shrug of the shoulders, "you mustn't ask me that. I'm a

[2] A name given to the epilepsy.

44

plain fellow, and it was Greek to me at any rate. There was more foolery besides, if I could remember it." "Will you dine with me to-morrow, Casca?" asked Cassius, for he saw cunning where Brutus saw bluntness only. Casca promised, and so they parted.

And during the next month Cassius was busy. He feared, on second thoughts, to trust Cicero; but he sounded others of his acquaintance—Trebonius, Ligarius, Cinna, Decimus Brutus, Metellus Cimber— who were ready to join the plot. Their main hope, however, rested on Marcus Brutus; for whatever their own several motives might be, they knew none but the highest would persuade him to lift a hand against Cæsar, and that the people would give him credit for this. Cassius, to influence his friend, had letters and scrolls carefully prepared in different handwritings, all hinting at Cæsar's ambition, and that Rome looked to Brutus for deliverance. Some of them would be thrown in at Brutus' window, others laid among the petitions in his prætor's chair, others again pinned to the statue of his great ancestor. Every day brought a fresh shower of these letters, which Brutus believed to come honestly from the people and express their wishes.

Indeed, as often happens when treason or conspiracy is in the air, the public mind began to be disquieted with vague rumours and whisperings. Whence they came, or what they meant precisely, none knew. But folk began to talk of omens, signs of heaven, mysterious fires and meteors. A lion had been found wandering loose in the streets; an owl had settled at noonday above the great market-place; a slave's hand had burst into flame, but when he had cast the flames from him the hand was found to be unhurt—such were the foolish tales spread and discussed. Certainly the heavens were unsettled and broke on the night before the Ides into a furious thunderstorm.

Cassius passing through the drenched streets, reckless of the lightning, to join his fellow-conspirators, ran against Casca, whom the storm and its horrors had completely terrified. He had left Casca to the last, knowing him to be easily pliable. But now the time was short. To-night the plotters were to come together and hear Brutus' final answer. It took Cassius but a few minutes to convince the shaking man that the portents at which he trembled were really directed against Cæsar, to whom in the morning, if report said true, the senators meant to offer the crown; and but a few minutes more to persuade him that he really was a bondman and owed Cæsar a grudge. "I am ready," he protested, "to dare as much as Cassius in putting down the tyrant. I am no tell-tale." Cassius had his own opinion about this; but now that the time for tale-bearing was past, disclosed the plot to him and bade him follow to the porch of Pompey's Theatre, where the conspirators were assembling to pay their visit together to Brutus' house.

Brutus meanwhile had been passing through a terrible time. The more he pondered the more clearly he seemed to see that Cæsar's life was a daily-growing menace to the welfare and liberties of Rome. "It must be by his death," he heard an inner voice whispering. Another voice would whisper that privately he could find no quarrel with Cæsar. And then a third would answer that Cæsar's tyranny must increase with his opportunities. "It is the bright day that brings forth the adder, and therefore," it said, "kill this serpent in the egg."

These were the thoughts which for days had kept him distracted. They allowed him no sleep to-night, but drove him from his bed long before daybreak. He wakened his young slave Lucius, and bidding him set a taper in the study, walked out into his orchard when the storm had spent itself and left the heavens clear enough for the eye to mark the meteors shooting above the dark trees.

But out here the same miserable doubts dogged and besieged him. The boy brought word that his taper was lit, and handed him a sealed paper which he had found by the window in searching for a flint. "Go back to bed," said his master, "it is not day yet. By the way, is not to-morrow the Ides of March?" "I know not, sir." "Go then first and look in the calendar, and bring me word."

He broke the seal of the paper, and read a sentence or two by the light of the trailing stars. It was another of the mysterious letters. "Brutus, thou sleepest. Awake and see thyself"—the very words might have told him who the author was. Another call to him in the name of his great ancestors to come to the rescue of Rome!

The boy, coming back to report the date, was interrupted by a knocking without. It was Cassius, with the rest of the conspirators, heavily cloaked and wrapped. By his master's order Lucius admitted them to the dark garden. Cassius made them known—Trebonius,

Decimus Brutus, Casca, Cinna, Metellus Cimber; and then drew Brutus aside while the rest fell into constrained trivial talk which barely hid their uneasiness.

But Brutus' mind was made up. After some whispering with Cassius he came forward. "Give me your hands—no oath is necessary. We are Romans, and a promise is enough." He laid great stress on this; to him it meant everything to read in their purpose the genuine old Roman spirit. Cassius recalled him to more practical matters. "What of Cicero? Shall we sound him?" "We must not leave him out," said Casca, and Cinna and Metellus agreed. Brutus urged that Cicero was not a man to follow what others began. "Better leave him out, then," said Cassius, who mistrusted Cicero on other grounds. "No, indeed, he won't do," chimed in Casca, ready as usual to contradict himself and echo the last speaker.

Decimus Brutus wished to know if Cæsar alone should be sacrificed. "Well urged," said Cassius; "if we allow Mark Antony to live, he is just the man to do us mischief. Antony must fall too."

But this counsel revolted Brutus. "We are sacrificers and not butchers," he dwelt again on the sober justice of their purpose—as it appeared to him. He abhorred bloodshed, and pleaded for no more than was necessary.

"Yet I fear him," urged the more far-sighted Cassius, "for the love he bears to Cæsar."

"Do not think of him," Brutus answered impatiently. He underrated Antony, and Cassius felt sure he was wrong, but gave way.

It was three in the morning and high time to disperse. There remained a doubt whether Cæsar, who had grown suspicious of late, would not be deterred by recent omens from going to the Capitol. Decimus Brutus engaged to override any such hesitation and bring him. They left promising to send another likely conspirator—Caius Ligarius—whom Brutus was to persuade; and with yet another reminder of the Roman part they were to play, he saw them through the gate.

As he turned and bent over the boy Lucius, who, having no plots or cares on his mind, had fallen into a sound sleep, Brutus' wife, Portia, came out from the house.

She was uneasy about her husband. He had been strange in his manner for many days. Men, she knew, had their dark hours, and she had waited and watched. But this trouble, it seemed, would not let him eat, or talk, or sleep. It had changed him so that only in feature was he the Brutus she knew. "Dear my lord, tell me the cause of your grief!"

"I am not well in health; that is all."

"Is it for your health, then, that you are here abroad on this cold raw morning? No, you have some sickness of the mind rather, which as your wife I have a right to share. See, I beg you on my knees, by the beauty you once commended and the great vow you swore to me—your other half—that you tell me the truth. What men were here just now—men who kept their faces hidden?"

Then, as Brutus hesitated, she reminded him that though a woman only she was Brutus' wife and Cato's daughter. "Listen," she said, "before asking to share your secret I determined to test myself, to prove if I were worthy of it. See, I took a knife and gashed myself here, in the thigh. The wound is very painful, but I have kept my lips tight, and not allowed the pain to overcome me. Now say if I cannot be trusted to keep my lips closed on your secret!"

Brutus, touched and amazed by his wife's heroism, took her in his arms, and would have told her the whole story then and there, but a knocking interrupted him, and with a hurried promise that she should know all, he dismissed her into the house just as the boy admitted the last of the conspirators, Caius Ligarius.

Nor was Portia the only wife who had slept ill on that ominous night. Cæsar's wife, Calpurnia, had been tormented with horrible dreams; dreams in which she had seen her husband's statue spouting blood from a hundred wounds, while a crowd of Romans came and bathed their hands in it; dreams so ghastly that thrice in her sleep she had started up crying for help—that Cæsar was being murdered.

To unnerve her further, close upon these dreams had come early reports of the night's portents, the horrid sights seen by the watch. A lioness had whelped in the streets; the very graves had been shaken; the men swore to hearing noises of battle, the neighing of horses, the groans of dying men, the squealing of ghosts among the voices of the storm, and that the clouds had actually drizzled blood on the Capitol. Calpurnia had not Portia's firmness of mind. She gave herself up to terror, and protested that Cæsar should not stir from the house that day.

Her fears even infected Cæsar, though he would not own it to himself. He gave orders that the priests should do sacrifice and report what omens the victim yielded. Then he turned to Calpurnia. "What the gods purpose men cannot avoid. These portents are meant for all men, not specially for Cæsar. But suppose them meant for me—well, cowards die many times before their death, but a brave man tastes of death once, and once only. It seems to me the strangest of all wonders that men should be fearful, seeing that a man must die and the end must come in its due time."

His servant returned with word that the augurs warned Cæsar against stirring abroad that day. On plucking forth the entrails of the victim they discovered yet another portent—the heart was missing. Cæsar would have made light of it. "'Tis the gods' reproof of cowardice," he said; "I, too, should lack a heart were I to stay at home for fear." But Calpurnia besought him to stay and send word by Mark Antony that he was not well; and Cæsar, divided between a belief that he was above danger and a sense of menace in the air, was promising to humour her, when Decimus Brutus arrived to accompany him to the Senate-house.

"Tell them," said Cæsar, "that I will not come. It were false to say I cannot, and false to say that I dare not. So say that I will not."

Decimus asked for his reasons; and being told of

Calpurnia's fears, so well enacted his promised part of flatterer, with hints of what the Senate might say or suspect, that Cæsar soon felt ashamed to have yielded to his wife's fears. "Give me my robe," said he, "I will go." And an escort of his supposed friends (for the conspirators were among them) arriving at that moment settled the matter. "Come, Antony, Cinna, Metellus!—what, Trebonius? You are the man I want to talk with. Keep near me that I may remember." "I will," muttered Trebonius darkly.

Cæsar was to have yet another warning. One Artemidorus, a teacher of rhetoric, had an inkling of the plot, and had posted himself in the crowd before the Capitol with a letter. The citizens cheered as the great man passed through the streets, while Brutus' wife, Portia, waited outside her door, straining her ears at every sound borne across the city from the direction of the Senate-house. She bade Lucius run thither, and broke off, forgetting she had given the boy no message to take. She read meanings into the talk of the passers-by. She breathed a prayer for Brutus, and then was terrified to think the boy had overheard it. "Run," said she, "any message! Tell my lord I am cheerful, and bring me back word what he answers."

Cæsar, arriving before the steps of the Senate-house, spied amid the crowd there the soothsayer who had warned him against the Ides of March, and halted to throw him a rallying word. "So the Ides of March are come!"

"Ay, Cæsar," answered the man, "but not gone."

Decimus Brutus stepped forward with a petition from Trebonius. At the same moment Artemidorus pressed close, and would have thrust his letter of warning into Cæsar's hand. "Read mine first," he implored. "Mine is a suit which touches Cæsar nearer." But Cæsar waved it aside with a truly royal answer. "What touches us ourself shall be served last." Artemidorus was thrust back into the throng, and so the great man went up the steps, with the attendant crowd at his heels.

However anxiously some hearts were now beating in that crowd, he—the unsuspicious victim—was at ease, possessed (as never before perhaps) by the calm consciousness of pre-eminence. The conspirators eyed each other nervously. When anyone not in the plot approached Cæsar it filled them with misgivings. They had laid their plan. Trebonius was to draw off Mark Antony, and presently they saw the two step aside together. Metellus Cimber was to kneel and present a petition for the recall of his brother from banishment. Then Casca was to strike; after him all the others. They pressed around as Cimber flung himself on his knees. Cæsar guessed the nature of his petition, and would have prevented him. "Courtesies such as these might have effect upon ordinary men, not upon Cæsar. If this plea be for thy brother, I spurn thee aside like a cur. Know that Cæsar doth no wrong, nor will be satisfied without cause." Brutus and Cassius here pressed forward. "What, Brutus! I tell thee that as the stars in heaven are past number, but among them only one, the pole star, is fixed and constant, so among men is only one who holds his place unassailably, unmoved and unshaken, and I am he. Hence!" as Cinna, in turn, knelt: "Wilt thou lift Mount Olympus?" he demanded; and turning on Decimus Brutus, "It is idle. Does not even Marcus Brutus kneel in vain?"

"Speak, hands, for me then!" cried Casca, and stabbed him fiercely between the shoulders. As Cæsar staggered, the rest ran upon him with their daggers, hewing and hacking. He turned at bay, but only to take the blow from the man he most trusted, and to look him in the eyes—

"Thou too, Brutus?"

And with that he covered his face and let them strike as they would, until his strength failed, and he sank in his blood upon the pavement at the foot of Pompey's statue.

"Liberty! Freedom!" shouted the conspirators, brandishing their daggers. But they shouted to empty benches. The scared senators had started from their seats, and were crowding in a panic for the open. The attack had been so sudden that for the moment none knew how many were in the plot, or could tell friend from foe. Cassius, turning and seeing one aged man who stood confounded and unable to flee, spoke a kind word, and hurried him after the rest. For the moment these men stood alone among the pillars of the deserted building, alone with the body of their victim. Antony had fled to his house with the running, screaming crowd. Thence he despatched a servant, who made bold to pass through the awe-stricken few who lingered outside and present himself before the group, as at

Brutus' command they smeared their hands and arms with the blood of their victim. To Brutus what they had done was still a deed worthy of old Rome, and as Romans he called on them to go forward and waving their red weapons, cry "Freedom and liberty!" through the market-place.

The message brought by the servant was merely a plea that Antony might be allowed to come in safety and learn what manner of burial would be granted to Cæsar's body. "Thy master," answered Brutus, "is a wise and valiant Roman. Tell him upon my honour that he may come and be satisfied, and shall go untouched." Brutus believed, as the messenger had indeed professed, that Antony could be won over to their side; but Cassius had his misgivings.

Antony soon arrived, and seeming not to hear Brutus' salutation, knelt first beside Cæsar's body. "I know not," said he, looking up from his farewell, and letting fall the cloak he had lifted from the dead face, "I know not what you intend, gentlemen, or what other blood must be shed. For myself there is no fitter hour to die than this, and no place will please me so much as here, by Cæsar."

Brutus assured him they had no such intent. "Though we must seem to you bloody and cruel, look not at our hands, but at our hearts rather. It is for pity we have done this, pity for Rome. Against you we have no malice at all."

"Join us," said Cassius, who better understood the man they were dealing with, "and your voice shall be as powerful as any man's in disposing of new dignities."

Antony put this aside. The part he had to play was that of a true friend and admirer of Cæsar stunned by the shock of the murder, yet willing to believe that other men were wiser than he in his fondness could be. He took the hand of each conspirator in turn, and then seemed to break down under the thought that these hands had just murdered his friend. "Pardon me, Julius! So it was here they brought thee to bay; here thy hunters stand red with blood, and thou liest among them like a royal stag struck down by many princes!"

"Mark Antony——" interrupted Cassius. But again Antony seemed to misunderstand him.

"Pardon me, Caius Cassius; even an enemy might say this. How much more a friend such as I was?"

"I blame you not for praising Cæsar. But I am impatient to know what compact you mean to have with us, and if we may depend on you."

"It was for that I shook hands with you; but the sight of Cæsar distracted me. Yes, I am friends with you all if you will tell me why and in what Cæsar was so dangerous."

"Certainly," put in Brutus, "this would indeed be a savage spectacle if we could give no reasons for it; but we can—reasons that would satisfy you were you Cæsar's own son."

"That is all I ask; except this, that I may carry his body to the market-place and, as becomes a friend, make my speech among the funeral rites in due course."

"You shall," promised Brutus; but Cassius drew him aside. "You know not what you are promising," he whispered. "Do not consent to this. Consider how he may move the people." But Brutus never doubted that, his own reasons being good, he had only to state them to convince everybody. "By your leave," said he, "I will myself mount the pulpit first and show what reasons we had for Cæsar's death; and explain that what Antony may say is said by our permission. It will do us more advantage than harm to show our wish that Cæsar should be buried with all lawful ceremonies."

Cassius was discontented, but gave way again; and Antony readily accepted the conditions. The conspirators left him to prepare the body. Sinking on his knees beside it, he begged its dumb forgiveness that he must behave so meekly and gently with "these butchers." Then after prophetic promise of the curse this murder should bring upon Rome and Italy, he rose, despatched a messenger to Octavius, Cæsar's adopted son, and, lifting the body, bore it out to the market-place.

Brutus had already mounted the rostrum and was addressing the crowd. And the crowd listened approvingly, because they respected his character; but his formal sentences did not kindle them. "Romans, countrymen, and lovers! my appeal is to your judgment. If there be any in this assembly, any dear friend of Cæsar's, to him I say that Brutus' love for Cæsar was no less than his. If then that friend demand why Brutus rose against Cæsar, this is my answer: not that I loved Cæsar less, but that I loved Rome more. Had you rather Cæsar were living, and die all slaves, than that Cæsar were dead, to live all free men? . . . Who is here so base that he would be a bondman? Who so rude that he would not be a Roman? Who so vile that he will not love his country? If any, speak; for him have I offended. I pause for a reply."

This was speaking "like a book," as we say. The impressed but slightly puzzled crowd, finding an answer expected, cried after a moment, "None, Brutus, none!"

"Then I have offended none," the speaker argued, and was enlarging on the necessity of Cæsar's death when Antony arrived with his fellow-mourners bearing Cæsar's body in sad procession. Here was a far more effective appeal than cold logic, had Brutus known men well enough; but he was blind to it. "With this I depart," he went on, "that as I slew my best lover for the good of Rome, I have the same dagger for myself when it shall please my country to need my death."

"Live, Brutus! live!" shouted the mob. And some were for escorting him home in triumph, others for giving him a statue with his ancestors. "Let him be Cæsar!" shouted one; while another, even more sapient, suggested "Cæsar's better parts shall be crowned in Brutus." Comments so ignorant might have warned him of the mistake he made in relying on their reasonableness. But the warning was wasted. Begging them to listen to what Antony might have to say, he stepped down from the rostrum and withdrew, chivalrously leaving the coast clear.

There was some disturbance when Antony mounted the steps to speak. The mob was persuaded after a fashion that Cæsar had been a tyrant, and that Rome was well rid of him. "He'd best speak no harm of Brutus here," threatened the sapient citizen who had suggested crowning Cæsar's better parts. But having obtained silence, Antony knew better than to begin by attacking Brutus.

"Friends, Romans, countrymen," he began, "attend! I am here to bury Cæsar, not to praise him. The evil which men do survives them; the good is often laid away under earth with their bones. Let it be so with Cæsar. He was ambitious, the noble Brutus has told you. If that were so, it was a grievous fault, and Cæsar has paid for it grievously. Here, by leave of Brutus and the rest—for Brutus is a man of honour, and so are they all, all men of honour—I am come merely to speak the last words over my friend.

"For he was my friend, and to me faithful and just; though Brutus—who is a man of honour—says he was ambitious. He brought, in his time, many captives home to this city, and poured their ransoms into the public coffers. When the poor have cried, Cæsar has wept for them. It is hard to detect ambition in all this; but Brutus—who is a man of honour—says he was ambitious. You all saw how at the Lupercalia I thrice offered him the kingly crown, and how he refused it thrice. Was this ambition? Brutus says so; and to be sure, he is a man of honour. But I am not here to disprove what Brutus told you. I am here merely to tell you what I know. You all loved him once—not without cause. Can you not mourn for him? Oh, have men lost all their judgment, all their reason!" He paused as one surprised at his own outburst. "Bear with me, friends; my heart is in the coffin there with Cæsar. Grant me a while to pause and recover it!"

His listeners were moved already. "There is reason in what he says." "Cæsar has had great wrong, if you consider." "We may have a worse master than Cæsar." "He refused the crown—so he did—so 'tis plain he couldn't have been ambitious." "Poor soul! look at his eyes, red as fire!" "There's not a nobler man in all Rome than Antony!" Thus they murmured together, while Antony conquered his emotion and prepared to speak again.

"But yesterday," he went on, "the word of Cæsar might have weighed against the whole world. Now he lies there with none—not the poorest—to do him reverence. Sirs, if I were disposed to stir you to mutiny and rage I should be wronging Brutus and Cassius— who, as you know, are men of honour. I will not do this. I choose rather to wrong the dead, to wrong myself, to wrong you, than to wrong such men of honour! But here I have Cæsar's will. If I were to read it to you—but, pardon me, I do not mean to—I say if I were to read it you would run to kiss Cæsar's wounds, to dip your handkerchiefs in his blood——"

"The will! read the will!" shouted the people; but Antony protested that he must not; it was not meet for them to hear how much Cæsar loved them; it would inflame them, make them mad. There was no saying what might come of it.

"Read the will! Read it!" they clamoured.

But again he protested; he had gone too far in speaking of it; he feared, indeed he did, that he was wronging the men of honour—whose daggers had stabbed Cæsar.

"The will! the will! 'Men of honour!' Traitors! Read the will!"

"You force me to read it? Then come, make a ring about Cæsar's corpse while I show you him who made the will." He stepped down from the rostrum, and as they gathered and pressed about him, he lifted the mantle from the body. "You all know this mantle. I remember the first time Cæsar put it on—one summer's evening, in his tent. It was the day he overcame the Nervii." He showed them the holes made by the daggers; where Cassius had stabbed, and Casca, and Brutus—"the well-beloved Brutus," "Cæsar's angel"—"ah, that was the unkindest blow! That was the heart-breaking stroke! Then it was that great Cæsar covered his face and fell!" His hearers were weeping by this time, and he could be bold. "Fell? Ay, and what a fall! My countrymen, then it was that I and you and all of us fell, while treason and bloodshed flourished over us. You weep at sight of his garments merely! Look you here then on *him*—marred, as you behold, by traitors!"

They were mad now. They shouted for revenge. "Fire!" "Kill!" "Slay!" "Death to the traitors!" But Antony, who had worked them to frenzy with such masterly art, must perfect that frenzy before letting them slip.

"Good friends, sweet friends, I must not stir you

up so. The men who have done this deed are men of honour. What *private griefs* they had against Cæsar to make them do it, I know not, alas! But as men of honour they will give you their reasons. You see, I am no orator like Brutus!"—indeed he was not!—"but, as you all know me, a plain blunt man, who love my friend, and have permission to speak. For I have no gifts of eloquence to set men's blood stirring. I only speak right on, telling you what you know already, shewing you Cæsar's wounds, and bidding them speak for me. Were I Brutus now I could put a tongue into every wound of Cæsar that should move the very stones of Rome to rise in revolt."

"And so will we!" "Burn the house of Brutus!" "Down with the conspirators!" Antony had to shout for a hearing. "Why, friends, you are going to do you know not what! Nay, you scarce know yet how much cause you have to love Cæsar. You have forgotten the will I told you of."

"True—the will! Read the will!"

"Here is the will, then, sealed by Cæsar. It gives to every Roman citizen a legacy of seventy-five drachmas,"—again the hubbub was deafening—"and to the citizens in general he bequeaths his gardens and orchards beyond Tiber, to them and their heirs for their recreation for ever. . . ."

They listened for no more. They rushed on the market-place tearing up benches, stalls, tables, and heaping the wreckage for a funeral pile. They laid the body of Cæsar on it and set fire to the mass; and as it grew hot they plucked out the blazing brands and rushed off towards the conspirators' houses, yelling for revenge. Antony could watch now. He had done his work, and done it thoroughly.

But the conspirators had been warned, and by this time were riding through the gates in hot haste. They drew rein at Antium. The mob, after all, was but a mob; and, though Antony doubtless coveted Cæsar's place, before he could aspire to it he must win the army. The senatorial party on the whole supported the conspirators; for when Brutus and the rest talked of Roman liberty, what they meant was the privileges of the old Roman families which still composed the Senate, not the rights of the populace. It was the Senate, not the populace, which had resented Cæsar's absolute power, and for their deliverance the blow had been struck. Officially the senators had, by law and in name at any rate, the army on their side; for by law the chief magistrates took command of the forces. So the conspirators had much in their favour.

Between these two parties—Antony and the mob on one side, and the majority of the Senate on the other—stood the young Octavius, Cæsar's grand-nephew and heir, with an army at his back; a young man, not yet twenty, but wiser than other young men, with a handsome, expressionless, inscrutable face, a heart without feeling, and a temper inhumanly cold and obstinate—an enigma to all, and as yet perhaps even to himself. Brutus and the rest had made the grand mistake of conspirators; they had supposed that by killing a great man they could destroy the forces which made him. Driven from Cæsar's dead body, these forces gathered again and centred upon Cæsar's young heir, and henceforth this statue of a youth is propelled by them and moves as a man of fate.

At first Octavius inclined towards the senatorial party. Brutus and Cassius went off to their provinces in the East. In Italy Antony might have been crushed had the Senate followed a fixed plan or dared to trust Octavius; but distrust and divisions palsied their policy and the movements of their troops. Octavius saw that he could make nothing of them. On the other hand, by combining with Antony he could crush them in Italy, and then turn upon Brutus and Cassius in the East. As for Antony—well, time would show.

The two chiefs met, and took into their counsels one Marcus Æmilius Lepidus—a weak man, but a name of weight and influence with the popular party. The three appointed themselves to a Triumvirate—in other words, a three-man dictatorship—and divided up the Roman Empire between them as though it had been their own inheritance. To effect this, however, certain prominent men had to be got rid of, and each Triumvir was naturally anxious to shield his own friends. At length, however, by bartering their separate friendships against their hatreds, they "proscribed," or marked down and put to death all who were likely to interfere with their plans. Octavius handed over Cicero to Antony; who in turn sacrificed Lucius Cæsar, his uncle on his mother's side; while Lepidus, to his peculiar shame, suffered his own brother Paulus to be pricked down on the list. Having thus by wholesale murder cleared the coast in

Italy, they could turn securely upon Brutus and Cassius in the East.

And in the East Brutus was beginning to learn that the philosophy found in books will not carry a man through the business of statecraft, especially when one is conducting a revolution. He wanted money, and pressed Cassius for money. He would have no unjust tolls levied in his own province, and disgraced his subordinate, Lucius Pella, on finding him guilty of pilfering the inhabitants of Sardis. Yet he must have known, had he considered, that if Cassius had money to spare it was only by behaving less scrupulously. This punishment of Pella annoyed Cassius, who took it for a reflection upon himself, having dealt leniently a few days before with two of his own officers similarly convicted. At Brutus' request he came with his army to Sardis to clear up misunderstandings. The two friends met coldly, for Cassius was genuinely incensed and made no secret of his feelings.

Brutus, however, led him to his own tent, and setting a watch on the door bade him speak out his complaints.

"You have wronged me," said Cassius, "in disgracing Lucius Pella and making light of the letters I sent appealing for him."

"You wronged yourself, rather, to write in such a case."

"This is no time for laying stress on every petty offence."

Now Brutus was suffering and hiding a private sorrow of which his friend knew nothing. Under such trials the tempers of good men grow infirm.

"Let me tell you," he broke out violently, "you yourself, Cassius, are accused of an itching palm—of trafficking your offices for gold to unworthy men!"

"I! an itching palm!" Cassius sprang up indignant, blankly astonished. "You know you are Brutus who utter the words, or by the gods that speech were your last!"

"The name of Cassius honours this corrupt dealing, and therefore it goes without chastisement."

"Chastisement!"

But Brutus was not to be checked. "Remember March—remember the Ides of March! Why did Cæsar bleed, but for justice? Was there a man of us stabbed him except for justice?" Cassius winced. "What! Shall one of us who smote down the foremost man in the world because he supported robbers shall *we*, I say, now be contaminating our fingers with base bribes? I'd rather be a dog than such a Roman!"

We may pity Cassius now. The ablest, shrewdest, most practical of all the conspirators, he had one soft place in his heart—his admiring love for his friend. Time after time he had given way to Brutus—in sparing Antony, in allowing Antony to harangue the crowd, he had given way against his judgment; and always the event proved that he had been right and Brutus wrong. His respect for Brutus was a kind of superstition. And here he was being preached at and pelted with opprobrious words by the friend who had been pressing him for money, being too moral himself to raise money in the only way it could be raised! It was intolerable, and he felt it so.

"Brutus, bait me not, for I'll not endure it. You forget yourself! I am a soldier, older in practice than you, and abler to make conditions."

Brutus caught him up. "What, *you* abler?" "Do not tempt me further," Cassius pleaded. "*You* abler?" Brutus replied with sneer upon sneer: "You a better soldier?" "I said an elder soldier, not a better one. Did I say better?" "If you did, I care not. . . . You threaten me? I am armed so strong in honesty, your threats go by me like so much wind,"—and Brutus began to twit him with refusing the money. "*I* can raise no money by vile means. *I* had rather coin my blood than wring the vile stuff from these peasants. You know this, and yet when I asked you for money you refused me! Was this done like Cassius?" Cassius answered simply that he had not refused the money (which, in fact, was true). "You did!" "I did not. It was a fool who brought you my answer. A friend should bear the infirmities of a friend, but you, Brutus, make mine greater than they are. Come, Antony! Come, Octavius! revenge yourself on Cassius alone! He is weary of this world; hated by the man he loves; checked like any slave; all his faults set down, noted, learned by rote, cast in his teeth. Here is my dagger and here my breast, naked! I denied you gold? Take my heart, then. Strike, as you struck Cæsar."

Brutus was softened, though as yet far from

convinced he was in the wrong. "Sheathe your dagger. I must bear with you; I cannot carry my anger long." "And must I live to be mocked and laughed at by Brutus?" "I was ill-tempered," Brutus admitted. "You confess so much? Give me your hand." "And my heart too." They had come thus near to being reconciled when a noise at the tent-door interrupted them, and in broke a crazy follower of Brutus, one Marcus Phaonius, who set up to be a philosopher, but from his eccentric behaviour was more often regarded as a fool. This fellow had heard that the two generals were quarrelling; and, pushing past the guards, he struck an attitude and began to recite certain verses of Homer, full of wise counsel, but with such extravagant gestures that Cassius burst out laughing while Brutus angrily hustled the fellow from the room.

Nothing cleanses the temper like a hearty laugh. Brutus, still frowning, called for a bowl of wine. "I did not think," said his friend, "you could have been so angry." "O Cassius," came the confession, "I am sick of many griefs."

"You—a Stoic—should make use of your philosophy."

"I do. No man bears sorrow better. Portia is dead."

"Portia!"

"She is dead."

So this was the explanation ... Cassius sat stunned. "How did I escape killing," he murmured, "when I crossed you so?"

Heart-broken with grief for her husband's absence and the forces gathering under Octavius and Antony to overwhelm him, Portia had lost her reason and taken her own life. Brutus told of it in a dull, level voice. It was Cassius who broke out with exclamations; not he to whom she had been dear above living things.

"Speak no more of her," he said, as the boy Lucius entered with the wine. The two friends drank to their love before admitting the captains to consider with them the plan of campaign.

At first, while Brutus discussed the latest news received of their enemies, Cassius sat dazed and inattentive, muttering of Portia's loss. He roused himself for a moment on hearing that Cicero too had perished—"proscribed" by the Triumvirs; but it was a direct question from Brutus which fully awoke him. "Octavius and Antony were marching upon Philippi, on the border between Thrace and Macedonia. What did Cassius think of crossing over to Europe and encountering them there?"

Cassius was opposed to this. It was better to let the enemy weary himself and exhaust his means on long marches than to go and save his labour by meeting him.

But Brutus made little of these reasons. The people in Asia Minor were disaffected already and grudged their contributions. Octavius and Antony would enlist recruits as they came, and therefore were better met and opposed as soon as possible.

Cassius would have argued. Once more he was right, and Brutus wrong; but either the old admiration blinded him, or he was passing weary of altercations. He gave way; the march was fixed for the morrow, and with the friendliest good-nights they parted.

It was late when the council broke up, and Brutus was left alone. A sense of calamity lay heavy on him. He called for two soldiers, Varro and Claudius, to sleep within his tent-door. They were willing to stand and watch; but he would not have it so, being always a kind master. His slave Lucius brought him his gown and book; the poor boy was heavy with want of sleep. With some self-reproach, Brutus begged him to take his lute and play. Lucius would do far more than this for the master he loved; and began to sing, touching the strings drowsily, while the two soldiers slept. The instrument almost slipped from his hand. Brutus took it gently from him, and the boy's head fell back on the pillow. And now the master alone kept watch, holding his book close to a solitary taper.

Minutes passed; by and by—was the taper burning ill, or was there a shadow deepening beyond it? He looked up. It was a shadow, but it had shape—likeness; it was dead Cæsar standing there! Brutus' blood ran cold as he stared at the apparition. It seemed to him that he found voice to challenge it. "Speak—what art thou?"

"Thy evil spirit, Brutus."

"Why comest thou?"

"To warn thee thou shalt see me again—at Philippi."

Between dread and scorn of himself and incredulity Brutus echoed the words stupidly, almost with a laugh.

"At Philippi," the vision repeated.

"Why, I will see thee then, at Philippi"—Brutus

brought his fist down on the table, calling "Lucius! Varro! Claudius! Awake there!"—and looked again. The vision had vanished.

"The strings are out of tune, my lord," muttered the boy Lucius drowsily.

Brutus awoke him; awoke the two soldiers. "Why had they cried out in their sleep? what had they seen?" They had seen nothing. Had they cried out? It was strange; but indeed they had seen nothing.

Had Brutus, too, seen nothing? Perhaps. But the spirit of Cæsar—all that Cæsar had stood for, all that he had meant upon earth—awaited them on the plains of Philippi towards which Brutus and Cassius set forth next day. They said little to one another as they and their legions marched deeper into what they felt to be the shadow of doom. When they had crossed the straits and were face to face with their enemies' tents, that shadow hung visible over them. During the march out from Sardis two eagles had perched on their banners and fed from the soldiers' hands. But at Philippi these birds of good omen had taken their departure, and now in their place the air was darkened with a flock of ravens, crows, and kites gathered from every quarter to forestall the grim feast preparing.

Nor did the two generals wear the mood of happy assurance. On the morning of the fight they took leave of each other bravely, as men should, but solemnly, as men prepared for the worst. If victory should be theirs, with the gods' help, then they might meet again with smiles and live all the rest of their days quietly one with another. If not—then this day would end the work begun on the Ides of March. No conqueror should ever have the joy of leading Brutus and Cassius in triumph. And upon this they took their farewells.

In the ordering of the battle Brutus found himself opposed by Octavius, Cassius by Antony. The two Triumvirs were never in hearty agreement from the first. Destiny alone bound them together for the time. Their natures were opposed in all respects. The elder man, eager, talented, and pleasure-loving, girded against the lad who was young enough to be his son but who went his own way so calmly and with a sort of bloodless self-possession. Antony had wished to oppose Brutus. "Why do you cross me?" he complained on finding that Octavius had arranged otherwise. "I do not cross you," replied Octavius, as if it did not admit of argument; "but I will have it so." Antony said no more.

Brutus finding Octavius' forces at a disadvantage, gave the word to charge; and his haste would have been justified—for his men at the first assault drove their enemies back with great slaughter—had it not taken Cassius unawares. As it was, Cassius' men gave ground before Antony's attack. He rallied them only to find himself hemmed round. Brutus should have relieved him at this point, and the day would have been won; but his men were plundering and killing among Octavius' tents, and he could not recall them in time. Cassius' cavalry were in full flight for the coast; he did what he could to hold his infantry firm, and snatching an ensign from one of the standard-bearers, planted it for a rallying mark, and fought on in hope of the assistance which did not come.

At length, however, he was forced to pluck up his standard and withdraw, with a few about him, to a little hill which gave a prospect over the plain. His sight was weak, but he could see his own tents blazing while Antony's soldiery pillaged through them. He made out also a troop of horsemen galloping towards him, and doubtful whether they were friends or foes, sent one of his companions, Titinius, to make sure. Meanwhile his servant Pindarus had climbed to the summit of the hill for a better view.

The advancing horsemen had in fact been sent by Brutus, though too late. Perceiving Titinius, and knowing him for one of Cassius' friends, they raised a great shout of welcome, with boastings of their victory. But Pindarus on the hill, hearing the noise and seeing Titinius surrounded, made sure that he was taken prisoner, and called down this news to Cassius. "Come down," commanded his master. The two were alone. "In Parthia I made thee prisoner, and in return for thy life took an oath from thee that whatsoever I might bid thou wouldst do. Take thy liberty now, and this sword— the sword that stabbed Cæsar. Smite, I command thee; now, as I cover my face." Pindarus drove the sword home, and then, as his master fell dead, cast it from him and ran; nor was he ever seen again.

So it happened that Titinius returning crowned with a wreath of victory and impatient to tell his good news, stumbled on his master stretched dead upon the hillside. The garland was useless now. Titinius bound it reverently on the senseless brow, and forthwith, like a stern Roman, slew himself upon the body; there to be found a little later by Brutus and his attendants. With bent head Brutus uttered the last farewell over his friend—"the last of all the Romans," he called him. "Friends, I owe this dead man more tears than ever you shall see me pay. I shall find time, Cassius; I shall find time."

In truth, as he said, the spirit of Cæsar still walked the earth and turned the conspirators' swords against themselves. Brutus' own time was not long. The first battle having proved indecisive, he offered fight again—to be driven from the field with a few remaining followers. One by one he drew them aside and entreated them to perform for him the office which Pindarus had performed for Cassius. Each shook his head; they loved him too well. It was a servant who at length, turning his head aside, held the sword on which Brutus flung himself—more gladly, he said, than he had lifted it against Cæsar.

Even his enemies respected the body, and gave it burial with full honours. "This," said Antony, "was the noblest Roman of them all. All the conspirators save him did what they did in envy of Cæsar's greatness. He alone joined them in honest motive and thought for the common good. His life was gentle, and himself so composed, that Nature might stand up and say to all the world, 'This was a man!'"

KING JOHN

HENRY II., King of England, was lord not of England only, but of a good third of what we call France. If you take a map of France and draw a line from Boulogne due south to the Pyrenees, you may say roughly that the country east of it was swayed by the King of France, and the country west of it by the King of England.

From his mother Matilda, daughter of our Henry I., he inherited the dukedom of Normandy as well as the crown of England; from his father Anjou, Maine, and Touraine; and his marriage with Elinor, Duchess of Aquitaine, brought him the seven provinces of the south—Poitou, Saintonge, the Angoumois, La Marche, the Limousin, Périgord, and Gascony.

Through his father—Geoffrey, the handsome Plantagenet, Count of Anjou—Henry came of one of the most notable and terrible races in history; a race descended from a wild Breton woodman who had helped the French king against the Danes and won for himself a grant of broad lands beside the Loire; a race half-savage, utterly unscrupulous, and abominably shrewd; great fighters to begin with, afterwards great generals, schemers, and controllers of men; outwardly good-natured and charming, but at heart lustful, selfish, monstrous in greed, without natural affection and indifferent to honour; scoffers at holiness, yet slavishly superstitious; and withal masterful men of affairs, sticking at no crime or treason which might help their ends. Such was the character fatally handed down from father to son. Henry inherited his share of it, and passed it on to his sons, who broke his heart by their hatreds and conspiracies against him; but the son whose treachery darkened his last hour was his favourite, John.

Of these sons we are only concerned with three—Richard Cœur de Lion; Geoffrey, Duke of Brittany; and John. On his father's death, Richard—who had hastened it by intriguing with the King of France—succeeded to the throne. Geoffrey was already dead, but had left a young son, Arthur, of whom we are to hear. Richard reigned for ten years, of which he spent just six months in England. He was a brave soldier but a detestably bad king. He looked on war as a sport, and to feed that sport in foreign countries he drained England by the cruellest taxes, which he repaid with misgovernment, or rather with no government at all. To him England, whose crown he wore, was a foreign land.

Now to John—who remained at home while Richard went crusading—England was not a foreign land, not a country of second importance. John was the shrewdest as well as the wickedest of his shrewd and wicked race, and alone of that race he valued England aright. We shall have to hate him; but let this be set to his credit against his black sins. He was the first of our kings to teach England—by bitter suffering, indeed, but still he taught her—to stand up for herself and defy the world.

When Richard died of an arrow-wound received while he was attacking the Castle of Châlus in the Limousin for some treasure he supposed it to contain, John, who had long been plotting against him at home, seized his opportunity and the crown of England.

He had no right to it. The true heir was young Arthur, son of his elder brother Geoffrey. But John was here on the spot, and he had his mother Elinor's support—for with her, as with the father he injured, he had always been the favourite son. England acknowledged him; Normandy acknowledged him; and in the south of France his mother held Aquitaine secure for him.

On the other hand Anjou, Maine, and Touraine did homage to young Arthur; and Philip, King of France, stood forward to champion his cause—not, as we shall see, from any burning sense of justice, but calculating perhaps that on his borders so young and gentle a lad would be a more comfortable neighbour than the ruthless and sinister John. At any rate, in answer to the entreaties of Constance, Arthur's mother, he made a fine show of indignation and sent his ambassador Chatillon to demand the surrender of John's claims.

"What follows," asked John grimly, "if we refuse?"

"Fierce and bloody war," replied Chatillon, "proudly to control you and enforce the rights you withhold by force."

"Here we have war for war, blood for blood,

controlment for controlment. Take that answer to France; and take it swiftly. For be you swift as lightning, the thunder of my cannon shall be quick on your heels."

And John was as good as his word. Chatillon, delayed by contrary winds, had scarcely time to reach France and report this defiance to his master before John had collected troops and was after him.

The ambassador found King Philip, with Constance, Arthur, and his forces, collected before the walls of Angiers, the capital of Anjou and birthplace of the Plantagenets. The unhappy citizens of that town saw themselves, as we say, between the devil and the deep sea. To acknowledge Arthur, to acknowledge John, seemed equally hazardous; and an error in deciding would assuredly mean their ruin. With admirable prudence, therefore, they had closed their gates against both parties, and postponed the ticklish business of declaring their preference until events should determine which side was likely to win.

This hesitancy of theirs naturally annoyed Philip, who had by his side, to support Arthur's cause, the Viscount of Limoges—though the real importance of this nobleman counted as nothing to his importance in his own conceit. As friend of the family to a Plantagenet he was enacting a new part. For it was by an arrow-shot from his Castle of Châlus that Richard Cœur de Lion had perished.

This was hardly an affair to brag about; but in honour of it Limoges ever after wore a lion's skin across his shoulders, and was swaggering now in this cloak while professing his love for Richard's nephew. But if the part he enacted was new, he seemed to feel it a magnanimous one, and promised Arthur his help and received the thanks of Constance with the air of a man who has reason to be pleased with himself and believe Heaven pleased with him.

While Philip was making up his mind to batter the obstinate town into submission, Chatillon arrived with his report and the news that John had crossed the Channel and was following upon Angiers by forced marches, bringing with him his mother Elinor, a very goddess of discord stirring him up to blood and strife; his niece Blanch, daughter of his sister Elinor and King Alphonso of Castile; and a whole crowd of dauntless volunteers who had sold their fortunes in England to equip themselves and win new and greater fortunes in France.

Chatillon spoke truth. Before Philip could bend his artillery against the walls, John arrived with his host and brought the French to parley. There was little to argue. Philip took his stand upon Arthur's plain right to inherit. "Geoffrey was thy elder brother, and this is his son. England was Geoffrey's right, and this is Geoffrey's." "Whence hast thou commission to lay down a law and condemn me by it?" was all that John could demand in reply. "From that supernal Judge," answered Philip, "who stirs good thoughts in the breast of any man holding strong authority, and bids him see to it when the right is defaced or stained. That Judge has made me this boy's guardian; under His warrant I impeach the wrong you are doing, and by His help I mean to chastise it." The parley might have ended here had not the dispute been fiercely taken up by the tongues of the women, Elinor on the one side, Constance on the other. Limoges in his character of family friend was ill-advised enough to interpose between them, crying "Peace!" "Hear the crier!" exclaimed a mocking voice at his elbow. The insulted noble turned round, demanding who dared thus to interrupt, and found himself face to face with a bluff and burly Englishman, a soldier commanding in John's army, Robert Faulconbridge by name.

Now this Faulconbridge was a son of Richard Cœur de Lion's, born out of wedlock. Like his father, he loved fighting for its own sake, and like a true Englishman he loved his country. So when John offered him service abroad, these two passions of his jumped together, and he readily gave up all claim to his estates at home and took the knighthood held out to him as his reward. The honour, as he confessed, he might learn to rise to. It was his humour to make himself out a rough and careless free-lance. But this blunt humour covered a real earnestness, and to see his father's memory insulted by this Limoges with the lion's skin was more than he could endure.

"Who is this fellow?" demanded Limoges.

"One that will soon let you know, sir, if I can catch you and that hide of yours alone. I'll tan that skin-coat for you, I promise you. So look to it!" and Faulconbridge rated him until the ladies of John's train began to join in the sport. "See," went on Faulconbridge, "the ass in lion's clothing! Ass, I'll take that burden off you, never fear, or lay on another that your shoulders shall feel!"

Limoges turned away in disgust; and Philip calling silence on this noisy diversion, demanded if John would resign his usurped titles and lay down his arms. "My life as soon!" John retorted, and called on Arthur to submit, promising him more by way of recompense than ever the coward hand of France could win for him. Elinor, too, urged Arthur to submit. "Do, child," mimicked Constance, using such prattle as is used to children. "Go to it grandam; give grandam kingdom, and grandam will give it a plum, a cherry, and a fig; there's a good grandam." The women's tongues broke loose again. Philip with difficulty cried them down at length, and bade a trumpet be blown to summon the citizens of Angiers to the parley.

The citizens appeared on the walls, and John and Philip in turn urged them by threats and persuasion to make their decision. The citizens made answer that they would acknowledge neither John nor Arthur until one had proved himself the stronger; for him they reserved their submission. In this resolution they were obstinate, and the two parties drew off to array their armies for the test of combat.

But the engagement which followed was indecisive. Each side claimed some trifling success, and on the strength of their claims the heralds of France and England were soon under the walls once more urging the citizens to decide. The citizens, who had watched the fight with impartial minds and from a capital position, made answer to the heralds and to the impatient kings who followed, that in their opinion no advantage had been gained by either party, and that they abode by their determination to keep their gates barred.

On hearing this answer it occurred to the pugnacious Faulconbridge to recollect that once upon a time the factions in Jerusalem under John of Giscala and Simon bar-Gioras had ceased their assaults upon each other to combine in resisting the Romans. He suggested that this example from history was worth copying, and that by first combining their forces to batter down Angiers, France and England would clear the ground for settling their own quarrel. To this wild counsel, as its author modestly called it, Philip and John were the more readily disposed to listen because in fact there appeared no other way out of a somewhat ludicrous fix.

Hitherto the citizens of Angiers had found the easiest policy—that of sitting still and waiting—the wisest. But now they saw clearly it was high time for them in their turn to make a suggestion; for if the two kings listened to Faulconbridge, as they seemed not averse from doing, Angiers was doomed.

So their spokesman craved leave for a word, and it was granted. This astute burgess saw well enough that the real decision for Angiers lay, not between Arthur and John, its rightful and its wrongful sovereign, but between the army of Philip and the army of John. From the beginning he had pledged the town to accept as in the right the claimant which should prove the stronger; and from this there was but a short step to the proposal he now made, which without any regard for right was simply aimed to get both armies on the same side.

"See," said he, "on one side here is the Lady Blanch, the niece of England; on the other, Lewis, the Dauphin of France. Where could be sought and found a couple more clearly suited each for the other? Unite them, and you unite two divided excellences, which only need union to be perfection; you join two silver currents such as together glorify the banks that bound them in." It was a shameless proposal, but the speaker was addressing shameless ears, and did not allow this to trouble him. Indeed his eloquence began to carry him away. "Marry them," said he, "and their union shall do more than battery upon our gates. But without this match the sea enraged is not half so deaf, nor are lions more confident, nor mountains and rocks more immovable; no, nor is Death himself in mortal fury one-half so peremptory, as we are to keep this city!"

"Dear, dear!" commented Faulconbridge, who had a natural prejudice against any scheme likely to dissuade from fighting, and perhaps a leaning of his own towards the love of the Lady Blanch, "here's a large mouth indeed! It spits forth death and mountains, rocks and seas, and talks as familiarly of roaring lions as maids of thirteen talk of puppy-dogs! Zounds! in all my born days I was never so bethumped with words!"

But the speaker knew what ears he was addressing. First Elinor advised her son to grasp the offer. She saw that Philip was wavering; perceived him already whispering with his advisers; noted that he glanced about him, and that Arthur and Constance were not present to harden him in the right. "Will their Majesties answer me?" asked the voice upon the wall. "Let England speak first," said wavering Philip. And John on this invitation spoke; offering Anjou, Touraine, Maine, Poictiers for the bride's dowry. The bribe was too much for Philip; the young couple professed themselves willing; Angiers opened her gates. Philip had one spasm of contrition for the widow and the widow's son he was betraying; but John quickly silenced his regrets. "Arthur shall be Duke of Brittany and Earl of Richmond, as well as lord of this fair town. If we cannot fulfil all the Lady Constance's wishes, we will at least give enough to silence her exclamations." The whole party passed through the gates to solemnise the contract without loss of time, leaving that rough soldier Faulconbridge to muse alone on the power of Self-Interest, that goddess who persuades men to break their vows, and kings to do off the armour which conscience has buckled on. But Faulconbridge had perhaps more than one reason for being out of temper.

To the Earl of Salisbury fell the thankless errand of carrying the news to Constance as she sat with her son in the French king's pavilion. Her outcries were terrible and pitiful too. "Gone to be married! Gone to swear a truce to join false blood with false blood!" She would not believe it. She turned fiercely on the Earl, and then reading the truth in his looks, fell to caressing and fondly lamenting over her boy. "Begone!" she commanded Salisbury, "leave me alone with my woes."

"Pardon me, madam," he answered, "I may not return without you."

"Thou mayst, thou shalt. I will not go. Grief so great as mine is proud," and she seated herself upon the ground. "Here," said she, "I and sorrows sit. Here is my throne; go bid kings come and bow before it!"

Terrible were the curses she uttered when the kings with the bridal train returned from the ceremony and found her seated thus; curses and prayers for discord between them, swiftly to be fulfilled. The officious Limoges again tried to pacify her, and again most ill-advisedly, for she turned on him in a fury and withered him with contemptuous fury. He was a coward, ever strong upon the stronger side; a champion who never fought but when fighting was safe; a ramping, bragging, fool; a loud-mouthed promiser, who fell away from his promises. "*Thou* wear a lion's hide! Do it off for shame, and hang a calf-skin on those recreant limbs!"

Limoges was stung. "If a man," he sputtered, "dared to say those words to me!"

"And hang a calf-skin on those recreant limbs," spoke a cool voice at his elbow, and there stood Faulconbridge ready for him.

It was maddening. "Villain! for thy life thou darest not say so!"

"And—hang—a calf-skin—on—those—recreant—limbs," repeated Faulconbridge imperturbably.

John had scarcely time to call peace between them

before a newcomer was announced—Pandulph, the legate of Pope Innocent the Third. The Pope had grave cause of anger against John. After the death of Hubert Walter, Archbishop of Canterbury, John had forced the monks of Christchurch to accept a creature of his own, John de Gray, Bishop of Norwich, as Primate. Innocent set aside the election, and consecrated Stephen Langton, a cardinal and thorough churchman, as archbishop. John refused to allow Stephen to set foot in England, drove out the monks of Christchurch, quartered a troop of soldiers in their cloisters, and confiscated their lands. Innocent threatened excommunication, and now sent Pandulph to demand in the Pope's name why John had not submitted.

This flung John into a fury. "What earthly name can compel the free breath of a sacred king to submit to questioning? Go, ask your master that; and further add, from the mouth of England, that no Italian priest shall take tithe or toll in our dominions. But as, under God, we are supreme head, so under Him we will uphold that supremacy without the assistance of any Pope!"[3]

"Brother of England, you blaspheme," put in Philip, shocked by this defiance.

"Blaspheme, do I? Though you and all the kings in Christendom are misled by this meddling priest—this man who sells divine pardon for money; though you

[3]Remember that Shakespeare, who puts this defiance into John's mouth, was writing for a Protestant England. Call it right or wrong, "England for England" was John's motto, and—black as Shakespeare must paint him—it is also the motto of this play.

and all the rest feed this juggling witchcraft with your moneys; yet I alone—alone, I say—will stand up against it and count the Pope's friends my foes."

This was enough. In the Pope's name Pandulph pronounced the terrible words of interdict—placing John without the pale of Christianity, blessing all who revolted from allegiance to him, and promising the name and worship of a saint to anyone who should by secret murder rob him of his hateful life. And the curses of Constance echoed the appalling sentences.

Then turning to Philip, Pandulph bade him, on peril of the Pope's curse, withdraw his friendship and join with the rest of Christendom against the heretic.

This demand, coming so soon upon his newly-knit compact, placed Philip in a truly pitiable plight. And standing there amid the clamours of the women between the imperious calm of Pandulph and dark face of John, who stood silent, waiting for his answer with the sneer ready on his lips, the King of France cut a sorry figure. In vain he protested and appealed to Pandulph. The legate answered him calmly, proving that to keep faith with John was to break faith with religion, that to be friends with both was impossible.

And in the end, as was certain from the first, Philip gave way. Though by doing so he must set discord between the young pair so newly married, he gave way. John had looked for nothing else. "France," said he, with curt contempt, "thou shalt rue this hour within this hour"; and turning to Faulconbridge, bade him draw the English forces together. Faulconbridge needed no second bidding.

And in the fight which followed, Faulconbridge, at least, had his revenge. It is not known in what part of the field he encountered Limoges, or what was said between them. But he returned nonchalantly bearing Limoges' head, and asserting that, by his life, it was very hot weather!

John, too, enjoyed some measure of revenge in taking prisoner young Arthur, whom he handed over into the keeping of his Chamberlain, Hubert de Burgh. In the camp of the beaten French there was little doubt now of the fate in store for the boy. His mother Constance cried for him, and refused to be comforted. Her body had become a grave to her soul, a prison holding the eternal spirit against its will. Her cries and calls upon death wrung the hearers' hearts. They deemed her mad wholly, but she denied it with fierceness. "I am not mad. If I were, I could forget my son, or cheat myself with a babe of rags. I am not mad." Binding up her dishevelled hair, she fell to wondering and asking Pandulph if 'twere true she should meet her boy in heaven. "For now sorrow will canker his beauty, and he will grow hollow as a ghost, and dim, and meagre; and so he'll die. And so, when he rises again, and I meet him in the court of heaven, I shall not know him—shall never, never again behold my pretty Arthur!" Philip and Pandulph tried to rebuke this excess of grief. She pointed to the legate, "He talks, that never had a son!" Then turned to the King—"Grief! It is grief that fills up the room of my absent child, lies in his bed, walks at my side, puts on his pretty looks, and repeats his words. Good reason have I to be fond of grief. Fare you well! Had you such a loss as I, I could give better comfort than yours." And she went her way to her chamber; but as she went she broke out crying again, "O Lord! my boy, my fair son, my Arthur!"

Lewis the Dauphin and Pandulph watched her as she went, the boy shallow of heart and head, the man deep-witted and just now thoughtful even beyond his habit. "Before the curing of a disease," he mused half-aloud, "ay, in the instant when health turns back towards repair, the fit is strongest. It is strange, now, to think how much John has lost in this which he supposes so clearly won. You are grieved, are you not, that Arthur is prisoner?"

"As heartily," said Lewis, "as John is glad."

"You are young. Listen; John has seized Arthur, and while that lad lives John cannot draw a quiet breath. Arthur will fall."

"But what shall I gain by Arthur's fall?"

"Simply this, that in the right of your bride, the Lady Blanch, you can then claim all that Arthur did. The times conspire with you. This murder of Arthur—which must be—will so freeze the hearts of men against John that every natural sign of heaven will be taken for an index of divine wrath against him."

"May be," Lewis urged, "he will not touch his life, but hold him a prisoner."

"Should you but move a foot," said the astute priest,

"even if Arthur be not dead already, at that news he dies. That death will set the hearts of all England in revolt. Nor is this all. Faulconbridge is even now in England ransacking the church and offending charity. A dozen French over there at this moment would whistle ten thousand Englishmen to their side. Shall we lay this before your father?"

The temptation was too strong. "Yes, let us go," answered Lewis. "Strong reasons make strong actions. What you urge my father will not deny."

On one point Pandulph was not mistaken. While Arthur lived John could not draw quiet breath. No sooner had he despatched Faulconbridge to England than he called Hubert de Burgh to him. Of murder he would not speak openly, but first he dwelt on Hubert's professed love for him, and went on to say that he had a matter to speak of, but must fit it to some better time. The day was too open. If it were night now, and a friend standing by—such a friend as could see without eyes, hear without ears, make reply without tongue, why then . . . and yet he loved Hubert well and believed himself loved in return.

"So well," protested Hubert, "that were it death to do bidding of yours, I would undertake it!"

"Do I not know thou wouldst? Hubert," he whispered, casting a glance over his shoulder at the boy, whom Elinor had craftily drawn aside. "Good Hubert, throw an eye on that boy yonder. I tell thee he is a serpent in my way. Wheresoever I tread he lies before me. Dost understand? Thou art his keeper."

"And will keep him so that he shall never offend your Majesty."

"Death." John muttered the word, half to himself.

"My lord?" Hubert heard, and half understood.

"A grave." John was not looking at him.

"He shall not live."

"Enough." John made show not to have heard. "Hubert, I love thee. Well, well, I'll not say what I intended. To England now, with a merry heart!"

When Hubert, however, had his young charge safe in England, John's commands became more precise. Arthur's eyes were to be burnt out with hot irons—an order which revolted even one of the executioners hired for the task. And when the dreadful hour came, and Hubert had the men stationed behind the arras with orders to heat the irons, his heart, as he sent for the boy, sickened at the thought of the black business. For Arthur with his gentle and confiding nature had soon given Hubert his love, and Hubert's rough nature was touched by the child who meant no harm to anyone and could not understand that anyone should mean harm to him.

Arthur saw at once that his friend was heavy. "Why should you be sad?" he asked. "I think nobody should be sad but I; and if only I were out of prison, and a shepherd-boy, I could be as merry as the day was long. I would even be merry here, if it were not for fear of my uncle. Is it my fault, though, that I am Geoffrey's son? I wish I were your son, Hubert, and then you would love me."

This innocent talk was torture to Hubert. He feared that more of it would steal all his resolution, and therefore pulled out the hateful paper at once and showed it, turning away to hide the tears that against his will came into his eyes.

"What!" cried the dazed child. "Burn out my eyes! Will you do it? Have you the heart? Hubert, when your head ached, I bound it with my handkerchief—the best I had—and sat with you at midnight to comfort you. If you think this was crafty love, you must. But will you indeed put out these eyes that never so much as frowned on you, and never shall?"

"I must. I have sworn," groaned Hubert, and stamped his foot for signal to call the executioners. It was pitiful how Arthur ran and clung to him at the sight of them with their cords and irons.

"Save me, Hubert, save me!" he screamed.

"Give me the iron, and bind him here," commanded Hubert.

"No, no—I will not struggle. I will be still as a stone. For Heaven's sake do not let them bind me! Hubert, hear me!—drive these men away, and I will sit as quiet as a lamb. I will not wince, will not speak a word. Only send these men away, and I will forgive whatever torment you put me to!"

"Go," said Hubert, "leave me with him." And the executioners withdrew, glad to be released from the horrible deed. "Come, boy, prepare yourself."

But Arthur pleaded on his knees. "Hubert, cut out my tongue, if you will, but spare my eyes! O, spare my eyes!" The iron, while he pleaded, grew cold in Hubert's hand. He could not do this monstrous crime. It was ruin for him if John discovered the truth, but he would take the risk, and spread the report that Arthur was dead. Thus resolved, he led the boy away to hide him.

His friends in the French camp were not the only ones who foreboded evil for Arthur. To make all sure, John on his return to England had himself crowned a second time. The barons who attended—the Earls of Pembroke, Salisbury, and the rest—were full of courtly phrases. This second coronation, they assured John, was superfluous as to gild refined gold, to paint the lily, perfume the violet, or seek to garnish daylight with a taper. But behind these polite professions they were whispering about Arthur's fate. And when John bade them state what reforms they wished for, the Earl of Pembroke boldly requested, for all, that Arthur should be set at liberty.

"Let it be so," answered John, who knew, or thought he knew, how idle a thing he conceded. At this moment Hubert entered, and the King drew him aside, while the lords whispered their suspicions.

"Good lords," announced John, coming back, "I regret that to grant your demand is beyond me. This man tells me that Arthur died last night."

There was an ominous silence. Then the Earl of Salisbury spoke. "Indeed," said he with meaning, "we feared that his sickness was past cure." "Yes," added the Earl of Pembroke, "we heard how near his death he was—before he felt himself sick. This must be answered for."

"Why are you frowning on me?" John demanded. "Do I hold the shears of destiny, or can I command life?"

"It is foul play," said Salisbury boldly, and Pembroke echoed him. In stern anger the barons withdrew. Already John began to repent his cruel order, or at any rate the haste of it.

Soon he had further cause. News came that France was arming mightily to invade England—nay, had already landed an army under the Dauphin; that his mother Elinor was dead; that death, too, had ended the frenzy of poor Constance. How could he meet the invaders? His barons were disaffected. Faulconbridge, who had been levying cruel toll upon the clergy, returned with word that the whole country was uneasy, full of vague fears, overrun with men prophesying disasters. In truth the interdict lay on the land like a blight. All public worship of God had ceased. The church-doors were shut and their bells silent; men celebrated no sacrament but that of private baptism; youth and maid could not marry; the dying went without pardon or comfort; the dead lay unburied by the high-roads; the corpses of the clergy were piled on churchyard walls in leaden coffins; the people heard no sermons but those preached at the market-crosses by priests who cried down curses, or wild prophets who uttered warnings and pointed to the signs of heaven for confirmation. With news similar to Faulconbridge's Hubert broke in on the King, as he sat muttering in dark sorrow for his mother Elinor's death. It was "Arthur," "Arthur," in all men's mouths. The peers had gone to seek Arthur's grave; all the common folk whispered of Arthur's death.

"Arthur's death?" John interrupted him savagely. "Who murdered him but you?"

"At your wish," retorted Hubert.

"It is the curse of kings to be attended by such over-hasty slaves."

"Here is your hand and seal for it," Hubert protested. But John, who by this time heartily wished Arthur alive again, broke out on him with craven reproaches. "Why had Hubert taken him at his word? Why had he not dissuaded, even by a look—a look would have been enough." So he ran on, until Hubert had to confess the truth, that Arthur was yet alive.

"Arthur alive!" The King sprang up. "Hasten! Report it to the peers! Forgive what I said in my passion; my rage was blind. Nay, answer me not, but hasten and bring these angry lords back to me!"

But Hubert was mistaken. Arthur was no longer alive. The unhappy prince, scheming to break from his prison, had escaped the watch by donning a ship-boy's clothes; but in a rash leap from the walls had broken himself upon the stones below, a little while before the barons—Pembroke, Salisbury, and Bigot—arrived in search of him. Before hearing Hubert's news John had despatched Faulconbridge to persuade them to return. He overtook them by the wall of the castle; and while he urged them, they stumbled together on the young body lying at the base of it.

"It was murder," they swore; "the worst and vilest of murder; nay, a murder that stood alone, unmatchable!" They appealed to Faulconbridge.

"It is a damnable work," he admitted indignantly. "The deed of a heavy hand; that is," he mused doubtfully, "if it be the work of any hand."

"*If!*" cried Salisbury. "There is no if! We had an inkling of this. It is Hubert's shameful handiwork devised by the King—whose service, kneeling by this sweet child's body, I renounce, and swear neither to taste pleasure nor take rest until I have glorified this hand of mine with vengeance!" And the two other barons said AMEN to him.

But hardly was the vow taken before Hubert himself arrived, hot with haste, and panting, "Lords, the King sends for you. Arthur is alive!" With that he stood confounded, staring down upon Arthur's dead body.

"Begone, villain!" Salisbury drew his sword. "Murderer!" "I am no villain, no murderer," Hubert protested. "Cut him to pieces!" urged Pembroke. Faulconbridge flung himself between them, threatening to strike Salisbury dead if he stirred a foot. "Put up your sword, or I'll so maul you and your toasting-iron that you'll think the devil himself has got hold of you!" And Salisbury, proud lord as he was, obeyed. But, though Hubert protested his innocence, the angry lords would not believe. Faulconbridge could do no more, and was forced, to his chagrin, to watch them galloping off to join the Dauphin.

When they were gone he turned to Hubert. "Know you of this work? For if this work be yours, Hubert, your soul is lost beyond reach of mercy; nay, if you but consented, despair. Hubert, I suspect you grievously."

Said Hubert: "If in act, or consent, or thought, I stole the sweet breath of this child, let hell lack pains enough for my torture! I left him well." He lifted the body and carried it in his arms into the castle, while Faulconbridge followed sorely perplexed. "I lose my way," confessed that honest soldier, "amid the thorns and dangers of this world."

By this time John's case was a sorry one. Pope Innocent had formally deposed him, and was urging on the crusade which the Dauphin led against England. Wales was in revolt, Scotland intriguing against him. But, worse than all, England herself could not be relied on. Betrayed by his barons, who flocked to Lewis' standard; denounced by the clergy; sullenly hated by all classes, who laid the miseries of the interdict to his account; the King felt the ground slipping from under his feet.

But he was an Angevin after all; that is to say, as diabolically clever as he was shameless. It only needed shamelessness, and by a bold stroke he could turn the tables on France, and perhaps win back all. John played it. He sent for Pandulph, and hypocritically tendered his submission to the Pope, on condition that the Pope called off the French and put a stop to the crusade against him. Like many a man without religion John was slavishly superstitious, and he had heard it prophesied that before Ascension-day he should deliver up his crown; and it pleased him to think that by this form of tendering it into Pandulph's hands he was cheating Heaven as well as his enemies.

Pandulph gave him back the circlet, and hastened off to compel the Dauphin to lay down his arms. Scarcely had he left before Faulconbridge arrived with news that London had thrown open its gates to the French, and the barons refused to return to their allegiance.

"What! When they heard that Arthur was yet alive?"

"They found him dead—done to death by some accursed hand."

"That villain Hubert told me he lived."

"On my soul," said Faulconbridge, "he did, for aught Hubert knew."

John informed him of the peace just made with the Pope. As might be expected, this news filled Faulconbridge with disgust. It was too much altogether for his English stomach. "But perhaps," he suggested, "the Cardinal Pandulph cannot make your peace,"—he had to call it "*your* peace"—"and, if he can, let them see at least that we meant to defend ourselves." And with

John's permission he hurried off to save what he could of England's honour.

Indeed, Pandulph was not prospering on his errand. He found the Dauphin entertaining the revolted barons with words as fair as they were deceitful, since, after using them to crush John, he meant to make short work with Salisbury, Pembroke, and the rest. Young Lewis had learnt his lesson too well. As Pandulph himself had once suggested, he was now by Arthur's death left with a good claim to the English crown. In short, he flatly refused to draw off his troops. "Am I Rome's slave?" he demanded. "Your breath kindled this war, but who maintained it? Who but I provided men and munition, and bore the sweat of this business? Here I am with England half-conquered, and all the best cards in my hand, and you ask me to retire! No, on my soul, I will not!"

In this temper Faulconbridge found him, and with the legate at a complete loss. It was the chance he had prayed for, and he made royal use of it. In the name of England he stood up to the angry Dauphin, defied him, and dressed him down with threats. "Our English King promises through me to whip you and your army of youngsters out of his territories. What! the hand that cudgelled you the other day at your own door till you jumped the hatch and hid yourself, and shook even when a cock crew—your own Gallic cock—thinking its voice an Englishman's—do you deem that hand which chastised you in your own chambers to be enfeebled here?" And having done with the Dauphin, he swung round on the revolted barons and gave them their rating in turn.

"Enough!" broke in Lewis at length. "We grant you can outscold us." Pandulph would have put in a word, but Faulconbridge bore him down, and with mutual defiance the parley ended.

It was war now, but a war which brought disasters to both sides. In the south of England the Dauphin met with small resistance; but the fleet which was to bring him supplies came to wreck on the Goodwin Sands, and the English barons, warned of the treachery he plotted against them, streamed away from him. On the other hand, John, though he kept the field fiercely, traversing the midlands by forced marches from the Welsh border to Lincoln and breaking up the barons' plans, was already touched with a fever which increased on him as he started from Lynn and crossed the Wash in a fresh movement northwards. In crossing the sandy flats his troops were surprised by the tide, and all his baggage and treasure washed away.

Shaking with the fever, which by this time had taken fatal hold of him, wet, exhausted, and sick at heart, the stricken tyrant took shelter in the Abbey of Swineshead. There, men said, a monk poisoned his food; but although the monks had reason enough to hate him, we need not lay this crime at their door. Panting for air, crying that his soul might have elbow-room for hell was within him, he was borne out into the abbey orchard. The tears of his young son Henry fell on his face. "The salt of them is hot," he complained; and so, at the height of his own misery and England's, he died.

His death put a new face on the fortunes of England. Against a young king, supported by the barons and the better hopes of his subjects, the troops of a foreigner could not hold their ground for long on this island. And the lesson of this "troublesome raigne" is summed up for us in the wise, brave, and patriotic words of Faulconbridge—lines which every English boy should get by heart:—

> "This England never did, nor never shall,
> Lie at the proud foot of a conqueror,
> But when it first did help to wound itself.
> Now these her princes are come home again,
> Come the three corners of the world in arms,
> And we shall shock them. Nought shall make us rue,
> If England to herself do rest but true."

KING RICHARD
THE SECOND

WHEN King Edward the Third died, the crown passed to his grandson Richard, son of the good and gallant Black Prince, whose untimely death all England lamented. And though Richard became King in his eleventh year, all England hoped much of him for his father's sake. In honour of his coronation London was gay with banners and arches, and the loyal merchants of Cheapside erected a fountain which ran with wine for the rejoicing citizens.

But the sons of strong men are not always strong, and as time went on Richard began to disappoint the hopes of his subjects. He was weak, partly no doubt by nature, partly perhaps by training; for he had too many advisers, some of whom flattered him whilst all were intent on their own ends. A boy may be weak and yet very wilful, and this boy-king naturally made favourites of those who flattered him most, and, being without experience, trusted to their advice. At first he was given twelve councillors; his three uncles, the Duke of Lancaster (called John of Gaunt), the Duke of York, and the Duke of Gloucester, being excluded;

but these three in their jealousy often interfered with the government, and at last one of them, the Duke of Gloucester, was put at the head of the council. Under him the Parliament—called "wonderful" by some, and "merciless" by others who admired it less—put to death two of Richard's favourites, De Vere and Suffolk, and stripped the rest of their properties. This incensed the young King, who waited his time, and at twenty-two, declaring he would be in leading-strings no longer, dismissed his guardians and for some years ruled his kingdom discreetly and well.

But he was not great enough to forgive those who had humbled him. Perhaps, too, he still feared the Duke of Gloucester. At any rate, after eight years of merciful rule he seized his uncle suddenly and had him carried off to Calais, where Thomas Mowbray, Duke of Norfolk, was governor; and in the prison there Gloucester came to a mysterious end. We cannot be certain that he was murdered by the King's order; but many believed this. And they believed it the more surely when Richard began to cast off pretence of ruling to please his people. He had chosen new favourites—Sir John Bushy, Sir Henry Green, Sir William Bagot—to replace his old ones; and now he called a packed parliament, which not only undid the acts of the detested "wonderful" Parliament, but entrusted all future government to the King and a little knot of his friends. So Richard for the time was absolute, and the kingdom suffered, as it always must when a King postpones its happiness to his private likes and dislikes.

Gloucester was dead, and of the other two uncles

(whatever they suspected) old Lancaster—or John of Gaunt—was too wise, and old York too pliable, to accuse the King openly of his murder. But John of Gaunt had a son Henry, surnamed Bolingbroke, Duke of Hereford, a soldierly man who was not so cautious. Henry's wife, too, was a sister of Gloucester's widow, and this no doubt made him more eager for revenge. Yet even Henry Bolingbroke did not dare accuse his cousin the King in so many words. He chose a more politic way. At first privately, and then openly, he charged Mowbray, Duke of Norfolk—who had been governor of Calais at the time of Gloucester's murder—as a traitor. The King summoned the appellant and the accused to confront each other in his presence, and there, after mutual defiance, the one protesting the truth of his charge, the other his complete innocence, and both their loyalty, they severally stated their quarrel. "I accuse Mowbray," said Bolingbroke, "first, that he has detained for his own use eight thousand nobles which should have been paid to the King's soldiers; next, that he has been the head and spring of all treasons contrived in this realm for these eighteen years; and further,"—and here lay the pith of his accusation—"that he did contrive the death of the Duke of Gloucester, whose innocent blood cries to me from the earth for justice and chastisement." "What sayest thou to this?" demanded Richard, hiding his feelings (whatever they were) and turning to Mowbray. "Fear not because the accuser is my cousin. Ye are equally my subjects, and the King's eyes and ears are impartial, the firmness of his soul unstooping." Mowbray gave Bolingbroke the lie in his throat. Each of the disputants by this time had thrown down his gage, and now each swore to uphold his cause upon the other's body. Richard endeavoured to appease them, and invoked the help of old John of Gaunt, Bolingbroke's father, who stood by. But Mowbray flung himself at the King's feet imploring to be allowed to defend his honour; and finding Bolingbroke equally stubborn, Richard ceased his mediation. "We were not born," he said, "to sue, but to command. And since our commandment will not make you friends, we charge you to appear at Coventry, on St. Lambert's day, and there decide your quarrel with sword and lance."

So at Coventry on the appointed day the lists were set with all the ceremony and circumstance of those times. The King attended with his train of nobles and favourites; and as they entered to the sound of trumpets and filed into their seats along the decorated balcony, they found both combatants armed and ready with their heralds. At a word from the King the Lord Marshal, to whom fell the solemn business of dressing the lists, approached Mowbray the defendant, and demanded his name and quarrel.

"My name," was the answer, "is Thomas Mowbray, Duke of Norfolk, and I come hither upon my knightly oath, to defend my loyalty and truth to God, my King, and my heirs, against the Duke of Hereford who appeals me; and by the grace of God and this arm of mine to prove him a traitor to my God, my King, and me. And as I truly fight, defend me Heaven!"

Bolingbroke, on being asked the same question,

declared, "I am Harry of Hereford, Lancaster, and Derby, who stand in arms here ready to prove in lists upon Thomas Mowbray, Duke of Norfolk, by God's grace and my bodily valour, that he is a traitor to God, to King Richard, and to me. And as I truly fight, defend me Heaven!"

The Lord Marshal thereupon (as the custom was) gave warning that no man should, upon pain of death, enter or touch the lists, except only the officers appointed to direct the duel. But before engaging Bolingbroke craved leave to kneel and kiss the King's hand; "for," said he, "Mowbray and I are like two men vowed to a long and weary pilgrimage, and it were fitting that we took a ceremonious and loving farewell of our friends." "Nay," said the King, when this message was reported; "we will ourselves descend and embrace him;" and he did so, saying, "Cousin of Hereford, as thy cause is right, so be thy fortune!" meaning "*as far as*," or "*if* thy cause is right," for he well knew that the charge against Mowbray was covertly aimed at himself. And he added, "Though thy blood and mine be kin, if thy blood be shed we may lament but not avenge thee." "Nay," answered Bolingbroke, who took his meaning, "let no man lament for me if I fall. But I go to this fight, and so I take my leave, confident, lusty, young, and cheerful. And do thou, my father," turning to John of Gaunt, "prosper me with thy blessing, that my armour may be proof against my adversary, and thy name take new brightness from thy son's lance." "God make thee prosperous in thy good cause!" answered the old man.

The King's farewell to Mowbray was purposely

more cold and brief. "However God or fortune may cast my lot," Mowbray protested, "there lives or dies a true subject, a loyal, just, and upright gentleman. Take from me the wish of happy years. And so, as a captive from prison, gentle and jocund, I go to this feast of battle. For truth has a quiet breast." "Farewell, my lord," the King answered; "in thine eye I read virtue and valour together."

With that he gave the word to the Lord Marshal. The two combatants received their lances, and the heralds on either side made proclamation: "Here standeth Harry of Hereford, Lancaster, and Derby, on pain to be found false and recreant, to prove the Duke of Norfolk a traitor to God, to his sovereign, and to him." "Here standeth Thomas Mowbray, Duke of Norfolk, on pain to be found false and recreant, both to defend himself and to approve the same on Henry of Hereford, Lancaster, and Derby."

"Sound trumpets! and set forward, combatants!" shouted the Lord Marshal; but as the pair couched lances and dug spurs for the charge, as the horses gathered pace for the shock, he glanced towards the royal balcony, and held up a hand.

"Stay!" he cried. "The King has thrown down his truncheon!"

For by this signal Richard, as president of the fight, arrested it.

The combatants reined up. "Let them," commanded Richard, "lay by their helmets and spears and both return here to their chairs." And while they obeyed, and the trumpets sounded a long flourish, he consulted, or seemed to consult, with his nobles.

"Draw near," he commanded again, "and hearken what with our council we have decided." And he went on to unfold his sentence—a sentence of banishment on both; for Bolingbroke ten years, but for Mowbray no date at all. "Never to return," were the hopeless words of Mowbray's sentence. "It is a heavy one," pleaded the unhappy man. "A dearer merit, and not so deep a maim, I have deserved at my King's hands. Can I unlearn my native English which I have learned these forty years? I am too old to go to school now. That to which you condemn me is a living death."

But the King answered curtly that the time had gone by for pleading. Yet, weak man that he was, he recalled Mowbray and desired both him and Bolingbroke to lay hands on his sword and vow never to meet and plot against him—a foolish vow, which suggested a fear, and the keeping of which he could never enforce.

Both took the vow. And on rising Bolingbroke made a last appeal to Mowbray to confess. But "No," said Mowbray, "I am no traitor. What thou art, God, thou, and I know; and all too soon, I fear, the King will learn and rue it." And so he departed into exile.

No sooner was he gone than weak Richard, reading the sorrow in the dimmed eyes of old John of Gaunt, impetuously relieved Bolingbroke of four years of his sentence. His banishment, he promised, should be for six not for ten winters. But this wayward leniency brought him little gratitude. Bolingbroke did not even thank him. "Four lagging winters," he commented grimly, "four wanton springs ended in a word! Such is the breath of kings!" Old Gaunt was more nobly rebukeful. "I thank my liege that for my sake he remits four years of my son's exile; though it will profit me little, since, ere the six years be gone, my inch of taper will be burnt out, and I gone into darkness where I shall never see my son." "Why, uncle," Richard would have reassured him, "thou hast many years yet." The old man turned on him grandly. "But not a minute, King, that thou canst give! Shorten my days with sorrow thou canst, kill me thou canst, but lengthen life or restore it thou canst not." "Thy son," said Richard, nettled to an unworthy taunt, "is banished upon good advice—which *thy* tongue joined in giving." "That is true," answered John of Gaunt; "I gave it as a judge, not as a father, and in the sentence destroyed my own life. Alas! I looked for one of you to say I was too strict with my own. But you did not; you allowed my unwilling tongue to do myself this wrong!" To this the selfish Richard could find no answer, but curtly left them to their leave-taking. And a sorry leave-taking it was, the good old man vainly casting about for arguments to cheat the bitterness of his son's exile. "Six winters are quickly gone . . . this absence will make home-coming all the more precious . . . to the wise man all places visited by the eye of Heaven are ports and happy havens . . . let necessity teach thee to reason thus, for there is no virtue like necessity." But the younger man brushed these flimsy consolations aside. "Can a man bear to hold fire in his hand by thinking of the frosty Caucasus, or cloy his hunger by imagining that he feasts? No; to apprehend happiness makes him feel more keenly the evil he suffers. But farewell England's ground—my mother and nurse! Where'er I wander, this I can yet boast, that though banished I am a true-born Englishman." And with this he took his leave.

But Richard, alone with his favourites—Bagot and Green and the rest—could confess he was glad to be rid of Henry Bolingbroke. For the King had no sons of his own, and this son of Lancaster had wooed the common people and practised such affability that to jealous minds he seemed to look forward with confidence to a day when the crown would be his. "Well, he is gone," said Green; "out of sight is out of mind." Thus relieved of present anxiety, and having no child for whom his love might have taught him that in the end a king's welfare and his people's are one, and having emptied his coffers by selfish extravagance, Richard fell in with the proposal to farm out the nation's revenues to these harpies, who undertook to provide him with ready money to suppress a rebellion in Ireland which for the moment was giving him trouble. One day, while they were discussing this, Bushy entered with the news that John of Gaunt had been seized with a grievous illness. In such company Richard could blurt out his feelings. "Now, may God," he cried, "put it in the physician's mind to help him to his grave immediately! The lining of his coffers shall make coats for our soldiers in these Irish wars. Pray God," he added cruelly, "that we may make haste—and come too late!" And all said "Amen."

John of Gaunt was sick indeed. His son's banishment

had been his death-blow; and now, at Ely House in Holborn, he lay in his bed and discussed with his pliable brother, old York, the last warning he intended to deliver to Richard. "Vex not yourself; counsel comes in vain to him," urged York. "But the tongues of dying men— these, they say, enforce attention like deep harmony. Men's ends are more marked than their lives. Though Richard would not hear my counsel in life, his ear may be unsealed now." "No," said York, "for it is stopped with flattery. Save the little breath thou hast remaining." But the dying man felt bound to speak; "for," said he, "I feel like a prophet inspired to foretell that this rash fierce blaze of riot cannot last;" and as he lay awaiting the King's coming, his lips began to mutter, over and over, words of love for England and pride in her.[4]

"This royal throne of kings, this scepter'd isle,
This earth of majesty, this seat of Mars,
This other Eden, demi-paradise,
This fortress built by Nature for herself
Against infection and the hand of war,
This happy breed of men, this little world,
This precious stone set in the silver sea,
Which serves it in the office of a wall
Or as a moat defensive to a house,
Against the envy of less happier lands,
This blessed plot, this earth, this realm, this England,
This nurse, this teeming womb of royal kings,

[4]This incomparable lament may only be rendered in Shakespeare's own words, which no English boy, who is old enough to love his country, is too young to get by heart, forgetting the sorrow in it. Tears such as Gaunt's are drawn from a well of joy and pride in England and of fierce love of her good name.

Fear'd by their breed and famous by their birth,
Renowned for their deeds as far from home,
For Christian service and true chivalry,
As is the sepulchre in stubborn Jewry
Of the world's ransom, blessed Mary's Son,—
This land of such dear souls, this dear dear land,
Dear for her reputation through the world,
Is now leased out, I die pronouncing it,
Like to a tenement or pelting farm:
England, bound in with the triumphant sea,
Whose rocky shore beats back the envious siege
Of watery Neptune, is now bound in with shame,
With inky blots and rotten parchment bonds:
That England, that was wont to conquer others
Hath made a shameful conquest of itself.
Ah, would the scandal vanish with my life,
How happy then were my ensuing death!"

While he mourned, the King was announced, with his Queen and train of courtiers. "How fares our noble uncle, Lancaster?" were the Queen's words; but Richard addressed York more roughly. "What comfort, man? How is't with old Gaunt?" The sick man heard the word, and his failing mind fixed and began to harp on it: "Ay, old Gaunt—old and gaunt—gaunt with keeping watch for sleeping England—gaunt as the grave to which I go." "Can sick and dying men be so witty?" sneered Richard. "Nay, King, 'tis thou who art sick, and thy death-bed no lesser than thy realm wherein thou liest and givest over thy anointed body to be cured by these flatterers, these physicians who dealt the wound." And rising on his pillow he began to call shame on his nephew's mad misgovernment. But Richard, white for the moment and scared, turned upon him in a fury. "Thou lunatic, lean-witted fool! Darest thou presume on an ague's privilege to admonish me thus? Now, by my throne, wert thou not brother to great Edward's son, thy tongue which runs so roundly should run thy head from thy shoulders!" "Spare me not for *that*," exclaimed Gaunt bitterly: "My brother Gloucester's end is good witness that thou regardest not shedding Edward's thy grandfather's blood!" And so having uttered at last the accusation which he had so long foreborne to utter, and for hinting at which he had consented to see his son exiled, Gaunt was borne out dying. "So be it," said Richard.

But so incensed was he—men of his nature being angriest when some fear underlies their wrath—that presently, when the Earl of Northumberland brought news that Gaunt's life had indeed flickered out, he rapped forth the order which he had discussed secretly with Bushy, Bagot, and the rest—to seize upon the dead duke's estate and moneys for his own royal use.

Even old York—weak worm as he was—turned at this. The nation's disgrace had not stirred him as it stirred Gaunt, but he could feel a family wrong; and for once he plucked up courage to speak out—so boldly, indeed, as to astonish Richard. "Why, uncle, what's the matter?" exclaimed the King incredulously, after a while. Even so small an interruption as this dashed the old man's spirit; but he persisted—only now with some abatement of vigour—in warning the King what danger he courted by confiscating Gaunt's property and thus dispossessing Bolingbroke. Richard quickly took the measure of this protest. "Think what you will, we seize his plate, goods, money, and lands." "Then I'll not be by to countenance it," was York's feeble conclusion, and with that he departed, muttering that no good could come of it.

He was scarcely gone before Richard betrayed how a little firmness might have carried the day. Almost in the same breath with which he gave instructions about confiscating Lancaster's property, he appointed York to be lord governor of England during his own absence at the Irish wars. For in truth he had been brought up in a wholesome dread of his uncles, and some of it still lingered to be transferred to this last surviving one, and the weakest of them all.

But if York scarcely knew his own mind, other nobles knew theirs. The Earl of Northumberland, head of the great house of Percy, only waited the King's departure to call shame on his conduct, or, as he preferred to put it (and men, when they meant business, have put it thus more than once or twice in English history), on the conduct of his misleading flatterers. He said enough, indeed, to make certain nobles present suspect that he had more to tell, and they pressed him to tell it—which he did. News had come from Brittany that Bolingbroke with a few noble followers and three thousand men-at-arms had set sail in eight tall ships with intent to make a landing in the north-east of England. They had been waiting only for the King's departure. "Then to horse!" cried Lord Ross; and "To horse!" echoed Lord Willoughby; and soon the conspirators were in saddle and galloping northwards.

It was true; Bolingbroke had landed at Ravenspurgh on the Humber. There the Earl of Northumberland joined him, with other discontented nobles; and no sooner was Northumberland proclaimed traitor than his brother, the Earl of Worcester, Lord Steward, broke his white staff of office and fled northwards to join the rising. The news reached the Queen as she sat talking with Bushy and Bagot. Her heart was heavy already after parting from her husband—for she loved him, poor lady!—and heavier yet with an unborn sorrow; for trouble often makes itself felt before it takes shape. And when Green came running with the ominous news, it sank like lead. Nor could she take comfort at the sight of trembling old York, who followed on Green's heels. "Uncle," she cried, "for God's sake speak comfortable words!" But York, though he had donned his gorget as if for war, could only wring his hands and cry feebly that he was old, and "Why am I, so weak that I can scarce support myself, left to underprop my nephew's kingdom? Would to God he had cut my head off first! Have no posts been despatched for Ireland? How are we to find money? Sure *I* cannot tell what to do in this tangle . . . on one side the King, my kinsman, whom oath and duty bid me defend; on the other, Bolingbroke, my kinsman too, whom the King has wronged. . . . Well, something must be done! Gentlemen, muster your forces and meet me at Berkeley. I ought to be at Plashy where my brother Gloucester's wife is lying dead at this moment. But there's no time; everything is at sixes and sevens!"

Clearly there was little to be hoped of so rambling

a commander; and no sooner had he departed than Bushy, Bagot, and Green resolved to save themselves by flight. Green and Bushy posted off for Bristol; Bagot to take advantage of the fair wind for Ireland—the wind which at once hastened the ill news towards the King and hindered his own return.

There was good cause for their dejection and terror. Escorted by Northumberland and his forces, Bolingbroke marched unimpeded down and across England from Ravenspurgh to Berkeley in Gloucestershire. Here with some show of boldness old York challenged his advance, and in an interview which he opened with great dignity upbraided his nephew roundly with this bold act of treason. Henry, whose action spoke for itself, was humble enough in words. "My gracious uncle, in what have I offended? I am Lancaster now; but my rights and revenues have—yourself knows how unjustly—been plucked from me and given away to unthrifty upstarts. I ask for my legal rights only; but lawyers are denied me, and therefore I am come to lay my claim in person." Behind all this, and behind the pleas urged on York by the other disaffected lords, stood the real argument which all were too polite to hint at—Bolingbroke's troops. York hemm'd and ha'd. "Well, I can't prevent you; but if I could I call Heaven to witness that I would. Since I cannot, I call you to witness that I am neutral. So fare you well—unless it please you to enter the castle here and repose you for the night." "An offer," answered Bolingbroke smoothly, "which we will accept. But we must persuade you a little further—and that is, to go with us to Bristol Castle, where I hear that

Bushy, Bagot, and the rest of these caterpillars of the commonwealth have sought shelter." "May be, may be," answered old York, who knew himself in no condition to refuse. "Things past redress are past care," was now the one reflection in which he could find any comfort.

There remained a last hope for Richard in the Welsh army, forty-thousand strong, which the Earl of Salisbury had collected in Wales. But already this strong force was weakening. A report ran among them that the King was dead; and in their superstitious minds this was confirmed by a dozen idle omens. A blight had fastened on all the bay-trees in the country, the heaven was full of meteors, the moon had taken a bloody tinge, and prophets whispered that such signs infallibly foreran the death of kings or their fall. One thing was certain; the King delayed to return. And before he landed on the Welsh coast, this army, which might have saved him, had melted away.

But as yet Richard knew nothing of the extent of these disasters. On his landing he wept for joy and touched the very earth affectionately, comparing himself to a mother who re-greets her child after a long absence and plays fondly with her tears and smiles at meeting. And in truth this was Richard's way; whether glad or sorry, he must play with his feelings and dress them up in fine words, and dandle and make a show of them. "Nay, do not mock me, my lords," said he (for they could not always conceal their impatience of this pretty habit); "this earth shall have a feeling and these stones turn to armed soldiers sooner than see her native King falter under foul rebellion." "No doubt, no doubt," answered in effect the trusty Bishop of Carlisle; "but none the less we had better be using all the means which Heaven puts in our way." And old York's son, the Duke of Aumerle, hinted even more roughly that this was no time for dallying. Richard turned on him petulantly: "Discomfortable cousin! knowest thou not that thieves and robbers range abroad boldly in darkness; but when the sun confronts them and plucks the cloak of night off their backs, they stand bare and naked and tremble at themselves! So, when I confront him, shall this traitor Bolingbroke tremble at himself and his sins. Not all the water in the rough rude sea has power to wash the balm from an anointed King, nor can the breath of worldlings depose the Lord's elected deputy. For every man impressed to aid Bolingbroke, God hath in his pay a glorious angel to fight for Richard!"

The entrance of the Earl of Salisbury interrupted these big words. "Ah, my lord, welcome!" Richard greeted him. "How far off lies your power?" meaning the Welsh army. "Alas," was the desperate answer, "no nearer and no farther off than this my weak arm. My gracious lord, you have come one day too late. Call back yesterday and you shall have twelve thousand fighting men. But to-day that army is gone. It heard that the King was dead, and has fled to make friends with Bolingbroke."

At this ominous news the blood left Richard's cheeks; but at a word from Aumerle he recovered himself. "Am I not King? Is not the King's name twenty thousand men? Arm then, my name, against this puny subject! Have I not York, too? And has not York power enough to serve my turn?"

But his high tone sank again as he caught sight of a new messenger, Sir Stephen Scroop, with ill-tidings written on his face; and (as men will) he tried to meet the blow he saw coming, and to soften it by talking humbly. "At the worst it will be worldly loss. Suppose my kingdom lost. Why, then, my care goes with it. Will Bolingbroke be great as we? He shall not be greater; for if he serve God, we'll serve Him too."

Poor flimsy arguments—and not even honest ones—to fortify a king's mind! For Scroop's tale was of disaster. "Bolingbroke covers the land with steel, and hearts harder than steel. Not strong men only, but greybeards, boys, thy very almsmen, yea, even women, are running to him." "What—what of my friends, the Earl of Wiltshire, Bushy, and Green? Have *they* made peace with Bolingbroke?" "They have made peace"— began Scroop. "O villains, vipers!" broke in the King, and fell to cursing them for dogs and Judases. As he took breath, Scroop explained that the peace these unhappy men had made was not this world's peace. Bolingbroke had taken them prisoners at Bristol, and already the grave covered them. "But where," asked Aumerle, "is my father, the Duke of York, with his power?" "No matter where," cried despondent Richard, and began again to play with his misery. "Let us talk of graves, worms, epitaphs—nothing but sorrow! For God's sake, let us sit upon the ground and tell sad stories of the death of kings, and of Death, the King of kings!" and so forth. "My lord," said the Bishop of Carlisle impatiently, "wise men never sit and wail their woes, but seek to meet and prevent them;" and "Yes," said Aumerle once more, "ask of my father York; he has a force to help you." Richard, as easily elated as cast down, caught at the suggestion he had rejected a minute before. He was not only hopeful again, but confident. "Thou chidest me well; to win our own is an easy task. Say"—he turned on Scroop—"where is our uncle York with his power? Speak sweetly, man, though thou lookest sourly!" "Alas!" said the messenger, "I look as I feel, and my tale is like a torture applied little by little. Your uncle York has joined Bolingbroke; your northern castles have fallen to him, and your southern gentlemen-in-arms have gone over to his side." Under this last blow of all Richard weakly faced around on Aumerle. "Beshrew thee, cousin, for leading me to comfort when I was so sweetly on the way to despair! By heaven, I'll hate him for ever who speaks another word of comfort! Discharge my followers! Let them hence from me to Bolingbroke!"

In this spirit the unhappy King set forth on his way to Flint Castle, where he was scarcely installed before Bolingbroke arrived with drums and colours and a force which included the willing Northumberland and the unwilling York. It was Harry Percy (or Hotspur, as men called him for his brave and heady temper), Northumberland's son, who brought the news that King Richard lay within the castle. Bolingbroke at once ordered a parley. His trumpet sounded and was answered, and presently Richard himself appeared on the walls, with the Bishop of Carlisle, Aumerle, Salisbury, Scroop, and the rest of his followers.

Bolingbroke did not himself advance to the parley, but remained below the walls and withdrawing a little apart sent Northumberland forward to be his spokesman. As this rough noble advanced, unceremoniously enough, the King drew himself up and his eye (as even the watchers below could see) flashed like an eagle's. There was a pause, and "We are waiting, my lord," said Richard; "You forget, it seems, the duty of kneeling to your lawful King. If we be not that, show us, pray, the hand of God that hath dismissed us from our stewardship. Go, tell Bolingbroke—who methinks stands yonder—that every stride he makes upon my land is dangerous treason. He is come to open war as it were a testament bequeathing him a crown; but before he enjoys that crown in peace, ten thousand bloody crowns of mothers' sons shall change the complexion of England to scarlet indignation."

To this Northumberland gave a smooth answer. "Heaven forbid our lord the King should so be assailed! Nay, Bolingbroke begs leave rather to kiss thy hand and swear that he comes only to sue for his revenues and his restoration as a free subject. This granted, he swears to lay aside his arms; and, as I am a gentleman, I believe him."

"Then tell him," said Richard, "that he is welcome, and his demands shall be granted,"—a galling answer for a monarch to utter, yet a wise one; for, as Aumerle said, "We must fight with gentle words till time lend us friends and sharper weapons."

And it was an answer which yet gave Richard a chance, had he kept a cool head. For by holding Bolingbroke to his oath he could have forced him to choose between disbanding his army and seizing the King by force, and so proclaiming himself a breaker of his word. But the sight of Northumberland returning so agitated him that he let slip the very offer which Bolingbroke dearly wished to receive, but hardly yet dared to demand. "Must the King submit?" he cried. "The King shall do it. Must he be deposed and lose the name of King? Why, then, let it go!" And turning to Aumerle, who could not withhold his tears (for many men yet loved Richard in spite of his waywardness), he confessed most pitifully and in words that might have moved a stone that his spirit was broken. "Let me now change my jewels for a set of beads, my palace for a hermitage, my gay apparel and my sceptre for an almsman's gown and such a staff as palmers carry, my large kingdom for a little grave—a little grave and obscure. Or bury me rather in the King's highway, some way of common traffic, where subjects' feet may trample, hour by hour, on their sovereign's head. Nay, my weeping cousin, let us weep together, and make a pretty match of our weeping. Shall we drop our tears until they fret a pair of graves for us to lie in, and men write over us how we dug them?"

While he played with these poor sorrowful fancies, came Northumberland with word that Bolingbroke desired to speak with his Majesty in the base-court below. The King descended; and, when the invader met him with due homage, would not suffer him to kneel. "My gracious lord," said Bolingbroke, "I come but for my own." "Your own is yours," Richard answered, "and I am yours, and all is yours. We must do what force will have us do; and that, cousin, is to set on towards London, is it not?" "Yea, my good lord." "Then I must not say no," sighed the King.

To London accordingly he was escorted, in name still King of England; but what he was in fact his reception there told only too surely. For, as the citizens crowded to their casements, all their eyes were for Bolingbroke, who rode ahead on a mettlesome horse—Richard's own horse, too, Roan Barbary by name—which paced as if proud of its new master; all tongues cried "God save Bolingbroke!" and Bolingbroke answered their salutations with bared head, bowing to this side and that. As it is on the stage when a well-graced actor leaves it and is succeeded by one whom the audience holds tedious, so poor Richard followed, drooping beneath the scowls of his "faithful subjects." No joyful tongue gave him welcome. No man cried "God save Richard!" But some even cast dust down upon his anointed head, dust which he shook off with a gentler, simpler sorrow than he was presently to show in laying off his crown.

For it was to come to this. Shortly, at Westminster, old York—who was learning his lackey-like business of compliance more and more easily—brought Bolingbroke word that Richard willingly resigned his sceptre to the "great Duke of Lancaster." "And long live Henry the Fourth!" wound up this venerable time-server.

"In God's name, then, I ascend the throne," replied Bolingbroke.

One voice only challenged his right—the voice of the trusty old Bishop of Carlisle, who, stirred up by God, as he asserted, boldly and at risk of his head protested against this dethronement as a sin against God, and prophesied the wars and bloodshed that this division of house against house would bring upon England in the end. "Well have you argued, sir," sneered Northumberland; "and for your pains we arrest you of high treason."

He was answered yet more effectually by the entrance of Richard, who humbly offered Henry the crown; and yet with a last reluctance which Henry bore down by quietly pinning him back from his wandering sentences to the point, "Are you, or are you not, contented to resign?" and with many pretty sad speeches too, which Henry (having gained his point) treated now with some humour and little ceremony, while Northumberland would have forced the King to read over the bald confession of his misgovernment. Unable to keep the dignity of kingship, Richard would fain have dallied with the dignity of his sorrow. "If my word be sterling yet in England, let it command that a mirror be brought to show me what face I have, since it is bankrupt of its majesty." "Go somebody, and fetch him a looking-glass," commanded Bolingbroke, with brief and biting contempt. It was brought. "Was this the face that every day kept under its household roof ten thousand men? This the face that faced so many follies, and was at last outfaced by Bolingbroke? Brittle glory and brittle face!" Richard dashed the glass on the ground. "I have done. I beg one boon, and will afterwards trouble you no more." "Name it." "Your leave to go." "Whither?" "Whither you will, only to be out of your sight." "Go, some of you, convey him to the Tower."

We left Richard's young Queen alone with her attendants and her foreboding heart. One day, as the poor lady sat with two of her maids in the Duke of York's garden at Langley, she heard the gardeners chatting as they went about their pruning and weeding; and one began to contrast their well-ordered plot of ground with England—"our sea-walled garden," as they called it,—so full of weeds, so unkempt, unpruned, with her hedges ruined, her flower-knots disordered, and her wholesome herbs swarming with caterpillars. "Hold thy peace," the head-gardener chid him. "He who allowed this disordered spring has now himself met with autumn and the fall of leaf; and the weeds which his once-spreading leaves sheltered—Wiltshire, Bushy, and Green—are by this time plucked up root and all." "What, are they dead?" "They are, and Bolingbroke has seized the King himself. 'Tis doubt he will be deposed before long. Letters arrived last night for a dear friend of the Duke of York's, and they tell black tidings."

The Queen, listening in the shadow of the trees, heard all that was said, and came running forward all distraught. "Wretch! Where got you this ill news? Speak!" "Alas! madam, and pardon me; it is all true."

Poor lady! She hurried to London, in time to post herself with her attendants in the street along which in a little while Richard came with the guard escorting him to the Tower. In her eyes, if not in others, he was kingly still. "Ah, see him . . . nay, rather, do not see him, my fresh rose withered; and yet, look up and behold him, that your eyes may dissolve to dew, and wash my rose fresh again with true-love tears!" "Sweet," said Richard, catching sight of her and halting, "this is Necessity, to whom I am now sworn brother. Hie thee to France, and there hide thee in some religious house, and learn to think of our former state as a happy dream. We two must win a heavenly crown now in place of the crown we squandered here."

Was this her royal husband, answering so tamely? Even her eyes of love could see that it was a changed Richard—changed in more than estate. "What!" she cried, "is thine intellect deposed too? Hath Bolingbroke usurped even thy heart? Does not the dying lion thrust forth a paw and wound the earth, if nothing else, in his noble rage at being overpowered? And wilt thou take thy correction mildly and kiss the rod and fawn—thou, the lion of England?"

She could not rouse him. "Go," he answered, "think that I am dead, and that here, as from my death-bed, thou takest leave for the last time." And he fell to fancying how her tale would move hearers in foreign lands, as she sat by the late winter's fire with good old folks and listened to their stories of woeful happenings in ages long ago, and in requital told them the lamentable history of Richard, and sent them weeping to their beds. "For," said he, dwelling with the fancy, "the very brands on the hearth will weep the fire out, and will mourn, some in ashes, some coal-black, for the deposing of a rightful king."

Their leave-taking was bluntly broken short by Northumberland, with news that Bolingbroke had now changed his mind and Richard must go, not to the Tower, but to Pomfret Castle in Yorkshire. An order too had come that the Queen must depart for France with all speed.

"Northumberland," said Richard, "the time shall not be long before thou, who hast planted an unrightful King, wilt desire to pluck him up again."

"My guilt be on my head," was the short reply. "Take your leave and part."

"Come then, my wife, let me unkiss our married oath—and yet not so, for it was made with a kiss. Part us, Northumberland; me towards the shivering north; my wife to France, whence she came to me adorned like May-time, and whither she returns like Hallowmas with its short daylight."

"Must we be divided? Must we part?" pleaded the Queen. "Ah! banish us both, or let me go whither he goes!"

But this was not allowed. With fond, unhappy speeches they kissed and tore themselves asunder, not to meet again in this world.

For even with Richard in prison Bolingbroke was hardly secure, and his friends felt that he was not secure. Already the Abbot of Westminster, with Aumerle, Salisbury, and others of Richard's friends, had hatched a plot against the new King.

It came, indeed, to nothing. Old York, discovering his son Aumerle's share in the conspiracy, lost no time in denouncing him to Bolingbroke. A different father this from old John of Gaunt, who had so heroically, yet sorrowfully, voted his son's banishment! Henry was not to be scared by plotters of this order; and at the Duchess of York's intercession he pardoned Aumerle, who lived to become Duke of York in his turn, and, later, to find a brave man's end on the great field of Agincourt. The Bishop of Carlisle, too, was pardoned, as his straight and fearless loyalty deserved. And with the death of the grand conspirator, the Abbot of Westminster, and the execution of Salisbury and some of the lesser men, this small rebellion flickered out.

But while Richard lived Henry's fears must live too; for any uprising would find an excuse in him, helpless prisoner though he might be. A certain knight, Sir Pierce of Exton, catching up some unguarded word of Henry's, resolved to set this fear to rest for ever.

In his prison at Pomfret Richard was already schooling himself to bear his calamity. For even calamity can be carried with an air, and—king or captive—a man of his nature must be a figure. Friends to visit him he had none but a faithful groom of his stable, who came with hardly-won leave to look upon the face of his late royal master; for Richard, with all his faults and weakness, was a lovable man, and could inspire devotion. The poor groom could talk of little besides horses, but his sympathy was none the less honest for that, and none the less grateful.

While they talked a keeper entered with a dish. "My lord," he said, setting it down, "will it please you to fall to?" "Taste of it first," answered Richard, who feared poison; and indeed it was the man's custom to do so; but this time he refused. "My lord, I dare not. Sir Pierce of Exton, who lately came from the King, commands the contrary." "The devil take Henry of Lancaster and thee!" cried Richard, and began to beat him soundly. "Help! help! help!" cried the keeper. And at this signal the door flew open, and Sir Pierce of Exton, with his armed servants, stood on the threshold.

With that Richard knew that his hour had come. Weak as his will might be, he had never lacked bodily courage; it has never been the way of English kings to lack it. In his youth he had faced a crowd of armed rebels under Wat Tyler, and cowed them with rare fearlessness; and the same spirit was alive in him yet. He snatched an axe from the first servant and clove him down with it. "Go thou, and fill another room in hell!" he shouted, turning on a second and smiting him dead. But this was his last blow. Before he could recover, Exton beat him to the ground with a fatal stroke.

Thus died Richard the Second, more nobly than he had lived. "I hate the murderer, love him the murdered," said Henry, when the coffin was brought to him at Windsor; and perhaps he was sincere. England had stood sorely in need of a firm and soldierly king, and now she had one. But the crown had come to him through bloodshed, and not without treason; and men who inclined to question the future saw the punishment for these things looming there sullenly, though as yet afar off.

KING HENRY THE FOURTH

I

BOLINGBROKE, now King Henry the Fourth, found no ease and little happiness in the throne to which he had made his way so crookedly. To begin with, Richard's death did not leave him the rightful successor. This was a youth named Edward Mortimer, grandson of the Earl of March, who had married Philippa, daughter of Lionel, Duke of Clarence. This Lionel was the third, John of Gaunt (Henry's father) the fourth, of Edward III.'s sons; and therefore, while young Edward Mortimer lived, the title of Henry was a faulty one.

He rested it, however, not on law but on the goodwill of his subjects. We have seen how as Bolingbroke he courted the opinions and flattered the hopes of Englishmen of all degrees. These hopes and opinions had given him the crown. He was the popular King; and now he must approve the people's choice by governing to please them.

Unfortunately by doing so he could not avoid offending the great nobles who had helped to exalt him; and especially the rough Earl of Northumberland, whom Richard had warned "the time will not be long before thou who hast planted an unrightful king shalt be longing to pluck him up again." There was nothing these feudal barons desired so little as to see the privileges of the common folk extended; for each was a little king in his own territory and a law to himself. But this happened to be just the mischief which Henry's first Parliament set about correcting, and in the course of its stormy debates no less than forty gauntlets of defiance were flung down on the floor of the House. We stand now at the beginning of the struggle which the Wars of the Roses completed by utterly breaking up the old feudal system. The first heavy blows against that system were dealt by this Parliament of Henry's. Bit by bit the Commons increased their power. Parliament took upon itself authority to declare what was treason and what was not; it forbade government by packed assemblies; it voted the supplies of money and claimed to know how they were spent; it tried to restrain the insolence of the great lords by forbidding any person except the King to give liveries to his retainers.

Naturally the barons began to ask themselves why they had seated this man on the throne, to consider they had been tricked, and to feel sore about it. And Henry, who read their thoughts, knew that he had no answer to give. But above all, the death of Richard lay on his conscience and haunted him continually. In two years this burden had changed "mounting Bolingbroke" into an old man shaken and wan with care; too much the man to faint or turn back from the path marked out for him, yet conscious all the while of a heavy debt which must be discharged some day, and praying that the settlement might be deferred.

Two years before, when the news of Richard's murder was first brought to him, he had meditated a pilgrimage to the Holy Land to expiate his guilt; but civil discord had kept him at home, and the purpose was yet unfulfilled. Now in a short breathing space his thoughts turned again to a crusade against the pagans in the

> "holy fields
> Over whose acres walked those blessed feet
> Which fourteen hundred years ago were nailed
> For our advantage on the bitter cross."

But again while his Council discussed the expedition came news to unsettle it. One Owen Glendower, a Welshman and descendant of Welsh princes, had been educated in London, and had served as an esquire at the Court of Richard II. In wrath at his master's death and the confiscation of his own estates, he had raised a revolt in Wales, and his harrying of the English border called out the forces of the shire of Hereford to resist him, under the command of Sir Edmund Mortimer, uncle of that Edmund Mortimer, Earl of March, whom we spoke of just now as legal heir to the throne. The encounter ended in a defeat of the English, over a thousand of whom were slain, and their dead bodies barbarously mutilated by the savage women of Wales. Sir Edmund himself fell into Glendower's hands. Close upon this came tidings from the North, more cheerful indeed, yet not wholly pleasing to Henry. A Scottish invasion had been roughly checked by a defeat on Nesbit Moor; but that brave Scot and inveterate foe of the Percies, Archibald, Earl of Douglas, had vowed vengeance, and invading England three months later, was faced at Holmedon (now Humbleton, in Northumberland) on Holy-rood day by the English under young Harry Percy, surnamed Hotspur, and was there utterly routed with the loss of ten thousand men, including three-and-twenty Scottish knights. Douglas himself lost an eye in the fight; and five hundred prisoners fell into Hotspur's hands, including Mordake (Murdach), Earl of Fife, eldest son of Robert, Duke of Albany, Regent of Scotland, and the Earls of Murray, Angus, and Athol.

Two thoughts at least poisoned Henry's pleasure in this victory. In the first place it must increase in the North the prestige of the House of Percy, already great enough to keep him uneasy. And secondly, whenever men spoke of the heir of that house, Harry Hotspur, he could not help reflecting upon his own graceless son, that other and very different Harry, who seemed deaf to every call of honour, and squandered his youth in taverns with all manner of dissolute company. "I would," he groaned, "it could be proved that some fairy had changed our two children in their cradles, and called mine Harry Percy, his Harry Plantagenet!" And he would try to dismiss the young scapegrace from his mind as he turned wearily to his business of state.

The Percies at any rate held that the time had come when they might bear themselves haughtily towards Henry. The ransom of the prisoners taken at Holmedon would amount to no small sum of money; and when the King sent to claim them, his messenger brought word that Hotspur flatly refused to surrender any but Mordake, Earl of Fife. In hot displeasure the King sent again to summon him, with his father Northumberland and his uncle Worcester, to Windsor, to answer for this refusal.

To Windsor accordingly they came, but their bearing was by no means humble. Worcester, indeed, who was ever a sour-minded noble, flatly told Henry that the House of Percy deserved no such treatment from one who owed his greatness to it, and was promptly dismissed from the presence. "When we need your counsel we will send for you," said the King, and turned to Northumberland for his explanation. "The prisoners, my good lord," the Earl said, "were not denied with the positiveness reported to you." But here his son broke in hotly. "My liege, I denied no prisoners. But I remember when the fight was over, and I leaning on my sword breathless, exhausted, and dry with rage and hard work, there came to me a certain lord, neat, trimly dressed, clean shaven, and fresh as a bridegroom. The fellow was scented like a milliner, and kept sniffing at a pouncet-box he held 'twixt finger and thumb, and smiling and chattering; and as the soldiers went by carrying the dead bodies, he rated them for unmannerly knaves to bring a slovenly, ill-looking corpse between the wind and his nobility. In this mincing speech of his he questioned me, and amongst the rest demanded my prisoners in your Majesty's name. Then it was that all smarting, with my wounds taking cold, to be so pestered with a coxcomb, I gave him out of my pain and impatience some careless answer—he should, or he should not—I forget what exactly. For he made me mad, standing there so spruce and dapper, scented and talking like a lady-in-waiting of guns and drums and wounds—save the mark!—and telling me that spermaceti was the sovereign'st remedy on earth for an inward bruise, and "it was a great pity, so it was, to dig that nasty saltpetre out of the harmless earth to destroy many a good tall fellow so cowardly!" and "but for these vile guns he would have been a soldier himself." This empty, idle chatter, my lord, I answered at random as I have told you, and beseech you not to take his report as any accusation of my love for your Majesty."

"Surely, my lord," pleaded Sir Walter Blunt, a gallant and loyal knight who stood among the listeners, "whate'er Lord Harry Percy said at such a time and place, and to such a person, may reasonably be forgotten and held in the circumstances void of offence, if he be ready now to unsay it."

"But I tell you he still denies me his prisoners!" insisted the King angrily; "or surrenders them only on condition that we promptly ransom at our own cost his foolish brother-in-law Mortimer, now held a prisoner by Glendower."

This was indeed Hotspur's stipulation, and one not at all pleasing to Henry. The King had no inclination at all to spend money in buying home a Mortimer of all persons in the world. And Mortimer did not seem to find his captivity intolerable, if the news were true that he had actually married Glendower's daughter.

From this to the suggestion that he had led his troops against Glendower with the set purpose of betraying them was no very long step, and Henry did not find it a difficult one. "Ask us to empty our coffers to buy back a traitor! No; let him starve on the barren mountains! He is no friend of mine who asks for one penny to ransom revolted Mortimer."

"Revolted Mortimer!" Hotspur flared up at the word. "He never did revolt, my liege; never fell off from you but by the fortune of war; and to that his many wounds can bear witness—wounds which he took in stubborn and bloody combat with Glendower on the banks of Severn. Treachery never yet took wounds of that sort, and therefore let him not be slandered with revolt."

"Tut, tut!" answered Henry lightly. "Mortimer fought no such combat; he durst as well have met with the devil alone as with Owen Glendower. Sirrah," he wound up sharply, "speak no more of Mortimer. Send me your prisoners speedily, or you shall hear from me in a fashion you won't care for. My lord Northumberland, we give you and your son leave to depart. Send us your prisoners, I repeat, or you will hear of it."

With these words the King walked out, and left Hotspur raging. "If the devil come and roar for his prisoners, I will not send them!" He would have run after Henry and shouted it, had not his father and his uncle, who re-entered at the moment, held him back while they tried to make him hear reason. "Not speak of Mortimer! 'Zounds, I *will* speak of him; aye, and let my soul want mercy if I don't join with him and lift him as high as this thankless King! He will have all my prisoners, will he? But when I urge him to ransom my wife's brother, when I speak the name Mortimer, then his countenance changes!"

"And good reason why," Worcester put in quietly. "Is not a Mortimer true heir to the crown, and was he not so proclaimed by King Richard before his death?"

"Ay? Then I don't blame this cousinly King for wishing a Mortimer to starve on the barren mountains! But you—you who set the crown on the head of this forgetful man—will you go on to abet this murder? Shall it be recorded of you that not only did you pluck down the rose Richard to plant this thorn, this canker, this Bolingbroke—as you did, and God forgive you for it!—but suffered the shame of being fooled and cast off by the man for whom you stooped to do it? Nay, while there is yet time redeem your good name and revenge yourself on this King, who would pay his debt by plotting to take your lives." "And so we will," said Worcester, "if you will hearken to the secret I have to whisper. But I warn you that what I propose will be perilous." "Perilous?"—Hotspur was off again: "Give me peril, adventure, anything so that it wins honour! Set honour shining in the moon and I will leap for her; sink her into unfathomed depths of sea and I will dive for her and pluck her up by the locks, so that I might have her for my own! It's this half-faced sharing of honour that I cannot stomach." "Pray listen!" "I cry your mercy; proceed." "These Scottish prisoners, then——" "I'll keep them all, I tell you! By heaven, he shall not have a single Scot of them, not if a Scot would save his soul!"

"Nay, but listen; you shall keep those prisoners——"
"Nay, I will, and that's flat! He won't ransom Mortimer,
won't he? forbids me to speak of Mortimer! I swear
I'll catch him asleep and holla "Mortimer!" in his ear;
nay, I'll train a starling to say "Mortimer," "Mortimer,"
nothing but "Mortimer," all day long, and make him a
present of it to keep his anger going. I'll make it my life's
business to torment this Bolingbroke; and as for that
Prince Harry, that son of his, if I didn't think his father
would thank me to be rid of him, I'd have him poisoned
with a pot of ale." Worcester was making for the door
in despair. "Why, what a wasp-stung impatient fool
thou art," cried Northumberland, "that wilt listen to no
tongue but thy own!" "Well, and it *does* sting me when
I hear of this vile politician and remember the candy
deal of courtesy the fawning dog proffered me once at—
where was it?—that place in Gloucestershire where we
helped to put him on the throne. How went it?—'When
my fortune shall be better established,' and 'gentle Harry
Percy,' and 'kind cousin.' The devil take such cozeners!
say I. God forgive me! Let's have your tale, uncle; I've
done." "Nay, if you have not, start afresh. We will stay
your leisure." "I have done, I tell you." Hotspur flung
himself into a chair, while Worcester unfolded his plot.
Briefly it was this—that Hotspur should return all his
Scottish prisoners without ransom and, crossing the
border, on the strength of this act of generosity invite
his old foe the Douglas to an alliance against Henry;
that meanwhile Northumberland should visit and make
cause with Richard Scroop, the powerful Archbishop
of York, who (it was understood) bitterly resented

the death of his brother, William, Earl of Wiltshire, at Bolingbroke's hands, and only waited an occasion to be revenged; and finally, that these two forces should unite with Glendower and Mortimer from Wales, a matter which Worcester charged himself to arrange presently when the time should be ripe. It was a strong plot, as Hotspur allowed. It suited his temper exactly, and soon the two Percies were riding north to put their revenge into action.

Here we must leave them and go in search of that Prince Harry of whom we have heard men speaking from time to time, but speaking nothing to his credit. While his father toiled and watched and schemed to preserve the crown against other ambitious men who threatened it, we shall find him at ease entertaining his pet crony, an old, disreputable, and immensely fat knight called Sir John Falstaff. There was much good in this old fellow, or rather, much that was amiable, in spite of his rascality and loose living. He was, in fact, a gentleman; a poor gentleman shaken loose from the lower degrees of feudalism when that edifice began to rock and totter. Shaken off, he had gone utterly astray, wasting his days in drinking and rioting among unworthy company, which in the end became a necessity to him. His round face and grotesque, fat belly were familiar in every low London tavern, and the butt of men far below him in birth and still farther below him in honesty. Yet with all his incurable frailty he kept so large a heart and so sweet a temper that at the sound of his infectious laugh—never so ready as at his own expense—men felt themselves drawn to him even in the act of despising him. The Prince found him the rarest of companions; for you could laugh at him, or laugh with him, or even both together.

For the moment their pursuit of folly left them a little repose, and for lack of anything better—or worse—to do, Falstaff sat drinking, while the Prince lounged and watched him.

"Hal, what time of day is it, lad?" demanded the old Knight.

"Thou art so fat-witted with drinking and snoring after supper and sleeping upon benches after noon that thou hast even forgotten to ask what it concerns thee to know. What in the world hast thou to do with the time of day?"

"True; the night is the time for us, who take purses. Sweet wag, let there be no gallows standing when thou art King. Do not thou, when thou art King, hang a thief. Phew!" he sighed, "I am as melancholy to-day as a gib cat. I prithee, Hal, trouble me no more with vanity. I would to Heaven thou and I knew where good reputations could be bought. An old lord of the Council rated me the other day in the street about you, but I marked him not; and yet he talked very wisely, but I regarded him not; and yet he talked wisely, and in the street too. But indeed thou art enough to corrupt a saint. Thou hast done much harm upon me, Hal—Heaven forgive thee for it! Before I knew thee, Hal, I knew nothing, and now I am, if a man should speak truly, little better than one of the wicked. I must give over this life, and I will. I'll not forfeit my soul for any King's son in Christendom."

The Prince looked across at him slily. "Where shall we take a purse to-morrow, Jack?"

"'Zounds, where thou wilt, lad. I'll make one, call me a villain and cut off my spurs if I don't!"

"I see a good amendment of life in thee," laughed his companion, "from praying to purse-taking!"

Sir John grinned amiably. "But hullo! here comes Poins. Now we shall know if that villain Gadshill have made an appointment,"—this being a notorious footpad named after a rise on the road between London and Canterbury in evil repute for highway robberies. And Poins indeed brought word of an appointment at this very spot. "My lads, my lads, to-morrow morning by four o'clock early at Gadshill! There are pilgrims going to Canterbury with rich offerings, and traders riding to London with fat purses. I have masks for you all. Bring your own horses. Gadshill spends to-night at Rochester, and I have bespoke supper for to-morrow night in Eastcheap. We may do it as secure as sleep."

"I'll go," promised Falstaff. "Hal, wilt thou make one?"

"What, I rob? I a thief? Not I, by my faith." Prince Harry had no prejudice against playing the madcap, but he kept a good share of common sense at the bottom of his follies, and highway robbery was too serious a jest altogether.

"I'll turn traitor then," growled Falstaff, "when thou art King," and assured him—having a pun handy as usual—that a man couldn't be half a sovereign if he dared not stand for ten shillings! But Poins got rid of the old Knight with a promise to persuade the Prince, and no sooner saw his fat back turned than he whispered a plan which made Harry rub his hands with delight.

So it was that while Harry Percy rode north with a secret in his breast and a plot to be executed, Harry Plantagenet took horse at nightfall and rode south, with a secret and a plot of far merrier complexion.

It was four in the morning and pitch-dark, and already in an inn-yard at Rochester the sleepy carriers were shuffling about with lanterns and harnessing their horses. Gadshill, the highwayman, who had slept in the house, was astir too, and soon enough to learn from the chamber-man of the inn (an accomplice) that in the party just setting forth was a franklin, or yeoman, from the weald of Kent with three hundred marks worth of gold[5] about him. "I heard him tell it to one of his company last night at supper. They are up already and calling for eggs and butter; they will away presently."

Gadshill smacked his lips. This was no ordinary piece of business, and he could not hang for a job in which, for sport's sake, no less a personage than the Prince of Wales was "gracing the profession," as he put it. To-night he was in league with no sixpenny rascals, but with the "nobility and tranquillity." So he saddled his nag with a quiet mind, and ambled off to Gadshill,

[5] £200.

where the Prince, Poins, and Falstaff were already at the rendezvous beside the dark highway. Poins had taken advantage of the darkness to untether Falstaff's horse, and tie him up at a little distance; and the fat knight was fuming up and down in search of him, while the other two lay a few paces off and shook with laughter. "Eight yards of uneven ground is threescore and ten miles afoot with me," he groaned, as he waddled to and fro; "and the stony-hearted villains know it well enough. A plague upon it when thieves cannot be true to one another!" At length they whistled from their hiding-place. "Plague on you! Give me my horse, you rogues; give me my horse, and be hanged to you!"

"Keep quiet, you fat paunch!" whispered the Prince. "Lie down, lay your ear to the ground, and listen if you can hear the tread of travellers."

"Lie down? Have you any levers to lift me up again if I do? Good Prince Hal," he wheedled, "help me to my horse, good King's son! Treatment like this, when a jest is so forward, and afoot too! I hate it."

Just then Gadshill arrived with Bardolph and Peto, two fellow-plotters he had picked up on the way. "On with your masks, quick! There's money a little way behind us, and now coming down the hill!"

The Prince made haste, and divided his company on the plan arranged. Gadshill, Bardolph, Peto, and Falstaff were to waylay the travellers close by in the narrow lane. The Prince himself and Poins would take their stand a little farther down the hill, and pounce upon any who escaped.

"How many be there of them?" asked Peto.

"Some eight or ten," Gadshill reported.

" 'Zounds!" Falstaff's voice had dismay in it. "Won't they rob *us*?"

But the footsteps were close by this time, and with a whispered word or two Prince Harry and Poins slipped off to their place of ambush.

Along came the unsuspecting travellers. They had finished the toilsome ascent, and were giving their horses over to the boy to lead down the hill while they stretched their legs, when out sprang our rascals from behind a thicket. "Strike!" bellowed Sir John. "Down with them! Cut the villains' throats! Ah, you caterpillars, you bacon-fed knaves! They hate us young fellows; down with them! fleece them!"

The poor travellers, thrown into confusion, and crying helplessly, were quickly robbed and secured. "Hang ye, you fat-bellied knaves! Young men must live!" panted Falstaff, while this was doing. The four seated themselves by the road to divide their spoil before taking horse. "If the Prince and Poins be not two arrant cowards there's no equity stirring. There's no more valour in that Poins than in a wild-duck!"

"Your money!" shouted a voice behind his shoulder. "Villains!"

They scrambled to their feet in the darkness. Gadshill, Bardolph, Peto broke away and ran for their lives; and Falstaff, after a blow or two, took to his heels also, leaving the booty scattered on the ground.

The Prince and Poins—for these and no other were the assailants—flung themselves down and laughed until they were tired. Still shaking with laughter at the thought of the dismayed four now running at the sound of each other's footsteps—each taking the other in the darkness for a constable—of Falstaff especially, larding the earth with sweat as he shuffled along, the pair gathered up their gains, climbed into saddle, and galloped away merrily towards London.

But the cream of the jest, they promised themselves, was to come when Falstaff should make his appearance next evening in Eastcheap, where Poins had ordered supper at the Boar's Head. The Prince and Poins were there early, you may be sure, and whiled away the time at the expense of Francis, a distracted waiter, whom the Prince held in talk, while Poins played the impatient customer, and kept bawling "Francis!" from the next room. "Francis! Francis!" "Coming, sir! Coming!" By this simple game they managed to drive the poor fellow half out of his wits before letting him go.

The Prince flung himself into a chair. "Men take their pleasures differently. Now I am not yet of that fellow Hotspur's mind—he that kills me some six or seven dozen Scots at a breakfast, washes his hands, and says to his wife, 'Fie upon this quiet life! I want work.' 'My sweet Harry,' says she, 'how many hast thou killed to-day?' 'Give my roan horse a drench,' says he; and answers, 'Some fourteen,' an hour after; 'a trifle, a trifle.'"

But here the door opened, and in walked Falstaff, Gadshill, Bardolph, and Peto, with the waiter at their heels carrying wine. All four were footsore and sulky, and Falstaff merely growled when Poins bade him welcome. "A plague of all cowards, I say, and amen to it! Give me a cup of sack, boy. A plague of all cowards!" He affected to disregard the Prince and Poins and their greetings. "Pah! this sack has been doctored too; there is nothing but roguery to be found in villainous man; yet a coward is worse than doctored sack. Go thy ways, old Jack; die when thou wilt, for manhood, good manhood, is forgot upon the face of the earth. There live not three good men unhanged in England, and one of them is fat and grows old. A bad world, I say. A plague of all cowards, I say still."

"How now, wool-sack?" demanded Prince Harry. "What are you muttering?"

"A king's son! If I do not beat thee out of thy kingdom with a dagger of lath, and drive all thy subjects afore thee like a flock of wild-geese, I'll never wear hair on my face more. You Prince of Wales!"

"Why, what's the matter, you round man?"

"Are you not a coward? answer me that: and Poins there?"

"'Zounds," threatened Poins, "call me coward again, and I put a knife into your fat paunch."

"I call thee coward? I'll see thee further ere I call thee a coward; but I would give a thousand pounds if I could run as fast as thou canst. You are straight enough in the shoulders, you care not who sees your back. Call you that backing of your friends? A plague on such backing!

Give me a cup of sack." Falstaff drained another cup. "A plague of all cowards, still say I."

"What's the matter?" asked the Prince again.

"What's the matter! There be four of us here have taken a thousand pounds this very morning."

"Where is it, Jack? Where is it?"

"Where is it? Taken from us it is: a hundred upon poor four of us."

"What, a hundred, man?"

"I am a rogue if I was not at close quarters with a dozen of them two hours together. 'Twas a miracle I escaped. I was eight times thrust through the doublet, four through the hose; my buckler cut through and through; my sword hacked like an hand-saw—look for yourself! I never fought better since I was a man; but all no good. A plague of all cowards!"

The Prince, in mock bewilderment, appealed to the others to tell their story, and all together plunged into the outrageous concocted tale. "We four set upon some dozen——" "Sixteen at least." "And bound them." "No, they were not bound." "Yes, they were bound, every man of them, or I'm a Hebrew Jew." "As we were sharing some six or seven fresh men set upon us——" "And unbound all the rest, and on they all came." "If I fought not with fifty of them, I'm a bunch of radish."

"Dear, dear"—the Prince kept a serious face—"pray Heaven you have not murdered some of them!"

"Nay, that's past praying for. Two I am sure I have

paid, two rogues in buckram suits. See here, Hal"—
Falstaff struck an attitude—"thou knowest my old
guard; well, I took it—so. Four rogues in buckram let
drive at me——"

"What, four? Thou saidst two a moment ago."

"Four, Hal; I told thee four. These four assailed me
in front, thrusting at me. I made no more ado, but took
all their seven points in my buckler, thus."

"Seven? Why just now there were but four."

"In buckram?"

"That was it; four, in buckram suits."

"Seven, by my sword-hilt, or else I am a villain."

"Let him alone," whispered Poins; "we shall have
more presently."

"Dost thou hear me, Hal? That's right, for it is worth
the listening to. These nine men in buckram that I told
thee of——"

The Prince whistled softly. "Two more already!"

"Their points being broken, began to give me
ground. I followed close, came in foot and hand; and
as quick as thought paid out seven of the eleven!"

"Monstrous!" groaned Harry. "Eleven buckram men
out of two!"

"But, as the devil would have it," went on Falstaff,
"three accursed fellows in coats of Kendal green came
at my back and let drive at me; for it was so dark, Hal,
that thou couldst not see thy hand——"

"Well, of all the lies!"

"Eh? What? Art thou mad? Is not the truth the truth?"

"Why, how couldst thou know these men in Kendal green, when thou sayst it was too dark to see thy hand? Come, explain, pray." And Poins joined in, "Explain, Jack, explain."

"What, upon compulsion! Tell you on compulsion! Give you a reason on compulsion! If reasons were as plentiful as blackberries, I would give no man a reason upon compulsion—not I!"

"Enough of this," said the Prince; "and now listen to me. We two—Poins and I—saw you four set upon four travellers, and bind them, and make yourselves masters of their wealth. Mark, now, how a plain tale shall put you down. Then we two did set on you four, and, with a word, outbraved you and took your booty; ay, and have it. We can show it to you here in the house. Why, Falstaff, you carried your fat paunch away and roared while you ran as lustily as ever I heard a bull-calf. And you hack your sword like that, and say it was done in fight! Come, what trick can you find now to cover your shame?"

"Ay, Jack," echoed Poins, "what trick can you find now?"

Sir John stood abashed for just a moment; then a twinkle showed in a corner of his eye, and spread slowly over his fat features.

"By the Lord, I knew ye all the time! Why, hear you,

my masters, was it for me to kill the heir-apparent? Should I turn upon a true Prince? Why, thou knowest I am as valiant as Hercules; but beware instinct! The lion will not touch the true Prince. Instinct is a great matter; I was a coward upon instinct. I shall think the better of myself and thee during my life! But, lads, I am glad you have the money. Shut the doors, hostess!"

But the hostess had a word of her own to say. "There was a nobleman of the Court at the door would speak with the Prince."

"Give him money and send him packing," said the Prince, not willing to be interrupted.

Falstaff offered to take him an answer, and while he was gone Bardolph and the others confessed how the knight had hacked his sword with his dagger, and persuaded them to tickle their noses with spear-grass, and make them bleed, and smear their clothes with the blood, to make believe it was all done in fight.

But Falstaff came back with serious news. The Prince hailed him lightly. "Well, how now, fat Jack? How long is't ago since thou sawest thine own knee?" "My own knee? When I was about thy years, Hal, an eagle's talons would have met round my waist. I could have crept through an alderman's thumb-ring. A plague of sighing and grief! it blows a man up like a bladder. But there's villainous news abroad. That was Sir John Bracy, sent by your father; you must go to the Court in the morning. That mad Percy of the north, and that wizard-fellow of Wales, Owen Glendower, and his son-in-law Mortimer, and old Northumberland, and that sprightly

Scot of Scots, Douglas, that never runs away———"

"Unless upon instinct, Jack."

"I grant ye, upon instinct. Well these, and one Mordake, and a thousand blue bonnets more, are up in arms. Worcester has stolen away to-night; thy father's beard is turned white with the news, and you may buy land now as cheap as stinking mackerel. Tell me, Hal, art thou not horribly afraid? Could the world choose for thee, as heir-apparent, three worse enemies than Douglas, Percy, and Glendower?"

"Afraid? Not a whit, Jack; I lack some of thy *instinct*."

"Well, well; thou wilt be horribly chid to-morrow, when thy father gives thee a talking-to. If thou lovest me, practise an answer."

Upon this, though the news was serious and the time short, Prince Harry could not resist setting the fat Knight in a chair to represent the King, and rehearsing to-morrow's scene with him in mockery; and afterwards taking the King's seat himself and rating the corpulent old man as a headstrong youth, rebuking him especially with his fondness for that hoary old reprobate, Sir John Falstaff. While the two were at this game a second knocking sounded on the outer door, and the hostess came running to say that the sheriff and watch were without, demanding to search the house. Guessing what brought them, the Prince cleared the room and had just time to stow Sir John behind the arras hangings before the sheriff appeared with the robbed carrier.

"Pardon me, my lord," explained the sheriff,

recognizing the Prince, "but a hue and cry has followed certain men to this house."

"What men?"

"One of them, my gracious lord, is a notorious character—a gross, fat man."

"Ha! I know whom you mean. He is not here, but I will engage he shall call upon you by to-morrow dinner-time, and answer any charge you may bring."

"There are two gentlemen, my lord, who have lost three hundred marks in this robbery."

"That may be. If he have robbed them, he shall be answerable"; and so with compliments the Prince bowed the sheriff out.

But when he and Peto, the coast being clear, pulled aside the arras, they found Sir John with his double chin sunk on his chest. Tired out with his last night's exertions he had dropped sound asleep. "Search his pockets," whispered the Prince; but Peto could find no money—only a tavern bill which read:

	s.	d.
Item, A capon	2	2
Item, Sauce	0	4
Item, Sack, 2 gallons.	5	8
Item, Anchovies and sack after supper . . .	2	6
Item, Bread	0	0½

"O monstrous! but one half-pennyworth of bread to this intolerable deal of sack!" The Prince looked down on the stertorous sleeper. "Let him snore on. It is late, and I must to Court in the morning. The money stolen must be paid back with interest. We must to the wars now, and I'll procure this fat rogue a charge of foot-soldiers; I know the marching will be the death of him. Good morrow, Peto," and Prince Harry stepped out into the cold dawn.

In truth the serious summons had come for him. Hotspur had prospered in the affair which took him north. Douglas had readily joined the conspiracy. Northumberland had no difficulty in persuading the Archbishop of York, who commended not only the attempt but the plan of campaign. And Glendower needed no persuasion, being already in active rebellion against the King. By the Archbishop's advice a paper was drawn up stating the several grounds which justified the revolt, and copies of this were secretly sent here and there throughout England to those barons whose affection for Henry stood in doubt. Many returned promises of help; though it may be said here that their promises did not amount to much on the day of trial. And indeed the conspiracy held grave elements of weakness. It had no roots in popular feeling; for the people as a whole looked upon the King as their friend, and justly; and read plainly enough in this revolt the jealousy and disappointment of a few big nobles. Nor was it knit together by a common purpose. Northumberland lagged behind his son, considering how he might save himself in case of failure. Douglas and Glendower had quite different aims; and Glendower especially was about the last man in the world Hotspur could understand.

Hotspur worked hard, and for a while his impetuosity carried the movement along. His plans laid, he set out for Wales; and his wife (who had pleaded vainly to be taken into his confidence) followed him to Bangor, where she met her brother Mortimer and his newly-wedded Welsh wife in company with Glendower and his wild troops. Worcester, too, had arrived. But from the first it was clear that Hotspur and Glendower could neither agree nor tolerate each other.

We know what Hotspur was—a blunt, headstrong, practical soldier, impatient of speech and curt, almost brutal, of manner even towards his own wife. Glendower was a fighter too, but he was also a chieftain over a wild and superstitious race; a dreamer and a visionary; gentle towards women; insanely proud of his barbaric sovereignty, and touchy at the least suspicion of ridicule; a romantic and dignified savage thinly varnished by his youthful training in the English Court.

So when the leaders met in council at the Archdeacon of Bangor's house, and began, with the map between them, to parcel out the realm of England, the first compliments were scarcely exchanged before Hotspur and Glendower began (as we say) to rub each other's temper the wrong way.

"Be seated, cousin Percy," Glendower began graciously; "or let me say cousin Hotspur, for when our enemy Lancaster hears tell of you by that name he turns pale and wishes you in heaven."

"And you in hell whenever he hears of Owen Glendower." Hotspur bettered the compliment with a brusque laugh.

But Glendower took it quite seriously. "I cannot blame him; at my nativity the heavens were full of blazing stars, and the whole frame and foundation of the earth quaked at my birth."

"Why so it would have done at the same season if your mother's cat had but kittened, though you had never been born."

"I say," repeated Glendower solemnly, "that the earth shook when I was born."

"Did it? Then I say that the earth couldn't have been of my mind, if it shook for fear of you."

"The heavens were on fire; the earth trembled."

"Oh, then the earth shook to see the heavens on fire; that explains it. The earth suffers from those spasms at times."

"Cousin," Glendower reproved him, "I do not permit many to cross me as you are doing." And having no spark of humour, he went on to adduce further proof that he was no ordinary man.

"I think no man speaks better Welsh." Hotspur soon had enough of this. "I'll to dinner."

"Peace, cousin," put in Mortimer, "or you will drive him mad."

"I can call spirits out of the deep," still went on the sonorous Glendower.

"Why so can I; so can any man. The question is if they'll come when you call them."

"I can teach you to command the devil himself."

"And *I* can teach *you* how to shame him. Tell the truth and shame the devil—that's the way, cousin."

"Thrice hath Henry Bolingbroke made head against me; thrice from the banks of Wye and Severn have I beaten him home bootless and weather-beaten."

"Home without boots, and in foul weather! How in the world escapes he the ague!"

Clearly Hotspur in this mood was intractable. Even Glendower saw this at length, and picked up the map sullenly. The Archdeacon of Bangor had divided off the future realms of the three parties in the revolt. To the Mortimers, as true heirs to the throne, fell the whole of England south of Trent and east of Severn. The Percies took the north of England from Trent to the Scottish border, and Glendower his native Wales. But Hotspur was now in a temper to pick holes in any arrangement. "It seems to me you have given me the smallest of the portions; look at this river here, this Trent, winding into the best of my territory, and cutting out a huge slice. I'll have the current dammed up here, and cut a straight channel across. It shall not wind so."

"Not wind?" cried Glendower. "But it shall, it must; you see that it does."

"Then I'll see that it shall not; it shall run straight."

Mortimer showed that another bend of the river gave Hotspur back as much as the first took from him. Worcester pointed out how a little engineering would make the channel straight. Glendower would not hear of any alteration. "Pray who will deny me?" demanded Hotspur. "I will." "Then you had better say it in Welsh, so that I shall not understand you." "I can speak English, my lord, as well as you. Yes, and I learnt in the English Court to turn many an English song to the harp, and give a new ornament to your language; an accomplishment which I believe you never possessed." "No, I'm glad to say, I'd rather be a kitten and cry 'mew!' than be one of your ballad-mongers." Glendower gave him up in despair. "Very well, you shall have Trent turned." "Oh, as for that I don't care; I'd give thrice so much land to any friend who deserved it; but when a man starts to bargain with me, look you, I'll dispute to the ninth part of a hair."

The compact was given into the secretary's hands, and Glendower withdrew with dignity, while the two others expostulated with Hotspur for so crossing the worthy gentleman. "I cannot help it," Hotspur protested; "he wearies and vexes me so with his lore and his crack-brained pretensions. He's worse than a smoky house." "And yet, let me tell you," said Mortimer, "my father-in-law has a real respect for you, and curbs himself when you cross his humour as he would for no other man in the world." "Well, well, I am schooled," said Hotspur, and bore himself good-humouredly enough until the moment of departure—hours spent in that peaceful happiness which made home so dear to Glendower, and was enjoyed by him so rarely. It was small wonder that Mortimer had fallen in love with his captor's daughter, and was loath now to leave his Welsh wife, whose language was strange to him, as his was to her, but who loved him and spoke it with tearful eyes while she sang him the soft songs of her native land, and he, laid on the rushes with his head on her lap, looked up and forgot for a while that the campaign called him and the moments were running away towards his departure. Even Hotspur, that hater of ballads and scorner of sentiment, was less brutal than his wont in announcing that the time was come to take leave.

We left Prince Harry on his way to answer his father's summons. The King wished to speak with him alone, for he read the anger of Heaven in the reports which reached him of his eldest son's misconduct, and fully believed that in this was laid up the punishment for his own past wrong-doing. "My father," said the Prince, "I would I could redeem all my offences as thoroughly as I can prove myself guiltless of many charged against me. But let me beg this, that if I disprove many falsehoods brought to your Majesty's ear by smiling but envious tattlers, I may in return for some youthful faults which I have indeed committed find pardon on making a clean breast."

"May God pardon thee, Harry! It is for me to wonder how my son can so differ from his father and all his blood. Struck out of the Council—thy place there given to thy younger brother Clarence—all but an alien to my Court and thy kindred of the blood!—What wonder that men think upon what they hoped and expected of thee before now, and shake their heads prophetically? Had I made myself cheap as thou, should I ever have won the crown? No; I husbanded myself, went abroad rarely, and when I did people would point and say, 'This is he!' or ask, 'Where? Which is Bolingbroke?' And with this I used such courtesy as won their allegiance, so that they raised cheers for me even in the King's presence. It was Richard, that skipping fellow, who made himself cheap and familiar; ambling up and down with shallow companions, laughing and sporting until the public eye grew utterly tired of him. And thou, Harry, art running the same gait. Not an eye but is aweary of thee"—the King sighed—"save mine, which hath yearned to see thee more; which even now does what I would not have it do, and grows dim with a foolish tenderness."

"My gracious lord," promised Harry, "from this time I will be more myself." But the King had more on his mind. That his son should be so different from Hotspur—there lay the wound which gnawed him—that he should be driven to envy this foe, and acknowledge him at every point superior to his own Harry, his nearest and dearest enemy. And in his bitterness he uttered a taunt equally cruel and unjust. "I could believe thou art base enough, degenerate enough, through fear of him or pettish wrath against me, to take Percy's pay and fall in at his heels to fight against me!"

"Do not think that!" cried Harry, shocked and indignant. "You shall not find it so; and God forgive those who have so warped your Majesty's good thoughts from me! There shall come yet the close of a day when, wiping off the blood of battle and with it my past disgrace, I shall be bold to tell you I am your son. And that day shall be when this much lauded Hotspur and your poorly thought-of Harry come face to face. Before God, sir, he shall render me up all my lost honours, if I have to tear the reckoning from his heart. Trust me this once, and I will die every death before breaking this vow!"

"I will trust thee," said the King slowly.

And the hour for proving that trust was at hand. While father and son still looked each other in the face, Sir Walter Blunt arrived with news that Douglas and Percy had already joined forces at Shrewsbury. Glendower would be following, and old Northumberland might be despatching reinforcements at any moment. The Earl of Westmoreland and young Prince John of Lancaster were already moving northward upon the rebels. "On Wednesday, Harry, you shall set forward; we ourselves the day after. Let your line of march be through Gloucestershire, and in twelve days' time we should meet and join at Bridgenorth." Smarting from this interview, but flushed now with a new resolve, Harry hurried off to prepare for the campaign.

In his preparations he did not forget his old promise to provide Falstaff with a command of foot. That worthy just now was in a melancholy humour, but doing his best to work it off by railing at Bardolph's red nose, a feature which did much service by engaging his attention in hours of slackness or despondency. The images—biblical and other—called up by it, the trains of thought suggested by it, were endless. "Thou art our admiral, thou bearest the lantern in the poop. . . . When thou rannest up Gadshill in the night to catch my horse, if I did not take thee for a will-o'-the-wisp or a ball of wildfire there's no purchase in money. . . . Thou hast saved me a thousand marks in links and torches, walking with thee in the night betwixt tavern and tavern; but what thou hast drunk would have bought me lights as cheap in the dearest chandler's in Europe. I have maintained that salamander of yours with fire any time this two-and-thirty years, Heaven reward me for it!" Sir John's commentary was peculiarly rich and pungent to-day; the fact (as he asserted) being that during his sleep he had been robbed of several valuable bonds and a seal-ring belonging to his grandfather. This charge against the credit of her house Mistress Quickly, hostess of the Boar's Head, shrilly resented, and the dispute was hot when the Prince arrived and proved the robbery to have been but a few unpaid tavern-bills. As for the money taken from the travellers, it had been paid back. "Ah!" quoth Sir John, not in the least out of countenance; "I do not like that paying back; 'tis a double labour." But the Prince was in earnest now. Sir John must attend in the Temple Hall to-morrow to receive his commission and money for his equipment. Bardolph must set out with a letter for Prince John of Lancaster. "To horse, Peto; thou and I have thirty miles yet to ride ere dinner-time." These tavern loafers took fire from him; their marching orders had come, and in a day or two they with their betters had left London and were pressing northward to Shrewsbury.

At Shrewsbury in the rebel camp all was not

prospering. Hotspur and Douglas had met in good fighting trim, but Glendower had not arrived and, worse still, Northumberland, whose name and influence in the north meant everything to their cause, was either sick or feigning sickness, and marched southward slowly, sending messages that his coming must not be relied on. "A bad time to be taken sick," grumbled Worcester. "His health was never so valuable as it is just now." Hotspur, for a moment depressed by the news, quickly recovered his spirits. It would be no bad thing in case of mishap to have a second force to fall back upon. Worcester shook his head; the great Percy's hesitation would have a moral effect—men would begin to doubt and question. Hotspur and Douglas alike scorned the notion of fear; and a report that the royal forces were approaching set the former on fire with impatience. Happiest of all was he to hear that the Prince of Wales was coming; for in truth, and for some time, these two Harrys had felt themselves to be rivals. Harry Percy might talk disdainfully, but the feeling was there. Harry, Prince of Wales, might listen to the other's praises with affected carelessness, but he had not been too careless to mark and remember even what kind of horse Hotspur rode. While men contrasted them, fate whispered to each of a day which should finally decide between them—"Harry to Harry, hot horse to horse."

So while Glendower tarried and Northumberland sent malingering messages, the royal troops pressed on towards Bridgenorth. It was lucky for his Majesty that his army contained few companies such as Falstaff's. Sir John had not left London too soon. The tale of the robbery on Gadshill had come to the ears of the Lord Chief-Justice Gascoigne, who was not a man to show favour to any friend of the Prince, or even to the Prince himself. It had been his duty before now to sentence Bardolph to imprisonment for a riot committed in the Prince's company, and Harry, being in court when the sentence was delivered, had so far forgotten himself as to draw his sword; whereupon the judge had promptly committed him to the King's Bench.

Falstaff, who had been reported as concerned in the Gadshill robbery, had to thank the confusion of the times rather than any weakness of Lord Chief-Justice Gascoigne that he was still free to abuse the King's confidence. And he abused it royally. Being licensed to "press" soldiers in the King's service, he had taken care to lay hands only on passably rich fellows—yeomen's sons, well-to-do bridegrooms on the eve of marriage, and the like—in fact anyone who seemed pretty sure to pay a round sum to escape serving. And with the money thus gotten he had hired in their place such a crew of scarecrows that he was fairly ashamed to march them through the streets of Coventry. "The villains," he growled, "march so wide between the legs as if they had fetters on; for indeed I had the most of 'em out of prison. There's but a shirt and a half in all my company; and the half-shirt is two napkins tacked together and thrown over the shoulders like a herald's coat without sleeves; and the shirt, to say the truth, stolen from my host at St. Alban's, or else from the red-nosed innkeeper of Daventry. But," he consoled himself, "that's all one; they'll find linen on every hedge. And as for the fellows themselves, they'll serve as food for powder; they'll fill a pit as well as their betters. Tush! mortal men, mortal men!"

The Prince, in whose army these rapscallions marched, joined the King at Bridgenorth, and the combined armies marched forward on Shrewsbury and halted within sight of the rebel forces.

Still Northumberland hung back, and Glendower tarried on the Welsh border. But although he knew himself outnumbered, although Worcester and even Douglas counselled delay, Hotspur was for prompt attack. Always a fierce fighter, in this crisis he showed himself an indifferent general. He had, however, a true general's power of swaying men, which he used now to override opposition; and when the King sent Sir Walter Blunt to offer generous terms, he returned the insulting message that he and his house had proved the King's promises before and knew what they were worth. Yet on an afterthought he promised that the King's offer should be considered, and that Worcester should bring a cooler answer on the morrow.

The morrow had scarcely dawned when Worcester, with Sir Richard Vernon by his side, rode into the royal camp for this last interview. The day was that before the feast of Saint Mary Magdalen, and the month July, but the newly risen sun hung red and angry in a cheerless sky, and a whistling south wind gave promise of stormy weather.

In the King's presence Worcester rehearsed once more his old tale of the promises given to the house of

Percy and unfulfilled. Prince Harry, standing beside his father, listened with impatience, and at the close of the recital stepped forward and offered to save unnecessary bloodshed and decide the quarrel between their two houses by single combat with Hotspur, to whose admitted prowess he paid many courtly compliments. This gallant proposal was of course not to be thought of; but the King, still clemently minded, again offered the rebels pardon if they would surrender, and a free inquiry into their grievances with a view to redress.

Vernon was for reporting this offer to Hotspur, but Worcester, morose and distrustful as ever, turned it over in his mind and decided that the King was not to be relied on; he would merely bide his time and find another occasion to strike. Hotspur's trespass might be forgotten for the sake of his youth and notoriously choleric temper; but his elders, who had spurred him on, would one day surely be made to pay for it. Thus reasoning, Worcester took a decision as fatal as it was dishonest, and returning to Hotspur and Douglas not only said nothing of the King's offer, but so misreported him as to throw his nephew into a new rage. One thing only he related truthfully, the Prince of Wales's challenge; and Vernon, not relishing the deceit which he was abetting, found some consolation in bearing witness to the courtesy with which that challenge had been uttered. "Courteous, was he?" answered Hotspur. "I hope before night to embrace him so with a soldier's arm that he will find himself shrinking under *my* courtesy." Without delay he set his battle in order, and with the famous cry of his house, "Esperance! Percy!" led them forward to the attack.

After a murderous exchange of archery, the two armies joined, and in the first shock Douglas with his Scots forced back the King's van, led by the Earl of Stafford, and very nearly broke their array. Distressed by a storm of arrows and harassed in flank by irregular bodies of Welshmen who had been lurking in the wooded hills and marshes and now came to the rebels' support, the Earl's men were wavering when Henry came up and relieved them with his main body. Now from the nature of the quarrel it had been foreseen that the rebels might direct their attack specially against the King's person, and to baffle this no less than four knights had taken the field that day in armour precisely like the King's. Two of these, the Earl of Stafford himself and Sir Walter Blunt, were cut down by Douglas in two separate onsets which carried to the very foot of the royal standard; and finding himself twice cheated, the Scot swore to cut his way through the King's wardrobe piece by piece until he found the real Henry, and to this vow our friend Falstaff no doubt owed his life. For, encountering with Douglas, and finding himself in peril of being spitted, this hero flung himself on the ground and shammed dead. It was not easy in any circumstances to mistake Falstaff for the King of England in disguise, and without pausing to make sure Douglas hurried forward in pursuit of higher game.

As we know, it was no light matter for Falstaff, once prostrate, to get on his legs again. On this occasion he was in no great haste to try, and so it happened that, stretched where he had fallen, he was witness of the encounter between the pair who had been seeking each other since first the battle joined.

Prince Harry had been fighting nobly. Early in the day an arrow had wounded him in the face, and his father, himself withdrawn from the hottest of the fight only by the vehement entreaties of the Earl of March, had vainly implored him to retire and have his wound dressed. To this he would not listen, and it was on the ground from which he had already beaten off an onslaught of Douglas upon his father that he and Hotspur at length came face to face.

"Two stars keep not their motion in one sphere." They fought, knowing that for one or the other his hour had come. And it was Hotspur, the formidable, the approved soldier, who fell. It was Prince Hal, the reputedly worthless, who stooped and laid his scarf respectfully over the face of his dead rival—so often envied! As he did so he turned and spied Falstaff. "What? Thou too, old acquaintance! Farewell, old Jack!—I could better have spared a better man. Lie there by Percy until I return and see thee duly embowelled and buried!"

Falstaff watched him out of sight, and slowly heaved himself on his feet. "Embowelled! If thou embowel me today, I'll give thee leave to powder and eat me too, to-morrow. Phew! It was time to counterfeit, or that hot, termagant Scot had paid me scot and lot too. The better part of valour is discretion, say I." He waddled over to Hotspur's corpse, and giving it a thrust or two with his dagger to make sure, hoisted it on his back.

By this time the rebel bugles were sounding retreat. Lacking Hotspur to put heart in them, their ranks were breaking, and the day was already won when Prince Harry and his brother, John of Lancaster, met the fat Knight staggering along under his burden. The Prince could hardly believe his eyes, or his ears either, when Falstaff cast the body on the ground and complacently claimed that he and no other had killed Hotspur. "There is Percy. If your father will do me any honour, well and good; if not, let him kill the next Percy himself."

"Why, I killed Percy with my own hand, and I saw thee dead!"

"Didst thou indeed? Lord, Lord, how this world is given to lying! I grant you I was down and out of breath, and so was he. But we rose both at an instant, and fought a long hour by Shrewsbury clock. See you this wound in his thigh!"

"Make the most of thy falsehood, if it do thee any good." The Prince had no time to waste in such disputing. The victory was now assured, the rebellion broken up. Douglas, chased from the field and spurring his horse at a desperate crag, was flung heavily and taken prisoner. Him the King pardoned without ransom at Harry's entreaty. Worcester and Vernon, captives too, he condemned to execution.

"Hadst thou borne back our true message of grace, many a gallant man now dead had been drawing life this hour." They were led forth, and the King, despatching his son John and the Earl of Westmoreland towards York to deal with Northumberland and the Archbishop, directed his own march upon Wales to complete his victory.

II

IN the orchard of Warkworth Castle, on the banks of the Coquet and handy by the sea, the old Earl of Northumberland paced to and fro, waiting for news of the battle he had been too "crafty-sick" to attend. And along the roads between Shrewsbury and Warkworth more than one horseman was spurring with rumours caught up in quiet towns far from the battle-field.

The first of these tired riders to dismount at the castle gate was Lord Bardolph, one of the heads of the conspiracy. Northumberland tottered out to learn the news.

"Certain news!" announced Lord Bardolph, "and as good as heart can wish! The King defeated and wounded almost to death, the Prince of Wales slain outright by your son, both the Blunts dead, and young Prince John, Westmoreland, and Stafford fled from the field! Never since Caesar's time was day so fought, so followed up, and so fairly won!"

"But whence have you this? From Shrewsbury? Saw you the field?"

"I had it, my lord, from a gentleman who was there and saw; one of birth and name, who can be trusted."

While Lord Bardolph spoke another rider appeared on the crest of the road.

"Here comes Travers," cried the Earl, "my servant whom I sent last Tuesday to seek news."

"I overtook him, my lord, and rode on ahead; he can bring no certain news but what I gave him."

But Travers had something more to tell. "My lord," he panted, dismounting. "Lord Bardolph turned me back with the joyful tidings and outrode me, being better horsed. But after him came spurring a gentleman on a horse over-ridden and lathered with blood. He reined up and asked the way to Chester; and I demanded what news from Shrewsbury. He answered that the rebellion had bad luck, and young Harry Percy's spur was cold. That is how he said it, and with that gave his horse the head and striking spur again left me at a furious gallop."

"What! tell it me again. How said he?—that Hotspur's spur was cold, the rebellion had ill luck?"

"My lord," insisted Lord Bardolph, "I'll wager my barony his story was false!"

But the Earl was not convinced, and presently a third horseman hove in sight. It was Morton, another retainer of the Percy; and his face told that his tidings were evil. He had escaped from Shrewsbury, he reported. The Earl forestalled more with a trembling string of questions, which Morton's white face answered only too surely. "Yes, the Douglas was living, and the Earl's brother—as yet; but as for my lord's son—" "Why, he is dead. Ah, I guessed it, I know it! Yet speak, Morton, and tell me my son is not dead!" "I cannot think he is dead, my lord," said Lord Bardolph.

But Morton had to answer that it was true. "Sorry am I to force you, my lord, to believe that which I would to God these eyes had not seen. But he is dead, slain by Prince Harry, and his death disheartened the troops and turned the day. Worcester fell a prisoner in the flight, Douglas was thrown from his horse and taken. In short, the victory was the King's, who has already despatched a force under Prince John and Westmoreland against your lordship."

Such in sum was the news, not to be doubted. And now the unhappy Earl, who had tarried and feigned illness when he could have saved everything, awoke to his loss and flinging his crutch away in a weak passion, called too late for his armour, and too late took heaven and earth to witness that he would be avenged. His listeners, who knew too well what his conduct had cost, yet reasoned with him that nothing could be gained while yet more might be hazarded by this outburst. The mischief at Shrewsbury was done; it remained for men who had counted the risks of rebellion beforehand to accept that reverse and put forth new efforts elsewhere. The Archbishop of York was up, with a strong army; and the rising which before had been in men's eyes a rebellion only, now had the sanction of religion to avenge the death of Richard, whose blood had been scraped from the stones of Pomfret Castle to incite the people. Let the Earl and the Archbishop join forces boldly and all might yet be redeemed.

From Warkworth Lord Bardolph posted south to York, where the Archbishop sat deliberating with Lord Hastings and Lord Mowbray. These had ready a picked force of twenty-five thousand men, and they had to consider if such a force could hold head without Northumberland's aid. With that aid they could feel reasonably safe, but Lord Bardolph knew too well to trust the Earl's energy. They were (he argued) planning a big enterprise, and ought to count the cost carefully, and be certain their means were equal to it. Hastings was more sanguine; the King, to be sure, had more than five-and-twenty thousand men, but his power must be divided against three separate dangers—against Glendower, against the French (who had landed twelve thousand men at Milford Haven in Wales), and lastly against this new revolt should they determine on it. The Archbishop decided for prompt action. "The country," said he, "is already sick and surfeited of this usurper. Let us go forward boldly and proclaim everywhere what calls us to arms!"

Meanwhile Prince Harry, whom the King had now learned to trust with the command of men, was pressing back the Welshmen; and it is enough to say here that by slow and careful campaigns, lasting over four years, during which he learned the art of soldiery and a scorn of hardships which was to stand him in good stead hereafter, Harry wrested the south of Wales from Glendower, and drove him back into the mountain fastnesses around Snowdon, there to maintain a stubborn and almost single-handed fight until his death.

But this was a kind of fighting which, sharp while it lasted, had its holidays; and now and again it gave Harry time to revisit London. Falstaff (who was of no build for Welsh campaigning) soon after the battle of Shrewsbury found himself back in the old haunts, with a boy to follow him for page (a gift from the Prince), but a purse barely sufficient to maintain this grandeur. Somehow his tailor fought shy of giving him credit, and demanded security; was even unkind enough to ask for better security than Bardolph's, which Falstaff offered. "The rascally knave! I looked he should have sent me two-and-twenty yards of satin, as I am a true knight, and he sends me security! I can get no remedy against this consumption of the purse; borrowing only lingers and lingers it out, but the disease is incurable."

So we find him back in London streets with seven groats and twopence in his purse, and a page at heel pompously bearing his master's sword and buckler, and openly poking fun at his master's broad back. "I know not how 'tis,"— Falstaff turned about on the pavement, and sticking his thumbs in his girdle, addressed the lad reproachfully; "but men of all sorts take a pride to gird at me; the brain of that foolish clay, man, is not able to invent anything that tends to laughter more than I invent, or is invented on me; I am not only witty in myself, but the cause of wit in other men."

Who should pass along the street at this moment but the man Sir John had best reason to avoid—Lord Chief-Justice Gascoigne? Sir John had, indeed, been sent for by this upright judge before marching north, to answer some awkward questions about the robbery on Gadshill, but had managed to put a convenient distance between himself and London. The victory at Shrewsbury had happened in the interval, and the Lord Chief-Justice was disposed to let bygones be bygones; though, at the same time, the sight of Falstaff suggested that a word of advice would not be out of place. So, knowing that the fat knight was to depart again northwards presently to join Prince John of Lancaster, he sent his servant to call him.

Falstaff at first pretended to be deaf, and then, as the servant plucked his sleeve, made believe to take him for a beggar. But the judge was not to be shaken off so. "Sir John Falstaff, a word with you," said he gravely, walking up.

Thus cornered, Falstaff could only push forward a hundred inquiries for his lordship's health. "I am glad to see your lordship abroad: I heard say your lordship was sick: I hope your lordship goes abroad by advice. Your lordship, though not clean past your youth, hath yet a touch of age. I most humbly beseech your lordship to have a reverend care of your health."

The judge waved aside all this solicitude, and would have begun, but Sir John was off upon another tack. "An't please your lordship, I hear his Majesty is returned sick from Wales. I hear it is that apoplexy again. This apoplexy is, as I take it, a kind of lethargy, an't please your lordship; a kind of sleeping in the blood, or pins-and-needles, as your lordship might say. It has its origin in much grief, in study, and worry of the brain. I have read the cause of its effects in Galen; it is a kind of deafness."

"I think you must be suffering from it, then," said Gascoigne drily; "for you hear not what I say to you."

"Say rather, my lord," Falstaff answered with a broad smile, "it is the disease of not listening that I am troubled with."

"Well, well, sir; I sent for you before the expedition to Shrewsbury to answer for a robbery upon Gadshill; your services in the wars have a little gilded over that night's exploit, and you may thank the unquiet times that the business was allowed to pass so quietly. But I warn you to let sleeping dogs lie. The truth is, you live in great infamy, and have been a bad companion for the young Prince."

"My lord, you that are old make no allowances for us youngsters. We are wags, I confess, we fellows in the prime of our youth."

"You a youngster! you, with every mark of age on you—a moist eye, a white beard, a decreasing leg, an increasing belly; with your voice cracked, your wind short, your chin double, your wit single, every part of you smitten with antiquity? And yet you call yourself young? Fie, fie, fie, Sir John!"

"My lord, I was born about three o'clock in the afternoon, with a white head and something of a round belly. For my voice, I have lost it with halloing and singing of anthems. The truth is, I am only old in judgment and understanding; and if any one will dance with me for a thousand marks, let him lend me the money and I'm his man. As for that box on the ear the Prince gave you, he gave it like a rude Prince and you took it like a sensible lord. I have rebuked him for it, and the young lion repents, not in sackcloth, but in old sack."

"Well, the King has separated Prince Harry from you. I hear you are going with Prince John of Lancaster against the Archbishop and the Earl of Northumberland."

"Yes, and I thank your pretty sweet wit for it." Falstaff was shrewd enough to put two and two together. "It seems there is not a dangerous action can peep out its head, but I am thrust upon it. Well, I cannot last for ever; but it always was the trick of our English nation, if they have a good thing, to make it too common. If you must have it that I am an old man, you should give me some rest. But there! I would to Heaven my name were not so terrible to the enemy as it is. I were better to be eaten to death with rust than scoured to nothing with perpetual motion."

Somehow the Lord Chief-Justice felt that he was not having the best of the encounter. He turned to walk away. "Well, be honest, be honest; and may your expedition prosper."

"Will your lordship lend me a thousand pounds to furnish me forth?" asked Falstaff blandly.

"Not a penny, not a penny. Farewell; commend me to my cousin Westmoreland." The judge was off in a hurry.

Falstaff looked after him. "Lord, how old age is given to covetousness!" he sighed.

Indeed Sir John's purse was at a low ebb. Mistress

Quickly of the Boar's Head Tavern would give him credit no longer, and had actually entered a suit against him to recover what he owed. "A hundred mark," she tearfully assured the sheriff's officers, "is a long one for a poor lone woman to bear; and I have borne, and borne, and borne, and have been fubbed off, and fubbed off, and fubbed off from this day to that day, that it is a shame to be thought on!" And so it happened that when next the Lord Chief-Justice came upon Falstaff it was to find him brawling with the sheriff's men, with Bardolph backing his resistance, and Dame Quickly dancing round the scuffle, calling names and crying for a rescue—or as she put it, "a rescue or two"—at the top of her shrill voice.

"Keep the peace here!" commanded the Chief-Justice. "What's the matter? How now, Sir John! You should have been well on your way to York by this time."

"Oh, my most worshipful lord," began Mistress Quickly, "an't please your grace, I am a poor widow of Eastcheap, and he is arrested at my suit."

"For what sum?"

"It is more than for some, my lord; it is for all, all I have. He hath eaten me out of house and home."

Gascoigne turned to Falstaff. "Fie, Sir John! Are you not ashamed to enforce a poor widow to so rough a course to come by her own?"

"What is the gross sum I owe thee?" Falstaff demanded.

"Marry, if thou wert an honest man, thyself and thy

money too. Thou didst swear to me upon a parcel-gilt goblet, sitting in my Dolphin-chamber, at the round table, by a sea-coal fire, upon Wednesday in Wheeson[6] week, when the Prince broke thy head for likening his father to a singing-man of Windsor, thou didst swear to me then, as I was washing thy wound, to marry me and make me my lady thy wife. Canst thou deny it? Did not goodwife Keech, the butcher's wife, come in then and call me Gossip Quickly? coming in to borrow some vinegar; telling us she had a good dish of prawns; whereby thou didst desire to eat some; whereby I told thee they were ill for a green wound? And didst thou not, when she was gone down stairs, desire me to be no more so familiarity with such poor people; saying that ere long they should call me madam? And didst thou not kiss me and bid me lend thee thirty shillings? I put thee now to thy book-oath; deny it, if thou canst!"

"My lord," said Falstaff compassionately, "this is a poor mad soul. She has seen better days, and the truth is poverty has driven her crazy."

"Sir John, Sir John," the Chief-Justice answered, "I know well your manner of twisting the true cause the false way. But neither your confidence nor your glib and impudent sauciness can prevail upon my level consideration. You have practised upon this woman's weakness. Pay her the debt you owe her, and undo the wrong you have done her."

Falstaff was stung. "My lord, I will take no such snubbing from you without an answer. You call

[6]Mistress Quickly means Whitsun.

179

honourable boldness impudent sauciness; if a man makes courtesy to you and holds his peace, he is virtuous. No, my lord, my humble duty remembered, I do not choose to be your suitor. I say to you I request to be delivered from these officers, being upon hasty employment in the King's affairs."

The reply was poor perhaps; but it showed that Falstaff, though careless with the low company of his choice, had shame enough left, being a gentleman himself, to wince under the rebuke of a gentleman. The Chief-Justice was here interrupted by a Captain named Gower, with letters from the King; and while he studied them, Falstaff applied himself to the task of wheedling Mistress Quickly—no very difficult one. Scraps of their talk only reached the judge, and he paid no heed to them. "As I am a gentleman, now." "By the heavenly ground I tread upon, Sir John, I shall have to pawn my plate and the tapestry of my dining-chambers." "Glasses, glasses are the only ware for drinking; and for thy walls, a pretty slight drollery, or the story of the Prodigal, or the German hunting in water-colours, is worth a thousand of these bed-hangings and these fly-bitten tapestries. Come, there's not a better soul in England than thou, if 'twere not for thy humours. Go, wash thy face and withdraw the action. Come, come, I know thou wast set on to this." "Let it be twenty nobles, Sir John! i' faith, I am loath to pawn my plate, I am. . . . Well, well, you shall have your way, though I pawn my gown. I hope you'll come to supper. You'll pay me in the lump—no instalments?" "As sure as I live!"—So Falstaff had his way, and the prospect of a good supper besides; and as Dame Quickly bustled off to prepare it, he turned to the Chief-Justice. "What's the news, my lord?"

But the Chief-Justice affected not to hear him. "Where lay the King last night?" he demanded of Gower.

"At Basingstoke, my lord," was the answer.

"I hope all is well, my lord. What's the news, my lord?" Falstaff repeated.

Still the Chief-Justice paid no regard. "Are all his forces returned with him?" he went on to inquire. Gower answered, "No; fifteen hundred foot and five hundred horse have marched to join Prince John against the Earl of Northumberland and the Archbishop."

"Is the King back from Wales, my lord?" Falstaff persisted. But still he addressed a deaf ear.

"Come with me, Master Gower," went on the Chief-Justice. "I shall have a letter presently to send by you."

Falstaff cleared his throat. "My lord!"

"Hey? What's the matter?" For the first time the Chief-Justice seemed aware of his presence. But now it was Sir John's turn, and he pointedly addressed Captain Gower.

"Master Gower, may I beg you to dine with me?"

"I thank you, Sir John, I must wait upon my lord here."

"Sir John," said the Chief-Justice sternly, "you loiter too long here, being bound to recruit soldiers on your way."

Not a word did Sir John seem to hear. "Will you sup with me then, Master Gower?"

The Chief-Justice stamped his foot. "What foolish master taught you these manners, Sir John?"

"Gower," said Sir John, with his bland smile, "if my manners become me not, he was a fool who taught them me." Then with a mock bow he turned on his adversary, "Tap for tap, my lord, as between fencers—and so part fair!"

So once more Chief-Justice Gascoigne had not all the best of it, and Falstaff supped merrily that night at the Boar's Head, hob-a-nob with Bardolph and Dame Quickly and a ranting follower of his named Pistol, whose gift lay chiefly in swaggering and mouthing fustian lines out of plays and books, of which he knew just enough to misquote them—a bragging rascal with the heart of a mouse. We shall meet him again and make his better acquaintance.

And in the midst of their feasting who should drop in but the Prince, newly returned from Wales, with his old comrade Poins? We do not change old habits in a moment; and now and again, even after his taste of a new self-respect and men's better opinions, Harry caught himself hankering after the old wild ways. As he put it to Poins, "It does my greatness discredit, but I must confess to a longing for small beer." He knew, too, that men did not seriously believe him reformed. In his heart he was deeply sorry for his father's sickness; but few, he felt sure, would give him credit for this, and the thought cast him back upon a reckless show of not caring. "Yet," he confided to Poins, "I could tell thee, as one whom it pleases me for lack of a better to call my friend, I could be sad, and very sad too."

"Scarcely," answered Poins incredulously, "upon such a subject."

The Prince sighed. "I see; thou thinkest me as deep in the devil's book as thyself or Falstaff. Let the end try the man. But I tell thee my heart bleeds inwardly that my father is so sick. What wouldst thou think of me if I should weep?"

"I should think thee a most princely hypocrite."

"And so would every man," said Harry bitterly; "and thou art a blessed fellow to think as every man thinks. And why, pray, should you and every man think so?"

"Why, because of your loose life and your attachment to Falstaff."

"And to thee; add that."

Poins protested. "The worst any one can say of me is that I am a younger son and a proper fellow of my hands." So surely it appears to every man that he is a good fellow really, though led astray by somebody else, or perhaps by circumstances.

The man they most blamed at any rate had resolved to lead the Prince astray no longer, nor be suspected of it. Falstaff had been stung by the Chief-Justice's rebuke, and learning of the Prince's likely arrival in London, sat down and wrote a letter, and despatched it by Bardolph.

Thus it ran: "SIR JOHN FALSTAFF, KNIGHT, *to the son of the King, nearest his father,* HARRY PRINCE OF WALES, GREETING: *I will imitate the honourable Romans in brevity. I commend me to thee, I commend thee, and I leave thee. Be not too familiar with Poins, who abuses thy favour. Repent at idle times as thou mayest; and so, farewell.—Thine, by yea and no, which is as much as to say, as thou usest him,* JACK FALSTAFF *with my familiars,* JOHN *with my brothers and sisters, and* SIR JOHN *with all Europe."*

"Is your master here in London?" the Prince asked Bardolph.

"Yea, my lord."

"Where sups he? at the old haunt?"

"At the old place, my lord, in Eastcheap."

"What company?"

"The old crew, my lord."

Prince Harry turned to Poins. "We will steal upon them there;" and after cautioning Bardolph not to report his arrival, he and Poins hurried off to procure a couple of waiters' suits, in which they appeared on the scene as the old riotous mirth was at its height. The old laugh went round, the old jests were played, but the Prince, though he entered into them, missed the old sparkle. In truth he had descended to this tavern world, but he had never belonged to it, and was just beginning to find this out. Even Falstaff, with the quick sympathy of a gentleman, felt a difference, and answered now and then with a changed note—a terribly sad note for all its defiant recklessness. It was Peto who put an end to the revelry, breaking in with news that the King had returned to Westminster, that a score of weary riders had come with tidings from the north, and that messengers were knocking up all the taverns to find Falstaff, and hurry him on his road. Sir John thrust his chair back from the table, and lurched off to pack his campaigning kit, while the Prince did on sword and cloak and passed out into the street, busy with the thought which had been in his head all day. "We play the fools with the moment, and the spirits of the wise sit in the clouds and mock us. Well, the end shall try the man."

In quiet Gloucestershire there lived at this time a country gentleman and Justice of the Peace, by name Master Shallow; a vain, petty, talkative person, well on in years, full of his own importance, and given to painting for his neighbours the most wonderful pictures of the dashing, dare-devil life he had led in London when he had studied at Clement's Inn, and before he had come back to settle down as a country squire.

He had not many listeners, and the best of them was his cousin Master Silence; for Master Silence either took, or seemed to take, all his stories for gospel, and seldom interrupted with talk of his own. Now it happened that he had come over for an early visit, and after the first handshaking he must answer for his health and his wife's and his daughter Ellen's (a godchild of Shallow's) and his son William's. Thus the talk ran on:—

"And William? I dare say now William is become a good scholar. He is at Oxford still, is he not?"

"He is, to my cost."

"He must be going then to the Inns o' Court shortly. I was once of Clement's Inn, where I think they will talk of mad Shallow yet."

"You were called 'lusty Shallow' then, cousin."

"By the mass, I was called anything; and I would have done anything indeed too, and never thought twice. There was I, and little John Doit of Staffordshire, and black George Barnes, and Francis Pickbone, and Will Squele, a Cotswold man; you wouldn't see another four such roisterers in all the Inns o' Court. There was Jack Falstaff, too, now Sir John, a youngster and page to Thomas Mowbray, Duke of Norfolk."

"Will that be the same Sir John who is coming here to enlist soldiers?"

"The same, the very same. I saw him break Skogan's head at the court-gate when he was a whipper-snapper not *so* high; and the very same day did I fight with one Sampson Stockfish, a fruiterer, behind Gray's Inn. Dear, dear, the mad days I have spent! And to think how many of my old acquaintance are dead!"

"We shall all follow, cousin."

"Certain, 'tis certain; very sure, very sure; death, as the Psalmist says, is certain to all; all shall die. What was a good yoke of bullocks fetching at Stamford fair?"

"To say truth, I was not there."

"Death is certain. Is old Double of your town still living?"

"Dead, cousin."

"Dear, dear, dead is he? 'A drew a good bow: and dead! 'A shot a fine shoot: John o' Gaunt loved him well, and betted much money on him. Dead, now? He'd hit you the white at twelve-score yards, and carry a long-distance shot fourteen and fourteen and a half, 'twould have done your heart good to see. What price a score of ewes now?"

"That depends; a score of good ewes may be worth ten pounds."

"And so old Double is dead, is he?"

This profitable talk was here interrupted by a visitor, who turned out to be our friend Bardolph, bearing Sir John Falstaff's compliments and the news of his arrival.

Master Shallow was delighted to hear it. "How doth the good knight? May I ask how my lady his wife doth?"

"Pardon, sir," answered Bardolph, "a soldier is better accommodated than with a wife."

"And that is well said, sir; well said indeed. 'Better accommodated,' very good indeed; good phrases are surely, and ever were, very commendable. 'Accommodated,' it comes of Latin 'accommodo'; very good, a good phrase."

"Please, sir?" Bardolph was puzzled. "I know nothing about phrase; but the word is a good soldier-like word, and that I will maintain with my sword.

'Accommodated,' that is, when a man is, as they say, accommodated; or when a man is, being, whereby he may be thought to be accommodated; which," Bardolph wound up, "is an excellent thing."

Before Master Shallow had done admiring this interpretation, Falstaff's arrival claimed his politeness. "Give me your hand, give me your worship's good hand. By my truth, you bear your years very well! Welcome, good Sir John.—This is my cousin Silence, a justice of the peace like myself."

"Good Master Silence," Falstaff bowed, "it is fitting that you should be of the peace. Phew! this is hot weather, gentlemen. Have you provided me here half a dozen sufficient men?"

"Marry, we have, sir." Master Shallow begged Falstaff to be seated. "Where's the roll? where's the roll? where's the roll?" He fussed about, fitting on his spectacles. "Let me see, let me see, let me see. So, so, so, so, . . . " He found the names at length and called up the six dispirited recruits one by one. They were a sorry crew, and Sir John had plenty to say about their looks. Two of them only had the makings of stout soldiers—Ralph Mouldy and Peter Bullcalf. "Is thy name Mouldy?" demanded Falstaff. "Yes, sir, an it please you," stammered the poor man. "'Tis the more time thou wert used then." "Ha, ha, ha!" tittered Master Shallow, "excellent, upon my word! things that are mouldy lack use: very good indeed! Well said, Sir John; very well said."

Falstaff passed the six in review, "Are these all?" he asked.

"They are two more than your number," Shallow reminded him. "You must have but four from these parts. And so, I pray you, go in with me to dinner."

But Sir John was pressed for time. "Come, I will drink with you, but I cannot stay for dinner. By my troth I am glad to see you again, Master Shallow," he added affably.

"Ah, Sir John, do you remember that wild night we spent in the windmill in St. George's Field?"

"Tut, tut, Master Shallow; no more of that, no more of that."

"Ha! that was a merry night. Ha, Cousin Silence, if thou hadst seen what this knight and I have seen! Eh, Sir John?"

"We have heard the chimes at midnight, Master Shallow."

"That we have, that we have, that we have; faith, Sir John, we have: our watchword was 'Hem boys!' Come, let's to dinner, let's to dinner. Dear, dear, the days that we have seen! Come, come . . . "

Now it suited Sir John's book very well that Bardolph should be left alone for a while with the recruits. As he fully expected, no sooner had he stepped into the house with the justices than a couple—Bullcalf and Mouldy— began to sidle up to the Corporal; for these two likely fellows were the ones who least liked the prospect of soldiering.

Bullcalf began, "Good Master Corporate Bardolph, stand my friend, and here's four ten-shillings in French crowns for you. In truth, sir, I had as lief be hanged as go to the wars. For my own part, sir, I don't care; but rather because I am unwilling, and for my own part have a desire to stay with my friends; else, sir, I would not care, for my own part, so much."

"Go to; stand aside," said Bardolph gruffly.

"And good master corporal captain," pleaded Mouldy, "for my old woman's sake stand my friend. She has nobody to do anything about her when I am gone, and she is old and cannot help herself. You shall have forty shillings from me too, sir."

"Go to; stand aside," commanded Bardolph in the same tone. Perhaps he expected some further bribes; but the others were either too poor or too reckless to offer anything. Indeed the feeblest scarecrow of them all protested that he for his part was ready to go. "A man can die but once: we owe God a death; and I'll never bear a base mind. If it be my destiny, so be it: if not, so be it: no man's too good to serve his king: and let it go which way it will, the man who dies this year is safe for the next."

"Well spoken," said Bardolph; "thou'rt a good fellow."

"Faith, sir, I'll bear no base mind."

So when Falstaff came out, Bardolph drew him aside. "Sir, a word with you," he whispered, "I have three pounds to let Mouldy and Bullcalf go."—From which it will be seen that the corporal took his pickings.

"Come, Sir John," demanded Master Shallow, "which four will you have?"

Falstaff eyed the six with his wisest air. "Mouldy and Bullcalf shall stay at home; I'll take the rest."

"Sir John, Sir John," Shallow twittered, "be better advised! They are your likeliest men, and I would have you served with the best."

"Master Shallow," replied Falstaff loftily, "are you pretending to teach me how to choose a man? What care I for limbs, thews, stature, bulk, or all the big total of these? Give me *spirit*, Master Shallow. Take that thin fellow yonder: he presents no mark to the enemy; the foeman might as well aim at the edge of a penknife. And that other fellow—what a pair of legs for a retreat! Or see this ragged man—what's his name?—Wart. Bardolph, give Wart a musket; now then, Wart, march! Come, show us how you handle your musket. So; very well; very good, very good indeed! O give me always a little, lean, old, wrinkled, bald marksman! There's a sixpence for thee, Wart."

"But," Master Shallow protested, "he's not doing it right! I remember at Mile-end Green, when I lived at Clement's Inn, I belonged to an archery club; and there was a little nimble fellow who would manage his weapon thus; and he would about and about, and come you in and come you in; 'rah-tah-tah,' would he say; 'bounce!' would he say; and away again would he go, and again would he come. I shall never see such a fellow!" sighed Master Shallow, pacing about and skipping to show exactly how it was done.

"These fellows will do well, Master Shallow," Falstaff assured him, and so took leave, vowing he had a dozen miles to march that night. The justice wished him prosperity. "And pay us a visit on your way back; let our old acquaintance be renewed. Nay, who knows but I may go up to London with you to court."

"Indeed, I wish you would, Master Shallow."

"There, there; I said it too hastily. Fare you well."

"Fare you well, gentlemen." Falstaff commanded Bardolph to march the recruits ahead of him. "As I return," he told himself, "I will have sport with these justices; I do see to the bottom of this Shallow. Dear, dear, how subject we old men are to this vice of lying! This same shrivelled-up justice hath done nothing but prate to me of the wildness of his youth and the feats he hath done about Turnbull Street—and every third word of it a falsehood! I remember him at Clement's Inn like a man made out of a cheese-paring, a forked radish with a funny little head carved on top. And now this miserable lath is become a squire, and talks as familiarly of John o' Gaunt as if he had been his sworn brother; and I'll swear never set eyes on him but once, in the tilt-yard, and then had his head broken for crowding among the marshal's men. I was there and saw it, and told John o' Gaunt he beat his own name. Well, well, I'll make his further acquaintance if I return, and it shall go hard if I don't turn him to some profit."

At home in his palace of Westminster the King lay sick in mind and body, wearing to his end under the cares of the crown he had once so eagerly seized, restless, wooing in vain on his pillows of down that sleep which the meanest of his subjects enjoyed as an easy boon—the labourer in smoky cabin on a hard pallet, the ship-boy perched on a giddy mast yet cradled by the rocking seas. And lying awake through the long night-watches he remembered Richard and Richard's prophecy—that Northumberland, who had made haste to overthrow one king, would not be slow in casting down another. Another prophecy he recalled; an old one which promised that his death should be in Jerusalem; and he prayed for an end of these civil wars, that he might sail, as he had so long purposed, for the Holy Land, and there meet it, not unwelcome.

And Northumberland, not less unhappy, still tarried in his castle of Warkworth near the sea. But for him his son Hotspur might be alive and Mortimer King of England; and it added a gnawing poison to his self-reproach that now, when too late he would have redeemed his honour, the voices that assured him how vain it was were the dispirited sad voices of Hotspur's mother and Hotspur's wife. "The time was," the young widow reminded him, scarce knowing how cruelly; "the time was you broke your word when it was dearer than it can ever be now; when your own Percy, Harry, my heart's dear, looked northward for his father's coming, and looked in vain. *His* honour was to him as the sun to heaven; by the light of him was all England's chivalry moved to do brave deeds. All copied him who sought to be noble; copied even his small tricks of manner and speech. Him you left at disadvantage to abide a battle hopeless but for the miracle of his name. Your honour? Ah, never now wrong his ghost by holding your honour more scrupulous with others than you held it with him! Let the Archbishop alone and his friends. They are strong. Had my dear Harry had but half their numbers, this day might I, twining my arms around his neck, be talking of that other Harry's—his slayer's—grave!"

"Beshrew your heart, daughter," groaned the unhappy father, "you draw the spirit out of my breast. I must go and face the danger, or it will find me elsewhere and worse provided." But wife and son's wife implored him together to escape to Scotland and wait; and knowing that they despised him, knowing that he despised himself, he took their advice, sent excuses to the Archbishop, and fled northward. It must be terrible for an old man to despise himself, and feel that the time for cure has gone by.

His message was felt as a heavy blow by the Archbishop and his partisans Mowbray and Hastings. But it reached them when they were in full march and committed to war. At Gaultree Forest in Yorkshire they came face to face with the King's army, led by Prince John and the Earl of Westmoreland; and again from the royal side came an offer of terms. But this time the offer was not so honest as it had been at Shrewsbury. Perhaps the King had Worcester's treachery in his mind when he gave Prince John his instructions, or perhaps that somewhat cold-blooded youth devised the snare which his brother Prince Harry would have scorned to lay.

It was Westmoreland who brought the rebel leaders to parley, demanding in the King's name their reasons for this armed rising. Once more the Archbishop repeated the old story. It was not with these men as with the Percies, a story of past services unrewarded. They had hated Bolingbroke and felt his hatred from the beginning. The Archbishop owed him a brother's death. Mowbray was the son of that Thomas Mowbray, Duke of Norfolk, who had faced Bolingbroke in the lists at Coventry, and gone from them into hopeless exile; he had been allowed, indeed, to inherit his father's estates, but he had inherited, too, the memory of that bitter sentence, and no man in England nursed a deeper detestation of Henry. "With my consent," he declared, "we will admit no parley." Hastings was less uncompromising. "Has the Prince John," he asked, "a full commission from his father to hear our complaints and grant conditions?" Westmoreland assured them that this was so. "I am come to learn these complaints, to tell you that his Grace will give you audience and freely grant those demands which shall appear to him to be just." On this assurance the Archbishop tendered a paper setting forth their grievances. "Let them be redressed, my lord," said he, "and all concerned in this movement granted due acquittal, and once more we are His Majesty's peaceful subjects."

The royal offer seemed a fair one, and Mowbray alone remained unconvinced. Westmoreland departed back with the document, and returned with word that Prince John would meet and confer with the malcontent leaders midway between the two armies.

In the conference which followed the Prince opened with a formal rebuke, but ended by confessing that the demands contained in the paper seemed to him fair.

"And I swear here by the honour of my blood that my father's intentions have been mistaken; that they and his authority alike have been abused by some about him. My Lord Archbishop, these grievances shall be speedily redressed; they shall, on my soul. If my word for it content you, we will here and now disband our forces on each side, and pledge our restored love and amity."

"I take your princely word that they shall be redressed," answered the Archbishop.

And now it only remained to pay and discharge the two armies. Hastings sent word to the rebel camp; and while the leaders drank and pledged one another, they heard the cheers of the dispersing soldiery. Prince John commanded Westmoreland to go and disband the royal troops. "My lord," said he, turning to the Archbishop, "if it please you, let the two armies march past us, that we may see the men we came so near contending with."

The Archbishop agreed, and sent Hastings to give the order.

But now Westmoreland came back with word that the royal army was not yet in motion. Its leaders had charge from Prince John to keep their station, and would not stir without his direct command.

"They know their duties," said the Prince calmly.

What he meant by this he made plain when Hastings returned and announced that it was too late to march the Archbishop's men past; they were already dispersed and hurrying homeward, east, west, north, and south, like boys when a school breaks up.

"Good news, my Lord Hastings," said Westmoreland ironically; "and so I arrest you, traitor, of high treason; and you, Lord Archbishop; and you also, Lord Mowbray."

Under this treacherous stroke, Mowbray, as he had most mistrusted, was the first to find his speech. He turned on Prince John. "Is this just and honourable?" he asked.

It was neither; it was the meanest and coldest crime the House of Lancaster had to pay for in its day of reckoning. "Will you break your faith thus?" the Archbishop demanded.

"I pledged none to *thee*," was the Prince's shameful answer. "I promised redress of these grievances, and by my honour I will perform it with a most Christian care. But for you rebels, you shall taste the doom of rebels. Lead these men to the block; and sound drums for the pursuit of their followers!" With the name of God on his lips the Prince hurried off to chase and massacre.

At home the thoughts of the sick King still ran on his voyage to Palestine, and again on the son he loved most but could never understand. The nearer he drew to his end the more his heart yearned over this Harry who should succeed him. Most of all he hated that others should share or even guess his own fears. To his other sons—and especially to Thomas of Clarence, who had succeeded to Harry's place in the Council, and cherished little love but no little contempt for his elder brother—he insisted pitifully on Harry's good qualities and kindness of heart.

There came a day when, stretched on his couch, he asked after Harry, and was told that the Prince had gone to hunt at Windsor.

"Is not Thomas of Clarence with him?"

"No, my lord, he is here." And Clarence came forward. "What would my lord and father?" he asked.

"Why, Clarence, art thou not with thy brother? Thou dost neglect him, and yet of all his brothers he loves thee best. Cherish that love, my son; and when I am dead it may knit you all together in brotherly affection, proof against envious whisperers who will seek to divide our house against itself. His is a generous nature, but quickly incensed, and then as stubborn as flint; therefore chide his faults carefully and in season, and again in his headstrong moods give him rein and let his passion work itself out. Study him, Clarence."

"I will observe him, my lord, with all care and love."

"But why art thou not at Windsor with him?"

"He is not at Windsor to-day, but dining in London—with Poins and his other constant companions."

This was just what Henry had dreaded to hear; and for the moment in his weakness he let slip the cry of his heart, the anguish he had been trying to hide, the perpetual haunting terror of the days to come, when he should be asleep in his tomb and his son misgoverning England without check or guidance. It was at this moment, while the Earl of Warwick, one of his wisest counsellors, sought to console him, that a messenger arrived from the north with happy news.

Northumberland at last had met the reward of paltering with fate. He had failed Hotspur; he had failed the Archbishop; both in the hour of need. Too late he had been forced to summon up courage and strike with Lord Bardolph and the remnant of the rebel leaders; and at Tadcaster, near York, had fallen on the field in the general rout of his troops.

This was the news which at another time might have put new life into Henry. But Henry was past rejoicing. Stretching out his hands, with one terrible call upon Good Fortune which had come too late, he sank back upon his couch in a swoon.

His sons rushed to his side, with Westmoreland and Warwick. They bore him into another chamber, and laid him there on a bed, standing beside him until the fit passed and his eyes opened. He was very weary, he whispered; let there be no noise made, unless it were soothing music. He begged them to set the crown on the pillow beside him, while the music lulled him—if it might be—to sleep.

While the musicians played softly in a near room, and the King's eyes closed, Prince Harry came in noisy high spirits along the corridor, eager to tell the good news from the north which he had heard outside. Warwick met him at the door, entreating, "Less noise, less noise!"

The sight of his brothers' grief and of the figure stretched on the bed sobered him. "Has he heard the good news?" he asked. "What? Overcome by it? If he be sick with joy, he'll recover without physic."

"Not so much noise," Warwick entreated again. "Prince, I implore you speak low; your father is disposed to sleep."

The others withdrew softly to the other room, but Harry sat down to watch alone by his father. While he watched his eyes fell on the crown resting on the pillow. "Why does it lie there, I wonder?" He went over, touched it, took it in his hands, laid it back again. "Sleep with it now; but of how much slumber has it not robbed thee, my father—this golden burden?" As he set it down something caught his attention. A tiny feather of down had escaped from the pillow and lay close to the King's parted lips. He bent; the feather did not stir. "This must be death!" He dropped on his knees. "My gracious lord! my father!" The figure on the bed neither answered nor moved. "Sleep? ay, the sleep that hath parted so many English kings from this golden circlet." He took the crown again from the pillow, and standing upright held it in both hands above him. "My due to thee, father, is a son's tears and heavy sorrows, and tenderly, fully, shall they be paid; thy due to me is this crown. Here on my head I place it; God shall guard it: the whole world shall not be strong enough to force it from me—the crown of England, to be my son's as it was my father's!"

By and by the eyes of the sick King unclosed, and gazed feebly about the room. It was empty. He raised himself on an elbow. "Warwick! Gloucester! Clarence!" he called; and as they came hurriedly, "Why have you left me alone here?"

"We left the Prince of Wales here, my liege. He

undertook to sit by you and watch."

"The Prince of Wales! Where is he? Let me see him; he is not here."

"He must have gone out by this door; he did not pass through the room where we have been sitting."

But the King's eyes were now turned upon his pillow. "Where is the crown? Who has taken it? Go, fetch the Prince. Is he so hasty to think me dead? O you sons!" he cried bitterly, "you for whom we fathers wake and scheme and toil, only to be thus rewarded!"

The Prince was not far to seek. Warwick found him overcome with grief, weeping alone in one of the rooms close by; and he came back joyful and amazed, while Henry dismissed the others with a motion of his weak hand.

"Father! I never thought to hear you speak again!"

"Thy wish, Harry, was father of that thought. It seems I stay too long and weary thee. What! So hungry after my empty chair that thou must needs put on my honours before thy hour comes? Couldst thou not have waited a little—a very little? but must steal that which in an hour or two would have been thine without offence? All thy life has proved that thou hadst never any love for me, and now thou wilt have me die well assured of it. What! Couldst thou not forbear one half-hour? Go, then, dig my grave; bid the bells ring for thy coronation." From terrible reproaches the dying father passed to yet more bitter, more terrible gibes. "Harry the Fifth is crowned! Long live the new king, and farewell to dignity and wise counsel! Assemble, all the apes of idleness, all the scum of Europe! Has any nation a ruffian ready to swear, drink, dance, revel, rob, murder, commit the oldest sins in the newest kind of ways? Be happy—he shall trouble you no longer. Send him to England—there are office, honours, power awaiting him here. For Harry the Fifth is King, and England goes back to her old inhabitants, the wolves!"

Harry was hurt beyond anger. "My liege, blame the tears that hindered my speech and have suffered you to speak, me to listen, so far. There is your crown; and may He who wears a crown everlasting long guard it yours! If I care for it more than as your honour and renown, let me not rise from these knees. God is my witness, when I came in and finding no sign of breath believed you dead, how cold it struck my heart; my witness with what thoughts I lifted the crown, accusing it and the cares of it for thy death, and put it on my head as moved by the moment to try with it, as with an enemy who had murdered my father, the quarrel of a true inheritor. But if I rejoiced, was puffed up, or hailed its possession, may God keep it from my head for ever, and abase me as low as the poorest vassal who kneels to it in awe and terror!"

These indignant words, spoken with honest looks, touched the King and convinced him. "My son, God must have put it in thy mind to take the crown, that thy words of excuse might win the more surely thy father's love! Come, Harry, sit by my bed, and hear my counsel—the latest, I think, that I shall ever utter. God knows, my son, by what devious ways I came to this crown, as I know too well what a weight it hath been to wear. But it descends to thee more quietly, better allowed by men's opinions, ay, and assured; for I carry to earth all the stain with which it was won. All my reign through I have been forced to defend it, and thou knowest with what peril I have done so. My death changes all, and by thee it will be worn as a fair inheritance. Yet beware; the power of those who advanced me and might have dragged me low again is but newly broken. It was to keep them busy, too busy to be idly prying into my title, that I had planned to lead them to Palestine. Do thou, Harry, keep them busy with wars abroad, and so may action wear out the old bad memories, and God, forgiving how I came by the crown, grant it may abide with thee in true peace!"

"My gracious liege," declared Harry, "as you won it, wore it, kept it, and have given it to me, so it is mine, and against all the world will I maintain it."

The King was exhausted and almost too weak for speech. "My lord," he muttered, as Warwick re-entered, "the chamber where I swooned—has it not some particular name?"

"It is called Jerusalem, your majesty." For so it was called from the paintings around its walls, and indeed is so called to this day.

Henry remembered the old prophecy that nowhere but in Jerusalem should his end be. "Praise be unto God! vainly I supposed it was to be in the Holy Land; but now bear me back to that chamber, and let Henry die in Jerusalem."

Now Falstaff had not forgotten his promise to revisit Justice Shallow on his way back from the wars; and a little while after these things happened at Westminster, in peaceful Gloucestershire Sir John was resting his unwieldy legs under the justice's table, drinking deep of his sack, listening to his endless empty discourse, and promising himself how Prince Harry would laugh over his description of this visit, a little dressed up. "It's a long way a dressed-up tale and a jest with a solemn face will go with a youngster who never had an ache in his shoulders. I will make Harry laugh over this Shallow till he cries."

And indeed after supper, when the justice led his guests out into his orchard, where their dessert was spread in a summer arbour—"a last year's pippin of my own grafting, with a dish of caraways and so forth"— the tale promised to be a very lively one. For Master Shallow had drunk too much sack, and Master Silence had unaccountably found his tongue and could not be restrained from trolling out snatches of song.

"I did not think," remarked Falstaff, observing him with a roguish cock of the eye; "I did not think Master Silence had been a man of this mettle."

"Who, I?" hiccupped Silence; "I have been merry once or twice in my time!" and again he broke into singing.

While they pledged each other and Falstaff egged Silence on to make himself more and more ridiculous, they heard from the orchard a knocking on the house door, and Shallow's man Davy ran to answer it. He came back. "An't please your worship, there's one Pistol arrived from the court with news."

"Pistol? From the court? Let him come in. Why, how now, Pistol?" demanded Sir John, as the visitor came swaggering across the turf. "What wind blew you hither?"

"Not the ill wind which blows no man to good. Knight, thou art now one of the greatest men in this realm."

"'Pon my word, now, I think he be," tittered Master Silence foolishly, "unless it be fat Puff of Barson parish."

"Puff!" Pistol rounded on him with a flourish in his loftiest manner, familiar enough to his friends, but highly disconcerting to an honest country gentleman pretty far fuddled with drink. "Puff in thy teeth, most recreant coward base! Sir John, I am thy Pistol and thy friend, And helter-skelter have I rode to thee, And tidings do I bring and lucky joys, And golden times and happy news of price."

"Come," said Falstaff, with a glance at Silence, who sat with his jaw dropped in sheer astonishment at a gentleman who talked blank verse, and such unusual blank verse, by habit, "I pray thee tell thy news like a man of this world."

"A farthing for the world and worldlings base! I speak of Africa and golden joys."

"Very well, then." Falstaff observing its effect upon the two justices, took up Pistol's manner with a grin.

"O base Assyrian knight, what is thy news? Let King Cophetua know the truth thereof."

"And Robin Hood, Scarlet, and John—"

warbled Silence.

"Shall dunghill curs confront the Helicons? And shall good news be baffled? Then, Pistol, lay thy head in Furies' lap!"

"Honest gentleman," quavered Shallow, "I don't know who you may be, but all this is very strange to me—"

"Why, then, be sorry for it," Pistol interrupted.

"Your pardon, sir," persisted the little justice; "if you come with news from the court, I take it there's but two ways, either to utter it or to conceal it." He drew himself up primly. "I am, sir, under the King, a person of some authority."

"Under which King, Besonian? Speak or die!"

"Why, under King Harry."

"Harry the Fourth or the Fifth?"

"Harry the Fourth, to be sure."

Pistol snapped his fingers. "That, then, for thy authority! Sir John, thy pet lamb is to-day King of England. And long live Harry the Fifth!"

"What!" Falstaff staggered to his feet. "The old King dead!"

"As a door-nail."

"Away, Bardolph! saddle my horse. Master Robert Shallow, choose what office thou wilt in the land, it is thine. Pistol, I will double-charge thee with honours."

"O joyful day!" Bardolph waved his hat. "I wouldn't swap my fortune to-day for a knighthood."

But Falstaff was all fume and bustle to be off towards London. "Carry Master Silence to bed. Master Shallow— my Lord Shallow—be what thou wilt, I am the dispenser of fortune now—get on thy boots! We'll ride all night. Bless thee, Pistol. Away, Bardolph! Come, tell me more, Pistol. Boot, boot and saddle, Master Shallow! I know the young King is pining for me. Let us take any man's horses; the laws of England are what I choose 'em to be. Blessed are they who have been Jack Falstaff's friends; and woe to my Lord Chief-Justice!"

The Prince's loose companions were not alone in believing that a merry time lay in store for them, and a sorry one for men of sobriety and good counsel. The Lord Chief-Justice, for example, had reason enough to fear what Falstaff so confidently promised. What could he look for from the youth he had been hardy enough to commit to prison? "I would he had called me with him," he sighed, when news came to him of the King's death. Whatever happened, it could not be worse than he had foreboded of late.

At the first audience of the new King which he attended at Westminster, the Princes Gloucester and Clarence gave this upright judge but cold comfort. "You will have to pay your suit to Sir John Falstaff now," the latter sneered.

Harry when he entered the audience chamber was quick to perceive the gloom on their faces. "Brothers," said he, "you mix fears with your sadness. This is the English court, not the Turkish; here Harry is succeeded by Harry, not one tyrant by a tyrant who slays his brothers. Yet be sorrowful, as I will be sorrowful; but let us as brothers wear for a common reason the sorrow that so royally becomes you." The young King cast his eyes around the chamber. "I see you all look strangely on me. *You* most of all"—he turned on the Lord Chief-Justice—"you are assured I have little love for you."

"I am assured," answered Gascoigne with humble courage, "that if I be measured rightly, your Majesty has no just reason to hate me." He had promised the Princes beforehand that he would sue for no half-hearted pardon, but if his uprightness and innocence availed nothing, would follow the dead King to his grave and tell him in another world who had sent him there.

"No reason?" demanded Harry. "Can a prince of my great hopes forget the indignity you once laid on me? What! rate, rebuke, pack off to prison the heir of England! Is that to be forgotten, think you?"

"My liege," answered Gascoigne firmly, "as judge I stood for your father. I represented the King. While I administered his law your highness was pleased to forget the majesty I stood for; you struck me there in the very seat of justice. In me you offended your father, and by his authority I committed you. If I did ill, you who now wear his crown cannot take it ill should a son of yours insult the law and, through the law, your royal person.

Suppose the case yours; imagine yourself so disdained by a son; imagine me silencing that son by the power I hold from you; and so after cold consideration pass sentence upon me, and say what I did that misbecame my place or my person or the majesty of my King."

"My lord judge," answered Harry, "you are right. Continue to bear the scales and the sword of justice, and may you increase in honour till you live to see a son of mine offend you and obey you as I did. Then shall I live to say as my father said: 'I am happy to have a judge so brave that he dares to do justice on my own son; and not less happy to have a son who can so submit himself to justice.' Yes, my lord, continue to wear that untarnished sword and to use it as boldly, as justly, as impartially as you used it against me. There is my hand; help me with your wisdom; and with the help of God and such counsellors as you, no one shall have cause to wish aught but long life to King Harry."

Had Falstaff known of this—had he and his companions guessed that while they spurred towards London the King's officers were ransacking the Boar's Head Tavern and dragging its hostess and others to answer for the life of a man mishandled there by Pistol and since dead of his wounds—their haste had been less confident. As it was, they reached the city and posted themselves near Westminster Abbey in time to hear the trumpets and to see the grooms strewing rushes along the roadway for the King's return from the coronation. Falstaff had already on the strength of his promises bled the justice for the loan of a thousand pounds, and his only regret was that time had not allowed him to array his men in new liveries. "Stand here by me, Master Shallow; I will make the King do you grace: I will leer upon him as he comes by, and you shall mark how pleasantly he'll look. Stand behind me, Pistol; I wish I had those liveries. But no matter, this poor show will prove what zeal, what devotion, I had to see him."

"True, true," Master Shallow agreed.

"As it were to ride day and night; and not to have patience, not to change my clothes, but to stand stained with travel and sweating with desire to see him; thinking of nothing else, putting all other business aside, as if there were nothing else important in the world but to see him."

"Very true."

Pistol indeed had heard disquieting news of the raid on the Boar's Head Tavern, and repeated it to Falstaff. The womenkind there, it seemed, had been taken and flung into prison.

"Tut, tut,"—Sir John waved him aside; "I will see them set at liberty."

And now the trumpets sounded, the throng raised a mighty shout, and forth from the great doors of the Abbey stepped the newly crowned King with his train of peers attending.

"God save thy grace, King Hal!" Falstaff thrust himself forward, cheering louder than any. "My royal Hal!"

"The heavens thee guard and keep, most royal imp

of fame!" chimed in Pistol.

"God save thee, my sweet boy!" Falstaff shouted, almost splitting his lungs.

The King heard his remembered voice, halted, flung him a glance, and turned to Gascoigne. "My Lord Chief-Justice, pray speak to that vain man."

"Have you lost your wits?" chided the judge. "Do you know whom you speak to?"

But Falstaff was not to be repressed. "My King! My Jove! I am speaking to thee, my heart!"

The King looked him up and down. Then, clearly and coldly, he spoke: "Old man, I know thee not. Get thee to thy prayers; for ill do white hairs become a fool and a jester. I have been a long time dreaming, and in that dream I have known such a man, one so swollen with indulgence, so old, and so profane. But now I am awake and despise my dream. Hence! leave gluttony, and learn that there is a grave gaping for thee and thrice as wide as for other men. Nay; answer me not with some foolish jest, nor presume that what I was I still am. For God knows, and the world shall know, that I have dismissed my old self, and with it I dismiss those who were my companions. When thou hearest that I am again what I was, then approach and be again my tutor and feeder in riots; but until then I forbid thee on pain of death, as I have forbidden the rest of my misleaders, to approach within ten miles of my person. I have granted thee a sufficient income for life, that poverty may not drive thee to evil, and as we hear of your reformation we will advance you. My Lord Chief-Justice, it shall be your duty to see this performed." And so King Harry passed on.

Falstaff turned a sad, very woeful face. "Master Shallow," he said, "I owe you a thousand pound."

"Yea, marry, Sir John," chirped Shallow; "and I beseech you let me have it to carry home with me."

"That can hardly be, Master Shallow," the old knight answered pitifully, and strove to reassure himself. "Do not you grieve at this. He will send for me in private. Look you, he has to appear like this to the world. Never fear for your advancement; I shall make you a great man yet."

Master Shallow shook a rueful head. "I cannot well perceive how. I beseech you, Sir John, let me have five hundred of my thousand."

"Sir, I will be as good as my word. Come with me to dinner; come, Pistol and Bardolph; I shall be sent for soon to-night."

But even this hope was shattered by Lord Chief-Justice Gascoigne as he came back along the street in talk with Prince John of Lancaster and followed by his officers. "Go," he commanded; "carry Sir John Falstaff and his company to the Fleet Prison!"

"My lord, my lord," stammered poor Falstaff.

"No more at present! I will hear you soon, at another time." He watched them as they were led off and turned to Prince John in silence.

"A good beginning," said the Prince quietly; "the

King has provided for his old followers, but they are banished until the world finds their conduct more reputable."

"They are," assented the Lord Chief-Justice grimly.

"My lord, he has called his parliament." Again the stern old judge nodded as a man well pleased. "I will lay odds," the Prince went on, "that before the year is out we shall be moving—perhaps as far as to France." The Lord Chief-Justice looked at him sharply. "I heard a little bird sing so," said Prince John.

KING HENRY THE FIFTH

PRINCE HAL was now King Henry V, and Prince Hal no longer. All trace of that madcap, that haunter of taverns and dissolute company, had vanished in the young man who now held the sceptre of England with a firm hand and serious purpose. The wildness seemed to die out of him as the breath left his father's body, and his people wondered, while they thanked Heaven for the change. Never, they told each other, had reformation come in such a swift and cleansing flood; and since the days of miracles had gone by, they were forced to believe that his thoughtfulness had been growing secretly under cover of his old wild courses, as a strawberry ripens under a nettle, or grass springs fastest while the night hides it.

For they saw him to be not sober-minded only, but shrewd; of strong will, yet just; masterful, while willing to listen to advice; at once a king with high thoughts for his country's welfare and honour, and a man with a mind of his own. He had not forgotten his father's dying counsel, to strengthen his throne by busying the minds of the nobles with foreign conquest, that so they might be the less tempted to plot mischief. They were restless, he knew. War was their chief and natural pastime; he must supply it abroad upon an honourable excuse, or they would find one for raising trouble at home. Already plots were hatching around the young Earl of March, who (as men did not forget) in strict law was heir to the throne. It was high time to confirm himself for the great struggle surely coming between the crown of England and big feudal lords. A successful war abroad would keep them busy, and (better still) busy in strengthening his hands.

And the chance lay open to him. France had let no occasion slip of thwarting and fostering treason against Bolingbroke; but France just now had an unhappy madman for king, under whom she was rent by the quarrels of two factions, the one headed by the Duke of Burgundy, the other by the Duke of Orleans; Burgundians and Armagnacs they were called. Under this strife she lay for the moment helpless. This moment was Henry's, and he seized it to claim the French throne.

The claim was in law a shadowy one; the shadow of a claim raised once before by our Edward III. It rested on this. Philip the Bold of France, who died in 1285, had left two sons, Philip the Fair, who succeeded him, and Charles, Count of Valois. Philip the Fair had three sons, each of whom held the throne in turn, and one daughter Isabella, who married our Edward II., and became the mother of Edward III. Now when these three sons died without heirs the crown did not pass to their sister Isabella, but to the son of Charles of Valois, the reason being that by a law (called the Salic Law) no woman could hold the succession. And with the descendants of Charles of Valois the crown had remained down to the madman Charles VI., who now wore it.

Edward III. had refused to accept this Salic law, arguing that it was of force only in Salic land, and that this did not include France. There had been much reason in his claim, but there was none in the claim now revived by Henry V., his descendant; because if Henry stood upon strict law, the throne of France belonged *not to him but to the young Earl of March, as first in direct descent from Edward.*[7]

He made his claim, however; and he had something more than the weakness of France to promise him success. For reasons of their own the clergy of England, headed by the Archbishop of Canterbury, were longing for a foreign war. As Henry wanted to keep his nobles busy, so the clergy wished to keep Henry diverted from prying into their affairs. The Church, in fact, was feeling the first of the pains and disquiet which in time brought the Reformation to birth. Men were beginning to look enviously on her great riches, and to ask how they were spent. In the last reign a bill had been brought before Parliament making the King master of the lands left to the Church by devout persons and "disordinately spent" by the clergy; the money to be used in maintaining earls, knights, and esquires for the defence of the realm, almshouses for the poor, and leaving a surplus of twenty thousand pounds for the King's own coffers. This, as the Archbishop put it, was not drinking deep, but drinking cup and all; and how the clergy felt towards the bill we need not say. Pressing troubles had pushed it out of

[7]A glance at the accompanying table on the next page will help to make plain the question of title.

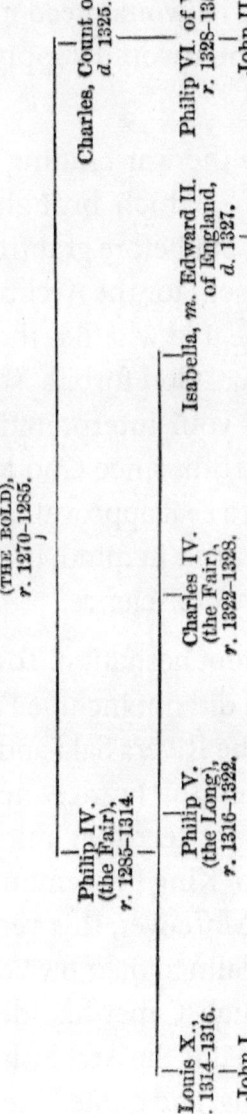

THE CLAIM OF HENRY V. TO THE FRENCH CROWN

question for the time; but now under the new King it was being proposed again. Something must be done to divert him; and what better for this purpose than a foreign war? For this to be sure he would need money. Very well; these wily Churchmen would supply him with money.

They did more; they made the war binding upon his conscience. The day came which brought the French answer to his demands; but before granting the ambassadors audience, Henry sent for the Archbishop of Canterbury and desired to be told whether the Salic law did or did not bar his claim. "God forbid," said he, "that you should wrest or bow your interpretation to that which suits not with the truth, since God knows how much blood will be shed to seal approval of what you say. Speak, my lord; but bear this in mind, I conjure you, and speak only with a pure conscience."

The Archbishop spoke without hesitation. To begin with (he argued), the Salic land did not include France, but lay in Germany, between the Rivers Sala and Elbe. The Salic law was never devised for France, nor did the French possess their present territory until 400 years and more after the death of King Pharamond, the supposed founder of the law. Moreover, this very law would upset the French king's claim to their own crown, since both King Pepin and Hugh Capet had derived their titles by female descent. All this the Archbishop set forth with much show of learning, and quoted the Book of Numbers to support him—"If a man die, and have no son, ye shall cause his inheritance to pass unto his daughter." "May I, then, with right and conscience make this claim?" demanded Henry. "The sin be on my head!" was the Archbishop's answer. Nobles and churchmen now vied in urging the King to uphold his claim, but Henry, having the answer he religiously sought, needed no urging. His mind made up on this main point, he turned his thoughts at once to ways and means. It would never do to leave his kingdom defenceless against the Scot, who would seize the moment of his absence to invade and harry. Said the old proverb—

> If that you will France win,
> Then with Scotland first begin.

The Duke of Exeter and the Archbishop met this difficulty. "My liege, a quarter of your fighting men, with you to lead them, will set France shaking. Leave us with the rest, and we promise to defend England for you."

It was enough. "Call in the Dauphin's messengers!" commanded Henry, and they entered. "Now we will know the Dauphin's pleasure, since it seems you come from him." "May we speak freely?" they demanded. "We are no tyrant," was the answer, "but a Christian King; our passions as securely chained as the wretches in our prisons. Be frank without fear."

Their first words made it clear that to the mistaken Dauphin Henry was still Prince Hal. "In answer to your claims, then, the Dauphin, our master, says that you savour too much of your youth; bids you be advised you cannot dance your way into French dukedoms; and sends you, therefore, as an offering more suitable for you—this chest of treasure."

"What treasure, uncle?" asked Henry, as the Duke of Exeter peered beneath the lid they lifted.

"My liege, it is—tennis-balls!"

Henry sprang from his throne, but mastered his rage in a moment and stood grimly staring down upon the tennis-balls, these insulting ghosts of his youth fetched up for a sorry joke. He turned upon the ambassadors. "We are glad," he said quietly, "the Dauphin is so pleasant with us. We thank you for his present and for your pains. When we have matched our rackets with these balls of his, by God's grace we will play a set which shall strike his father's crown into the hazard! Yes, we understand him and how he twits us with our wild youth. But tell him that when I rouse me *in my throne of France* he shall see and know for what I reserved my majesty! And tell him," Henry's voice rose, "tell the pleasant prince this mock of his has turned his tennis-balls to gun-stones, shall mock wives out of their husbands, mothers from their sons, shall mock castles down, and give men yet unborn cause to curse the pleasantry. But all this lies in the will of God, to whom I appeal. Go in peace. Let the Dauphin know that I follow, and add that his jest will savour of a shallow wit when bewept by thousands more than it made laugh." He turned to his attendants, "Give these men safe conduct hence."

"It was a merry message," said the Duke of Exeter when the ambassadors had taken their leave.

"We hope to make the sender blush for it," answered the King. Having committed the main issue to God, whose will upon the best advice he was following, this thorough Englishman turned to business. All his thought now was to get to France swiftly and in good time.

And all the fighting spirits of England took fire from him. They cared little for the right or wrong of the excuse; they looked back across years of galling peace and French insult and intrigue, and remembered Cressy. No more silken dalliance! Noble and knight, squire and serving-man, took down their weapons and looked to their equipment. The poor man sold his pasture and bought a horse to carry him to the wars and win wealth. All was noise and bustle about the armourers' forges. The taverns of Eastcheap felt the stir. The war would bring plunder for rascals. "Profits," as Pistol put it, "will accrue"; and he and the rest of Falstaff's hangers-on began to furbish up their swords and scour their stained armour, eager as crows at the scent of carrion, thirsty as horse-leeches. Pistol himself had lately patched up a marriage with Dame Quickly, greatly to the disgust of a late crony, Corporal Nym, to whom that lady had already plighted her troth; and red-nosed Bardolph had much ado to keep the peace between the rivals, who drew when they met and deafened him with their abuse, Pistol ranting in the old braggart fashion, Nym sheepish but persistent and vindictive, and the one as cowardly as the other. "Come, shall I make you two friends?" proposed Bardolph. "We must to France together. Why should we keep knives to cut one another's throats?"

"Let floods o'erswell, and fiends for food howl on!" foamed Pistol.

Nym was more matter-of-fact. "You'll pay me the eight shillings I won of you at betting?"

"Base is the slave that pays!" was all the satisfaction to be had at first; but presently relenting, Pistol promised six-and-eightpence, money down. Such are the quarrels of rogues, quickly patched up on the chance of preying together upon honest men. Within a minute this pair were sworn brothers for the campaign, in which Pistol proposed to serve as sutler—with pickings.

But Falstaff had come to the end of his campaignings. He lay at Mistress Quickly's, sick (as his hostess described it) of "a burning quotidian tertian"; but in a wiser moment she came nearer the truth. "The King has killed his heart"; there lay the secret of the disease, and before the King embarked the old reprobate had died of it. "A' made a finer end," was Mistress Quickly's account, "and went away an it had been any christom child; a' parted even just between twelve and one, even at the turning o' the tide: for after I saw him fumble with the sheets and play with flowers and smile upon his fingers' ends, I knew there was but one way; for his nose was as sharp as a pen, and a' babbled of green fields. 'How now, Sir John!' quoth I; 'what, man! be o' good cheer.' So a' cried out, 'God, God, God!' three or four times. Now I, to comfort him, bid him a' should not think of God; I hoped there was no need to trouble himself with any such thoughts yet. So a' bade me lay more clothes on his feet . . . . " In short, Falstaff was dead. "Would I were with him," groaned Bardolph, "wheresome'er he is, either in heaven or in hell!" and even Pistol heaved an honest sigh before kissing his wife and bidding her keep good house and give no credit during his absence.

The King, before setting sail from Southampton, had to cast off other and better trusted friends than Sir John. On the very eve of departure a plot was discovered for murdering him and setting the young Earl of March on the throne. To this treason French gold had tempted three men in Henry's inmost counsels—his cousin Richard, Earl of Cambridge, Sir Thomas Grey, and even Lord Scroop of Masham, his bedfellow. And they, not suspecting themselves discovered, gave Henry opportunity to condemn them out of their own mouths. Before the nobles, who already knew their guilt, he first consulted them on the firmness and loyalty of his troops, and having listened to their false assurances, turned to the Duke of Exeter, bidding him set free a man who the day before had been imprisoned for railing against the King's majesty. The three plotters each in turn pressed for severity upon the offence, though a trifling one and committed in drunkenness. "Let us be merciful," said Henry. "Your highness," urged Cambridge, "may be merciful and yet punish him." "Nevertheless, we will set him free, although Cambridge, Scroop, and Grey, in their dear care to preserve our person, would have him punished. And now to our French business!" He handed to the three plotters the parchments they supposed to contain their commissions, and watched them break the seals. "Why, how now, gentlemen? What read you in those papers that so changes your complexion?"

The unhappy three were staring at their death warrants. Mercy was not for them. Their punishment must be extreme as the trust reposed in them. In solemn sorrow Henry sent them out to their doom. "I will weep for thee," he said to Scroop, the most trusted of all, "for *thy* revolt is like another Fall of Man." And they confessed that they deserved the death which Henry prayed God to give them patience to endure. They were led forth; and that same night the King put his puissance in the further keeping of God and cheerfully hoisted sail for France.

Already in the French court some minds were growing uneasy. The Dauphin, to be sure, consented to follow his father's advice (for Charles, now enjoying one of his short spells of sanity, observed the vigour of the English approach and recalled bygone disasters and the memorable shame of Cressy) and to repair some of the weaker fortresses. But he persisted in his fatal error that Henry was but a vain shallow boy, not to be taken seriously, still less to be feared. "As for fear," he urged, "we have no more cause to show it than we should if we learned that England were busy with a Whitsun morris-dance." The Constable of France, Charles d'Albert, was wiser. "Prince, you are mistaken. Question your ambassadors, and they will tell you how royally, yet modestly, he received them; how careful he showed himself in taking counsel, yet how resolute. These vanities you speak of are spent and done with." "You are wrong, my lord," was the Dauphin's reply; "but there's no harm in esteeming an enemy more formidable than he seems, and our defences shall be looked to."

Quick on the heels of the message returned to the Dauphin, Henry had despatched an embassy of his own, headed by the Duke of Exeter, bearing his conditions with documents in support of his claim. He would endure no delay. He whom we first found rallying Falstaff for wanting to know the time of day, had now learnt (as Exeter said) to weigh time even to the uttermost grain. The Dauphin was for prompt defiance. His father pleaded for a night's respite. "Despatch us with speed," Exeter insisted, "or he will be here in person to know why you are loitering. Already he and his men have landed." Charles could find no conditions to stay the invasion already launched, and the Dauphin had his wish therefore, with what fatal results to France we are to see.

Henry's fleet had crossed from Southampton with a fair wind, and made the mouth of the Seine; and there, at Caux, he landed his thirty thousand soldiers and marched upon the town of Harfleur. It was a motley and miscellaneous army he commanded. English of all ranks and classes were there, from nobles down to sturdy yeomen, and from these down to such needy rascals as our friends Bardolph, Pistol, and Nym. These three worthies owned one page between them—the boy given by Henry to Falstaff in the old days—but, indeed, as the lad consoled himself, "three such antics do not amount to one man." He was not long in discovering their arrant cowardice. Bardolph was red-faced, but white-livered; Pistol had a killing tongue and a quiet sword; while as for Nym, "he never broke any man's head but his own, and that was against a post when he was drunk." Plunder, not fighting, was their game. "Bardolph stole a lute-case, bore it twelve leagues, and sold it for three half-pence, Nym and Bardolph are sworn brothers in filching, and in Calais they stole a fire-shovel." Rogues all, and when all was said and done, very futile rogues! The lad, being honest as well as shrewd, promised himself a quick dismissal from such service.

But the ranks were not made up of Englishmen only. Scotsmen, Irishmen, Welshmen had taken service with Henry as common soldiers and petty officers, and the shouts and calls of command under the walls of Harfleur made up a babel of dialects comic enough for those who listened to it, but more than merely amusing to us who know of what this was the beginning; how men of these races have since fought side by side, or back to back, with what traditions of glory and with what splendid results. They were good fighters even at Harfleur, these men of strange dialects. There was Captain Fluellen, for instance, a self-conceited, peppery, and pedantic little Welshman, scolding, arguing, criticising orders, but sweating and fighting like a hero. In Captain Fluellen's neighbourhood our London bullies found it unpleasantly difficult to shirk danger. "Up to the breach, you dogs!" was his exhortation, backed with blows of the sword. A moment later would find him wrangling with the messenger sent by the Duke of Gloucester to fetch him to the siege-mines. "Tell the Duke it is not so good to come to the mines; for, look you, the mines is not according to the disciplines of the war: the concavities of it is not sufficient; for, look you, the adversary, you may discuss unto the Duke, look you, is digg'd himself four yard under by countermines: I think a' will plow up all, if there is not better directions." Captain Gower, the messenger, had to remind him that the siege was being conducted by the Duke of Gloucester, under the direction of an Irishman, one Captain Macmorris. "He is an ass. He has no more directions in the disciplines of the wars, look you, of the Roman disciplines, than is a puppy dog!" This amiable opinion Fluellen had occasion to repeat to Macmorris himself, who came up at this point. "Captain Macmorris, I beseech you now, will you vouchsafe me, look you, a few disputations with you, as partly touching or concerning the disciplines of the war, the Roman wars, in the way of argument, look you." Macmorris first pleaded that the day was too hot for argument, and went on to lose his temper, but without the least effect. "Look you, if you take the matter otherwise than is meant, Captain Macmorris, peradventure I shall think you do not use me with that affability as in discretion you ought to use me, look you; being as good a man as yourself, both in the disciplines of war, and in the derivation of my birth, and in other particularities."

It was the King who controlled these jarring elements and knit them into an army; the King, now proving himself a born commander, and not least by the ardour of devotion his mere presence kindled. Englishman, Welshman, Irishman, Scot, each caught fire from him. Did he hold them back? they stood ready, eager, like greyhounds straining at the leash. Did he cry them on? they flung themselves into the breach again and again, resolute to force it or close the wall up with their bodies, for he called on their pride of birth in the name of home and the pastures which had bred them brave men. He never spared himself. He rode here, there, everywhere, and as he rode from point to point kept alive the battle-cry, "God for Harry, England, and St. George!" around Harfleur.

Moreover, though merciful by nature, he had hardened his temper to war as every great general must. When after five weeks' siege he summoned the citizens to the last parley, there was no lack of sternness in his conditions. "Submit yourselves, or defy us on certainty of the worst; for, as I am a soldier, if you force me to begin the battery once again, I will not leave Harfleur until she is buried in her ashes. Before shutting the gates of mercy, I bid you take pity on your town, on your people, while I have my soldiers in control. Refuse, and you shall see their hands defiling the locks of your screaming daughters; your old men taken by their beards and brained against the walls; your babes spitted upon pikes, while their maddened mothers shriek as the wives of Jewry before King Herod's slaughterers. Choose, then."

There was no other choice. Hopeless of aid from the Dauphin, Harfleur flung open its gates. But the city had been won at terrible cost. Dysentery and fever ravaged Henry's camp, and his men were falling like sheep. It was with an army reduced to half its old strength that he determined to follow the example of his great-grandfather Edward and insult the enemy by a bold march upon Calais. He found the bridges of the Somme broken down, and the fords rendered impassable by lines of sharp stakes; but after some days' delay an unguarded point was discovered high up the stream, and by forced marches he flung his army rapidly across, and pressing forward to Blangy, captured by a sharp skirmish the bridge over the little river Ternoise, just beyond which, at the village of Agincourt, lay the French army of more than sixty thousand, barring the road to Calais.

The bridge was gallantly seized and held. To quote Fluellen, who esteemed himself a judge, "I assure you there is very excellent services committed at the pridge. . . . The Duke of Exeter has very gallantly maintained the pridge; the French is gone off, look you; and there is gallant and most prave passages. . . . The perdition of th' athversary hath been very great, reasonable great: marry, for my part, I think the duke hath lost never a man, but one that is like to be executed for robbing a church."

This was indeed the unhappy Bardolph. Though his men were half-starving, Henry had given express orders that the villages were not to be plundered, nor the inhabitants insulted, nor anything taken without payment. He presented himself to France, let us remember, not as a ruthless conqueror but as a lawful sovereign interposing to heal her dissensions. Towards such an offence as Bardolph's he was least likely to show mercy, for Bardolph had stolen a pax.[8] "A pax of little price," urged his crony Pistol, who came to persuade Fluellen to make intercession for the thief. Now Fluellen had been not a little impressed by Pistol's loud boasting at the bridge, and was inclined to think him a very

---

[8]That is, a picture of Christ on a piece of wood or metal, kissed by worshippers in token of brotherly peace and unity.

valiant soldier; but he could not stomach indiscipline. "For if, look you, he were my brother, I would desire the duke to use his good pleasure and put him to execution; for discipline ought to be used." Whereupon Pistol fell to abusing him, and stalked off in a huff. "It is well. Very good."—Fluellen shrugged his shoulders with much calm. "Why," said Captain Gower, who stood by, "I remember that fellow; an arrant counterfeit rascal and a cutpurse." "I assure you, a' uttered as prave words at the pridge as you shall see in a summer's day." "Ay, the kind of rogue that now and then goes to the wars, to return and swagger about London as a soldier. Such fellows are pat with the names of great commanders; they have the campaign by heart, and would teach you what happened at such and such an earthwork, breach, or convoy; who was shot, who disgraced; what terms the enemy stood out for; they have it all in the right war-like phrases, which they trick up with new oaths. You'd hardly believe how far a suit of campaigning clothes and a beard cut like a general's will go among foaming bottles and listeners whose wits ale has washed out of them!"

But a campaign so grim as this of Henry's was like to prove sadly fatal to these swashers. Indeed it was fast thinning the ranks of honester men; and the French, while they wondered at Henry's daring, were almost sorry to see him come on with troops so sick, weary, famished, and (as they were bound to believe) dispirited. The glory of beating him would be the less. They never doubted to have him at their mercy; and

King Charles sent his herald Montjoy from Rouen to demand the invader's surrender. "Say thou to Harry of England"—thus ran the message—"though we seemed dead, we did but sleep. We could have rebuked him at Harfleur, but that we thought not good to bruise an injury till it were full ripe. Now we speak, and our voice is imperial. England shall repent his folly, see his weakness, and admire our long-suffering. Bid him, therefore, consider his ransom, which must be proportionate to our losses in wealth, and men, and the disgrace we have digested. Our losses he is too poor to repay; and for our disgrace his own person, kneeling at our feet, will hardly give satisfaction. Tell him, for conclusion, that he has betrayed his followers, whose doom is pronounced."

"Fairly rendered," was Henry's answer to Montjoy. "Turn back and tell your King I am not anxious to meet him between this and Calais. To speak frankly, my men are weakened by sickness, lessened in numbers; the few I have scarcely better than so many Frenchmen—nay, God forgive me! that was boasting, and I am sorry for it. Tell your master my ransom is but this body of mine, and my army a weak and sickly guard for it; yet, before God, we will come on, though King Charles and another as mighty as he stand in our way. If we may pass, we will; hinder us, and French blood shall pay for it. We desire no battle; but weak as we are we will not shun it."

"I hope they will not come on us now," muttered Gloucester, the King's brother, when Montjoy had departed. "We are in God's hand, brother," was Henry's answer; "not in theirs." He gave the order to cross the river.

There was very different talk in the French camp. While Henry spoke of trusting in God, the Dauphin was boasting of his horse and armour. Says the Psalmist: "Some trust in chariots, and some in horses; but we will remember the name of the Lord our God." "I will trot to-morrow a mile," promised the Dauphin, "and my way shall be paved with English faces." The young French nobles cast dice for the prisoners they were to take in the morning. The English, they agreed, were fools; if they had any apprehension they would run away. "By ten o'clock, let me see," said the Duke of Orleans, "we shall have a hundred Englishmen apiece."

The English had found a camping-ground but fifteen hundred paces from the French outposts. Drenched and exhausted they lit their watch-fires and cowered over them to ruminate on the morrow; so lank and gaunt in their worn coats that they seemed beneath the moon's rays a gathering of ghosts rather than of men—a gathering, at any rate, of men devoted to the sacrifice on which the enemy counted. So close lay the two camps, that across the belt of darkness where the outposts listened, between the glow of the watch-fires, each army could hear the other's confused hum, the horses neighing and challenging, the armourers' hammers busily closing the rivets for the morning, now announced to be near by the cocks crowing from unseen farmsteads along the countryside.

Henry knew even better than his soldiers how nearly

desperate was the prospect for England. Weariness aside, he was outnumbered by five to one. But in him the greater danger awoke the greater courage; nor did his own weariness prevent him going the rounds before dawn with his brother Gloucester. "Good-morrow," said he, finding his other brother, Bedford, upon a like errand; "there must be some sort of goodness in evil, for, see, our bad neighbour makes us early risers, which is both healthful and thriftful." Then greeting a stout old soldier, Sir Thomas Erpingham, "A good soft pillow," said he, "were better for that good white head than the churlish turf of France." "My liege, I like my lodging better as it is, since now I may say, 'I am lodged like a king.'" Henry borrowed the old knight's cloak, and wrapping himself close in it went forward alone. He wished to observe quietly and in disguise those feelings which his men would be loath to disclose in the presence of their King.

The first sentry to challenge him in this disguise was our friend Pistol, still chewing his disgust at that unfeeling man Captain Fluellen. "What's thy name?" demanded Pistol. "Harry le Roy." "Leroy? a Cornish name, eh?" "I am a Welshman,"—which was true enough, for Henry's birthplace was Monmouth. "Knowest thou Fluellen?" "Yes." "Then tell that leek-eating Welshman I'll knock his leek about his pate next St. David's day." "You had better not wear your dagger in your cap that day, lest he knock that about yours." But Fluellen just now had more important matters to think about. Presently the King passed him in earnest talk with his English friend, Captain Gower; chiding, in fact, Captain Gower for raising his voice too loudly. "It is the greatest admiration in the world, when the true and aunchient prerogatives and laws of the wars is not kept: if you would take the pains but to examine the wars of Pompey the Great, you shall find, I warrant you, that there is no tiddle taddle nor pibble pabble in Pompey's camp; I warrant you, you shall find the ceremonies of the wars, and the cares of it, and the forms of it, and the sobriety of it, and the modesty of it, to be otherwise." "Why," pleaded Gower, "the enemy is loud; you hear him all night." "If the enemy is an ass and a fool and a prating coxcomb, is it meet, think you, that we should also, look you, be an ass and a fool and a prating coxcomb?" "There is much care and valour in this Welshman," thought Henry, and passed on unobserved.

But he heard another aspect of war discussed by the next group he fell in with, a group of three common soldiers standing and watching the dawn. As he strolled up in the uncertain light, they asked to what company he belonged. "To Sir Thomas Erpingham's." "A good old commander and a kind-hearted gentleman; tell us, how does he think we stand?" "As men wrecked on a sandbank, who look to be washed off by the next tide." "He has not told the King so, surely?" "No," replied Henry, "nor is it fitting he should. For, though I speak it to you, I think the King is but a man as I am; a man with a man's senses; a man like any other when his royal pomp and rich clothes are laid by. His feelings may soar higher, maybe; yet when they swoop back to earth, they swoop much as ours. No doubt he tastes fear as we do; and yet men should be chary of imparting their fear to him, lest by showing it he should dishearten his whole army." "He may show what outward courage he will," growled one of the three, a fellow named John Bates; "but I believe, cold as the night is, he could wish himself in Thames up to the neck! And I wish he were, and I beside him, so we could win out of this." "I swear I don't believe the King would wish himself anywhere but where he is." "Then I would he were here alone. So would he be ransomed, and a many poor men's lives saved." "I dare say," said Henry, "you love him better than to wish any such thing, howsoever you say this to feel other men's minds. For my part, I could die nowhere so contentedly as in the King's company, his cause being just and his quarrel honourable." "That's more than we know," put in another, Michael Williams by name. "Ay," said Bates, "and more than we should seek to know. It's enough that we're his subjects; if his cause be wrong, we are only obeying him, and that clears us." "But," Williams objected, "if the cause be wrong, the King has a heavy reckoning to make, when all those legs and arms, chopped off in a battle, shall join together at the latter day, and cry all *We died at such a place!*'; some swearing, some crying for a surgeon, some upon their wives left poor behind them, some upon the debts they owe, some upon their children left without provision. I'm afeard few men die well in battle; for how can they quit themselves in goodwill towards men while their business is shedding blood? And if they do not die well, it will be a black matter for the King who led them to it, and whom they could not disobey."

"Nay," said Henry, "suppose a son went after merchandise by his father's orders, and in his seafaring perished in a state of sin, by your argument his father must be held responsible! Or if a servant, carrying money for his master, be set upon by robbers and killed before he can make his peace with God, you would call his master to blame for his soul's damnation! Not so; nor in fact can any king, be his cause never so spotless, if it come to be decided by swords, try it out with unspotted soldiers. Every subject's duty is the King's; but every subject's soul is his own. Therefore, should every soldier in the wars do as every sick man in his bed, wash every mote out of his conscience. So, if he die, his death is gain; and if he do not, he has lost his time blessedly in gaining such preparation. And in him that escapes it were no sin to think that God, to whom he made so free an offering of himself, let him outlive that day to see His greatness and teach others how they should prepare."

They were honest fellows. "I do not desire," said Bates, "the King should answer for me; and yet I determine to fight lustily for him." Yet they could not quite believe Henry's word that the King would never allow himself to be ransomed. "Ay, he said so, to make us fight cheerfully; but when our throats are cut, he may be ransomed, and we never the wiser." Henry rallied the gloomy Williams, and played at pretending to lose his temper when they jeered at him—a common soldier—for his impudence in promising "if I live to see the King ransomed, I'll never trust his word again." But as he parted from them his spirits felt suddenly the terrible weight laid upon him. "Yes; they laid it all on the King: their lives, their souls, their debts, their wives and children, their sins—all on the King! He must bear all. To this hard condition greatness is born, and can never escape from it—to bear the reproach of every fool who has only sense to feel his own wringing. Kings must neglect the heart's ease of private men; yet for what recompense? Is ceremony a recompense? Let be the hollowness of it: can it repay a king for the sleep which slaves enjoy, but he misses upon his gorgeous bed?"

The moment found him weak, but it was a moment only. It passed when Sir Thomas Erpingham came with news that the English nobles were seeking him. "Collect them at my tent," he commanded; and falling on his knees he besought the God of battles to steel the hearts of his Englishmen—yes, and to forget for this day the sin by which his father had won the crown. That sin, he knew in his heart, had not been retrieved; the blood of Richard was yet to be answered for. He had done much; would do more: the debt of divine wrath must be met, but "Not to-day, O Lord! O, not to-day!"

And again while he prayed the French were boasting of their horses and armour. In the gathering light they paraded, sixty thousand strong. The ground favoured them too. Flanked on either side by thick woods, they showed the English so narrow a front as to offer nothing to assault but a pack of men drawn up thirty deep. While they kept that position they could defy attack, and Henry had no choice between attack and surrender. Day found his ragged horsemen already in saddle and planted in face of this host "like fixed candlesticks," each with a torch in his hand; their armour rusty, their horses shrunken in flesh, with a tell-tale droop of the hind-quarters and heads lolling forward on their fouled bits. And over this spiritless cavalry wheeled flock upon flock of crows, sinister and impatient.

"They have said their prayers, and they stay for death," cried the French Constable.

"God's arm strike for us!" said the pious Earl of Salisbury among the English lords; "the odds are fearful." "O," sighed Westmoreland, "that we had here but ten thousand of those men who stand idle in England to-day!" Henry overheard him. "I would not have a single man more! If we are to die, the smaller loss to England; if to live, the greater our share of honour. Before God, as I love honour I would not have one man more to lessen the honour of this day's work! Go, make it known through the ranks that any man who will may depart; shall have a passport home and money to take him. We would not die in company of that man who fears his willingness to die in our company. To-day is St. Crispian's feast. I tell you the man who outlives this day and comes safely home shall stand an inch higher and feel his heart leap whenever he hears the name of Crispian; ay, if he live to see old age, yearly he shall call his neighbours to feast on this day's eve, and tell them 'To-morrow is St. Crispian!'—shall strip back his sleeve, show his scars, 'These wounds I had on Crispian's day.' Old men forget; yet when all's forgotten he shall remember and brag of his feats performed this day; and then our names—King Harry, Bedford and Exeter, Warwick, Talbot, Salisbury and Gloucester—will rise to his lips familiar as household words, and as the cup goes round be freshly remembered. Good man! he shall teach his son the tale, and Crispin Crispian never go by from this day to the world's end but we shall be remembered in it—we, we happy few, we band of brothers! For the man who sheds his blood with me to-day shall be my brother; by that raised a gentleman, however low his estate. And gentlemen now a-bed in England shall curse themselves that they were not here, and stand abashed when any man speaks who fought beside me upon St. Crispian's day!"

Once more before the armies engaged the Constable sent Montjoy to offer Henry the chance of ransom; and again Montjoy carried back a firm refusal. The Duke of York—known to us in Richard's reign as Aumerle, but now under a higher title a better and braver man—craved the honour of leading the English van. Henry granted it, and for the last time commending the battle to God, gave the order to advance.

The English archers bared their breasts and arms for free play and charged forward with shout. It is likely enough their charge would have had small effect on the French defence, had the French been contented to defend. But the sight of this audacious advance was too much for their patience; and, disregarding the Constable's plan of battle, the dense, heavily-weighted mass of men-at-arms broke ground and came floundering forward into the open over the sodden ground, which they trod into a quagmire. As they came, Henry called a halt. Each of his archers carried a sharpened stake; and now at a word planting a rough and ready stockade, from behind it they poured their arrows into the throng where no arrow could miss a mark. The slaughter was terrible; yet the French blundered on and by sheer weight drove the archers right and left into the woods, only to find the deadly rain now pouring on either flank from behind the trees, among which they could not pursue. While they swayed mire-bound and exposed to this cross-fire, Henry flung his heavier troops straight on their front, himself charging like a hero and setting an example to all. Once he went down under the blow of a French mace; again, while stooping to lift the Duke of York, felled by a blow of Alençon's, he took a stroke from the same hand which shore away a piece of the crown on his helmet. But the French masses were breaking up. The first to take to flight was a body of horsemen, some six hundred in number, who, hearing that the English camp lay undefended, rode round upon it and through it, pillaging and hacking down the lackeys and boys who showed fight. The news of it reached Henry as he drew breath after the great charge. There was no gentleness in him now. Stung by this outrage, and perceiving the French cavalry attempting to rally, he gave the stern order to show no quarter but kill all prisoners taken.

But the French rally came to nothing. The day was Henry's, as the herald Montjoy admitted, who came by and by to sue for leave to bury the French dead. "What," asked Henry, "is the name of the castle standing yonder?" "Agincourt." "Then we will name this the field of Agincourt."

On this field of Agincourt more than ten thousand Frenchmen lay dead, and among them one hundred and twenty-six princes and nobles bearing banners. The Constable himself had fallen, Chatillon, Admiral of France, the Duke of Alençon, felled by Henry's own hand, the Dukes of Brabant and Bar, the Duke of Burgundy's brother, the Earls Grandpré, Roussi, Fauconberg, Foix, Beaumont, Marle, Vaudemont, and Lestrale. The Dukes of Orleans and Bourbon were prisoners, with fifteen hundred lords, barons, knights, and esquires, besides common men. England had lost the Duke of York and the Earl of Suffolk—they had dropped side by side, and shaken hands like gallant brothers-in-arms before death parted them; one knight, one esquire, and but five-and-twenty rank and file. "O God, thy arm was here!" cried Henry as his eye fell on the short list. "Accept this victory, God, for it is thine only!" He forbade his men, on pain of death, to boast of their triumph; even the numbers of the killed were only to be published with the acknowledgment that God had fought for England. The army fell into line of march and moved in procession to the village, there to chant the "*Te Deum*" and "*Non nobis*"—"Not unto us, O Lord, not unto us, but unto thy Name give glory...."

But England was less disposed to make light of her soldiers' prowess. Henry's army, too weary to pursue its victory, made its way unopposed to Calais, and there shipped for home. Crowds lined the beach at Dover to welcome him, and even rushed into the sea to touch his ship. London poured forth her citizens on Blackheath to fetch home the victor. Henry behaved throughout as a modest man, rejecting even the proposal that his battered helmet and sword should be borne through the city of London before him. His work was not done yet. He had struck but the first blow, if the most effective, and was content for two years to watch France as between the Burgundians and Armagnacs she went from bad to worse. For a time the Emperor Sigismund occupied himself in an attempt to patch up terms between the two countries, but with no result; and in 1417 Henry sailed once more for Normandy, this time with forty thousand followers.

The discipline of the former campaign had been a stern discouragement of weeds and wastrels in the English soldiery. Men of true stuff—Gower, Fluellen, and their likes—were eager enough to serve again; Fluellen, for example, was ready to follow wherever led by his modern Alexander the Great, or Big, or (as he preferred to pronounce it) "Pig." Henry was born at Monmouth, and "I think it is in Macedon where Alexander the Pig is porn. I tell you, if you look in the map of the 'orld, I warrant you sall find in the comparisons between Macedon and Monmouth that the situations, look you, is both alike. There is a river in Macedon; and there is also moreover, a river at Monmouth: it is called Wye at Monmouth; but it is out of my prains what is the name of the other river; but 'tis all one, 'tis alike as my fingers is to my fingers, and there is salmons in both." But the day of Sir John Falstaff's merry rascally crew was over. The march upon Calais had weeded out Bardolph and Nym—both hanged for pilfering. At home Dame Quickly lay dying while her husband took ship for the wars, the last of the gang.

Even for Pistol there was waiting retribution of a

sort. Still nursing his grudge against Fluellen, he had been ill-advised enough, soon after landing on French soil, to insult the little Welshman before company by bringing him bread and salt to eat with his Welsh leek. "It was in a place where I could not breed no contention with him; but I will be so bold as to wear it in my cap till I see him once again, and then I will tell him a little piece of my desires."

So Fluellen still wore the leek in his cap, though St. David's day was long past, and at length he caught his man. "God pless you, Aunchient Pistol! you scurvy, lousy knave, God pless you! I peseech you heartily, scurvy, lousy knave, at my desires, and my requests, and my petitions, to eat, look you, this leek; because, look you, you do not love it, nor your affections and your appetites and your digestions doo's not agree with it, I would desire you to eat it." "Not for Cadwallader and all his goats!" swore Pistol: "Base Trojan, thou shalt die!"—as Fluellen fell to and began to cudgel him lustily. "You say very true; I sall die when God's will is. In the mean time I will desire you to live and eat your victuals." Here, still holding out his raw leek, he banged him again. "I pray you fall to; if you can mock a leek, you can eat a leek." Pistol began to whine. "Must I eat it?" "Yes, certainly, out of doubt, and out of question too, and ambiguities." The unhappy man began to nibble. "By this leek I will most horribly revenge: I eat and eat, I swear—" "Eat, I pray you. Will you have some more sauce to your leek?" Seeing Fluellen's cudgel lifted again, he ate obediently. "Throw none away," insisted Fluellen; "the skin is good for your broken coxcomb." He flung the poor wretch a groat, to heal his pate. Pistol pocketed it and slunk away, swearing horribly; slunk away to sink lower as such men will. We see no more of him. With him, as he goes, passes the old order of the Boar's Head, Eastcheap.

He who had once been the spoilt child of that order was now riding at the head of an army from victory to victory. He stormed Caen, was received by Bayeux, reduced Alençon, and Falaise, Avranches and Domfront; marched through Evreux, captured Louviers, flung his troops across the Seine, and sat down before Rouen. This, the wealthiest of all the cities of France, fell after a long, hideous siege. "War," said Henry, "has three handmaidens to wait on her—Fire, Blood, and Famine. I have chosen the meekest maid of the three." With Rouen fallen, and his kingdom hopelessly at variance, there remained but one course for the poor mad King of France. It was the young Duke of Burgundy who finally, at Troyes, brought about a meeting between the unhappy Charles and his conqueror. Henry listened unmoved while the miseries of France were recounted. The recital over, he laid down his terms like a man of business. He must be regent of France during Charles's life; he must receive the crown as his own upon Charles's death; and he must have Charles's daughter Katharine to wife.

Rather, this last was his first and his capital demand. It remained to learn what Katharine would say.

She was a lady of great good sense. From the first she had been curious to hear of this brave soldier from the north who won battles and spoke a language so barbarous. It was still as a soldier that he came wooing her. She was one of his terms of truce; and between this assurance and a perception of the ludicrous figure he cut as a wooer with scarcely a dozen words of French, he performed his courtship bluntly enough. Katharine could speak English but a very little better. "Faith, Kate, I am glad of it; else thou wouldst find me such a plain king thou wouldst think I had sold my farm to buy my crown. I know no ways to mince it in love, but directly to say 'I love you.' If thou canst love such a downright fellow, whose face is not worth sun-burning, and who never looks in his glass for love of anything he sees there, why well and good. I speak like a plain soldier. If thou canst love me for this, take me; if not, I shall not die of it; and yet I love thee." He essayed a French sentence, but broke down in comic despair. Katharine smiled at his perplexity, and liked him; and in this manner the conqueror of France won a French wife, and a charming one. We met him first as a wild scapegrace youngster, little better than a boy. We have seen him confirmed, step by step, in strength and a better judgment; become a wise king, a God-fearing man, a triumphant warrior. Here, at the height of achievement, we leave him; happily married, worshipped by his subjects, seated on a throne securely established, and looking forward to a still more splendid inheritance.

The Ballad of Agincourt

Fayre stood the winde for France,
When we our sailes advance,
Nor now to proue our chance
  Longer not tarry,
But put vnto the mayne:
At Kaux, the mouth of Seine,
With all his warlike trayne
  Landed King Harry.

And taking many a forte,
Furnish'd in warlike sorte,
Comming toward Agincourte
  (In happy houre),
Skermishing day by day
With those oppose his way.
Whereas the Genrall laye
  With all his powre.

Which in his height of pride,
As Henry to deride,
His Ransome to prouide
  Vnto him sending;
Which he neglects the while,
As from a nation vyle,
Yet with an angry smile
  Their fall portending.

And turning to his men,
Quoth famous Henry then,
"Though they be one to ten
  Be not amazéd:

Yet haue we well begun;
Battailes so brauely wonne
Euermore to the sonne
   By fame are rayséd.

"And for my selfe," (quoth hee)
"This my full rest shall bee,
England nere mourne for me
   Nor more esteeme me:
Victor I will remaine,
Or on this earth be slaine;
Neuer shall she sustaine
   Losse to redeeme me.

"Poiters and Cressy tell,
When moste their pride did swell,
Vnder our swords they fell:
   Ne lesse our skill is,
Then when our grandsyre greate,
Claiming the regall seate,
In many a warlike feate
   Lop'd the French lillies."

The Duke of Yorke soe dread
The eager vaward led;
With the maine Henry sped
   Amongst his hench men.
Excester had the rear,
A brauer man not there.
And now preparing were
   For the false Frenchmen.

And ready to be gone,
Armour on armour shone,
Drum vnto drum did grone,
   To heare was woonder;

That with the cries they make
The very earth did shake:
Trumpet to trumpet spake,
    Thunder to thunder.

Well it thine age became,
O, noble Erpingham!
That didst the signall frame
    Vnto the forces;
When from a medow by,
Like a storme, sodainely
The English archery
    Stuck the French horses.

The Spanish vghe[9] so strong,
Arrowes a cloth-yard long,
That like to serpents stoong,
    Piercing the wether:
None from his death now starts,
But playing manly parts,
And like true English harts
    Stuck close together.

When down theyr bowes they threw,
And foorth theyr bilbowes drewe,
And on the French they flew,
    No man was tardy.
Arms from the shoulders sent,
Scalpes to the teeth were rent;
Downe the French pesants went,
    These men were hardye.

When now that noble King,
His broade sword brandishing,

[9]Yes.

Into the hoast did fling,
　　As to or'whelme it;
Who many a deep wound lent,
His armes with blood besprent,
And many a cruell dent
　　Bruséd his helmett.

Glo'ster, that Duke so good,
Next of the royall blood,
For famous England stood
　　With his brave brother:
Clarence in steele most bright,
That yet a maiden knighte,
Yet in this furious fighte,
　　Scarce such an other.

Warwick in bloode did wade,
Oxford the foes inuade,
And cruel slaughter made
　　Still as they ran vp.
Suffolk his axe did ply,
Beaumont and Willoughby
Bare them right doughtyly,
　　Ferrers and Fanhope.

On happy Cryspin day
Fought was this noble fray,
Which fame did not delay
　　To England to carry.
O! When shall Englishmen
With such acts fill a pen,
Or England breed agen,
　　Such a King Harry?

MICHAEL DRAYTON

KING HENRY THE SIXTH

I

HENRY V. was granted but two years to enjoy his glory. He lived to see a son born to him; and with the help of the young Duke of Burgundy—who since the treacherous murder of his father by the Armagnacs, had in revenge flung the full weight of his support on the English side—to make himself complete master of Northern France to the banks of the Loire. When, as regent of France and heir to the crown, he celebrated the feast of Whitsuntide at Paris in the palace of the Louvre the splendour and gaiety of his court far outshone that of the real king.

And then, at the height of his fortunes, death claimed him. What the disease was is not known. It struck swiftly, baffling the physicians; and at Vincennes near Paris, on the 1st of September 1422, Henry died. His body was borne home in state and laid in the vaults of Westminster Abbey.

While the echoes of his dead march were still rolling through the Abbey aisles, men's ears caught the murmur of coming trouble. The inheritor of the two heavy sceptres of England and France (for the mad

King Charles had died a few weeks after his conqueror) was an infant nine months old, whose welfare, with that of England, was placed in the hands of his uncle Humphrey, Duke of Gloucester, as Protector, and a Council of twenty headed by Henry Beaufort, Bishop of Winchester. Another uncle, the Duke of Bedford—a general only inferior in skill to the dead King—was made Regent of France.

In other words, the kingly power which Henry IV. had fought so hardly for, and Henry V. had kept and increased by his own winning qualities and the fame of foreign victories, was now by force of circumstances given back to the great nobles. We shall see how they used it to wreck their country and in the end to work out their own perdition. The story we have to tell reminds one of the house swept and garnished of the Gospel parable. Such a house the conqueror of Agincourt had prepared; his sudden death left it open to a company of evil spirits far "worse than the first." "The violence and anarchy which had always clung like a taint to the baronage, had received a new impulse from the war with France. Long before the struggle was over it had done its fatal work on the mood of the English noble. His aim had become little more than a lust for gold, a longing after plunder, after the pillage of farms, the sack of cities, the ransom of captives. So intense was the greed of gain, that only a threat of death could keep the fighting-men in their ranks, and the results of victory after victory were lost by the anxiety of the conquerors to deposit their plunder and captives safely at home."[10]

[10]Green's *Short History of the English People*.

For a while the firm hand of Bedford kept this mischief in check. Summoned from the funeral rites of his great brother by the first of those messengers of disaster whom in a short time every wind was to bring across the Channel, he soon gave the French provinces proof that they were over-hasty in revolting. The Dauphin on his father's death had at once proclaimed himself King with the title of Charles VII., but it was long before he saw the end of the struggle on which he now entered. Still helped by the Duke of Burgundy, Bedford reduced the North of France back to its submission, and nobly upheld the honour of England in the victories of Crevant (1423) and Verneuil (1424). The latter crushed a daring advance of the French, who had pushed northward from the Loire, which separated the English from the French provinces, and offered battle on the very borders of Normandy—most rashly, for they were hurled back leaving a third of their knighthood on the field. In this moment of their utter discomfiture Bedford should have thrown his troops across the Loire.

He did not, and the reason why he did not is to be found at home. The Protector, "the good"—but certainly not too good—"Duke Humphrey," was at loggerheads with the Council from the first, and especially with its president, Henry Beaufort, a rich, ambitious, and quite unscrupulous churchman, son of John of Gaunt by a second marriage. The hatred of these two men broke into fierce words even over the coffin of the late King. "Cease your wranglings and live at peace!" Bedford had implored them; but with Bedford away in France they paid little heed to his counsel. By Henry's will

Gloucester should have been Regent of England as well as Protector. By Beaufort's influence in the Council he was refused the title. The serving men of the two nobles—Gloucester's in blue, and Beaufort's in tawny livery—never met without a skirmish; they flourished clubs and hurled paving-stones in the very streets of London, to the sore scandal of the Lord Mayor and all peaceable citizens; they brawled and their masters bandied insults and threats in the presence of the boy-king, who already began to show a gentle, timorous nature, devout, wishing well to all men, but weak and quite unfit to rule—least of all to rule the selfish and turbulent crowd which surrounded him.

Utterly selfish it was, every man in it; the "good Duke Humphrey" no less than the rest. Sick of the Protectorate in which the Council persistently tied his hands, Gloucester sought his own ambition abroad. He had married Jacqueline of Bavaria, the divorced wife of the Duke of Brabant, and claimed a large portion of the Netherlands as her inheritance. The Duke, her first husband, opposed this claim, and was supported by the Duke of Burgundy, who looked upon himself as Brabant's heir. For Gloucester to persist in his claim meant estranging the Duke of Burgundy from the English alliance, a most serious loss. But England's interest came second to her Lord Protector's. He himself soon had enough of the struggle; but it dragged on for three years, and meanwhile Bedford had to sit helpless before the chance of a splendid success, and watch his late allies the Burgundians marching away from him to fight his brother. Even without them he might have done much, had the quarrels of Gloucester and Beaufort at home allowed them time to provide him with the supplies of men and money he begged for. It was not until 1428 that, peace being restored in Holland and the Duke of Burgundy once more free to help his old allies, it was resolved to push southward across the Loire and reduce the provinces owning the sway of Charles.

The English had let their golden opportunity slip; but for all their fortunate delay the plight of the Dauphin, as we may yet call him, was very nearly desperate. As his first step Bedford laid siege to Orleans, and while he invested it with ten thousand men Charles had to look on and own himself powerless to relieve the city. The besieged themselves lay under a spell of terror, cowed as it were by the names of Bedford and his two gallant lieutenants, the Earl of Salisbury and Lord Talbot. Behind the English all the North of France, as far eastward as the border of Lorraine, lay ravaged and starving, the crops burnt, the peasantry destitute.

It was from Domrémy, a village near that Lorraine border, that while Orleans meditated surrender and Charles had shut himself up at Chinon to weep helplessly, help arose for France; a girl to put courage into a nation of men, a saint to match her unselfish devotion against the utter selfishness guiding the counsels of England, and against all expectation, almost against hope, to perform the miracle and win.

Jeanne d'Arc, or Joan of Arc as we call her, was a shepherd's daughter in this village of Domrémy, at the foot of the wooded slopes climbing towards the

Vosges mountains. She was a dreamy child, fond of wandering alone in these woods, and making friends with the birds and wild creatures she met; the folk at home saw nothing more in her than "a good girl, simple and pleasant in her ways," fonder of indoor tasks than of work in the fields, tender towards all suffering, very devout, a child living very near to God and loving Him passionately.

The war, of which she had heard echoes in the talk of the villagers, but very vague echoes, came sweeping by Domrémy at length. Then she knew what it meant, saw the ruin and misery it left in its wake, and while she nursed the wounded her heart swelled with pity for France.

It seems a little thing, pity in the heart of one peasant girl among thousands who saw this war and suffered from it. But there lies the miracle; it was a little thing. While she brooded she recalled an old prophecy that a maid from the Lorraine border should arise and save the land. In her walks now she saw visions—the mother of God walking between the trees; St. Michael standing in a slant of light between the green boughs and calling on her to save France; there was pity in Heaven (said he) for the fair realm of France. How might she save France? "Messire, I am but a poor maiden; I know not how to ride to the wars or to lead men-at-arms." She thought with shuddering of warfare and wounds; she shrank even from facing the rough men of the camp with their coarse greetings and brutal oaths. Yet her duty led thither, and lay plain before her—"I must go to the King." Her parents threatened, the villagers mocked her.

"It is no will of mine to go," she pleaded; "I had far rather stay here among you. But I must go to the King, even if I wear my legs to the knees." At length the captain of the near town of Vaucouleurs took her by the hand, and swore to lead her to Charles. At Chinon the churchmen refused to believe in her mission, but she won her way to the Dauphin at length, and he received her in the midst of his despairing nobles. "Gentle Dauphin," said she, "my name is Joan the Maid. The heavenly King sends me to tell you that you shall be anointed and crowned in the town of Rheims, to be lieutenant of Himself who is the King of France."

Had his case been only a little less desperate, the Dauphin would no doubt have dismissed her lightly. As it was, his French were so completely cowed by past defeats, and stood in such awe of the very names of mad-brained Salisbury and Talbot who, made prisoner in an engagement when the odds against him were four to one, had effected his ransom, and taken the field again more fiercely than ever, that even though the English before Orleans numbered but three thousand, the swarms of soldiery in the starving city dared not come out and fight. The coming of Joan broke this spell. Riding at the head of ten thousand men, clad cap-a-pie in white armour, with the great white banner of France studded with fleur-de-lys waving above her, she appeared to the citizens of Orleans as an angel from heaven. "I bring you," she told Dunois, the commander of the besieged, as he sallied out to greet her, "the best aid ever sent, the aid of the heavenly King." Scarcely opposed, she rode in through the gates and round the walls, bidding the citizens look on the ring of English forts and fear them no longer. The French generals plucked up heart and marched out to the attack. Salisbury had already fallen, killed by a shot as he surveyed Orleans from one of the forts. Talbot fought like a lion, but was utterly outnumbered. The French reduced fort after fort. Joan herself fell wounded before the last and strongest. They carried her into a vineyard, and Dunois would have sounded the retreat. "Not yet! As soon as my standard touches the walls you shall enter the fort." It touched, and the French burst in. Orleans was saved.

Talbot, however, was not the leader to be daunted by a single reverse, nor could the spell his prowess had built up be destroyed so summarily. Famous stories gathered about his name as they now began to gather about Joan. One ran that the Countess of Auvergne, professing a wish to see and speak with so renowned a warrior, invited him to pay her a visit and accept the hospitality of her castle. Talbot obeyed, and arriving was led to the Countess, who had given orders to lock and bar all the doors behind him. "What! is this the man?" was her greeting. "Is this the redoubtable Talbot, the scourge of France? I looked to have seen a Hercules, or a Hector at least; not this puny fellow." "Madam," answered Talbot, but moderately abashed, "it is plain that I have come at an unwelcome moment; I must take leave of you and choose some fitter occasion." "Take leave? No, my lord, excuse me, you are my prisoner." Talbot laughed. "Your ladyship should have chosen Talbot's substance, not his shadow, to treat so severely." "Why, are you not Talbot?" "I am indeed; and yet but the shadow of Talbot. As for his substance——" He put his horn to his lips and blew, and at once, with beat of drums, his soldiers came bursting through the gates and poured into the castle. "These, madam, are Talbot's substance." The discomfited lady sued for mercy. "Nay, you have not offended me. Some food and wine for my soldiers will be satisfaction enough."

A warrior of this humour will hardly be persuaded that he is beaten. Even after Joan had entered Orleans with colours flying, in the midst of the French rejoicings Talbot with his handful of English had escaladed the walls by night and fought his way to the market-place. The death of Salisbury, the hero of thirteen battles, called upon him to be avenged. He had read this command on the face of his great comrade as he bent over him; and over the body, which had been carried up the scaling-ladder and advanced to the middle of the great square, he could claim that his vow had been paid by the death of five Frenchmen for every drop of Salisbury's blood. Forced from the town, and at length (as we have seen) from the forts surrounding it, by overwhelming numbers, he withdrew his troops northward in good order.

Until reinforcements arrived he was powerless. But the French generals still feared him heartily, and, remembering Verneuil, would have remained inactive on the Loire. Joan refused to hear of this. Her mission was not yet over; and while the English waited around Paris she left the river at Giens and marched through Troyes, her army growing as it advanced, to Rheims. Here, with the coronation of Charles, she felt that her promise had been fulfilled. "The pleasure of God is done," she said, kneeling at the King's feet, and besought leave to go home. She was told that she could not be spared yet.

Though far differently inspired, these soldiers of France and England thought first of their duty; Joan following a heavenly vision, Talbot fighting under no such lofty enthusiasm, but doggedly and as a man should who loves his country. The selfishness lay at home in England with the wrangling nobles who kept him short of supplies; and among these was one whose growing ambitions, secretly nursed as yet, were to cost England even more dear than the disputes which already weakened her fighting arm.

We have seen that when Henry IV. deposed Richard and seized the throne, he was not the true heir to it even after Richard's death. The true heirship rested with the Mortimers, descended from Edward III.'s third son, Lionel, Duke of Clarence; whereas the house of Lancaster descended from his fourth son John of Gaunt. This fault in their succession they had cause enough to bear in mind, and fear that one day it would come to be paid for. It had been in Henry's mind when he prayed before Agincourt, "Not to-day, O Lord!"

The day, though for long averted, was coming. The last of the Mortimers, Earls of March, lay wasting to death in the Tower of London; but his sister, Ann Mortimer, had married Richard, Earl of Cambridge, son of the old Duke of York who so feebly defended the kingdom from Bolingbroke; and thus in her son,

Richard Plantagenet, were united the two lines of Mortimer and York, both derived from Edward III., and the elder claiming the true succession to the throne.

He was heir, too, to a great revenge; for his father, the Earl of Cambridge, had been one of the three whose treason Henry V. had discovered on the eve of sailing from Southampton (and we can guess at what the husband of Ann Mortimer would be aiming). His death and attainder left his son without title; but Richard meant to get his title and his revenge too, in time.

Meanwhile, he must walk warily, for to all appearances the odds were heavy against him. The house of Lancaster had possession—which is proverbially nine points of the law—and a record of three reigns in unbroken succession, one at least a reign of which England was proud. For all their differences, the rulers of the state were Lancastrian to a man, and Lancastrian by birth. Gloucester and Bedford were the King's uncles. Beaufort, now created a Cardinal, was a son of John of Gaunt, and only a little below him in influence came another Beaufort, his nephew the Duke of Somerset. These Beauforts, moreover, had a game of their own to play. Though belonging to a junior branch of Lancaster, and barred from the succession by a special clause in the Act which confirmed the marriage of John of Gaunt with their ancestress Katharine Swynford, they had hopes that, should the young King leave no heir, their claim would be made good.[11] The Beauforts, therefore, were the last to whom Richard could look for help.

[11] The table on the next page will illustrate the hopes of the Beauforts.

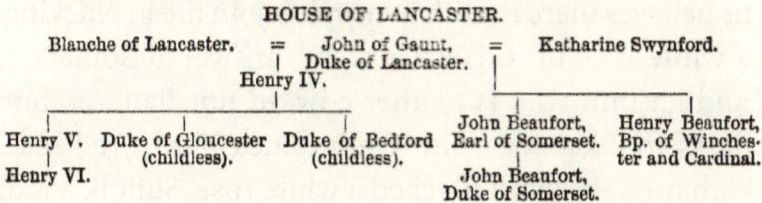

There remained two powerful nobles, who might or might not be of service to him—the Earls of Suffolk and Warwick. Both were astute, ambitious, selfish; each sought his own increase and sought it along his own path. It remained for Richard to see if those paths would run for a time with his.

A quarrel with the young Earl of Somerset in the Temple Hall—"where now the studious lawyers have their bowers"—brought this to the test. No fitter spot could have been found for setting forward Richard Plantagenet's claim, which rested on law. Stung by a taunt of the heir of the Beauforts in the presence of Suffolk, Warwick, and others, Richard lost control of his tongue and spoke boldly of his rights. The argument grew loud, and at Suffolk's suggestion they left the hall and walked out into the quiet garden by the river, where each disputant appealed in turn to his hearers. But the hearers felt they were on ticklish and dangerous ground. Suffolk evaded Richard's appeal. "Faith," said Warwick, "ask me to judge between two hounds, two swords, two horses, two girls, and I may have something to say; but these nice sharp quillets of the law are beyond me." "Since you are tongue-tied then," said Richard, "leave words alone and proclaim your thoughts by token. Let him who values his birth as a true-born gentleman, if he believes there is truth in my plea, join me in plucking a white rose off this brier." "Ay," answered Somerset, "and let him who is neither coward nor flatterer, but dares to take sides with truth, pluck here a red rose with me." Warwick plucked a white rose, Suffolk a red. A gentleman called Vernon who stood by, chose a white rose, and a lawyer of the party did the same; "for," said he, "unless my study and my books tell me false, the Earl of Somerset's argument will not hold." "*Now* where is your argument?" Richard asked tauntingly. "Here in my scabbard," answered Somerset; "and it meditates that which shall dye your white rose crimson." The dispute broke out afresh, and Warwick and Suffolk found themselves drawn into it. Somerset took his stand on the death and attainder of Richard's father. Richard insisted that his father had been no traitor, "and that I will prove on better men than Somerset." The champions of the red rose withdrew from the garden, uttering defiance. "This slur they cast on your house," promised Warwick, "shall be wiped out speedily. The King has summoned his Parliament to patch up a truce between Gloucester and Beaufort; and if he do not then and there make thee Duke of York, my name shall no longer be Warwick." Pinning on their white roses, Richard's supporters left the garden.

Warwick was as good as his word. But before Parliament met, Richard had visited the Tower and received a blessing from the lips of his dying uncle Mortimer. The unhappy prisoner, whose youth had flowered and wasted behind bars, rehearsed the woes of his house. "I am childless, dying; thou art my heir, but tread warily. I ask for no mourning, only see to my funeral. And so farewell, depart with fair hopes and prosper!"

Death had quenched Edmund Mortimer's "dusky torch" before his nephew hurried to the Parliament House, where the young King was attempting once more the endless business of reconciling Gloucester and the Cardinal. This time he indeed persuaded them to shake hands, but only after an open brawl which proved how little they respected their sovereign's presence; and the Cardinal, at any rate, had no intention of keeping his promise. Richard's turn came after this difficulty had been composed. Warwick presented a petition for his restoration to title and inheritance; the Protector joined in urging it. Henry gave way readily. "I grant it, with all the inheritance belonging to the house of York." Richard vowed obedience till death. "Stoop, then; set your knee against my foot. For this homage I gird thee with the sword of thy house, and bid thee rise Duke of York."

Henry had a special reason just now for desiring concord among his nobles, being on the point of crossing the sea to Paris, there to be crowned King of France in answer to Charles's coronation at Rheims. But their amity was as insincere and short-lived as the homage of York, between whom and Somerset the feud of the two roses broke out in sharp words during the hollow ceremony.

No ceremony could have been hollower, for the English cause in France was doomed already, and soon to be doubly doomed by a hateful crime. Joan of Arc had been detained in the French court while the towns in the north opened their gates to Charles. But Bedford, relieved by the efforts of Cardinal Beaufort, who poured his own wealth into the English treasury to raise fresh troops, took the offensive in his turn and drove Charles back behind the Loire, while the Duke of Burgundy set about reducing the revolted towns. This new call brought Joan upon the scene again. Her mission from God had ended, as she felt, at Rheims. But she could be brave still, and she still led the French ranks gallantly, until in a sortie from the city of Compiègne she was pulled from her horse by an archer and made prisoner. Her captors sold her to Burgundy, and he in his turn to the English. To them she was a sorceress and her triumphs procured by the Evil One. After a year's imprisonment she was tried as a witch before an ecclesiastical court presided over by the Bishop of Beauvais. Their questions failed to entangle her. They forbade her the mass. "Our Lord can make me hear it without your aid," she told them, weeping. That she was a witch she denied to the last. "God has always been my Lord in all that I have done. The devil has never had any power over me." In the end they condemned her. A pile of faggots was raised in the market-place of Rouen, where her statue stands to-day. The brutal soldiers tore her from the hands of the clergy and hurried her to the stake, but their tongues fell silent at her beautiful composure. One even handed her a cross he had patched together with two rough sticks. She clasped it as the flames rose about her. "Yes!" she cried; "my voices were of God!" and with those triumphant words the head of this incomparable martyr sank on her breast. "We are lost," muttered an English soldier standing in the crowd; "we have burned a saint."

Burgundy, who had sold her, was already wavering. Very tenderly Joan had pleaded with him in a parley for France, and against the unnatural wounds he inflicted on France. "Consider her, thine own country, France once so fertile! Consider her towns and cities defaced, her wasting ruin. As a mother looks on her dying babe, so look upon France as she pines to death." And to Burgundy her words might well have brought echoes of a day when he himself had pleaded for France with Henry V., painting the decay of her husbandry and the savage misery of her inhabitants. It had taxed all the diplomacy of Beaufort to pin him so long to the English cause. But even the Cardinal's persuasions failed in the end, and soon after Joan's death the Duke deserted back to Charles. This blow was followed by a second and yet more fatal one in the death of Bedford. Paris rose, drove out its garrison of English, and declared for Charles. The English possessions shrank at once to Normandy, portions of Anjou and Picardy, and Maine. At home the policy of England was distracted between Gloucester, who strove to continue the war, and Suffolk, who, following his own ambitious career, had become master of the Council when age and infirmity forced Beaufort to give over the active conduct of affairs, and was now scheming for peace. Abroad, York had succeeded Bedford as Regent of France, but was hampered at every turn by his deadly foe, Somerset.

If Talbot, now Earl of Shrewsbury, had been supported, our tale might have been a different one. He fought a hopeless cause with magnificent courage, at one time fording the Somme with the waters up to his chin to relieve Crotoy, at another forcing the passage of the Oise in face of a whole French army. Driven from Normandy, which in 1450 was wholly lost, he sailed for the south and landed in Gascony. Twenty-thousand men should have followed to reinforce him, but were delayed, and while Somerset hung back in spite against York, Talbot found himself confronted before Bordeaux by an overwhelming army of French. "The feast of death is prepared," said he; and turning to his son, young John Talbot, bade him mount his swiftest horse and escape. Hotly the young man refused. "Is my name Talbot? Am I your son, and you ask me to fly?" "To stay means death for both of us." "Then let me be the one to stay. By flight I can save nothing of Talbot but will be a shame to me." Father and son embraced and made ready to die together. Far from help, yet not too far if Somerset had made haste with his cavalry, the fighting Earl saw his troops mown down in swathes by the French cannon, and charging into the press rescued his son from the sword of Orleans. "Art not weary, John? There is time yet. Fly and avenge me." "Talbot's son," was the answer, "will die beside Talbot." In the next charge the Earl fell, and the lad rushed forward after his assailants. Some soldiers brought back his body and laid it in the arms of his dying father. "Now I am content. My old arms are my boy's grave." So passed indignant from France to heaven the last surviving spirit of Agincourt.

Elsewhere the end had been ignoble enough. The young King—had his will counted—detested the war. To his pious and contemplative nature such strife between peoples of one faith was abhorrent. Gloucester, awake at length to the hopelessness of the struggle, was for accepting the intervention of the Pope and the Emperor, concluding peace on good terms, and sealing it by a marriage between Henry and the daughter of the Earl of Armagnac. This, however, did not suit his opponent, Suffolk, who had a scheme of his own for marrying Henry to Margaret, daughter of Reignier, Duke of Anjou and titular King of Naples—a beautiful and almost penniless lady with whom, indeed, Suffolk himself had fallen more than half in love. In wooing her for his sovereign his tongue now and then spoke for his own heart. But if fond, he was above all things ambitious. Her being Queen of England would not prevent his paying court to her, while it would give her power to support his schemes. Reignier was a grasping father and drove a hard bargain, naming nothing less as the price of the match than the cession of Anjou (which by this time was not England's to give) and Maine, which Suffolk knew well to be the key of Normandy. To Suffolk this weighed little in comparison with his private advantage. He posted back to England and plied Henry and the Council with his praises of Margaret's beauty. Gloucester was outvoted again, and the contract with the Earl of Armagnac broken off. Henry listened wearily to their wrangling. "I am sick," said he, "with too much thinking." He had lost his father's conquests. Even the great southern province which had belonged to England ever since Henry II. had married Eleanor of Aquitaine was preparing to pass from him. If peace could be purchased by ceding Anjou and Maine, he was ready to spare them. Marriage he did not desire, yet (as he told Gloucester) would be content with any choice tending to God's glory and England's welfare. His mind, utterly irresolute, was sensitive enough to be distracted by these perpetual quarrels; and in this condition, as weak men will, he decided suddenly, almost pettishly; despatched Suffolk to France to arrange the betrothal with Margaret; in the very act of disregarding his advice, begged Gloucester to excuse this sudden enforcement of "my will"; and withdrew from the Council to shut himself up and meditate on the cares which afflict a king.

So Suffolk departed triumphant, following a vision of still greater personal triumphs. Margaret should be Queen and rule Henry; but Suffolk should rule her, and through her the King and the whole realm.

II

BUT one thing Suffolk had left out of account, the temper of the English people. He and his peers might treat the national honour as a chattel to be bartered for their private ends; but the mass of his countrymen had learnt under Henry V. to be proud of England, and this pride broke into furious resentment when they saw her greatness dishonoured by weak hands and trafficked away with a selfish unconcern. Duke Humphrey might be an imperfect patriot, but he was for continuing the fight rather than surrendering on such terms. When Suffolk brought Margaret home to London in state, the Protector's voice faltered as he read over the contract. At the clause ceding Anjou and Maine he fairly broke down.

The Cardinal, Suffolk's chief supporter, took the scroll from him and read on. Henry listened, professed himself well pleased with the bargain, and made Suffolk a duke for his services. He had no sooner withdrawn, however, with Margaret and her conductor to prepare for the coronation, than Duke Humphrey found speech. "What! was it for this my brother Henry spent all—his youth, his valour, money, and men,—lodging in the open field, winter and summer, to conquer France? Was it for this my brother Bedford laboured with his wits to keep what Henry had won? Yourselves—Somerset, Buckingham, York, Salisbury, Warwick—have earned honourable scars, while the Cardinal and I have sat toiling in Council early and late, and all to keep France. Is this to be the undoing and shameful end of your prowess and our policy?"

He had England behind him in speaking so; but the conscience of Englishmen had not yet discovered how to make itself heard. For the moment he spoke to men of opposing aims, and they listened with very different minds. Beaufort, his old enemy, openly censured his boldness; but then Beaufort's interest lay with the King's party and the new favourite, Suffolk. Somerset and Buckingham (another duke of the blood royal, descended from Thomas of Gloucester, the youngest of Edward III.'s sons) distrusted the Cardinal as their rival in craft, but were more concerned just now in hating and scheming against Duke Humphrey, the actual Protector, and were ready to join forces to pull him down from his seat. That Somerset took one side was reason enough for York's taking the other. But York, we must remember, considered himself the rightful heir to the throne, and that these were his dukedoms which Suffolk had given away. Warwick and his father Salisbury,[12] as supporters of York, were angry on his account, and also indignant at the loss of provinces they had helped to win.

For the moment, then, these diverse factions fall into two. On the one hand we see Gloucester, supported by York, Salisbury, and Warwick, all indignant at the King's marriage and the bargain it stood for, and representing in this the general silent feeling of England. On the other we have Suffolk, who made the bargain, favoured by the Queen, upheld by the Cardinal, and joined by Somerset and Buckingham, for the present purpose of unseating and destroying Gloucester.

And for the moment this second party could use the King's favour, and so held the upper hand. The stroke

[11] To show the descent of the King maker, we may extend the table given earlier.

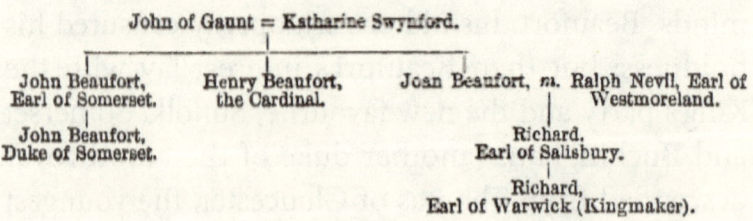

against Duke Humphrey must be dealt, and quickly; but how? They found their opening in the indiscretion of his second wife, Eleanor Cobham. This aspiring dame was guessed, and shrewdly enough, to nurse ambitions which flew higher than her husband's. She was a good hater, at any rate, and found a hater to match her in the young Queen, with whom she soon started a fierce quarrel. It maddened Margaret to see Gloucester's wife parading the Court with a troop of ladies and a duchy's revenue on her back, flaunting her riches, and not careful to hide her disdain of the penniless upstart from Anjou. She had boasted (so Margaret heard) that the train of her meanest gown outvalued all the Duke Reignier's estates. It was a woman's quarrel, and the storm burst in a very feminine fashion. Somerset and York were quarrelling again; this time over their claims to be regent over what remained of French territory. York, who had held the office, looked to be reappointed. Somerset opposed him. Duke Humphrey supported York. "Why should Somerset be preferred?" was the natural question urged by the Protector's party. "Because," answered Margaret imperiously, "the King will have it so." "Madam," replied Gloucester, "if so, the King is old enough to speak for himself." "Then," came the retort, "if he be old enough, he does not need you for Protector." "At his pleasure," said Gloucester, "I am ready to resign." "Resign then!" broke out the tongues of his enemies in turn—Suffolk, the Cardinal, Somerset, Buckingham, the Queen herself. Gloucester choked down his rage for the moment and withdrew, not trusting himself to speak. His Duchess remained. Margaret dropped her fan. "My fan, if you please!" she commanded, and, as the Duchess delayed to pick it up, caught her a box in the ear; then, feigning to have mistaken her for a maid-in-waiting, "I cry your mercy, madam. Was it you?" The Duchess flounced out promising vengeance.

She meant it too. But Suffolk had already prepared a trap for her, and when the Queen complained impatiently of her husband's subjection, Suffolk could promise a speedy deliverance. "I tell thee, De la Pole," Margaret confessed, "when I saw thee at Tours riding a tilt in my honour, and stealing away the French ladies' hearts, I thought thy master had been as brave and handsome and as gallant a wooer. But his thoughts are all given over to holiness. His beads and his sacred books are more to his taste than tilt-yard and weapons, and saints' images all the lady-loves he cares for." She stamped her foot. "I wish to Heaven the Cardinals' College would elect him Pope and carry him off to Rome!" Suffolk besought her to be patient. "And as for the Duchess," he promised, "I have limed a bush for that bird. When I have caught her, as I presently shall, never fear that she'll mount again to trouble you."

Eleanor Cobham, in fact, had over-reached herself. Since her husband would not make a snatch at the crown, she had set her own wits to work, and tempted by an opportunity which Suffolk cunningly threw in her way, had called in the help of sorcery. She was now, as her enemy knew, consulting with Margery Jourdain, a witch, a conjurer named Bolingbroke, and two priestly confederates, Hume and Southwell. Hume was actually in Suffolk's pay; the rest, it is most likely, were but foolish impostors who made a living by trading on superstitious folks. To such knaves the rich Duchess would be a gold mine, if only they could keep her bemused by jugglery and specious prophesying. Unfortunately for them Suffolk proved as prompt in striking as he was careless of what became of his tools after they had served him. As soon as ever he felt the moment ripe he used his information and despatched York and Buckingham with a guard to Duke Humphrey's London house. They broke into the garden and surprised the victims in the midst of their incantations—Margery Jourdain and Bolingbroke pretending to raise the Spirit of Evil, while Southwell took down its answers and the Duchess, with Hume, watched from a balcony. "Lay hands on these traitors and their trash!" commanded York; and then glancing aloft, "What! You there, madam? The King and commonwealth are deeply indebted to you for these pains of yours!" The papers seized by the guard contained the following prophecies:—

(1) Of the King—
"The duke yet lives that Henry shall depose;
But him outlive, and die a violent death."

(2) Of Suffolk—
"By water shall he die, and take his end."

(3) Of Somerset—
"Let him shun castles."

To seek information concerning the King's death was plainly treasonable. York marched his captives to prison, and despatched Buckingham post-haste to St. Albans, where he found Henry hawking and distracted as usual in the midst of his sport by the quarrelling peers, of whom Gloucester and the Cardinal were at the moment within an ace of coming to blows. Buckingham's news, as may be supposed, wholly confounded the Protector, and fetched the King hurriedly back to London to inquire into the Duchess's treason. There was, of course, no defence; the culprits had been taken red-handed. Henry pronounced judgment, sentencing Margery Jourdain to be burned at Smithfield, Bolingbroke, Southwell, and Hume to be hanged, while the Duchess—saved from the worst by her noble birth—was condemned to do three days' open penance through the streets of London, and then to live in banishment in the Isle of Man, under care of the governor, Sir John Stanley.

The day of her penance came, horrible alike for her and for Duke Humphrey, who on hearing her condemnation had knelt and with tears rendered up his Protector's staff into the King's hands. In mourning dress, with his attendants in black about him, the unhappy husband waited and watched the street along which his wife came in her degradation. She came bare-footed, draped in a white sheet pinned with insulting placards, holding a taper alight. A jeering crowd followed her. "Are you come, my lord, to look on my open shame? It is penance for thee too." She pointed back at the crowd. "Ah! Gloucester, hide from their hateful looks!" "Patience, Nell!" the poor Duke pleaded; "be patient and forget this grief." "Teach me, then, to forget myself. For while I think I am thy wife, and thou art a prince and ruler of England, methinks I should not be led along thus! Ah, Humphrey! can I bear it? Believest thou I shall ever look forth on the world again and deem it happy to see the sun! To remember what I was—there will lie the hell: to say 'I am Duke Humphrey's wife. He was a prince and a ruler of England; yet so ruled and was such a prince that he stood by whilst I, his duchess, was made a shameful jest for the street.' No!" she went on bitterly, "be mild as ever! Do not blush at it! Stir at nothing until the axe of death hang over thine own neck—as it will! For Suffolk, all in all with her who hates thee and all of us, and York and the false Cardinal have set the snare for *thy* feet. Go thy way, trusting as ever, and never seek to prevent them!"

But Gloucester would not believe. "I must offend before I can be attainted. Had I twenty times the foes I have; had each of them twenty times his present power, I cannot be harmed while I rest loyal, true, without crime. I beseech thee, Nell, be patient, and leave this to wear itself quickly away!"

While he talked with her a herald arrived to summon him to the King's Parliament, fixed to be held at Bury St. Edmunds on the first of the next month. "The date fixed! My consent not asked!"—Duke Humphrey forgot that he was Protector no longer. "This is close dealing," mused he, but prepared to obey. Hastily husband and wife took their sorrowful farewells and parted; she towards her exile, he for Bury St. Edmunds, where before his arrival his enemies were arranging his downfall.

For while Henry wondered at his delay in coming, Margaret, Suffolk, the Cardinal, and Buckingham were together poisoning his ear with evil charges and worse hints against the late Protector. "Should Henry die now and without child, Gloucester would be next heir to the throne." "It was he who must have set his wife upon her devilish practices." To come to more definite charges: "He had taken bribes from France." "As Protector he had visited small offences with savage punishments." "He had levied money to pay the armies in France and had never sent it." It was York who brought this last charge; for although York had disclosed his aims to Salisbury and Warwick, and although they had secretly sworn to make him King of England, he saw more clearly than they that Duke Humphrey's fate was now sealed, and the time had come to abandon him. Between them the plotters so wrought on the weak King, that when Gloucester entered at length and, wishing the King health, prayed to be forgiven his delay, Suffolk felt able to step forward boldly and arrest him of high treason. Duke Humphrey did not blench. "A clean heart is not easily daunted," said he, and denied, as he honestly could, the charges his enemies now repeated against him. "I never robbed the soldiers of any pay, nor have ever received one penny from France as bribe. So help me God, I have watched night after night studying good for England! If I have stolen one doit from the King, or hoarded one groat of his for my own use, let it be brought against me in fair trial. Nay, rather than tax the poor commons, I have poured out my own money to pay the garrisons, and never asked for repayment.

As for my punishment of offenders, it is notorious that my fault, if any, was too great clemency." Suffolk cut him short. "These are trifles. It is for heavier crimes I arrest you, and hand you over to my Lord Cardinal here, who will keep you until your trial." The hunted man turned to Henry, but Henry could give little help. "My lord," said he, "it is my especial hope that you will clear yourself of all these suspicions; for my conscience assures me you are innocent." "Ah, my liege! I know that they want my life; and if my death could make England happy, they would be welcome to it. But my death is the prologue only. Thousands, who as yet suspect nothing, will die and yet not conclude the tragedy here plotted. I see the Cardinal's malice in his red ferret eyes; Suffolk's brow clouded with hate; I hear Buckingham's sharp tongue unloading his envy; York dogged as ever— York whose ambitious arm I have held back from the moon he would grasp—levelling false charges against my life. And you, my sovereign lady"—he turned to Margaret—"have joined them in stirring up my true liege to hate me. Oh, I have had notice of your meetings, your conspiracies! I shall not lack false witnesses to condemn me!"

Henry stood powerless while the Cardinal's guards hurried away their prisoner; then he moved sadly towards the door. "My lords, I leave it to your wisdom. Do or undo as if I myself were present." "What?" cried Margaret; "will your Majesty leave the Parliament?" "Ay, Margaret; this grief overwhelms me. Gloucester is no traitor; he never wronged you, or these great lords, or any man, that his life should be sought." He could make pretty, touching speeches about his old friend and counsellor; but what, though King of England, he could not do was to find manhood enough to stand by him. His lamentations proved that he guessed only too well what was threatened; yet in the act of uttering them he was moving towards the door, and betraying Duke Humphrey to his fate. The savage and more intrepid hearts he left behind him in the Parliament House had already decided that fate, and were not long in discovering their agreement. Duke Humphrey must die.

York was spared whatever small dishonour remained, after consenting, in actively compassing the murder. While Gloucester's enemies deliberated, news came of a rebellion in Ireland, and to York was given the task of shipping an army at Bristol and sailing to suppress it. He could have desired nothing better. It removed him out of the way of the popular rage which he foresaw would follow the crime. And it gave him an army, which was precisely what he lacked. The golden opportunity had arrived and he grasped it. He would nurse his army in Ireland and wait, while Suffolk and the rest did his dirty work and incurred the odium of it.

For Suffolk was short-sightedly eager to strike. He had always made the mistake of undervaluing the opinion of England at large. His strength lay in his favour with Margaret and the influence this gave him in the narrow inmost circle around the King. He forgot, or thought he could neglect, that which no English king, even, has forgotten or neglected without disaster. Margaret, as a French-woman, might be forgiven for ignoring this; Suffolk's ignorance belonged to the tradition by which the great feudal lords treated the commons and their feelings as of no account, and by which they came to their ruin.

Two murderers hired by Suffolk strangled Duke Humphrey as he lay sick on his bed at Bury. As the King took his seat to try the accused, Suffolk, who had been sent to fetch him, returned with a white face. "He is dead, my lord! Dead in his bed!" The King swooned back in his chair. They revived him, and he fell to petulant, weak ravings; poor cries of a heart to which grief is half a luxury, something at least to be tasted. Margaret, who spoke up boldly for her pet Suffolk, would have made short work of this lamb-like rage; but as she ended a stronger wrath hammered at the door. A crowd of the commons stood outside. They had heard of the crime, and they had Salisbury and Warwick to speak for them and exact vengeance. While Henry wept impotently, these two nobles thrust themselves in, bearing the dead body on its bed. "View it, my liege! See, the blood black in his face—his eyeballs staring, his nostrils stretched with struggling—look on his hands, spread as they must have grasped for life! And on the sheets—see—his hair is yet sticking! By the Lord who died for men, this is foul play! This is Suffolk's work—the murderous coward!"

Suffolk and Margaret together hotly denied it. The favourite had long ago warned his Queen that the Nevils would have to be reckoned with; that Salisbury, the father, and Warwick, the son, were no simple peers; but as he now followed Warwick out to make good his denial by the sword, he found on the further side of the door a more terrible enemy than the Nevils. The throng there shouted for his blood, and he could not face it. With difficulty Salisbury forced the commons back while he spoke their mind. "Either Suffolk must be banished, or the crowd would enter and hale him forth to torture and lingering death. It was for the King's own sake they insisted, but the King must choose." "A mob of tinkers!" sneered Suffolk; but the time for sneering was past. These despised commons had fixed his doom for him, and clamoured impatiently while the King seemed to hesitate. He pronounced it at length. Suffolk was given three days in which to quit the kingdom for ever.

Margaret flung herself on her knees, but in vain. Henry had found a will stronger than even hers. This stormy, masterful woman could love, and she loved Suffolk as he had loved her from the day he wooed her for the husband she could neither understand nor respect. Before him she could be weak, and she wept as she took leave of him. He would stay, he swore, and face death rather than cry for death in a foreign land, cry for her to close his eyes and take his last breath on her lips. But no, she insisted, he must go and take her heart with him. Whithersoever he might wander her messengers should find him out. And he went, to an exile shorter than either of them guessed.

For the vengeance of Heaven was not tarrying. Already the Cardinal lay on his death-bed writhing in torments of conscience, clutching and gasping for breath, now blaspheming God and now cursing his fellow-men. Above all, he kept crying aloud for the King; but when Henry was summoned and stood by his bedside the dying wretch failed to recognise him. "Death? Art thou Death? I'll give thee all England's treasure—enough to purchase another such island—only let me live and feel no pain!" He passed to wilder ravings. Warwick bent and spoke in his ear: "Beaufort, it is the King come to speak to thee." "Bring me to my trial when you will! He died in bed, did he not? Where should he die? Can I make men live whether they will or no? . . . O! cease torturing; I will confess . . . . Alive again? Show me where he is—I'll give a thousand pounds to have a look. He has no eyes; the dust has blinded his eyes! Comb down his hair! Look! look! it is standing upright! . . . Give me drink, . . . bring the poison. Where is the poison I bought? . . . "

Henry, kneeling and praying for the divine mercy on this terrible end, cried to the Cardinal as he sank into silence to make some sign—to lift a hand—in token that his last thoughts were of heaven. The hand was not lifted. The breathing ceased. "O God, forgive him! We are sinners and may not judge him. Close up his eyes and draw the curtains."

Vengeance, passing onward from this bedside, overtook Suffolk as he reached the coast in disguise—he dared not travel openly, knowing the temper of the people. Near Dover he hired a small craft and put out to sea, trusting to be allowed a landing at Calais. He had sailed but a little way when a fleet of armed ships bore down on him. Forced to heave-to, he was summoned on board the *Nicholas of the Tower*, and as he climbed up the side the captain received him with the words, "Welcome, traitor!" Two days later, as the ship hung off the English coast, a boat came alongside, carrying a headsman, a block, and a rusty sword. This was the end of Suffolk—"by water," as had been prophesied.[13] His head was conveyed to Margaret, who mourned for it passionately. "I fear me, love," remonstrated Henry, "thou wouldst not have mourned so for me had I been dead." "Nay, my love, I should not mourn but die for thee."

The ships which seized Suffolk had put out from the Cinq Ports; and the men of Kent, who had furnished them, heard whispers that a terrible revenge was preparing. They were fiercely discontented, because they had prospered on the spoil of the French wars and their prosperity was at an end. Under John Cade, a soldier of some experience in those wars, they now determined to be beforehand with the royal anger, and rose in open revolt. There is more than a suspicion that York had a hand in this rising, though by reason of his absence in Ireland his hand did not appear; but Cade took the name of Mortimer, and although very few even of his ignorant followers believed him to be the true Mortimer, the name was significant.

They were a rough, incoherent crew, having at the bottom of their discontent a dull sense of injustice—a dull feeling that they were misused, that England was disgraced by misgovernment, and that somehow these two things were connected, though they were quite incapable themselves of reasoning this out. But

[13]Some found a punning confirmation of the prophecy in the name of his executioner, a certain Walter (or Water) Whitmore.

their sense of it broke out in a brute rage against the governing class. "It was never merry world in England since gentlemen came up"; "The nobility think scorn to go in leather aprons." Yet as happens with men of their class, flashes of mother-wit, narrow but very shrewd and practical, lit up their absurd arguments; as when Cade—himself, except in fighting, as ignorant as any of them—proclaimed that his father was a Mortimer. "That Mortimer," growled his right-hand man, Dick the Butcher, "was an honest man and a good bricklayer." Cade promised a thorough reformation of the realm. "There shall be in England seven half-penny loaves sold for a penny; the three-hooped pots shall have ten hoops; and I will make it felony to drink small beer. When I am king all shall eat and drink and chalk it up to me, and all shall go dressed in one livery, that they may agree like brothers and worship me, their lord." "The first thing we do," suggested Dick, "let's kill all the lawyers." "Nay," answered Cade, "that I mean to do. Is not this a lamentable thing, that of the skin of an innocent lamb should be made parchment? that parchment, being scribbled over, should undo a man? Why, I set my seal once to such a thing and was never my own master since!" They brought him a prisoner they had taken. "Who's this?" "The Clerk of Chatham; he can write and read and cast accounts." "O monstrous!" "We took him setting of boys' copies." "Here's a villain!" To Sir Humphrey Stafford, who came with the King's forces to suppress the rising, Cade boldly announced himself a genuine Mortimer, and boldly proceeded to prove it. "Edmund Mortimer, Earl of March, married the daughter of Lionel, Duke of Clarence, hey? Well, he had two children, twins, and the elder was stolen away by a beggar-woman and grew up to be a bricklayer. I am his son, and you may deny that if you can." "Indeed, sir," put in a rebel, "he made a chimney in my father's house, and the bricks are alive to this day to testify it. Therefore you cannot deny it." But Cade could fight better than he could argue. Stafford, finding persuasion vain, gave battle. His troops were defeated and himself and his brother slain, and the rebels marched triumphantly upon London, which they entered without resistance, Cade cutting the ropes of the drawbridge with his sword as he passed. Henry and his court had already escaped to Kenilworth, and for two days the city lay at the rebels' mercy. Their chief rage, now that Suffolk had fallen, was against Lord Say, as the royal adviser most guilty of the surrender of Anjou and Maine. Him they seized in his London house and brought to a rough trial—an old tottering man shaken with the palsy. "I'll see if his head will stand steadier on a pole or no," promised Cade. He charged Say—who denied that he was chargeable—with the loss of Normandy, besides lesser misdemeanours. "I am the besom that must sweep the court clean of such filth as thou art. Thou hast most traitorously corrupted the youth of the realm in erecting a grammar-school; and whereas before our forefathers had no other books but the score and tally, thou hast caused printing to be used; and, contrary to the King's crown and dignity, thou hast built a paper-mill. It will be proved to thy face that thou hast men about thee that usually talk of a noun, and a verb, and such abominable words as no

Christian ear can endure to hear!"

Such—a little distorted perhaps in jest—were the charges brought against Lord Say, and from treason of this sort he could hardly be expected to clear himself. He was led forth and executed; his head set on a pole, and the head of his son-in-law, Sir John Cromer, on another. The rebels enjoyed the brutal sport of making the two heads kiss.

But the term of Cade's triumph was a brief one. On the third day the Londoners, roused by the pillage of their shops and houses, seized London Bridge and held it gallantly for six hours. They were relieved by Buckingham and Clifford of Cumberland, a great noble of the north, who came not only with troops, but with promises from the King, on the strength of which they addressed Cade's rabble and promised pardon to all who dispersed. Cade saw his men wavering. "Believe them not!" he shouted. "What, has my sword broken through London gates, that you should leave me at the White Hart in Southwark?" Clifford, however, knew the men he was addressing. The King after all was the son of their adored Harry the Fifth. "Will you by hating him dishonour his father? Is Cade a son of King Harry, to lead you through the heart of France? Or will you quarrel at home till the French pluck up heart to cross over the seas and lord it in London streets? To France! and recover what you have lost!" "A Clifford! a Clifford!" shouted the mob: "We'll follow the King and Clifford." Cade turned on them. "Was ever feather so lightly blown to and fro as this multitude? The name of Henry the Fifth will lead them blindfold." While his late followers laid their heads together to seize him, he broke through their ranks and escaped, heading southwards. After days of hiding in the woods of Kent, hunger drove him to break into the garden of an honest esquire named Iden, who was rambling in his quiet walks when, to his astonishment, he came on this scarecrow intruder. Cade, utterly desperate with famine, showed fight at once, and Iden cut him down before recognising the rebel. Through this chance encounter he found himself suddenly the richer by knighthood and one thousand marks, the price set on the outlaw's head.

But the unhappy Henry had a short relief from his troubles. "Never," he lamented, "did a subject so long to be a king as I long to be a subject." He was no sooner rid of Cade, than there arrived the worse news that the Duke of York had landed with his Irish troops and was marching on London. York's proclaimed purpose was to remove from the King's side his inveterate enemy, Somerset, whom he declared a traitor. Somerset by this time had become a favourite with Margaret, but York's approach was too formidable to be defied, and the King had to send word by Buckingham that his enemy had been removed and committed to the Tower. This left him no excuse but to disband his Irish levies, and indeed for a while events took away all temptation to use force. To be sure, in 1453 a son was born to the King, and this might well have seemed fatal to the Yorkist chance of succession; but about the same time Henry sank into a state of idiocy which made his rule impossible, and York was entrusted with the business of government under the title of Protector of the Realm.

Margaret, however, who had now her infant, Edward, to scheme for, waited her time. Henry recovered, and his recovery deprived York of office. She seized this chance to release Somerset from prison and restore him to his old power. "For a thousand Yorks," she boldly announced, "Somerset shall not hide his head." This was too much. York denounced it as a breach of faith, denied the King's fitness to govern, and collecting again his scattered troops, openly took the field, supported by the Nevils. Clifford's great power in the north enabled Margaret and Somerset to get an army together to oppose him and set up the royal standard at St. Albans.

Upon this camp York marched with Salisbury and Warwick and a force of thirty thousand men. The battle which followed, though ostensibly fought over the question of dismissing Somerset or keeping him in power, was really the first fought to decide whether the English crown should go to the White or the Red Rose, and in the blood of Clifford, whom York slew with his own hand, it sowed a hatred which, inherited by Clifford's son, was to grow to a terrible harvest. The death of Somerset on the field, as the Yorkists swept victorious into St. Albans, removed the pretended cause of the quarrel. But York had proved his strength. Henry and Margaret were now in full flight for London, and thither he must follow with speed. In London he would learn how to act, would choose his next step.

III

YORK had four sons, the fortunes of whom we are to follow—Edward, Earl of March, soon to succeed his father as head of the House of York, and in time to become King of England and the first soldier of his age; Edmund, Earl of Rutland; George, afterwards Duke of Clarence, the false and fleeting; and Richard, the youngest, a hunchbacked lad, already giving promise of that sinister and malignant genius which was to carry him to the throne of England, and set him there in a white glare of hatred, the master-fiend of her history. In his crooked body, with its colourless, twisted face, eyes which repelled and fascinated, and snarling mouth (he had been born, the tale went, with all his teeth) there dwelt something of the wild animal, a monster hatched out of the worst and corruptest passions of Feudal England, to be its own scourge, and in the end its destroyer. Even as youth he feared neither God nor man nor devil. He had started for St. Albans with a blasphemy on his lips; in the battle he had thrice rescued the old Earl of Salisbury by his reckless courage, had cut down Somerset with his own hand,[14] and striking off his head, had carried it off and flung it down before his father in triumph. York gazed on the features of his lifelong enemy. "Richard," said he, "has done best of all

---

[14]Under the signboard of the Castle Inn in St. Albans. Those who will may see in this a confirmation of the prophecy mentioned in the chapter on Henry IV, Part 2.

my sons." "I hope to shake off King Henry's head in the same fashion," said Richard.

For this, as for other things, Richard's time was to come. For the moment he stood in the shadow of another great figure on the side of the White Rose—Richard, Earl of Warwick, the strongest of the strong Nevils, the "King-maker," the "Last of the Barons." Feudalism was doomed, but in Warwick it died, if not nobly, at any rate magnificently. He was its fine flower and its grandest type. Heir to the earldom of Salisbury, he had doubled his wealth and added the earldom of Warwick by his marriage with the heiress of the Beauchamps. When he rode to Parliament six hundred retainers, wearing his badge of the bear and ragged staff, followed at his heels. Thousands feasted daily in his courtyard. He could raise whole armies from his own earldoms. In generalship and (some said) in personal courage he might fall short of York's two sons, Edward and Richard, but he was an active warrior none the less, and for intrigue and politic dealing the first head in the kingdom. In the end the two lads outplayed him, but for the present he supported their cause, and it was by his support that in time they found themselves strong enough to challenge him.

This array of power and ability on the Yorkist side would have left Lancaster weak indeed had it not been for Margaret. Fierce and implacable as her husband was weak, she took the place of a man at the head of the Red Rose faction. Clifford could fight, but it was Margaret who commanded; and hereafter whenever success falls to the arms of Lancaster, it is always Margaret who is in the field, fighting like a tigress for the rights of her boy, again and again putting fresh life into her husband, and with undefeated tenacity lifting a beaten cause and renewing the struggle.

For a brief while after the battle of St. Albans a return of the King's malady gave the two parties a respite. York became Protector again, and Margaret pretended, at least, to be reconciled. But once more Henry's recovery raised the question "Who, after all, is to rule England?" and in 1460 York took the bold course and openly, in the presence of Parliament, asserted that the crown belonged to him. "My father was King," protested Henry, "and my grandfather was King by conquest." "Not so," answered York, "by rebellion." There, of course, lay the weakness of the Lancastrian title. "But a king may adopt an heir, and Richard in the presence of many nobles resigned the crown to my grandfather." "Yes, under force. Now, as well as right, we have force on our side." Warwick stamped his foot, and the Parliament-house was filled in a minute with soldiers. "Let me reign for my lifetime," pleaded Henry, too weak either to be a true king or to resign with a good grace. On this ground a compact was patched up. Henry should be allowed to reign during his life, and the crown should then pass to York and his heirs.

Young Clifford and the other barons of the north were furious at Henry's faint-hearted bargain, and marched out of the Parliament rather than consent to it. But their fury was nothing to Margaret's when the word came to her that her darling son had been disinherited. "Wretched man," she broke out, "would I had never seen thee! 'Enforced?' What! art thou a King and wilt consent to be forced—consent to reign on sufferance with York for Protector, Warwick for Chancellor and lord of Calais, and his uncle Falconberg in command of the Channel? Had I been there—I, a silly woman— Warwick's soldiers should have tossed me on their pikes before I let them disinherit my boy. Until that compact be repealed, thou art no husband of mine. The northern lords have forsworn thy colours; they shall follow mine. Come, my son, let us leave this talker!"

Poor Henry sat down to write letters entreating Clifford and the rest not to forsake him. But Margaret called on their loyalty in a more heroic fashion, and seeing her take the field Clifford raised the royal standard for her in the northern shires, while the new Duke of Somerset levied an army in the west. York, leaving Warwick in London to watch over the King, hastily gathered a force and marched northward until he encountered Clifford's army at Wakefield in Yorkshire. There he found himself outnumbered by four to one, and disaster fell on the White Rose. His second son, Edmund, Earl of Rutland, wandering the battlefield in charge of a tutor, fell into Clifford's hands. While the soldiers hurried away his protector, the poor boy begged for life. But Clifford had taken an oath of vengeance. "Thy father slew my father," was the answer, "so will I kill thee." And he drove his dagger into the young breast.

York's hour, too, was at hand. His two sons, Edward and Richard, fighting beside him, had made a lane for him through his foes, shouting, "Courage, father! fight it out!" But as their overmatched troops broke and fled, father and sons were swept apart, and at length the Duke found himself, faint and alone, hedged around by his deadly enemies. He could hope for no quarter. But Margaret held back Clifford's sword while she made her prisoner taste the full bitterness of death. She enthroned him on a molehill—this man who had reached at mountains. "Where are your sons now, to back you?—wanton Edward and lusty George, and your boy Dicky, that crook-back prodigy? Where is your darling, your Rutland? Look, York,"—she held out a crimsoned napkin,—"I dipped this in your boy's blood. If you have tears for him, take this and wipe your eyes." They called on him to weep for their sport. They brought a paper crown and set it on him. "Marry, now he looks like a king!" Clifford, in his father's memory, claimed the privilege of dealing the death-stroke. The doomed man's indignant protest moved even his enemy Northumberland to pity. "Woman, worse than tiger, I take thy cloth and wash my sweet boy's blood from it with my tears. So, keep it. Go boast of it, and have in thine own hour of need such comfort as thou art offering me!" Margaret had no pity. She taunted Northumberland's compassionate weakness. With her own dagger she followed up Clifford's stroke. "Off with his head! Set it on York gates, and let York overlook his city of York!"

It was in Herefordshire, near Mortimer's Cross, that news of York's fate reached his sons. Young Edward was hurrying to avenge the reverse at Wakefield with the army collected by Somerset in the west; and the soldiers told of an omen, an apparition at day-rise of three suns which, after shining separate for a while in the clear sky, joined and melted into one. The three heirs of York read it as promising them a triple yet united glory, and Edward from that time took three suns for the cognizance of his arms. It was Richard who recovered first from the blow of the heavy tidings. "Tears are for babes. I choose blows and revenge. As I bear my father's name, I'll avenge him."

In Herefordshire they were met by Warwick, who on learning the issue of the fight at Wakefield, guessing that Margaret's next move would be on London to rescue the King from his keeping, had promptly collected a force of Kentishmen and marched out to oppose her. For the second time St. Albans had seen a conflict between the Red and White Roses, but after a fierce day's fighting the Yorkist forces had broken under cover of the night, and Henry fallen again into the hands of his own party.

Such was the tale brought by Warwick, who had collected his broken regiments and marched post-haste to join with young Edward's fresh forces. The tidings might have been fatal had not Margaret paused in her march upon London to indulge her thirst for vengeance in a savage butchery of prisoners and allowed her northerners to scatter for pillage. As it was, Edward had just time to overthrow a body of Lancastrians barring his way at Mortimer's Cross, and hurrying forward to dash into London ahead of her. It was a stroke which proved him a born general. The citizens received him with shouts of "Long live King Edward!" as—a gallant handsome youth of nineteen—he rode along their streets. Margaret and her army fell back sullenly upon their northern headquarters at York, where Henry winced at the sight of his late enemy's head impaled over the gate. Edward, now secure of the support of the capital, lost no time in hurrying with Warwick to compel them to a decisive battle.

A parley at York between the leaders ended as usual in open threats and defiance, and the two armies met on Towton Field, near Tadcaster, to contest the bloodiest and most obstinate battle fought in England since Hastings. Together the armies numbered almost a hundred and twenty thousand men, and from daybreak, when the Yorkists advanced to the charge through blinding snow, for six hours the tide of success swayed to and fro undecisively. At one moment Warwick, as his men gave ground and their commanders began to consult gloomily, stabbed his horse before their eyes, and, kneeling, swore on the cross of his sword-hilt to revenge his brother (borne down and thrust through by Clifford) or to die on the field.

As the daylight grew, Henry, the unwilling cause of all this carnage, wandered forth on the outskirts of the fight. Margaret and Clifford had chidden him back out of danger, swearing that they prospered best when relieved of his presence. Seating himself on a hummock—just such a molehill as that on which York had been mockingly enthroned—in kingship scarcely less impotent and forlorn, he watched the ebb and flow of the battle. "Let the victory go to whom God wills it! Would that, by God's good will, I were dead!" Heartily he envied a shepherd's lot in just such a pastoral land as this, which, but for him, had been bloodless and smiling. To sit upon just such a hill, in the hawthorn shade, and carve out rustic dials while his sheep browsed—*that* to this gentlest of monarchs seemed true happiness. And while he sat he saw and understood what this horrible civil war meant for pastoral England, a war in which, forced by no will of their own to take sides, sons slew their fathers and fathers their sons. While at a little distance slayers such as these lamented over their slain, Henry wept for the unnatural error of it all.

At length Norfolk arriving with reinforcements turned the scale in favour of the White Rose. The Lancastrians were beaten back to the river which lay in their rear, and there the retreat became a rout. No quarter was given. All that night and through the next day the killing went forward. Clifford, desperately wounded, died before his enemies could overtake him, but the sons of York seized the body and exulted over the man who had slain their father and brother, and set his head to decorate the gates of York in its turn. Twenty thousand Lancastrians lay dead on the field, and almost as many Yorkists; but the victory made Edward king for the time beyond dispute. Henry and Margaret escaped over the Scottish border, Somerset into exile. Northumberland was dead. Devonshire and Wiltshire followed him as soon as the murderous reprisals began. Edward created his brother George Duke of Clarence, and Richard Duke of Gloucester. Richard had wished the dukedom of Clarence for himself. "That of Gloucester is too ominous," said he, between earnest and a jesting glance at the fate of Duke Humphrey. He took it, however, and waited his time for something better.

Edward was now Edward IV., crowned King of England, and could reign for a time in something like security. Yet Margaret kept up the struggle. Leaving Henry in Scotland, which had been their refuge after the disaster of Towton, she crossed back over the border and stirred up the north to a new rising, only to be crushed by Warwick at Hedgeley Moor and again at Hexham. Still indomitable, she set sail for France to beg help from the young king Lewis XI.; and there met face to face again with her enemy Warwick, who had come upon a rival mission.

Warwick by this time had reached the height of his power. He was Lord Admiral of England, and maintained in the Channel ports a fleet devoted to his service. He was Captain of Calais and Warden of the Western Marches. A brother, Lord Montague, ruled the northern border; a younger brother was Archbishop of York and Lord Chancellor; while his uncles Lords Falconberg, Abergavenny, and Latimer had all drawn rich spoils from the Yorkist triumph.

But if for three years the King-maker seemed all-powerful, the King (as his march on London had proved) was no Henry, but a young man of brain and will, and a leader of men. In private life abominably dissolute, and to all appearance an idler, a lover of costly wines and meats, a follower of vicious pleasures which in the end bloated his body and killed him before his time, amid these pursuits he could scheme as cunningly as Warwick, and when war summoned him it found him always the first general of his age.

Sooner or later between these two strong men the struggle was bound to come. It began silently, and Edward struck his first blow when Warwick was absent in France negotiating for him a marriage with the Lady Bona, sister of the French Queen. Lewis found himself between two petitioners; on the one side Margaret, passionately pleading for aid to restore her boy to the throne; on the other Warwick, temptingly offering a rich alliance with the actual King of England. Even poor Henry in his Scottish hiding could forecast how the contest would go. Margaret had come to beg, Warwick to give. Lewis might pity the weaker side, but he would surely decide for the stronger.

So indeed he did, but in the act of deciding he was interrupted by news from England. Edward had flouted Warwick and made his mission idle by privately marrying Dame Elizabeth Grey, the widow of a slain Lancastrian and daughter of a knight named Woodville. The King's brothers resented the match; but while Clarence openly inveighed against it, Richard kept a stiller tongue in his head. An heir to Edward, should one be born, would be one more life between him and the crown on which he had set his heart; but what was done could not be undone. He would have the crown, with time and patience.

To the Lady Bona, and through her to the French King, this marriage was a deliberate insult. Nor did it improve the temper of the befooled Warwick that

Edward at once began to shower favours on the Woodvilles, the greedy and vulgar-minded family of his new wife, and raise them to power in opposition to the proud Nevils. The King-maker and Queen Margaret whom he had ruined, now discovered that they had a common cause, and King Lewis in his anger was ready to back them. They swore alliance, and to cement it Warwick betrothed his eldest daughter, the Lady Anne Nevil, to Margaret's boy, the young Prince of Wales.

Warwick thus stood pledged to unmake the king he had made, and restore the House of Lancaster to the throne, in the person either of the young prince or of the deposed Henry who—tossed to and fro like a shuttlecock in the game—had once more passed abjectly into his enemies' hands. Stealing across the Scottish border to indulge in the sorrowful luxury of gazing on the realm he had lost, he blundered upon a couple of deer-keepers, who promptly secured and marched him to London, where, on horseback with his feet tied to the stirrups, he was paraded thrice round the pillory and then cast into the Tower.

Warwick could feel no real affection for anyone of the House of Lancaster. He had a second daughter, Isabel; and, while playing with the hopes and demands of the Lancastrians, he gave her in marriage to the discontented Clarence, whom he secretly proposed to set on the throne in Edward's place. Clarence had no scruple now in betraying his brother. He left the court and raised a revolt in the Midlands. Edward, marching hurriedly to cope with it, was surprised by Warwick and Clarence one night in his own camp, made prisoner, and confided to the keeping of Nevil, Archbishop of York. From this captivity he was cunningly stolen by his brother Richard, and Warwick's schemes for crowning Clarence were defeated by the Lancastrians, who demanded Henry's restoration and would do nothing under that price. In the following spring a new revolt broke out in Lincolnshire, but this found Edward better prepared. Marching northwards, he crushed the rebels and turned swiftly on their abettors. Clarence and Warwick could gather no force to meet them, and were forced to escape over-sea.

Desperate now of setting up Clarence, Warwick calmly abandoned him and fell back on the plan—which he had taken so long to stomach—of staking all on Margaret's side. To her he engaged his word to liberate Henry, and crossing once more to England at a moment when a fresh revolt had drawn Edward off to the north, he pressed on his heels with an army which gathered so ominously that Edward in turn was glad enough to escape out of the kingdom and take shelter in Flanders.

He retreated, however, but to return and strike effectively. Warwick had indeed liberated Henry and led him from his cell to the throne, but the unhappy King enjoyed a very brief freedom. He asked no more than to place the substance of power in the joint hands of Warwick and Clarence. The shadow was enough for him, might he share it with Margaret and his son, whom he summoned from France, where King Lewis was providing fresh troops to uphold the advantage which Warwick had gained for them.

But before they could obey, Edward—whom the Duke of Burgundy had supplied with an army—landed at Ravenspurgh and came marching down the length of England, making proclamation that he had surrendered his claim to the crown and sought only to be restored to his dukedom. But the name of Ravenspurgh and the terms of his proclamation sounded ominously to those who recalled where and how, and under what pretext, Bolingbroke had landed and wrested the sceptre from King Richard II. By the time he reached Nottingham sixty thousand men marched under the White Rose. Warwick, rallying his supporters under the Red Rose banner at Coventry, waited long but waited in vain for Clarence to join him. Oxford, Montague, Somerset, one after another, came trooping in with their drums and colours; still Clarence tarried. He had deserted back to his brother as lightly as he had deserted from him. Edward knew his levity; and, too cold perhaps to feel any deep resentment, certainly too politic to show it at this moment, gave him an affectionate greeting. Richard echoed it with a sneer—"Welcome, Clarence; this is indeed brother-like!"

The brothers, once more united, marched rapidly on London, the gates of which were opened to them; and for the last time Henry passed back from the throne to the Tower. Warwick followed, and the deciding battle was fought at Barnet, on the north side of London, April 14th, 1471 (Easter Sunday). Three hours of furious and confused slaughter, in which the Lancastrians, amid flying rumours of treachery and desertion, scarcely knew their friends from their foes, left Warwick, Montague, and all their ablest leaders dead on the field. The cause of the Red Rose was lost.

Somerset and Oxford escaped and fled westward to join Margaret, who on that very day had landed with her son at Plymouth. Three weeks later, as they marched to join the troops which the Earl of Pembroke was raising in Wales, their army was overtaken at Tewkesbury by Edward, who by a brilliant piece of strategy had hurried from Windsor to intercept them. Footsore and weary, they reached Tewkesbury on May 3rd, and took ground in a strong position close by the Abbey there. From this, on the following day, they were enticed by Richard, cut to pieces and slaughtered like sheep. Hundreds ran screaming into the Abbey for sanctuary, were seized, dragged forth, and executed in batches at the town cross; hundreds were chased down into the River Avon and drowned. Margaret and her son were taken and brought before Edward, who, angered by the gallant boy's defiance, smote him across the mouth with his iron glove. The daggers of the three brothers silenced him more effectually. Edward struck first. "What, sprawling?" sneered Richard. "Take that, to end your agony." "And that," added Clarence, "for twitting me with perjury." "Kill me too!" pleaded Margaret, broken at last, as his blood ran from their daggers. "Marry, that will I." Richard was ready, but Edward held his hand. When she recovered from her swoon and would have besought him again, Richard had galloped from the field. "The Tower! The Tower!" had been his last whisper in Clarence's ear. "He's sudden, when a thing comes into his head," was Edward's cynical comment when Clarence told him.

Henry sat reading in his cell in the Tower, when Richard was announced and entered with a sneering smile. The sad King knew his errand at once. His eyes were opened; he saw that death had entered with Richard and stood behind his crooked shoulder; and he saw in that crooked figure incarnate the final curse begotten in the long struggle and bred for the blight of all its shadow was to fall upon. His lips were opened too, and he prophesied. Richard leaped on him with his dagger. "For this I was ordained—among other things!" he snarled, and drove home the blow. "Ay, and for much more slaughter to come," gasped Henry: "God forgive my sins, and thee!" He was dead; but Richard, like a wild beast mad with the taste of blood, struck again and again. "Down—down to hell, and say I sent thee!" he growled over the body.

Richard II. was avenged. The curse against which Henry V. prayed before Agincourt had overtaken the House of Lancaster at length, and was fulfilled. But the curse on the House of York was yet to fall. At Westminster Edward could feel himself secure; could turn all his thoughts to pleasure and courtly shows. Margaret was banished; his strong foes, from Warwick downward, were dead one and all. A son had been born to inherit the crown. He bade his two brothers kiss their nephew. Clarence and Richard bent over the child in turn. We shall see that child again with Richard's shadow bent above him and over-arching.

KING RICHARD THE THIRD

At length England was at peace. The long struggle of the Roses had exhausted her and drained her of blood. When the great peers met in Parliament, the long empty benches told them at what cost to their order they had fought. They, the survivors, sat as it were with ghosts, representing the shadow only of those civil liberties their ancestors had won, had abused, and had lost again. In his palace King Edward could give himself up to indolence and pleasure; and he did so in the sight of all men, but he did also many things which they failed to mark. Few understood this curious cynical King who so carelessly cast his handsome body away to perdition, yet all the while was patiently and cunningly strengthening the monarchy, and making it all but absolutely powerful. In war he had never lost a battle; when it came to treachery, he had outplayed his master, the great Warwick; at one time and another almost one-fifth of the whole land in the kingdom, stripped from the nobles, had fallen into his hands; and now while he appeared to take his ease, content only to be gay and popular, his eyes under their drooped lids never relaxed their vigilance. Stealthily, surely, his toils closed around new sources of wealth; his ships multiplied on the seas;

his spies were everywhere; his will made itself silently felt in every court of law.

So his masterly brain went on working; but for himself he was weary of soul. He had reached his own ambition early. The most selfish of men, when it occurred to him to desire a thing, he heeded no opposition. It had been his fancy to marry Dame Elizabeth Grey, and he did so though it insulted the King of France and mortally offended Warwick. Her kinsfolk, the Woodvilles, were a base and greedy crew. Edward ennobled and enriched them one after another, enjoying the disgust of Clarence and Warwick and the great families, and afterwards watched with contempt, half-amused, half-tired, the vulgarity of these newcomers as they intrigued about him. For his children, indeed, he was anxious and even over-anxious; he had two sons and five daughters, and from their cradles he schemed to make marriages for them. Oddly enough, while his other projects succeeded, these always failed. For the rest, he had come to the end of his desires; nothing remained but to fall back on eating and drinking and coarse bodily pleasure, and with these he wore himself out.

While he was doing it, still, as always, his brother Richard stood by his side watching, waiting. He had not reached the end of his ambitions.

Our tale has brought us to a time when the darkness of the Middle Ages was breaking up. Already Caxton had set up his printing-press at Westminster, and soon, as the Turks took Constantinople and its Greek scholars fled for refuge to Italy, a flood of old Greek learning was to come pouring over the west of Europe. In that queer twilight, while the old faith was dissolving and before a new one had fairly dawned, there were born—it is one of the wonders of history—numbers of men with utterly pagan souls. They disbelieved in God and scoffed at Him; they were wicked, knew themselves to be wicked, rejoiced in it, and took a pride in their wickedness as if it had been a sort of fine art. Nowadays a wicked man usually tries to persuade himself that he is not so bad after all, that the world has used him ill, that he is "more sinned against than sinning"; but these men were wicked from choice and strove to be devilish. In the history of Italy about this time you may find many such. In England for several reasons this deliberate villainy has never been common; but if there ever lived in England a deliberate villain, by all accounts Richard was he.[15]

Let this be said for him—though it does not excuse him: it was no fault of his that Nature had made him

---

[15]I say "by all accounts"; but it is possible or even likely that if the truth about Richard had ever been allowed to come down to us, we should hold quite another opinion of him. When the first Tudor King slew him and took his crown, it became the business of the Tudors to blacken his memory and represent him as a fiend in human shape; and the Tudor historians did this handsomely. It is believed that Henry VII.'s chronicler, Polydore Vergil, destroyed documents wholesale, with his master's connivance, to remove all that might tell in Richard's favour. This was overshooting the mark. It left the picture too black to be credited when in course of time Tudor prejudice disappeared. But Shakespeare wrote under a Tudor queen and for a prejudiced audience; and lacking the means to correct it, we must take what he gives us—with more than a grain of salt.

so monstrous to the eye that the very dogs in the street barked at him. He felt his deformity keenly. "Very well," he resolved, "men shrink from me in loathing. They shall find me what they expect." He had still to learn that his terrible face could fascinate as well as repel.

He learned it in this way. The corpse of King Henry VI., after lying in state in St. Paul's, was being conveyed to the river-side, thence to be carried by boat to Chertsey in Surrey for burial. Richard strolled out into the street to feast his eyes on the small procession— the body of his victim, the bier, the few gentlemen of birth walking with halberds beside it, and one only mourner—the Lady Anne, daughter of the King-maker, and widow of the young Prince of Wales, over whose death agony the Yorkist brothers had gloated at Tewkesbury.

While she walked lamenting, cursing the man who had murdered father as well as son, the procession halted, and Richard himself stood before her.

"Set down the corpse," he commanded; and as the halberdiers hesitated, "By St. Paul, I'll make a corpse of any man of you who disobeys!"

"My lord," entreated one of the gentlemen, "stand back, and let the coffin pass."

"Stand thyself, thou unmannerly dog! Lower thy halberd, or, by St. Paul, I'll strike thee down and trample on thee."

The Lady Anne came forward. "What, gentlemen! Are you trembling? Are you all afraid? I cannot blame you, alas!—that your mortal eyes cannot endure such a devil." She turned on Richard. "Hence! minister of hell! Thou hadst power over his mortal body, but his soul thou canst not have."

"Be not so shrewish, sweet saint," Richard leered on her. In truth a wild scheme had come into his head, and he stood with his eyes on her and a smile twisting his face, while she cursed and accused him, pointing to Henry's wounds.

"Fair but most uncharitable lady," he answered at length, "give me leave to excuse myself."

"Excuse! Foul beyond power of thinking, what excuse canst thou give but to hang thyself? thou slaughterer!"

"Ay; but suppose I slew them not? It was not I who killed your husband, but Edward."

"Liar! Margaret saw thy dagger hot in his blood; nay, and it was turned against her own breast when thy brothers beat it aside."

Richard shrugged his shoulders. "She provoked me, with her tongue."

"Thine own bloody mind provoked thee! Didst thou not kill Henry, here?"

"I grant it."

"You grant it? Then God grant me thy soul's damnation for that wicked deed! Oh, he was gentle, so mild, so virtuous!"

"And the fitter to go to heaven. Heaven will suit him better than earth," Richard sneered.

"Thou art unfit for any place but hell."

"I grant it again. But let us be reasonable, gentle Lady Anne! Is the executioner of these untimely deaths more blameworthy than the cause of them?"

"Thou wast the cause of them."

"Not so." He fixed his eyes more intently upon hers. "Your beauty was the cause," he said slowly; then with a sudden passionate haste, "Your beauty, which has haunted my sleep, bidding me murder all the world if only to live for an hour on your sweet breast."

Anne shrank back, putting up her hands to cover her eyes; her fingers pressed the flesh until they left white marks. "If I thought that," she gasped, "these nails should tear that beauty away."

"Nay," said Richard coaxingly, "not while I stood by. I could not see the light of my life so blemished."

But Anne recovered herself, loathing herself that she could not free her eyes from his gaze. Breaking into curses again, she spat at him. "Would it were poison!" she panted. "Oh, if these eyes could but strike thee dead!"

"I would they might," Richard went on blandly, his own playing with them as a cat with a mouse; "then I should die at once: now they are killing me with a living death. They have drawn salt tears, lady, from mine—mine, which had no tears even when Rutland, my tender brother, moaned under Clifford's sword; none even when thy father, warlike Warwick, told us like a child the sad story of my father's death, and twenty times broke down in sobs while his hearers wept with him." Again Anne drew herself up and forced her mouth to smile scornfully; but he held her eyes. "Teach thy lips no such scorn, lady; they were made for kissing, not for contempt. If thou be too full of revenge to forgive me, see"—he drew his sword, and kneeling tendered it to her by the blade—"plunge this in this true breast, and let forth the soul that adores thee."

She took the sword by its handle: still kneeling, still with his eyes on hers, he pulled open his shirt. She pushed forward the point, then wavered.

"Nay, pause not. I did kill King Henry—but it was thy beauty provoked me; I did stab young Edward—but it was thy heavenly face set me on."

The sword dropped from her hands with a clang. Still Richard knelt.

"Nay, take it up again, or take me."

"Rise," stammered the poor woman. "I wish thy death, but I cannot kill thee."

"Then bid me kill myself. I will do it."

"I have done so."

"Tush, that was in thy rage. Come, say it again; and the hand which for thy sake killed thy love shall for love of thee kill a far truer love, and thou shalt be accessory to both murders."

She peered at him shuddering. "I wish I could read thy heart."

"My tongue utters it."

"Well, well," she sighed hopelessly; "put up thy sword."

"Tell me then that my peace is made."

"You shall know hereafter." For the moment she was vanquished, yet still she fought for time. But he stepped to her, caught her hand, and slipped his ring on her finger. "So," he persisted, "thy breast encloses my poor heart. Wear both, for they both are thine. For the moment I beg but one thing more: leave to me these sad rites, go quickly to my palace in Bishopsgate; and when I have seen King Henry interred at Chertsey monastery, I will repair back thither with all the swiftness of my regard. Grant this: I have reasons for asking it."

And Anne obeyed. Under his will she was powerless: it thrilled her, yet to be mastered in this fashion was not all unhappiness.

"Bid me farewell," Richard commanded.

She, poor soul, could even play at archness, or perhaps caught at it to steady herself. "'Tis more than you deserve," said she; "but since you must teach me to flatter you—imagine that I have done so already."

Richard watched her along the street, then turned abruptly to the bearers. "Sirs, take up the corpse," he commanded.

"Shall we bear it on to Chertsey, my lord?" asked one.

"No; to Whitefriars. Wait for me there at the river-side."

The mourners lifted the bier and passed on, leaving Richard alone. It had been the strangest wooing. "Was ever woman wooed or won in this humour?" he mused. "I'll have her!" he paused, and added, "but I will not keep her long."

Why had he wooed her? That answer at any rate is simple. She was one of the richest women in England. She and her sister, his brother Clarence's wife, were heiresses of all the vast possessions of their father, the King-maker. Clarence would be a heavy loser by this, and his wrath something worth witnessing. Well, Clarence would have to be dealt with.

But—it was wonderful! It amazed Richard himself. "What! I who killed both her husband and her father, to take her so in the moment of her bitterest hate, with curses in her mouth, with tears in her eyes, over the very body of Henry; with God and her conscience and all these witnesses against me, and I with nothing to back my suit but the sheer devil in me and a few dissembling glances; and to win nevertheless against every odds! Ha!" He took a long breath. He had learnt something—a power of mastery in him beyond his dreams. He had proved it in these few minutes; and yet, so wonderful was it, he glanced down his withered body as though prepared for a surprise there. "Has she already forgotten her Edward, young, gallant, and royal, whom I stabbed not three months ago? And can she condescend to be taken by me—poor, limping, misshapen me? Upon my life, I must be mistaken in my person. She must find me a marvellous good-looking fellow. I wish I could; but it seems I must buy a looking-glass."

But if he meant to marry Anne there would be Clarence to reckon with. This would not be hard. In his heart Richard despised Clarence wholly. Richard, with all his faults, had ever stood loyally by Edward's fortunes; whereas Clarence had betrayed him once in a baffled attempt to grasp the crown for himself and his children, and was even now scheming again.

This was the card which Clarence held or supposed himself to hold.—When Edward had first declared his intention of marrying Dame Elizabeth Grey, his mother, who (like the rest of his kin) hated the match, tried to prevail on a certain Lady Elizabeth Lucy to come forward and swear that she had been privately married by the king. When it came to the point, however, the lady had to admit that the contract was not a regular one. Of course if it could be proved valid, Edward's second marriage would be void and his children illegitimate, and the crown on his death must go by law to his next brother Clarence and to Clarence's heirs. That there was more in it than Edward owned was made the likelier by his touchiness on the subject; which went so far that once having heard that a London grocer who plied his business under the sign of "The Crown" had jestingly spoken of his son as "heir to the Crown," he had the unhappy tradesman hanged for his joke.

So when Clarence became troublesome, Richard had to his hand an easy means of removing him. He had simply to go to the King and report that his brother was prying into this business and raking up the old scandal. Edward, who as he felt his end near grew more angrily suspicious than ever of any hint against his children's legitimacy, was worked into a greater rage by the production of a prophecy which said that "G" should disinherit the King's heirs. Now Clarence's name was George, and George begins with a G. (So, by the way, does Gloucester, but Richard did not point this out.) As for the Queen and her kinsfolk, they were furious, as was only natural.

"So much the better," thought Richard; "Master Clarence, when he suffers, will put it down to them and never suspect me."

Everything fell out as he planned. Clarence was arrested and marched off to the Tower.

Richard lay in wait for him on his way thither and expressed a painful surprise. "This is the Queen's— that woman Grey's—work, with her pestilent kin," he declared; and when told by Sir Robert Brakenbury, Lieutenant of the Tower, that speech with the prisoner could not be allowed, "We are the Queen's abjects," sneered he, slurring over the two words so that Brakenbury might hear it as "the Queen's subjects" if he chose: "We must obey"; and he sent Clarence away with a promise that he would leave no stone unturned to obtain a release. Having watched him down the street he hurried to the palace where Edward, sick and alarmed, desired his presence, hoping to reconcile him with the Queen and her party so that when the end came they should all stand together and support the young heir to the throne.

Could the King have looked into the antechamber where presently they assembled he might have known how vain was that hope. The Queen was there, restless with apprehension; her brother, Earl Rivers; her two sons by her first marriage—Thomas, newly created Marquis of Dorset, and Richard, knighted as Sir Richard Grey. With them were Hastings, the Lord Chamberlain, but newly released from an imprisonment he owed to the Queen's hatred; Buckingham, Richard's most thorough-going and least scrupulous supporter, himself of the blood-royal by descent from Edward III.'s youngest son Thomas of Woodstock; and Stanley, Earl of Derby, a politic peer with an opportunity ahead and waiting for him. For out of the wreckage of the House of Lancaster there survived only one child, for the time safe in Brittany, who might in time be able to challenge the right of the House of York to the throne. This was the young Henry, Earl of Richmond, son of Edmund Tudor and Margaret Beaufort, and through her descended from John of Gaunt. And on Edmund Tudor's death Stanley had married the widow. But as yet he served the House of York, not guessing the fortune in store for his stepson.

Such was the incongruous company found by Richard in the anteroom. His line for the moment lay in a fine show of grievance against the Queen and her kinsfolk (as if they, and not he, had compassed Clarence's ruin), and before such hearers as Buckingham and Hastings he could afford to let them feel the rough side of his tongue. "A pretty state of things," he grumbled, "this tittle-tattling to the King! Who are they who spread such complaints? Cannot a plain man go his own way and think no harm of anybody, but his honest meaning must be abused by a lot of sly, insinuating upstarts?"

"To whom in the room is Your Grace speaking?" Rivers incautiously asked.

"To thee," snapped Richard. "And to thee—and to thee," turning from one to another of the Queen's party; and, fairly started, he rated them high and low for a set of low-born vulgar schemers until, after a worse taunt than the rest, the Queen protested she would stand it no longer; she would acquaint the King with these gross insults; she had rather be a country serving-maid than a queen on such terms.

But while they scolded there had stolen into the room a dark figure which, unperceived by them, hung back against the dim arras. It might have been taken for a ghost. In a sense it was indeed a ghost—the spectre of a terrible past crept back from exile—Margaret, once Queen of England. And yet it was no longer Margaret; no longer the fierce woman who had traversed England with troops and banners battling desperately for her child; nor even a childless widowed woman; but a body from which love, hope, ambition had departed, leaving only hate to burn in the wasted frame and keep it alive. She in whose arms, years ago, the ambitious Suffolk had prayed to die, had now no interest tying her to earth but to stand by and gloat over Heaven's vengeance. Upon all in the room lay the shadow of that vengeance; from each in turn the penalty would be exacted; and while they bickered she cursed each in turn under her breath, and having done, stepped forward before their faces. "Hear me, you wrangling pirates! you that fall out in sharing what you have pillaged from me. Yes, tremble; if not as subjects before their reigning queen, then as rebels before their deposed one——"

Richard was the first to recover speech. "Foul, wrinkled witch! what hath brought thee here? Wast thou not banished on pain of death?"

"I was, but for me death has no pains." She turned from one to another. "Where is my husband? my son? my kingdom? Yours should be the sorrows I bear."

"Thou bearest the curse laid on thee by my father in that hour when thou didst crown him in mockery and offer to dry his tears, the kerchief steeped in his child's innocent blood. God, not any of us, has scourged thee." And all forgot for a moment their quarrels and joined in cursing their common enemy.

"What! You were snarling, all of you, till I came. You were ready to fly at each other's throat, and now you turn all your hatred upon me! Curse, can you? and believe your curses reach the ear of Heaven? Nay, then, listen to mine." She faced upon the Queen, "May Edward thy son, now Prince of Wales, die for Edward my son who was Prince of Wales—and die young and by violence! Mayst thou outlive thy queenly glory as I have done, and live long to lament thy children as I lament mine; live, as I live, to see another decked in thy rights, and so end—neither mother, nor wife, nor Queen of England! Rivers and Dorset, you stood by—and you, too, my Lord Hastings—when my boy was stabbed. I pray God that none of you live to reach your natural end!"

"Have done!" Richard commanded.

"What, and leave thee out? Stay, thou dog, for thou *shalt* hear me. If God have in His store any punishment exceeding the worst I can wish for thee, I pray Him to keep it until thy sins be ripe and then visit thee, thou troubler of the peace of this poor world! May the worm of conscience then gnaw thy soul; mayst thou suspect thy friends for traitors, and take traitors for thy friends; let no sleep visit thee save with dreams of devils in torment—thou twisted, monstrous, rooting hog, sealed at thy birth to be hell's own son! Thou——"

Richard alone had courage to interrupt her curse with a jeering laugh; the others cowered before her. "Have done!" protested Buckingham; "for shame if not for charity's sake!"

She turned upon him, too, but without anger. "I have no quarrel with thee, princely Buckingham. Fair befall thee and thy house! Only beware of yonder dog"—she pointed a finger at Richard—"When he fawns, he bites; when he bites his tooth is poisonous, and the wound mortal. Beware, have not to do with him; for sin, death, hell, have set their marks on him, and all their ministers wait on him. What?"—for Buckingham shrugged his shoulders—"you scorn my warning? O, but remember it in the day coming when he shall split your heart with sorrow! *Then* say that Margaret was a prophetess!" In one long final gaze of hatred she gathered up all the others. "To Richard's hate I commit you, and Richard to yours, and all of you to God's!"

They stared after her in silence, or muttering that such curses made the hair stand on end. "Poor soul!" Richard heaved a sigh, "she hath been heavily wronged, and I repent my share in her wrongs." The others suspected no mockery in his creaking voice. "I never did her any wrong to my knowledge," the Queen protested. "But you have all profited by her wrongs," Richard answered. "For my part I was too hasty to help some one who seems to have forgotten my help; while as for Clarence"—he sighed again—"he is near his reward. May God pardon them who are to blame for it!"

With this most Christian conclusion, while the others passed in to the sick King's room, Richard lingered to give audience to two ruffians whom he had kept in waiting. In a few words he gave them their instructions, with the warrant for Clarence's death, and then he too passed into the sick-chamber.

In his cell in the Tower Clarence still trusted that Richard would gain his release. He guessed nothing of this treachery, or of the doom surely approaching. Yet horrible dreams haunted his sleep. "O," he confessed to Brakenbury, who came in the morning to wake him, "I have passed a miserable night!—a night of dreams so hideous, so full of dismal terror, that, as I am a Christian, I would not spend such another were it to purchase a whole world of happy days."

Brakenbury begged him to recount his dream.

"I dreamed," said Clarence, "I had broken from the Tower here and taken ship to cross over to Burgundy; and that my brother Gloucester was with me, and tempted me from my cabin to walk on the hatches, on the poop. Standing there we looked back upon England, and called up in talk the thousand times we had stood in peril during the wars between York and Lancaster. As we paced side by side on that giddy foothold methought Gloucester stumbled, and in falling, as I tried to save him, struck me overboard into the billows. God! what pain it seemed to drown! What dreadful noise of waters roared in my ears! What ugly shapes of death passed in my eyes! Brakenbury! I saw there a thousand fearful wrecks—ten thousand bodies of men on whom the fishes were gnawing—wedges of solid gold, great anchors, heaps of pearl, gems, and jewels beyond price scattered on the floor of the sea. Some of these lay in dead men's skulls, shining in the sockets where eyes had been, and leering on the dead bones strewn by them along the slimy bottom."

"What! In the moment of death you had leisure to mark these things?"

"It seemed so; and often I strove to yield up the ghost, but the flood held in my soul, and would not suffer it to escape forth on the empty wandering air, though I choked and panted to cast it free. Nor with this was the horror ended. For when my soul at length burst free and passed across the ferry of death and stood shivering and strange on the dark bank beyond, the first to greet me was my great father-in-law, Warwick; and he cried aloud, 'What scourge can hell afford for

Clarence, perjured Clarence?' So he vanished: and then came wandering by a shade like an angel, with bright hair dabbled in blood, and lifted a thin voice crying, 'Clarence is come! False, fleeting, perjured Clarence is come, who stabbed me in the field beside Tewkesbury! Furies, seize on Clarence and drag him to your torments!' And with that a legion of foul devils were about me howling in my ears so shrilly that with the noise I awoke trembling, and for a while could not believe but that I was truly in hell."

"My lord, I cannot marvel that you were frightened; for it frights me even to hear."

"O Brakenbury," groaned Clarence, "I have done those things, which now bear witness against my soul, for my brother Edward's sake. See how he requites me! Yet, O God, if my prayers come too late to appease Thee, and for me there is no forgiveness—yet spare my innocent wife and my poor children!" He begged Brakenbury to sit by him; and Brakenbury drew a chair beside the bed and watched until the eyes of the unhappy man closed and he slept.

Brakenbury was still watching when the sound of a harsh voice startled and fetched him to his feet. In the open doorway of the cell stood two ruffianly-looking men. "In God's name," the Lieutenant asked, "what are you, and how came you hither?" They handed him a warrant. It briefly commanded him to deliver over to the bearers the person of the Duke of Clarence. "I must not ask," said he, "what is meant by this"—though he knew only too well. "Here are my keys; there lies the

Duke sleeping." He left to report to the King that he had resigned his charge.

"Shall we stab him while he sleeps?" They were in two minds how to do it when Clarence awoke and sat up, rubbing his eyes. "Keeper, a cup of wine!" he called; and his eyes falling on the intruders, he demanded, as Brakenbury had done, "In God's name, who are you?—Who sent you hither, and why?" As his eyes sought theirs and the two men stammered, he read their purpose. "To murder me?"

"Ay, ay," growled the pair.

"But how, friends, have I offended you?"

"You have not offended us, but the King."

"I shall be reconciled to him."

"Never, my lord. You had best prepare to die."

"But what is my offence?" the Duke pleaded. They could answer little but that they were obeying the King's orders. "I love my brother Edward," he insisted. "If you are hired to do this thing, go back, seek out my brother Gloucester. He shall pay you better for my life than ever the King will to hear of my death."

"You are deceived," said the softer-hearted of the two. "Your brother Gloucester hates you."

But Clarence would not believe this. "When I parted with him he hugged me in his arms, and with sobs swore that he would labour to set me at liberty."

"My lord, make your peace with God," commanded the sterner ruffian. But the other was moved by pity and more than half regretted his errand. Clarence read this in his looks and turned to him with a piteous appeal, thus giving his back to the resolute one, who crept up knife in hand. "Look behind you, my lord!" cried the man he addressed. But it was too late. Before Clarence could turn, the knife entered his back and he dropped without another word. In the next room there stood a butt full of Malmsey wine. "He called for wine," said the murderer grimly; "and he shall have it." He dragged out the body and plunged it into the butt. The other stood conscience-stricken. "Take the full fee," he told his comrade; "I will have none of it."

Nor was he alone in repenting the deed. Edward, feeling his end near, had already sent to revoke his warrant. He wished to die in peace with all men, and to leave them in peace one with another; and the court factions had met beside his bed and been reconciled, at any rate to all appearances. Hastings had shaken hands and embraced with Rivers, Dorset and the Queen. Buckingham, conjured by Edward to join this league of amity, had sworn to the Queen an oath which she and he had afterwards good cause to recall. "Madam," said he, "if ever I fail to cherish you and yours with all duteous love, may God punish me with the hatred of those to whom I look for love! When I have sorest need of a friend and turn to him most confidently, may he prove hollow, treacherous, guileful. This is my prayer to God if ever I am cold in zeal to you or yours."

While he spoke, Gloucester entered; and he too entreated to be friends with all assembled. "I do not know an English man living with whom I have more quarrel than a new-born infant. I thank God for my humility," he concluded unctuously. Said the Queen, "This shall be kept hereafter as a holy day. I would to Heaven that all quarrels were healed, and I beseech your Majesty to take our brother Clarence back to your loving favour."

Richard gave a start of well-feigned indignant surprise. "Madam, have I offered love for this—to be mocked in the King's own presence? Which of you knows not that Clarence is dead?" It was now their turn to start. There was not one in the room but turned pale at the word. "You should not insult a corpse," he added quietly.

"Dead?" "Clarence dead?" They stared at each other.

"Clarence dead?" gasped the dying King. "But the order was reversed."

"Ay, my lord: but the second messenger ran too slowly. God grant that some, less noble than he and less loyal, nearer in thoughts of bloodshed if not so near in blood, deserve no worse than poor Clarence and yet escape suspicion!"

Now while they yet stood aghast, Lord Stanley came hurriedly into the presence-chamber and without observing their faces cast himself at the King's feet. He had a boon to beg. A servant of his had slain a gentleman in the Duke of Norfolk's service, and he had come hastily to plead for the man.

"Oh, peace!" groaned the King. "Can'st thou not see that my soul is full of sorrow?" But Stanley could not see how untimely his interruption was, and refused to rise. Edward groaned again. "And I who doomed my brother to death must with the same tongue pronounce pardon on a slave! My brother slew no man; yet he is dead, and who sued for his pardon? Who kneeled at my feet and bade my rage be better advised? Who spoke of brotherhood or of love? Who reminded me how the poor soul forsook Warwick to fight for me? or how he rescued me at Tewkesbury from under Oxford's sword? or of the night when we lay side by side in the open field, half-frozen, and he plucked off his own garments and wrapped me in them while he shivered? All this my wrath took from my remembrance, and not a man of you had the grace to put me in mind of it. But when your carters or serving-men have done some drunken murder and defaced Christ's image, then you are on your knees at once crying 'Pardon, pardon'; and I, as unjust as you, must grant it! But for my brother not one of you had a word; no, nor had I a word to plead with myself for poor Clarence. God, I fear Thy justice will seize on us and on ours for this!" And moaning, "Clarence! O poor Clarence!" Edward was borne to his chamber, never to leave it alive.

The Queen herself carried the news of his death a few days later to the old Duchess of York, Edward's mother, as she sat in her own apartments mourning for her other son Clarence, with Clarence's children beside her. Elizabeth's younger boy, Richard, Duke of York, was at home in London; but the elder, Edward, Prince of Wales and now heir to the throne, had been sent to Ludlow Castle in Shropshire. Thence he must now be fetched home to be crowned, and Gloucester, who had whispered his plans to Buckingham, undertook this duty. "We had better bring him with a small escort," Buckingham suggested.

"Why with a small escort?" asked Rivers.

"Because, my lord, in times so unsettled a multitude would merely provoke enemies and give them moreover a dangerous suspicion that we are afraid."

"I hope," put in Richard with meaning, "the King made peace between all of us. I at any rate abide by my pledged word."

Rivers agreed. "Yes, as you say, a big escort would suggest strife, and so I vote with my lord of Buckingham for a small one." He was the better pleased that this small escort included by arrangement all the young prince's uncles—himself and Grey as well as Gloucester. And so they set out.

But two of the uncles never returned. While the Queen sat expecting news at Westminster, and with her Archbishop Rotherham of York, the Chancellor, waiting to surrender the Great Seal to the new King, there arrived a messenger with the heavy news that Rivers, Grey, and Sir Thomas Vaughan, another kinsman of the Woodvilles, had been arrested at Northampton and sent under guard northward to Pomfret Castle. Richard and Buckingham had struck their first blow. At once Elizabeth's heart told her of other and worse blows to come. "I see the downfall of all our house," cried she; and taking the Seal from the hands of the

Archbishop she fled with her younger son to the Abbey for sanctuary.

The young King was sad and dispirited as he drew near the capital, as though he felt himself stepping into the shadow of doom. He missed his uncles Rivers and Grey. "You have not yet fathomed this world's deceit," Gloucester assured him; "those uncles of yours were dangerous. God save your Majesty from all such false friends!"

"God keep me indeed from false friends!" sighed the boy; "but they were none."

Nor could he hide his dejection when the Lord Mayor came out in full state to welcome him. "I thank you, my Lord Mayor, and all of you. I thought my mother and my brother would have met us on the way long before this. And where is Hastings, who should bring news of them?"

At this moment Hastings appeared, but with ill news. "Your mother and your brother York have taken sanctuary in the Abbey. The young duke wished greatly to come, but his mother would not allow it."

"What peevish caprice is this of the Queen's?" exclaimed Buckingham, and turned to the Archbishop of Canterbury, Cardinal Bouchier. "Will your Grace persuade her to send the Duke of York at once to the Prince, his brother? If she refuse—my Lord Hastings, go you with the Cardinal and take the child from her."

The Cardinal shook his head. "My lord of Buckingham, if my weak oratory can persuade her, you may expect the Prince; but I cannot, for all this land is worth, be guilty of infringing the holy privilege of sanctuary."

"You stand too much upon ceremony, my lord Cardinal. These times call for blunter methods. The benefit of sanctuary is granted to those who either deserve it or have the wit to claim it. But of a child's claiming or deserving it I never heard yet."

The Archbishop accepted the argument and departed on his cowardly errand.

"Say, uncle"—the boy-King turned to Gloucester— "if our brother comes, where will you lodge us until our coronation?"

"Wherever your Majesty pleases. If I may advise, though, let it be the Tower for a day or two, and thereafter in whatever place you choose as best fitting your Majesty's health and recreation."

"I do not like the Tower of all places. Did not Julius Cæsar build it, my lord?"

"He began the building of it, my gracious lord," Buckingham answered; "later ages have rebuilt and added to it."

"That Julius Cæsar," mused the boy, "was a famous man." His eyes brightened; "I'll tell you what, cousin Buckingham——"

"What, my gracious lord?"

"If I live to be a man, I'll win back our ancient rights in France, or else die a soldier!"

"Short summers have forward springs," muttered Gloucester under his breath.

Young Richard of York, whom Hastings and the Archbishop now brought from the Abbey, was forward in a different way. Less melancholy and reflective than his brother, he had a sharper tongue, and made no secret of his dislike for his uncle Gloucester, who in return listened to his childish, pert sayings and answered them with grim humour. "Will it please you to pass along, my lord?" he said at length; "my cousin Buckingham and I will go to your mother and beg her to go to the Tower and welcome you there."

"The Tower!" The poor lad turned to his brother. "What, are we to go to the Tower?"

"Our uncle will have it so," said Edward sadly.

"I shall not sleep quietly in the Tower," young Richard declared.

"Why? what should you be afraid of?" asked Gloucester.

"Marry, of my uncle Clarence's ghost. My grandmother told me he was murdered there."

"That boy is his mother's own child," Gloucester growled, as the procession moved on. He would deal with these boys in time; for the moment it sufficed to have them safe under lock and key while he turned to a preliminary piece of work. Buckingham—he was not quite sure how far Buckingham would go in the end— but Buckingham would help in this. He thought he could count too on another accomplice present, one Catesby, a lawyer, who had owed his rise to Hastings, and was known to have Hastings's confidence. Buckingham had already sounded Catesby on Richard's behalf, and had assured himself the man was ready to turn traitor to his old master; and now on Richard's behalf he put the all-important question, "Will it, think you, be an easy matter to persuade Lord Hastings to join us in setting the Duke of Gloucester here on the throne?"

"It will not," Catesby answered confidently. "The Lord Chamberlain loves the young King for his father's sake, and cannot be won to move a finger against him."

"H'm . . . and Lord Stanley?"

"Lord Stanley will follow Lord Hastings."

"Well, well, no more of this then. Go you and sound Lord Hastings discreetly, and bid him attend a Council to-morrow at the Tower. Be cautious with him and bring us word. There will be two Councils to-morrow, Catesby; and you shall have an important share in them."

"Ay," said Richard, breaking silence at length, "go, Catesby; commend me to my Lord Hastings, and tell him from me that his old enemies the Woodvilles will be let blood to-morrow at Pomfret Castle."

Catesby hurried off with a promise to return ere evening and report. Buckingham gazed after him. "My lord," he turned to Richard, "what shall we do if Hastings prove stubborn?"

"Chop off his head, man," was Richard's short answer. "And look you here; when I am King you may claim of me the Earldom of Hereford with its properties which the late King, my brother, enjoyed."

"I will claim that promise," said Buckingham, and the pair went off to arrange the plot over supper.

That night, while Hastings lay asleep, there came a knocking at his door and a messenger entered from Lord Stanley. Stanley had been troubled by an ugly dream, and some news which might or might not be uglier. In his dream he had encountered with a wild boar, and the brute had shorn away his helm with its tusks. Now a wild boar was the Duke of Gloucester's private badge. The news was that two Councils had been determined on for the morrow. "My master," said the messenger, "fears that one Council may determine that which may make him and you rue attending the other; and he sends to know if you will take horse at once and post northward with him out of danger?"

Hastings laughed at these fears. "Return to your master and bid him not be afraid of these separate Councils. He and I will attend the one, and my servant Catesby the other, who may be trusted to report anything which concerns us. His dream is a foolish one. Bid him rise and come to me and we will go to the Tower together."

The messenger had scarcely departed when Catesby entered.

"Ha, Catesby? You are an early riser. What news of this tottering state of ours?"

"It is a tottering state indeed," said Catesby gravely; and then with a sharp look at his master, "I believe it will never stand upright again until Richard wear the crown of England."

"How! Richard the King of England? I'll lose my head first. Is that what he aims at, think you?"

"I am sure of it; and, moreover, he hopes for your good help, and on the strength of it sends you word that this very day your enemies, the Queen's kinsmen, are to die at Pomfret."

"Well, I am not sorry to hear it; they were always my enemies. But if Richard thinks I'll help him to oust my late master's true heirs, God knows I'll die sooner."

"And may God keep your lordship in that mind," said Catesby. Hastings suspected no irony. His mind was running on the fate of his old enemies. "I shall laugh at this a year hence. To think that those who once thrust me out of my master's favour have come to this, and I live to see it. Catesby, I tell thee that before I'm a fortnight older I shall send some folks packing who little expect it."

"It is a vile thing to die, my lord," said Catesby musingly, "when it takes men unprepared."

But the confident Hastings still suspected nothing. Indeed for a moment he saw no bearing in the remark. "Eh? Oh, monstrous, monstrous! And so it happens to Rivers and Vaughan and Grey; and so it will happen—mark my words—with some others who think themselves as secure as you and I, friends as we are with Richard and Buckingham." He looked up to welcome Lord Stanley, who entered at this moment, and to rally him. "Come on, come on; why, man, where is your boar-spear?"

"Good-morrow, my lord; good-morrow, Catesby. You may jest as you will," said Stanley, "but for my part I don't like these separate Councils."

But Hastings pooh-poohed his fears, even when reminded that the Queen's kinsmen had been jocund and confident too as they rode from London. He set forth in the highest spirits. On his way to the Tower he ran against a pursuivant who had once escorted him prisoner along this very road. "I am in better case, man, than when last I met thee. Then I was going to prison through the malice of the Queen's party; to-day—hark ye, and keep it to yourself—those enemies are to die and I am in better state than ever." He flung the fellow a purse. A little further he met a priest, and stopped to arrange with him for a service in his private chapel. Buckingham coming along the street just then found them conferring.

"What, talking with a priest, my Lord Chamberlain? Your friends at Pomfret will be needing a priest this morning; but you surely have no need for shriving."

"Faith now," said Hastings, as they walked on towards the Tower together, "when I met the holy man those you mention came into my head."

Up in Yorkshire in the same cold dawn, Rivers, Grey, and Vaughan were being led out to die; Rivers calm, Grey reviling, Vaughan prophesying a retribution to come, but all remembering Margaret's curse and hugging in their last hour the remembrance that with them she had cursed others—Hastings, Buckingham, Richard . . . "O God, remember her prayers for them as for us!"

In London the Council—the second Council—had met. Buckingham, Hastings, Stanley were there, with Morton, Bishop of Ely, Ratcliff and Lovel (two partisans of Richard), and others. Richard himself was late, and they fell to business without him. They had to decide on the young King's coronation; or, rather (said Hastings, coming to the point at once), to fix the day for it.

"Is everything ready for it?" asked Buckingham casually.

"Certainly," answered Stanley, reading no second meaning in the question; "the day only needs to be named."

"To-morrow, then, seems to me none too soon," said Bishop Morton.

Buckingham glanced round. "I wonder now if any one knows the Lord Protector's mind on this matter? Who is most in the Duke of Gloucester's secrets?"

"We think your Grace should know his mind sooner than any one," said Morton.

"Who? I? He and I know each other's faces, my lord; but as for our hearts, he knows no more of mine than I do of yours; nor I more of his than you of mine,"—and this was truer than the speaker guessed. "Lord Hastings, you have his loving confidence."

"Well, I believe so," agreed that deluded man. "It is true that I have not sounded him on this matter; but if you will name the time, my lords, I will take it on myself to agree in the Duke's name and feel sure he will approve."

But at this moment Richard appeared in the doorway with a smile on his face. With an apology and a light compliment to Hastings, he turned towards the Bishop, "My lord, when last I was in Holborn I saw some famous strawberries there in your garden. Might I beg you to send for some?"

"With all my heart," said the Bishop, and went off to give the order. No sooner was his back turned than Richard drew Buckingham aside and whispered to him what he had heard from Catesby—that Hastings would not join them against the young King. The pair left the Council together.

So when Bishop Morton returned, having sent for the strawberries, he looked around and inquired what had become of the Lord Protector. "He looks in good temper to-day, does he not?" said Hastings; "I believe there's no man whose face hides his love or hatred less than his Grace of Gloucester's." The fond man was rubbing his hands with satisfaction when Richard and Buckingham came hurriedly back into the room, and this time Richard's face was twisted with passion. "Tell me,"—his vicious eye swept the Council—"what do they deserve who are caught planning devilish witchcraft against me, and have actually prevailed upon my body with their hellish charms?"

In the general astonishment, Hastings was the first to find his tongue. "The love I bear your Grace makes me most forward to speak. I say that such persons deserve death."

"See here, then." Richard pulled up his sleeve and showed his withered arm; he was making his deformity help him now. "See this arm of mine shrivelled up like a blasted sapling! It is Edward's wife who hath done this—that monstrous witch!"

"If they have done this, my lord—" stammered Hastings.

"*If!* Thou talkest of 'ifs'! Thou art a traitor! Lovel and Ratcliff, off with this fellow's head! By St. Paul, I will not dine till I see it. You that are my friends here, rise and follow me!"

He dashed from the room. Too late the befooled man saw the trap, and repented his vain confidence, and called out upon his murderers. With a brutal jest, Ratcliff and Lovel hurried him to the block. Meanwhile Richard and Buckingham had sent Catesby in hot haste for the Lord Mayor, and employed the interval in disfiguring their clothes until they looked like men under some blight of witchcraft. The Lord Mayor came hurrying as fast as his legs would bring him, and not in the least knowing why he was summoned. They called to him from the walls, and claimed his protection. They were in danger—victims of a plot. "Look behind thee!" called Richard, as the Lord Mayor halted by the drawbridge completely puzzled. "Here are enemies!" But the newcomers were Lovel and Ratcliff bearing the head of the unhappy Hastings. Richard heaved a mock sigh of relief. "I loved the man so dearly, I must weep. I took him for the plainest, most harmless creature——" Buckingham caught up the cue: "He was the subtlest most covert traitor that ever lived! Would you believe it, my Lord Mayor, were it not that by a miracle we have escaped to tell it, that traitor had plotted to murder me and the good Duke of Gloucester to-day in the Council-house?"

"Eh? What? Had he indeed?" The Lord Mayor could only stammer astonishment.

"What? Can you think for a moment we would have had the villain executed without form of law had not the instant peril to us and the peace of England compelled us?" Richard was virtuously indignant.

"Dear me, dear me! No doubt you did well and he deserved it," agreed the Lord Mayor.

"And yet," Richard went on, "we had not intended that he should die until your lordship should be present to witness his death. The zealous rage of our friends here somewhat outrun our intention. We wished, my lord, that you should hear him confess his treason, and report to the citizens, who may perhaps misconstrue what we have done."

"Not at all," said this very foolish Lord Mayor. "Your Grace's word shall serve as well as though I had been here and heard him confess. Be assured I will acquaint our dutiful citizens with the step you have justly taken." And he departed on his errand.

Now was the moment for action. The pair had prepared their plans well—and almost too well, since it was discovered later that although the indictment of Hastings was published within five hours after his arrest, the scrivener employed to draw it up had done his work so elaborately and in such beautiful penmanship that the veriest child could see it had taken twice that time at least to prepare, and therefore that the whole plot must have not been arranged long beforehand. But just now men did stop to think. Richard was ready with his trump-card—Edward's early contract of marriage and the consequent illegitimacy of the two young Princes. He was of course too clever to play it himself. He sent Buckingham off on the Lord Mayor's heels to hint it to the assembled citizens in the Guildhall; he had provided eloquent preachers—notably two named Doctor Shaw and Friar Penker—to proclaim it publicly; and having fired the train he withdrew quietly to his mother's house, Baynard's Castle by the Thames' side, to await results and plan a further piece of villainy which he doubted might be too strong even for Buckingham.

And yet the business did not proceed quite so smoothly as he had hoped. Buckingham in the Guildhall cast away reserve, and spoke boldly of Edward's early contract of marriage, winding up with "God save King Richard!"—but the citizens were dumb. They desired above all things peace; they feared that under a boy-king the country must be torn by new dissensions; the Wars of the Roses had exhausted and wearied them utterly. It would be a blessing to be ruled by a strong man. And yet they had liked Edward and guessed that injustice was intended against his children.

Buckingham demanded the reason why they kept silence. The Lord Mayor answered that the citizens were accustomed to be addressed through the City Recorder, and did not understand being talked to by a stranger. So the Recorder was brought forward and rehearsed the arguments, not as his own, but as Buckingham's, speaking in his most formal voice—"The Duke says this," "The Duke argues so and so." At the conclusion some hired followers of Buckingham at the lower end of the hall tossed up their caps and cheered for Richard. It was little enough, but Buckingham made the most of it. "Thanks, my friends—thanks, gentle citizens!" said he, bowing; "this general applause proves your wise affection for Richard," and with this he managed to bring the Lord Mayor with a considerable following to Baynard's Castle.

The position was ticklish; but the pair were clever enough to save it. When the Lord Mayor craved audience, Richard at first sent Catesby to refuse it. The Duke of Gloucester (so ran the message) was at his devotions with two reverend fathers of the Church. He was loth to be disturbed on a matter of worldly business. Could not his lordship defer it to some other day? Buckingham sent Catesby again with word that the matter was urgent, and used the interval to dwell on Richard's godly graces—so different from the idle wantonness of their late King! At length, with feigned reluctance, Richard made his appearance on a balcony above, standing between two bishops and with a book of prayer in his hand. This mightily impressed the Lord Mayor. Buckingham began with an apology for interrupting his Grace's devotion, and went on to press him to accede to the popular wish and accept the crown. Gloucester gravely rebuked him. He would depart in silence, but for the fear that his silence might be misconstrued. He thanked them for their affectionate zeal; but felt himself unworthy of it. He was poor-spirited, perhaps; conscious of his defects, at any rate. But, thank God! he was not needed. The late King had left an heir—young, no doubt, but time might be trusted to better that. And in short he would not wrest the child's right from him.

Buckingham plunged into a speech arguing against young Edward's legitimacy, and wound up by offering the crown again. The Lord Mayor joined in the petition. Again Richard refused. "Then whether you accept or no, your nephew shall never reign King of England. Come, citizens; I'll entreat him no more!" Buckingham flounced out with an oath. "Nay, my lord of Buckingham, do not swear,"—Richard was piously shocked—hurt even. Well, Buckingham was gone; but Catesby and others implored the arch-hypocrite to call him back. "Will you force me to bear this grievous burden?" he sighed. Buckingham was recalled, and came with his following.

"Cousin, and you other sage, grave men, since you will bind this load upon me, I must find patience to bear it. Should scandal arise from my acceptance, remember that you forced it on me. For God knows, and you in a measure must see, how far I am from desiring it."

The Mayor and his silly crowd waved their hats and, led by Buckingham, cheered for King Richard. He should be crowned on the morrow, Buckingham proposed. "When you please, since you will have it your own way," said Richard, and turning to the bishops— "Come, it is time we applied ourselves again to our holy task."

Early next morning two separate trains of ladies met at the Tower gate. They were on the one side the Queen and the old Duchess of York, escorted by the Queen's son, Dorset; and on the other the Lady Anne, now Richard's wife, leading with her the young daughter of Clarence. Both companies had come to wish joy to the young Princes; both were ignorant of what had happened at Baynard's Castle.

Brakenbury came out to meet them. "Pardon, madam," said he, addressing the Queen, "I may not allow you to visit the Princes. The King has given strict orders to the contrary."

"The King! why, who's that?"

"Your pardon, madam, again—I should have said the Lord Protector."

"The Lord protect him from being King! I am their mother."

"And I their father's mother," said the Duchess.

"And I," said Anne, "their aunt-in-law, but I love them as a mother. Take us to them, sir, and I will take to myself the blame."

Still Brakenbury shook his head; and, looking up,

the ladies were aware that Lord Stanley stood before them with a message to deliver.

"Madam," said Stanley, addressing Anne, "I am sent to conduct you to Westminster, there to be crowned Richard's Queen."

Then Elizabeth understood. For the moment half-stunned by the news, she recovered, and turned on her son Dorset. "Fly!" she panted. "Thou too art my child, and my name is ominous to my children. Quick—cross the seas and seek shelter with Richmond. Fly from this slaughter-house, lest thou be added to the number of the dead, and I bow to the full curse of Margaret, and die neither Queen nor wife nor mother."

"Wisely counselled," said Stanley. "Make haste, my lord, and you shall take from me letters to my son Richmond." He turned to Anne, "We too must hasten, madam,—to Westminster."

And the poor lady went unwillingly enough, un-envied even by the Queen whom she was to supersede. "Ah," she confessed, "when beside Henry's corpse I set eyes on the man who is now my husband, I cursed him and the woman who should marry him. 'May she be made wretched as I am wretched,' I prayed; and before I could repeat it his tongue had beguiled me and I had basely surrendered—to be his wife—to inherit my own curse! I swear to you that never since then have I enjoyed one quiet hour, one hour of easy slumber beside him. He hates me; soon, I know, he will murder me."

So they parted; one to be crowned, the other to

forget that ever she had been a Queen, yet the one as heavy of heart as the other. The old Duchess after eighty years of calamity was almost past grieving. As they started to go their sorrowful ways Elizabeth suddenly stood still. "Stay," she cried, "look once back with me!" She pointed towards the walls of the Tower. "O have pity, you ancient stones, on those tender babes by envy immured behind you. Rough cradle are you for such little pretty ones. Harsh and rugged nurse—old and sullen playfellow—ah, use my babies kindly!"

So Richard had reached his ambition, and was King of England; yet he could not feel safe while the boy lived who was King by right. Would Buckingham help him to get rid of Edward? Richard was not sure. He dropped a hint or two, eyeing his fellow-conspirator stealthily; but somehow Buckingham was less quick than usual in taking a hint. Perhaps he was considering that the time had come to be thinking of his own reward.

"Cousin," said Richard sharply, "you were not wont to be so dull. Must I say it plainly? Well then, I wish the boys dead, and quickly. What say you? Come—promptly, man!"

"Your Grace may do as you please," Buckingham answered evasively.

"Tut, tut; your zeal must be cooling. Yes or no, do you consent to their death?"

"Your Grace must give me time—some little time—before I can answer positively. I will think of it and bring my answer without delay,"—and so Buckingham made his escape.

Richard frowned. "H'm; ambitious Buckingham is growing circumspect." It was as he had more than half guessed. There were limits to Buckingham's wickedness, and he lacked either the heart or the nerve for this. Richard took account of all the dangers ahead. To begin with, there were the Princes; well, he could manage them without Buckingham's help. But their death would leave the succession to their sister, the young Princess Elizabeth; and after her came Clarence's children, a boy and a girl. The boy was half-witted and not dangerous; the girl could be married to some one of mean birth, which would keep her out of the way. But what about young Elizabeth? He considered, and his brow cleared. Why might he not marry her himself? She was his niece, and he had a wife living. Well, Anne must die. He called Catesby, and ordered him to have it rumoured about that she was dangerously ill—he would see to the rest. Even Catesby was staggered, but obeyed.

This marriage with a niece would be monstrous. "Murder her brothers and afterwards marry her!" Richard muttered it over in a kind of awe of himself; but if awed he was not afraid. He made inquiry and learned of a man likely to suit his purpose—a gentleman by birth and by name Tyrrel, poor, discontented, and ready to sell his soul for money. Richard sent for him. Their conference was short. That night Tyrrel, with two accomplices, named Dighton and Brobyn, entered the Tower and crept to the room where the young Princes lay in bed, cheek to cheek, their arms girdling each other, the book of prayers in which they had both been reading open on the pillow beside them. The sight almost melted the murderers' hearts; the wretches wept afterwards when they told what they had done—how they had drawn the pillows tight over the young lips and smothered them. Tyrrel handed the bodies over to the chaplain of the Tower, who buried them secretly, and dying soon afterwards took the secret to the grave with him.[16]

Tyrrel had scarcely left the King's presence before Buckingham returned. He found Richard in talk with Stanley, who had come to report that Dorset had escaped to join Richmond.

"My lord," began Buckingham, "I have considered the suggestion concerning which you sounded me."

"Well, well, let that pass," Richard was no longer interested. "Dorset has escaped to join Richmond."

"So I hear, my lord," said Buckingham; and would have said more, but the King turned to Stanley.

"My lord Stanley," said he, "Richmond is your wife's son. You had best be careful."

Buckingham was not rebuffed. "My lord, I have come to claim my reward, the Earldom of Hereford, which you faithfully promised me."

---

[16]Two hundred years later, in 1674, in the course of some alterations in the White Tower, the workmen discovered the bones of two children. These were at once guessed to be the bones of the two Princes, and by Charles the Second's orders they were removed to Westminster Abbey and placed in Henry the Seventh's Chapel there.

"Stanley," pursued Richard, "look to your wife. If she be found conveying letters to Richmond you shall answer for it."

"May I have your Highness's answer to my demand?" Buckingham persisted. Richard paid no heed to him, but still addressing Stanley began to discuss the prophecy once uttered by the unhappy Henry the Sixth that Richmond should one day be King of England.

Still Buckingham persevered, until the King turned on him sharply: "You annoy me with your interruptions. I am not in the giving vein to-day." He walked out and left Buckingham standing. "And it was for this I made him King!" muttered the disappointed man. Suddenly there came into his mind the thought of Hastings—of his confidence in Richard's favour, and of his fate. He took horse in haste and posted away towards Wales and his manor of Brecknock.

Now Morton, Bishop of Ely, lay in prison in Brecknock, having been removed by Richard as an obstacle in his path and put there under Buckingham's custody. Prisoner and gaoler had now a common cause; and the bishop presently escaped over sea to Richmond, but not before arranging the half of a dangerous plot. Buckingham was to raise a revolt in Wales; Richmond to sail from Brittany with an invading army, and on reaching England, to confirm his somewhat faulty title[17] to the throne by marrying the young Princess Elizabeth.

[17]His Lancastrian descent was derived from John of Gaunt's marriage with Katherine Swynford; and the issue of that marriage had been expressly debarred from the succession.

We shall see how the revolt fared. As we know, Richard had resolved to forestall one dangerous move in the plot by marrying the Princess himself; and before many days had gone by the country learned that the unhappy Anne was no longer living. Murders by this time were crowding thick and fast. Even Margaret as she haunted the court, hungry for revenge, could say that her appetite was almost cloyed. Margaret, Elizabeth, the old Duchess—these three had passed beyond hatred; they could seat themselves on the ground together, and recount and compare their woes, too far crushed under calamity to bandy reproaches. Only Margaret, whose wounds were older, could now and then break out into taunts. "Ah, triumph no more in my woes, thou wife of Henry!" pleaded Elizabeth; "God is my witness that I have wept for thine." "Bear with me," Margaret answered; "only Richard remains now, and his time is drawing near. Dear God, grant me life until I can say that dog is dead!" "Ay, thou didst prophesy the time when I should call on thee to help me in cursing him. Do not leave me, thou who art so skilled in cursing; stay, and teach me how to curse." "Shall I teach thee how? Put away sleep at night; fast by day; compare thy dead happiness with thy living woe; think upon thy lost babes—deem them fairer than they were, and their destroyer even fouler than he is. That," said Margaret, "is the way to learn to curse," "My words are dull," wailed Elizabeth; "oh, put life into them with thine!" "Thy woes will make them pierce," said Margaret, and left the two women alone. While they sat, Richard came by in state, and they lifted their accusing voices together—"Where is Clarence? Where is young Edward? Where are Hastings, Rivers, Vaughan, Grey?"

"Silence!" snarled Richard, and turning commanded the drums and trumpets to sound and drown their cries. "Now then," he said, as the hubbub died down, "either speak to me fair or your voices shall be silenced again."

The old Duchess, his mother, arose and pointed a finger at him. "Grievous thy birth was to me; thy infancy peevish and wayward; thy school-days frightful, desperate, furious; thy prime of manhood daring and venturous; thy full age proud, subtle, bloody, treacherous, milder but more dangerous, masking hatred with kindly looks. Canst thou name one hour in which I have had joy of thee? Nay, let me speak—for the last time. Thou art going to war, and either thou wilt die in it, or I shall be dead of age and sorrow ere thou returnest. Therefore take my heaviest curse with thee, and in the day of battle may it weigh thee down more than thy heaviest armour. My prayers go with thy enemies: may the little souls of Edward's children whisper success to them and cheer them to victory! Bloody thou art; bloody shall be thy end, and shameful as thy life hath been shameful!"

She tottered away and left Richard and Elizabeth face to face. Was it dogged defiance of shame—or was it faith in his star—that he stopped Elizabeth as she too turned away, and began to woo her for her daughter, very much as he had once wooed the Lady Anne for herself? Was it owing to this difference—that he now wooed a woman for her daughter, not for herself— or was it through some failure in his own hateful fascination—that success this time eluded him? And yet he seemed to be repeating his success. Again the woman cursed and the man cajoled; again the woman seemed to weaken while against all odds, in the face of hatred and loathing, his hands red with the blood of her dearest, the man fought and fought for his end with an unwearied persistence such as benumbs a rabbit and forces it in the end to lie down and wait for the weasel. And again the woman to all appearance yielded. She left him with a promise to bring her daughter round to his mind.

"Relenting fool! shallow, changing woman!" sneered Richard as he gazed after her. But in fact she had overreached him; or rather he had overreached himself. He had killed too much in Elizabeth; killed the ambitious intriguing woman and left only the woman with a mother's heart. It was the old Elizabeth to whom he had been appealing; the new Elizabeth—the woman he had made—listened and promised and went her way—to give her daughter to Richmond.

For Richmond was on the seas, intending to land on the coast of Devon, and win a kingdom. The men of Devon and the men of Kent were ready to rise, and by agreement Buckingham marched in open rebellion to cross the Welsh border. This was in October, 1483. As he started, a heavy and extraordinary storm broke over the country. It rained and blew for days. He reached Severn only to find it sweeping in a flood which is spoken of to this day as "The Great Water," or "Buckingham's Water." The King's supporters had broken down the bridges; and he found it hopeless to think of uniting his Welsh forces with the insurgents from Devon, for the whole country down to Bristol was under water. The same gale drove Richmond's ships back towards France. An eclipse of the moon terrified Buckingham's Welshmen still further, and the army melted away. The rebellion had been drowned out. Buckingham fled to the house of a retainer named Bannister, was betrayed—some say by his host—and executed in the market-place of Salisbury.

He had begged—but in vain—to see Richard; it is believed, in the hope of a chance of stabbing him. The day of his execution was All-Souls' Day (November 2nd), and as he was led forth he thought on the many souls hurried out of this life by his wickedness and remembered Margaret's curse. "All-Souls' Day is my body's doomsday. This is the day I wished might befall me when I was found false to Edward's children and his wife's kin. All have perished with my aid, and the curse has come upon me." He went to the block muttering the words of Margaret's warning.

So ended the man who had been Richard's most useful friend. Richard, the incarnate curse of the House of York, had fulfilled his terrible mission; in him the House of York had devoured its own children; he had executed judgment, he stood alone on the stage he had drenched with blood, and now Heaven had no further need of him and his own hour was at hand.

Richmond, driven back on the French coast, bided his time, and in 1485 sailed for England again. His voyage prospered, and on the 1st of August his ships dropped anchor in Milford Haven. Richard, warned that he had started, had pitched his camp at Nottingham as a central point of the kingdom, and horsemen sat in saddle along all the chief roads to gallop with tidings of the invader's approach.

Treachery was now what he had most to fear, and on Stanley, as Richmond's stepfather, his suspicions rested heaviest. He had good grounds for them; but Stanley was the wiliest fox in England. He detested Richard, he knew himself suspected, and yet he had lived among bitter enemies and never given the King a fair excuse to lay hands on him; had kept his level head on his shoulders, and seen Rivers, Vaughan and Grey, Hastings and Buckingham each fall in his turn. His sympathies lay with Richmond, but he could not declare himself since Richard held his son George Stanley as hostage, and would have chopped off his head at the first sign of revolt. So the father followed his master for the moment and bided his time.

In a fortnight after Richmond's landing the two armies came face to face on Bosworth Field to the south of Market Bosworth in Leicestershire. Desertions had weakened the King's army in spite of his savage watchfulness. Yet he kept the advantage of numbers and his old untameable courage. There was this difference, however, that he, who all his life long had feared neither God nor man nor devil, was beginning at last to be uneasy about God. On the eve of the battle he left his supper untasted, but drank great bowls of wine. Catesby, Ratcliff, and Lovel remained faithful to the master they had served so wickedly; better men stood by him in the staunch old Duke of Norfolk and his son the Earl of Surrey. With a parting injunction that Stanley should be watched and ordered to parade his troops before sunrise, and some commands about preparing his armour and saddling his charger White Surrey for the morrow's battle, Richard dismissed his friends and flung himself on the bed to sleep.

Hideous dreams haunted his sleep; visions of his many victims passed by the bed, and leaning over it bade him despair. There stood young Edward, stabbed at Tewkesbury, dabbled in blood, pointing to his wounds; there stood Clarence; there stood Rivers, Grey, Vaughan; there stood Hastings; there stood the two murdered Princes; there stood his wife Anne; there stood his first friend and last victim, Buckingham. "Let me sit heavy upon thy soul to-morrow"—"Let me"—"And me"; one after the other took up the terrible imprecation. "To-morrow—despair and die!"

"Jesu, have mercy!"—Richard started from the bed in a bath of terror. The candles burned blue by the bedside, but the tent was empty. "I was dreaming . . . conscience it is afflicting me. Oh, I am a villain! . . . No, it is too late to repent, to face the truth . . . I am no villain! . . . Fool! do not flatter thyself, when conscience has a thousand tongues and each one denounces thee villain. . . . Perjury, murder, sin upon sin thronging to the bar, each crying 'Guilty! guilty!' . . . I must not despair; not a creature loves me; and if I die not a soul shall pity me."

He was wiping the sweat from his brow when a hand lifted the flap of the tent.

"My lord!" said a voice.

"'Zounds!" Richard swung around fiercely. "Who is there?"

"It is I, my lord—Ratcliff. The cocks are crowing, and thy friends buckling on their armour."

"O Ratcliff, I have had fearful dreams! Will our friends prove true to us, think you?"

"I have no doubt of it, my lord."

"Yet, Ratcliff, I fear—I fear——"

"Nay, my lord, do not fear shadows."

"By Saint Paul, shadows have done more to-night to frighten the soul of Richard than can ten thousand armed soldiers led on by that shallow Richmond."

He did on his armour. The day hung back dark and ominous as he set his battle in order and rode down the ranks. He heard the advancing drums of the enemy and looked around him. "Where is Stanley?" he demanded.

"My lord," said a messenger, "Lord Stanley will not come."

"Off with his son George's head!" shouted Richard; but the enemy had already crossed the marsh, and Norfolk, who led the King's van, pointed out that there was no time now for small revenge. The troops swung forward, and then it grew clear that Stanley was not the only deserter. The Earl of Northumberland drew his men out of call and so passed over, foot and horse, to the invader. "Treason! treason!" shouted Richard, and dashed into the thick of the fray seeking for Richmond. He had never fought so splendidly, because never so desperately. White Surrey was stabbed and sank under him. "Another horse!" he yelled; "my kingdom for another horse!" While his men gave ground, he yet pressed forward; hewed his way to the Lancastrian standard, tore it from its pole, trod the pole in the ground, and still fought forward like a demon into the very presence of Richmond. And there—a foot or two only dividing them—as he aimed a murderous stroke at his rival, a score of men rushed on him together and bore him to the ground by sheer weight of numbers. Under that struggling mass he took his death-stroke. They drew off; the body did not move. They had pulled the wild boar down at last, and the great curse was ended.

As he went down the crown had fallen from his head and rolled beneath a hawthorn bush. Stanley picked it up and set it on the brows of the conqueror.

APPENDIX

THE HOUSES OF YORK AND LANCASTER

EDWARD III.

"Seven phials of his sacred blood."

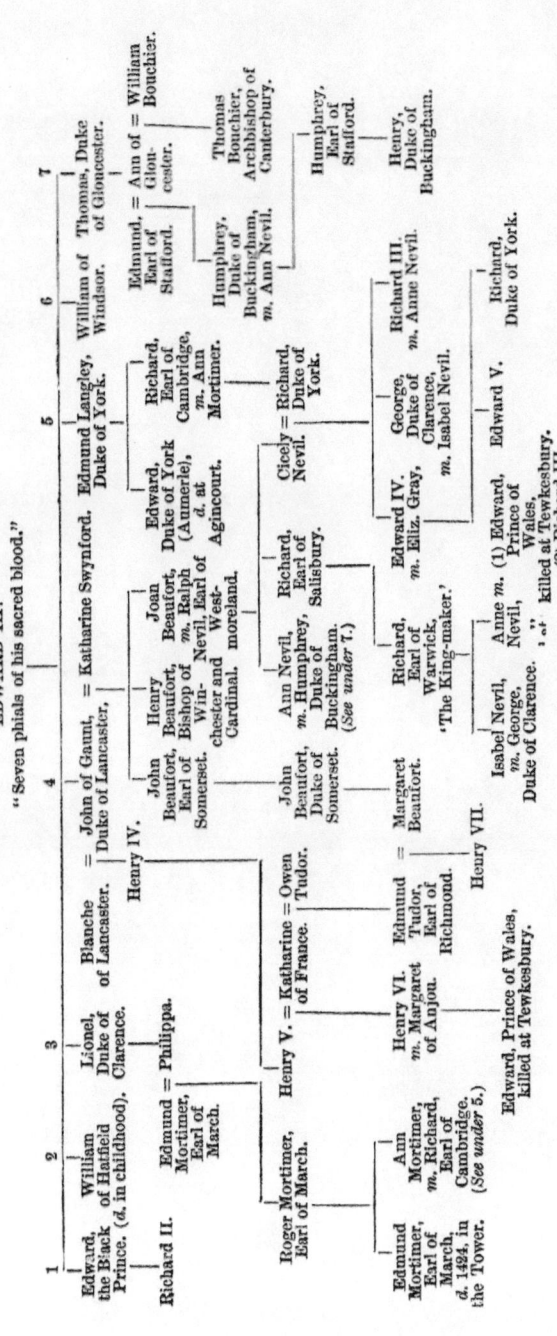